I0762282

THE RUNEMASTER HOMICIDE

THE RUNEMASTER HOMICIDE

THE DEMON-SLEUTH SCROLLS BOOK ONE

DAN JOLLEY

Cover Design by S. H. Roddey

For Tracy. Always.

I

THE DEMON

1

The demon's face floated up to him, unreal, like the ragged remnants of a hazy dream.

Covered in the blood of the men who'd sworn to protect him, Wendell Anwar lay on the icy dock, his cheek grinding into the rough planks, wrists bound tight against the small of his back.

One of the brigands had stabbed him. He couldn't tell how bad it was. It felt bad, lancing through him with each shallow breath, every thump of his heart spilling pain-infused blood. He could hear each drop as it fell into the river below him.

Shuddering, teeth chattering, Anwar tried to calculate his chances of living through the night. The depth of the knife wound would tell the tale. If the blade hadn't nicked any major vessels, they'd hold him for ransom. If the blood dripping down between the planks proved to be more his than his guard detail's, the brigands would dump him into the frigid water.

Anwar lay on his right side, his body twisted, his face no more than thirty centims from the river's surface. The fight had led into the shallows, just off the rocky bank, men grunting and swearing and screaming beneath the three bright moons overhead. Anwar couldn't tell how much of the liquid soaking his clothes was water, but his shivering was growing worse. He wondered if he might freeze to death before the brigands could make up their minds about what to do with him.

Beyond the dock, a black, frigid forest stretched away, klik after klik, until it fetched up at the base of the far mountains. Anwar spotted the dark clouds building that afternoon and had hoped they could make it to the next town before the rain began, but such luck was not to be. This far north, the nights got cold, even this early in Hexember. The tiny, desperate sound of his blood leaking away got lost as another freezing shower let loose, the impact of each raindrop on the water a whisper that built into a collective roar.

He couldn't turn his head, so he couldn't see which of his Imperial soldiers died last. He could only listen as the final man spat and cursed, struggling to the end—could only imagine two of the vile, fur-covered heathens holding him by both arms, the leader of the raiding party sheathing his knife in the soldier's throat.

The brigands talked quietly among themselves, long enough for the shower to end. As he blinked rainwater out of his eyes, Anwar had no doubt they were discussing his fate—*Do we loot the corpses and be done with it? Or do we take the prancy nobleman back to camp, and gamble over how much he might mean to someone?*

Anwar couldn't feel his toes anymore. Or his fingers. He wondered how much of that was thanks to the blood loss, and how much to the freezing night air. His nose seemed to have turned to fragile crystal, such that it might shatter and fall away from his face were he to press it against the dock.

With half his face hanging over the dock's edge, only his left eye peered down into the water. His right saw nothing but frozen, dirt-encrusted wood.

He narrowed that left eye as he gazed down into the river's depths. Did blood loss cause hallucinations? He couldn't remember ever hearing such a thing, and yet, as he stared, two spots of soft, luminous green appeared in the gloom directly beneath him. They rose slowly, carefully, and just before he realized those soft green spots were eyes, two black, dagger-pointed, sharp-ridged horns broke the surface, the rest of the demon's face following a heartbeat later.

The soft green snapped away, revealing yellow eyes as bright and hot as candle-flames, and Wendell Anwar's body became a living ice sculpture as the demon raised one long, elegant finger and laid it across her lips.

Sshhh.

The demon didn't have to make any sound. Anwar simply couldn't, because whatever scream he might have dredged up from inside him lodged and died in his windpipe.

If all three moons hadn't hung so full and bright overhead, he would never have seen anything but her eyes, as her skin from her nose to the soles of her feet was a deep, rich violet. Even with the moons' radiance, he could take in only the outlines of her lean, rippling body as she passed him by. The demon rose noiselessly from the water, wearing not a stitch of clothing, and slipped onto the dock as gracefully as a snowflake settling onto a blade of grass.

She paused, only for a second, only long enough to place a hand on his shoulder—a fleeting pressure, one that Anwar might have found reassuring had he not seen the moon-flash on the broad-bladed knife in her other hand.

Anwar tried to move as the demon padded down the dock's length away from him. He tried to squirm and twist and bring himself up far enough to see what was happening, but he'd grown too cold and too weak, had lost too much blood, and could only listen, motionless.

Another icy cloudburst swept over the dock as, once again, men screamed and cursed and died. Their voices reached the swift-flowing river and drowned there, just as the woods on the other side of the highway swept them up and smothered them.

Anwar didn't hear the demon approaching. Hands as strong as those of a blacksmith grasped his shoulders, and his head swayed as she hauled him up to a sitting position. When the world had stopped spinning, he tried to focus on the demon, but instead his eyes fell on the twisted pile of mangled corpses at the far end of the dock. A few meters past them, the coach had overturned and caught fire. Both draft horses lay dead, still strapped to the shafts.

The demon trailed her knife in the water. Anwar thought he might have seen the blood coursing away from it, a tiny black rivulet.

"Am I dead?" he asked, taking in the demon's blood-spattered nakedness. She didn't seem to feel any need to cover herself. Neither did she seem to feel the cold.

"Not yet," she said, and her voice hung in the winter air, a smoky presence that made him think of the whiskey his father had favored. Anwar had been present when envoys had spoken of the flowing precision that colored demons' words, but he'd never heard the accent himself before. The demon said, "I'm taking you to the fire," and the lyrical color she put to the words came close to making him forget about the cold and the pain and the blood.

Anwar expected the demon to offer him her hand. Or anchor his arm around her shoulders and support him as he limped toward the burning coach. He expected to have to protest, to tell her that he was too weak to walk. Instead, the demon slid her arms around him and picked him up, carrying him—cradling him—as easily as she might have carried an infant.

The ridged black horns that protruded from her forehead, to his quiet astonishment, took nothing away from the beauty of her face. Narrow it was, fine-boned and sharp, though he saw something around the lines of her jaw—something he couldn't put into words—that struck him as even less human than the horns. At first, he'd thought her yellow eyes glowed with some kind of infernal inner light, but this close, he saw that they simply reflected any light shined upon them. Firelight. Moonlight. He wondered how dazzling they might be in the sun. She inclined her head, and those eyes settled upon his own very, very plain brown ones, and she said, "How bad is the pain?"

He tried to answer her, but his teeth chattered, and all he could do was shake his head. As they arrived at the coach-fire, he managed, "Aren't you c-cold?"

The corners of the demon's mouth flickered up, and he got a glimpse of bold white teeth. "Don't concern yourself."

He swallowed hard, and then once more. "My n-name is Wendell Anwar. It's—you've—you saved m-my life."

The yellow of her eyes caught the fire's flicker and danced like twin stars. "Am I going to regret that?"

He clung to her. To the impossible warmth and sinful smoothness of her skin. "I p-*promise* you. You won't."

The demon set Anwar down with his back against a half-buried boulder and crouched beside him. "Show me the wound."

Anwar gestured weakly at his side. She pulled up the edge of the sodden fur jacket, then the silk shirt underneath, and her eyes narrowed in an unreadable expression. She tilted her head, and for the first time Anwar became aware of the mass of hair that started just behind her horns and fell to the middle of her back. While her skin absorbed the light of the fire, her lustrous, straight black hair gleamed in it, like a million perfect strands of onyx. When she moved again he saw, among the black, a streak of breathtaking metallic blue. It left him wondering if such a color could sprout naturally from her scalp alongside the onyx, or if such a thing were a demon's concession to vanity.

"It's not deep," the demon said. "But it will require stitches. Do not move."

He clutched at her arm. The warmth from her body and the heat radiating from the burning wagon had restored a fraction of his equilibrium—enough not to let his voice quake as he said, "You're not *leaving* me here?"

This time her lips parted fully, her white teeth revealed in a grin that made his belly tremble, and the quality of her jaw and mouth that he hadn't been able to identify before came to him.

It was *strength*. Power. Physical might that would let those teeth tear through flesh and bone as easily as through a slice of crusty bread, he had no doubt of it.

"Do not worry, Wendell Anwar. Those men..." She nodded toward the pile of dead brigands, "...were the only threat in these woods. You will be safe until I return."

Anwar nodded, and the demon turned and disappeared into the woods. He winced as a fresh stab of pain shot through his torso, and he tried to think of how he would describe all this to the territorial officials in Tember.

Anwar let his head drop back against the boulder and wondered what Emperor Valco would have to say about his current situation.

With a flare of shame to mirror the pain in his side, he wondered what his mother would have to say as well, since it was on her word that he'd gained this post in the first place. He imagined the criers in the squares bellowing the news to all who would listen: *Governor Pro Tempore slain by brigands before arriving in Tember to take office.* He let his eyes slide shut, grimacing at the imagined pain and humiliation.

Anwar jerked awake and gasped at the sound of soft footsteps approaching. He had no idea how long he'd been asleep, but darkness still filled the spaces between the trees, and the fire had only burned down a little.

The demon knelt beside him. Now she was covered from neck to heels in what appeared to be skillfully sewn fur garments, including tight leather gloves and a fur-lined hood that nestled against her shoulders. She opened a leather pouch and produced a length of fine line, a set of small, hooked bone needles, and a couple of little ceramic jars. "Here," she said, the warmth and husky texture of her voice washing over him again. "Lie on your side." Her gloved hands helped him as he stretched out on the frozen ground, his wound facing the firelight. He hissed as an icy wind sliced across his bared flesh.

"What are you doing? Exactly?"

The demon had begun humming a soft tune, and Anwar was suddenly sure his wound had to be much worse than he'd been led to believe, because he heard her answer him *over* the tune—the notes and the words reaching his ears simultaneously, and without interruption. "I need to put a bit of medicine in the wound before I sew it up." The melody hummed and flowed through a tiny pause. "Now lie still."

Anwar wondered if this were naught but the height of folly, trusting this strange, deadly, spectacular creature to perform such intimate duties. And yet he couldn't help returning to the knowledge that without the demon, he'd be dead or worse by now…and that he had no other option.

A few minutes later, with the pain in his side steadily abating, the demon helped him upright again, and sat down less than a meter in front of him, gracefully folding her legs. "How do you feel?"

Anwar tilted his torso in small, ginger movements. "Better? I believe? What kind of medicine is that?"

The demon shook her head. A small, dismissive gesture. "Just a few herbs. There is little choice but to tend to one's own needs out here." She paused, and though her lips did not move, he thought there might have been the tiniest flash of amusement in her brilliant yellow eyes. "Is it not impolite to stare in human society?"

He realized that he had, indeed, been staring, and dropped his gaze, his cheeks abruptly hot. "Sorry. I'm sorry. You save my life, and I repay that grace with rudeness." Carefully he looked up at her again. "I've never met…one of you…before. Please forgive me, but I—well, I —if you don't mind, may I know your name?"

The amusement dropped away from the demon's face. She did not look exactly hostile, but Anwar thought it would be a short journey to get there. "Wendell Anwar, those stinking, lice-infested men I killed tonight have been a pain in my tits for half a year. A trade caravan comes through once every full moon and stops here, so that I may sell my wares. Four of the last six times, the 'Rock Knives,' as they called themselves, attacked the caravan and disrupted my trade. Tonight was the first night I was able to catch them all in one place *and* distracted enough for me to rid myself of them. I did not set out to rescue you." Her nostrils flared. Settled. Her eyes darted to the burning coach as she said, "My name is Nysska Stonegate."

Anwar had been struggling, as she spoke, to take in and process all the words, so overwhelmed was he with the sudden barrage of the demon's unparalleled voice. He blinked a couple of times and ordered his thoughts. "Well…Miss Stonegate…what, if I may ask, *are* your wares?" Out of habit he wanted to add, *And why has it not been reported that an Imperial trade caravan is doing business with a demon on the Tember Road?* but kept that to himself.

"Furs," she said, and plucked at the lapel of her coat. "I catch them. Cure them. Cut and sew them, if requested."

Anwar blinked again. "And you live out here—in the wilderness? Alone?" When she didn't immediately answer, he said, "I thought all of your—that is, all the refugees—had congregated in the Crags? Mainly around Slocum?"

She shrugged.

"And...please forgive me if I sound impertinent. Are you, ah—satisfied with this? With such a solitary life?"

Nysska Stonegate leaned forward. She sniffed once, quietly, leading Anwar to wonder what a demon's sense of smell constituted, and whether anything about his scent betrayed more than he would've liked. "Why do you ask?"

Anwar took a breath to speak, thought better of it, and took another one. The wheels had indeed been spinning in his head, as the ancient saying went, and even as the words left his mouth, the vision he saw in his mind took more and more solid a shape.

Wendell Anwar, Governor *Pro Tempore* of the Green Needles Territory, said, "Because, Nysska Stonegate, I would like to offer you a job."

Nysska returned to the place she had reluctantly come to think of as home just as the sky began to turn gray in the east. Built onto the front of a shallow cave in the side of a hill, the log structure might have qualified as a house. Nysska thought of it as *barako.* "The shack." It kept the rain off her head, though, and the wind at bay, and the crude hearth she'd fashioned out of stones from the river provided warmth during the cold months when the nights stretched out so long.

The nights like tonight.

She pushed the door open and stepped inside, and a weak voice almost drowned out by the crackling of the flames reached her from the back. "Nysska? *Cxu estas vi?"*

Nysska crossed the floor and knelt by the bed of furs where her mother lay. "Of course it's me, *panjo*."

Simana, Nysska's mother, had gone blind not long after the *Krizo*, when she and Nysska and all of their brothers and sisters—the ones who'd survived, which hadn't been many—had fled Fortikajxo, running for their lives. The disaster had affected Simana's skin and muscles as well. For far too many months, Nysska had watched in powerless horror as her mother's skin turned gray, peeling off bit by bit, while her muscles atrophied and collapsed. Only in the past few weeks had she seemed to turn a corner—skin healing, muscles returning, but only so, so slowly. Nysska hoped her sight would come back. It hadn't yet. Simana's eyes, once a fiery orange, had changed to a smooth, unseeing white.

Her mind, unlike her body, had never lost even a single step, no matter how much she had suffered. "Where have you been?" Simana asked quietly, in Plainish now. They both knew the value of maintaining fluency in the human tongues.

Quickly, concisely, Nysska related what had happened with the Rock Knives, and the Imperial caravan, and the man she'd saved.

Simana nodded. A near-imperceptible motion. Her brow creased in a thoughtful manner Nysska recognized. "What did he look like? This human?"

Nysska grunted noncommittally. "Like most humans. A collection of various shades of brown. Hair like..." She made a spiral in the air with one finger, despite knowing her mother couldn't see it. "...springs."

"Young? Old? How was he traveling?"

"Grown, but still young. He had a wagon, and eight men guarding him. What is all this?"

"Tell me where this man is now."

"Back at the site. It was only a few meters from the road, and he's well enough. He'll be able to call out to the next travelers he sees. They'll take him to Tember."

Simana's white eyes narrowed. "You saved this man's life...and left him unattended?"

Nysska sighed. "I will tell you the same thing I told him. The Rock Knives presented the only threat in these woods. Now that they're all dead, he has no reason to worry."

"Perhaps not from any other *human* threat. But what do you think will happen should a beast scent all that fresh-killed flesh? Would your Wendell Anwar be able to defend himself?"

"I never asked to be involved in his affairs. I have already done him one service. Should that not be enough?"

"You never asked...? *Shame* on you, daughter. You involved *yourself*.

And you know the teachings of Atiina at least as well as I do. That man is now your responsibility. Never mind that you've left him, alone and vulnerable. What would prevent him from going to Tember and telling everyone of the..." Simana paused at the word. Her lip wrinkled in distaste. "The demon who abandoned him? What if he comes back with fifty soldiers and burns down the woods until he finds you?"

Nysska shook her head. "I do not believe he would do that. In fact, he..."

Simana turned her head to face Nysska fully. "He what?"

"He suggested that I...could...take up a position."

Simana's voice took on an edge, weak though it was. "What do you mean by 'position'?"

"He offered employment. In the human—in the *Imperial* government. He said that I could become an...*ambassador*...for my people."

Simana's hand quested out until it touched Nysska's arm and clamped around her wrist. "You must. You *must*. Return to this Wendell Anwar at once and tell him you will do as he asks."

Nysska pulled her arm away, scowling. "How can you even suggest that? The humans want no more to do with us than we do with them! They call us demons, yes, but better than half of them believe it *fact*!" Her tone softened. "*Ne*. I will stay here, *panjo*. With you. As we agreed."

Simana opened her mouth to speak, but only sighed. "I know that tone. Little can be done to change your mind now." With great effort, she rolled over onto her side, her back to her daughter. "We can discuss it further in the morning."

"There is nothing to discuss," Nysska said moments later, but Simana's breathing had already gone deep and even.

After a few minutes, during which Nysska decided to wake her mother and then decided not to at least five times, she stepped out into the sharp night air, headed for the latest latrine she'd dug.

"Hello, Nysska," a deep, smooth voice said, halting her in her tracks no more than two meters from the shack's door. She watched as five tall, lean columns of darkness detached themselves from the shadows and stepped closer, yellow eyes shimmering, ridged horns limned by moonlight. The one who'd spoken moved closer still, until he looked Nysska dead in the eye. "What a fascinating conversation we just overheard."

Wendell Anwar had asked Nysska Stonegate repeatedly not to go, and then asked her to take him with her, wherever her destination, but he wanted to believe that he hadn't quite resorted to begging.

"Stay here," she'd said. "Another caravan should pass this way tomorrow. The day after at the latest. They will take you."

"But...what about..." Anwar had eyed the pile of corpses the demon had built, and beyond them, the bodies of his guards scattered near the river. "What about other brigands?"

"There are no others," Nysska had said, plainly and simply. "Good luck to you."

She'd left him with a full skin of water taken from the river and a handful of strips of dried meat. He'd watched her vanish into the darkness between the trees, beyond the fire's reach, and had taken a breath to call out to her one last time but bit it off.

Now that she had faded into the woods, it was as if she had never been there at all. As if he had somehow been deposited by a mercurial god at the scene of the massacre, the only living human for hundreds of kliks, nothing but slowly draining cadavers to keep him company.

Anwar considered the possibility that this might have been a nightmare, but just as quickly rejected the thought. Yes, he was a world away from his warm bed in the Senatorial. Yes, he had just encountered a being that far too many citizens of the Empire still believed mythical. Yes, the scenario as a whole struck him as absurd.

He had only to run his fingertips across the skillful stitches the demon had left in his skin to know how real it all was.

A day, she had said. Perhaps two. If he kept the fire going, he might not freeze to death. If he rationed the water in the skin carefully or, if he got very lucky, managed to make his way back to the riverbank without tearing open the sutures in his side, he might not die of thirst. If the demon—Anwar caught himself. *Use the proper term.* If the *sethyd* was right, and no other thieves or murderers lurked along the edges of the highway, he might not awaken to the sensation of a blade slicing across his throat.

A board—once part of the side of the now-destroyed coach—turned loose of its nails and fell into the center of the fire, sending a shower of sparks skyward. The glare of the flames prevented him from seeing any of the stars he knew to be overhead. Often, as a boy, he'd made his way onto the roof of his father's grand home outside Caulspring and stretched out on the tiles, staring up into the vast darkness. Picking out the brightest stars and watching them shimmer. Tracking the paths of the three moons as they lumbered across the sky. It had always made him feel tiny. Insignificant.

But there on the side of the Tember Road, leaning against a boulder, watching a fire burn, he felt more minuscule, and more *alone,* than he ever had before in his life.

His twenty-second birthday was coming up in a few weeks.

Wendell Anwar wondered if he'd be around to see it.

Slowly he chewed one of the strips of meat Nysska had given him. He'd contemplated the possibility of her poisoning him but couldn't see any point to it. If she'd wanted him dead, he would've been cold and rotting already. Just like the Rock Knives. He wished he could have seen how she had dispatched them, instead of only hearing the brutal sounds of breaking bone and opening skin. He thought perhaps witnessing the carnage might have let it seem more...more *normal.* Instead of the hideous, demonic wrath conjured by his imagination.

Anwar took another bite, chewed, swallowed—

And froze.

A sound had reached his ears. Not from the fire, not from his own breath, not from the grinding of his teeth, and yet he still felt the sound in the marrow of his bones.

A heavy, grunting *chuff*. Somewhere behind him.

Anwar put one hand on the ground, about to try to leverage himself up to his feet, sutures or not, but as his palm pressed flat to the earth, he *felt* something. A vibration—and then another—and he knew. Not from any school-learned knowledge, not from any lived experience, but on a deeper level, an awareness that rose up from the bottom of his soul. Instinctual. Primal. He knew, and he abandoned any thought of running and simply pulled his knees up to his chest and wrapped his arms around them.

The great gray bear took another step, sending more tremors into the earth, and came around the boulder. It *chuffed* again. Anwar felt the punishing heat of its breath. The scent of blood and raw meat filled his nostrils like a carnal fog.

He'd never seen a bear that big before. Not in books, not in zoos. The animal moved past him, swaying by as if Anwar were nothing, negligible, and its mass seemed so great that it made Anwar feel as if an entire building had invaded the camp, as if the bear's flank were a wall stout enough to withstand the assaults of armies.

Anwar kept very, very still, and tried not to breathe.

The bear approached the fire first, but lingered near it for only a few moments. Its mammoth head swung toward the dead horses, and a few more seismic footsteps took it to them. Another *chuff*. The bear sniffed the dead animals. The nose lifted, still tasting the air, and guided it to the pile of slaughtered brigands. Once more it sniffed, and used one massive paw to shove a couple of the bodies to one side. The firelight glinted off its claws, each of one of them easily as long as one of Anwar's fingers.

Anwar racked his brain for information. *How to survive a bear attack.* Was this the kind of bear that didn't want to deal with humans? If he struggled to his feet and raised his arms high and bellowed at it, would it shamble off into the woods? Or...was this the kind that a human's only hope of surviving was to flatten out and play dead and hope against hope that it wouldn't maul him *too* badly?

The bear swung around and, for the first time, faced Anwar head-on. Its eyes fixed on his.

Anwar lost a small amount of control over his bladder.

The bear's eyes *glittered silver*. Its colossal skull swung back and forth as the immense clawed feet padded toward him. Anwar whimpered, and wished he hadn't.

The word rang in his brain.

Seraphic.

He wanted to call out—to the demon, to the Great Silver Dragon, to his mother—but the breath had locked tight in his lungs.

The bear stopped no more than a meter away. It exhaled, long, casually, and its summer-heat breath washed over him. The bear's skull, on its own, easily weighed as much as Anwar's entire body, and he watched as the great gray head tilted to one side, then the other, the glimmering silver eyes narrowing.

"I kn-kn-know what you are," Anwar said, surprising himself for saying *anything* out loud. "Y-you're a seraphic animal. You've got argonium running all through your v-veins. I know—" He choked, and coughed, and swallowed hard. "I know how smart you are. And I—I beseech you. Don't kill me. Please."

The bear closed the distance between them. The metallic eyes had not changed, giving Anwar no reason to believe that the beast had understood him, but he was too petrified to move, too petrified even to close his own eyes as the bear lifted a paw and reached forward—

One dagger-like claw, only one, snagged the hem of his tunic and raised it, exposing the stitchwork Nysska had performed on his flesh. The bear chuffed. Let the tunic fall back into place. The silver eyes bored into him.

Anwar swallowed again, his mouth abruptly dry as cotton. "Do you understand me? Do you—do you understand language? My language? Plainish?" The bear didn't move. Anwar tried again. "Estmani? No? Do you—do you speak the sethyd's language? Oh, uh, no, forget I asked that, I don't speak her language either, so it wouldn't do me any good."

From somewhere far down in the bear's body, a low growl emerged. Anwar got the rock-solid impression that the beast was losing patience with him.

"All right—all right! We can do this without language! Maybe." He picked up a twig and drew a couple of long, gently waving parallel lines in the dirt next to him. "Look, this is the river, yes?" He pointed. "That river. That's what I mean with this." He drew another line. "And here's the highway, running alongside it. With the forest—" a series of short lines, "—coming right up to it. And here's the dock, the one right over there. And here's the dead horses, and the dead brigands, and the fire." More scratching in the dirt, with points in between each. "And here's us! See?" He drew two figures, one much larger than the other. "See, this is you. And this is me." Anwar made a slow, sweeping gesture that he hoped and prayed would appear non-threatening. "This is this place, right here, where we are. Maybe you could nod if you understand me?" He nodded, an exaggerated motion. "This means 'yes.' Do you get it? This area. This is where we are. Right now."

The bear gazed down at his scratchings in the dirt and, after a moment, glanced around at the surrounding area, then back at Anwar. *Now* something had changed. Something deep in the beast's eyes.

"Fucking hell, you *do* understand me, don't you? All right—all right. Listen." Anwar drew a large circle around the rudimentary map. "I can see to it that no humans come into this area. Ever. I—" He paused, wondering if the word *governor* would mean anything more than a random collection of sounds to this animal. "Other humans will do what I say. I will make sure no more humans..." He patted his chest. "No more men or women or children come into this territory. *Your* territory. If you let me live. I have to go to the city, and there I can make this law."

The bear's eyes never left his. The colossal skull moved closer, closer still, and when the mouth opened only centims from Anwar's face, he wanted to squeeze his eyes shut and say a prayer, but he couldn't move, couldn't make even a single muscle twitch, and the bear's roar blew Anwar's hair back—

And cut off.

The bear sat down, and reached out one massive paw, and patted Anwar on the head. From somewhere in the creature's chest a sound emerged.

His eyes huge, jaw hanging open, Anwar said, "Are you—are you *laughing?*"

The bear patted Anwar again, on the side of the head and on the shoulder. Still making the sound that may or may not have been a great seraphic beast laughing at a puny, helpless human, the bear lumbered over to one of the horses, cut the leather belly band with an efficient swipe of a claw, and dragged the horse's body away into the night.

Wendell Anwar stared after it for a few minutes, silently, before he burst into tears.

Anwar awakened with the dawn's light, and mourned the loss of the last of the dried meat strips Nysska had left him. The fire had finally died away, all the wood of the wagon burned through, and he examined his fingers and toes for signs of frostbite. None showed itself. He even had sensation in most of them.

His stomach growled as he carefully, gently got to his feet and relieved himself at the edge of the woods, his eyes darting everywhere. The great gray bear had not put in an appearance since it had left with the horse carcass. Neither had he seen any other animals, besides birds in the trees overhead and the occasional squirrel. Still, Anwar wasn't sure he would ever feel relaxed again, and so Nysska's approach did not startle him. She came out of the woods, still covered in her fine fur clothing, and now had a large leather pack slung between her shoulders. He gave her a chattery, almost-frozen kind of smile. "Miss Stonegate! I'm so glad you came back! I—"

Anwar fell silent at the grim lines on her face.

Nysska came to him and, for the first time, he appreciated just how *tall* the sethyd was. Cranking his head up to look her in the eye, he said, "Miss Stonegate—are you all right?"

"I have changed my mind," she said, all the smoke and dark, dusky sensuality of her voice drained away, replaced with bitter exhaustion. "And I accept your offer."

2

A pounding at the door brought Henrik Gazer up from an alcohol-induced stupor. He lay in bed for a few seconds, blinking into the darkness as the wind rattled the rafters and whistled through the thatched roof. Lora, his wife of ten years —*Ten years too long,* he was fond of telling his friends at the tavern—stirred beside him. The pounding came again, and Lora's wiry fingers dug into his shoulder. "Who is it?" she hissed, and Henrik wanted to slam his fist into her mouth again.

"The fuck should I know?" he managed, hardly slurring his words at all, and shook her hand loose. "Whoever they are, they can fuck right off."

He sat up and swung his legs over, bare feet slapping down on the hard-packed dirt floor, and grunted at Cinda to get out of the way. Of course the girl was already awake and underfoot. As Henrik's eyes adjusted to the near-darkness—a few stray flashes of lantern light making their way through the far window from the town—he saw Cinda scoop up the filthy mat she slept on and scuttle into a corner.

Henrik rose to his full height and stretched as the godforsaken bastard outside bashed what sounded like a metal bar into the wooden door, rattling it in its frame. He stomped the width of the house's single room and threw the door open, his ice-shard eyes flaring under fearsomely beetled brows.

It was a glare that had won many fights, and many more arguments, stabbing out from beneath his thick mane of shaggy black hair. Henrik banked the coals behind that evil glower, peeled his lips back from the gappy teeth visible between his enormous black beard and moustache, and shouted, *"What?"*

The man standing in his doorway didn't flinch. Henrik blinked, confused, his brain still waking up, and as it registered that the man was both as tall and broad as he was himself, the sight of the bronze armor sank in. Henrik bit back any further words.

"Henrik Gazer?" the soldier asked, lifting the lantern in his left hand to get a better look at Henrik's face. "You Henrik Gazer?"

From off to his left, near one of the windows, Cinda whispered, "Daddy."

He glanced over and saw the girl peering out into the darkness beyond the lantern-carrying soldier, but a powerful wave of nausea swept over him, and he ignored her. Henrik let out a wet belch and steadied himself against the doorframe. "What if I am?"

"We got some questions for you, Mister Gazer. Mind if we step inside?"

A little louder: *"Daddy."*

Henrik squinted at the soldier. Yeah, he was big, but Henrik knew the type: a little shit who got handed his rank by some high-placed relative. Not a man accustomed to hard work. Fuck, soldiers never worked at all, that's what Henrik's father had always said. Another wave of nausea swept over him, and he silently acknowledged that the evening's ale hadn't finished with him. "No, you fucking well can't come in," he growled. He wanted to say more, something like, *Wake me up out of a dead sleep, fuck you and your Empire, leave us alone or I'll have my thumb in your eye,* but though Henrik was still very drunk, he did not believe himself to be stupid.

The soldier's eyes narrowed. He held up a tightly-rolled piece of paper. "Mister Gazer, I got here an edict from—"

A spasm in Henrik's gut didn't let the soldier finish. Blasting a cone of ale fumes and halitosis in the soldier's face, Henrik grabbed the man by the shoulders and vomited a flagon's worth of ale and stomach acid all over him. The soldier took one quick step backward, cursing, arms flailing, and toppled onto the grass with a great clanking impact.

Cinda shouted, "Daddy!"

Something reached out of the darkness behind the prone, befouled soldier and struck Henrik Gazer square in the breastbone, directly over his heart, with a force not unlike the kick of a mule.

The heel of Henrik's right foot left a drag-mark in the dirt floor as he skidded across the house's width and slammed into the rough stone wall. He sank to the floor, his body alight with pain in his chest and the back of his head, and the rest of the ale he'd consumed before falling asleep came spewing out of him, spraying his chest and lap and legs down to the knee. Some vague, distant part of his brain registered that Lora and Cinda were both screaming, and he tried to say, "Shut up shut up shut your stupid cunt mouths," but he could do little more than groan and dry-heave.

Henrik let his head tip back against the wall, squinting even as he blinked, trying to get his vision to come clear, and so it was that he saw a pair of glittering yellow eyes emerge from the darkness outside. Henrik gasped, sucked frothy spew into his lungs, and entered a coughing frenzy as the demon stooped to come through the door and into the house.

The demon's horns reached out from underneath a bronze Imperial helmet just like the one the other soldier wore. More armor encased its midnight-violet body, which grew taller and taller as it rose up to its full height, the tips of the ridged black horns brushing against the ceiling. One long, black-nailed hand curled around the pommel of a sword at its hip, and on the end of that pommel…

Henrik began to cry.

A faceted white jewel as big as a hen's egg adorned the end of the longsword's pommel. Henrik's eyes flashed back and forth between the jewel and the demon's face. The world felt as if it had just fallen away from beneath him, even though he knew full well he was still sitting on his ass on the cold dirt.

Lora's voice hissed from a far corner. Henrik turned his head to see his wife, their daughter clutched tight in her arms, eyes locked on the demon. Lora whispered prayer after prayer, begging and pleading for her soul and the soul of her child to be saved from eternal damnation as she crowded into a far corner.

Henrik tried to get to his feet, but pain chiseled into his skull, and his legs refused to work, and he dry-heaved again. Dimly, he recognized that some of the liquid soaking the backs of his thighs and his buttocks came from his abruptly empty bladder.

The demon looked back at the young soldier, who had gotten to his feet and now hovered in the doorway. She gestured at Henrik and said, "If I may, sir?" and Henrik realized it was a female.

A female demon.

Serving in the Thaumetallicon.

He began to cry harder. His sobs drowned out the sound of Lora's desperate prayers.

The demon crossed the room and crouched in front of him. Her hand never strayed from the hilt of the longsword, and this close, the white jewel seemed to glow with a silver inner radiance not unlike the twinkling light of the stars overhead.

"What'd you hit me with?" Henrik mewled. "Some demon magic? Infected me with your stench now? Will I turn into a worm, so you can eat me?"

"I hit you with my fist," the demon said, her voice low and rich and rough, with an accent he'd never before heard. "Are you going to be calm now, and answer our questions? Or will you force me into more unpleasantness?"

Henrik blinked at her. He licked his lips and dragged the back of one hand across his mouth. "You'll not kill me?"

The demon rolled her luminous yellow eyes. He thought they might have been reflecting some of the light from the pommel-jewel. "I won't beat you to death," the demon said. She reached out a hand, gathered a fistful of his collar, and stood up, lifting him off the floor as if he weighed no more than a modest trout out of the stream. "Whether you survive the night depends on you."

From the corner, Lora's prayers continued. They'd grown in intensity until she sounded like a hissing cat. The demon steadied Henrik on his feet and, as the soldier on whom he'd vomited came into the house, she turned to face the woman and child. "I'm going to approach you," she said, and Cinda started crying. "Please remain calm. I mean you no harm."

"Stay back, monster!" Lora cried as the demon moved closer to her. Henrik thought Lora might lash out, either with a poker from the fireplace or with her own bare hands, but she froze in place as the demon crouched down in front of them.

"We need you both to be quiet and calm," the demon said. "The process will move much more smoothly if no one is in hysterics."

Lora and Cinda both fell silent. Tears still rolled down the cheeks of woman and girl alike—and then the first soldier balled up his fist and drove it into the pit of Henrik's stomach. Henrik doubled over, gasping and heaving, and the last thing he remembered before he passed out was the sound of the soldier's disgusted curses.

"All right," Brux said, as Nysska stretched Henrik Gazer's unconscious body out on the grass. "Morrin. Do it." He stepped back and watched, wiping at his vomit-splashed chestplate with a bit of cloth he'd taken from inside the house. Brux had removed his helmet, putting his commander's band on display—he loved few things more than showing it off—and the bronze-inlaid leather strap encircling his huge, bald head bobbed up and down as his expression shifted from rage to disgust and back.

The wind pushed at Nysska. Frigid, wet, insistent fingers that wormed their way through the joints of her armor and moved the heavy braid of her hair. Seven long months had passed since that night in Hexember when she'd saved Wendell Anwar's life. *Seven months I'll never regain,* she thought, with a bitterness that matched the wind's cold. It was late March now, and the snow had only just decided to stay gone.

Nysska stood apart from the other three members of her Crucible, as she normally did. The four of them had, over the course of those seven months, developed a grudging, spiteful sort of shorthand that kept them from having to interact with each other more than absolutely necessary.

Not that they didn't communicate. Brux hated her, almost as much as he feared her, though his fear was so tied up with his insecurity that it often came across a bit muddled. Nysska knew there was no way the Cathedral would ever make her a Commander. Brux's job was safe, despite all of his suspicions and paranoia. Though tonight, as she watched his jaw ripple, teeth grinding in his skull at what he surely perceived to be her joy at his humiliation, the hatred might have edged out the fear.

Morrin, the Crucible's Sensor, simply feared her. But then, Morrin feared most things. She spoke almost as infrequently as Nysska did, her tiny mouse-squeak voice trampled under Brux's noise any time she tried to say anything. Nysska sighed—a private, weary sound. One she made often when thinking of Morrin.

The Keeper known as Staige didn't seem to care about Nysska any more than he cared about the other members of the Crucible, or about his own position in it, or about Greta, the big, friendly scent-hound he'd been hired to handle. He sat on the ground under a nearby tree, his back to the trunk, and tipped the metal flask he always carried. Greta paced back and forth in front of him, uncertainty in canine form, panting and licking her chops. Staige had hit the liquor early that day, and Nysska wondered if he was sitting because he didn't care about procedure, or because he was no longer able to stand.

Morrin gave Brux and his big fists a wide berth as she made her way to Henrik Gazer's side. She knelt near his shoulder, leaned down, and the argonium runes implanted on either side of her considerable nose glimmered a soft silver.

The silver gleam highlighted the bruise on her cheek, in the shape of one of Brux's knuckles.

Morrin took in Henrik Gazer's scent with three long inhalations. The runes on her face glowed a tiny bit brighter with each breath. Finally, she sat back, cast weak, watery eyes up at Brux, and nodded.

Brux said, "Staige. Get that mutt over here."

Staige didn't move from beneath the tree. He did belch, and wave one hand. "Greta."

The dog hesitated. Staige pointed at Morrin, and Morrin said, "Here, girl, come here, that's a good girl," and finally Greta whoofed and scampered over to her. Morrin said, "Sit," and Greta sat, and Morrin put her face close to the dog's muzzle and blew a long, slow breath into Greta's nostrils. Tiny silver motes swirled and danced in the exhalation.

Greta whined, and didn't move.

"Come on, girl," Morrin whispered.

Brux snapped, "What's the trouble?"

Nysska saw tears start in Morrin's eyes. Morrin said, "Staige, uh—he didn't give her the—the command word. Again. Same reason she lost the scent this afternoon."

Brux's neck muscles creaked as he swiveled his head toward the Crucible's Keeper. Staige had slid down onto his back beneath the tree now, and as the rest of his team stared at him, he began to snore.

Brux grabbed Morrin by the shoulder and hauled her to her feet in one rough yank. Greta whined and paced. "So, what, that's it? Because he didn't say the right word, now we're just *stuck*? Because this goddamn dog is too stupid to do its job, we all just sit here holding our cocks?"

Greta whined again. Brux shoved Morrin away, and said, "Goddamn worthless pile-of-shit dog," and drew back one heavy-booted foot, aimed squarely at Greta's ribcage.

Nysska said, "Don't."

Brux's foot came to an abrupt halt in mid-swing. He planted his feet again and swung to face her, his mouth open, the hatred he'd never bothered to hide pouring out of his eyes, but Nysska didn't move.

Brux all but vibrated with his loathing. That loathing boiled over, and he spun back to Morrin, who stood but had drawn in on herself, head tucked down, arms up around her head. Brux brought his foot back up. He didn't kick Morrin, but he did plant the sole of the bronze-reinforced boot in her stomach and shove her to the ground.

Morrin fell as if she had no bones, and only made a tiny, frightened sound on top of the thudding impact.

"What the fuck is wrong with you?" Brux screamed at Morrin, who stayed crumpled on the ground next to the unconscious Henrik. "She's a goddamn scent hound, ain't she? And you gave her the goddamn scent? How'd you fuck it up? Why the fuck can't you do your job?" He bellowed loud enough for the entire village to hear him. A few of the dozen or so other houses showed signs of life—a light in a window here, a stirring in a doorway there—but no one had come out to get any closer to the scene of the crime.

Nysska had seen this drama play out before, whenever Staige got too drunk to perform his duties. Brux never confronted Staige about his drinking, but he took any excuse he could find to punish Morrin. The bruise on her face gave mute testimony to that, just as the regular grunts and moans that had issued from Brux's tent over the last seven months had painted a picture of how he used Morrin for other purposes.

Nysska hadn't witnessed him land the latest blow. Brux rarely paid that kind of attention to Morrin when anyone else could see them. Nysska and Staige both knew what was going on, but while Staige displayed the sheerest apathy at Morrin's plight, Nysska had made repeated attempts to help.

On a cold October evening, Nysska had taken Morrin aside. She'd steered the young human to the edge of the encampment where they'd stopped for the night and sat her down on a broad tree stump. "Morrin. How long has Brux been abusing you?"

In hindsight, Nysska thought she should have known better than to think Morrin would open up.

"I don't want to talk about it."

Nysska had crouched in front of her, putting them eye to eye—or it would have, if Morrin had ever met Nysska's gaze. Not once in the half-year Nysska had been a part of Brux's Crucible had Morrin ever looked her straight in the eye. Even there, on the stump, away from everyone else, the girl had trembled like a tiny wet dog.

"Morrin. Listen to me. You do not have to endure this. It is against the Cathedral's code. You can report him."

Morrin had simply shaken her head and continued shivering.

"All right, then. You can do what *I* would do, should I find myself in the same situation. You know where Brux sleeps. I can show you where to put the knife—which ribs to slide it between. I know you're not strong, but a sharp enough blade will part muscle as easily as butter. Or, if you do not choose the heart..." Nysska had drawn a needle-sharp stiletto from a sheath on the inside of her forearm. "Simply plunge this into his ear. All the way to the hilt. Your body weight would be more than enough."

Morrin's shivers had turned into sobs. "I can't," she'd finally managed. "I'm not—not like you. I just—*can't*."

Now, in the middle of the night outside Henrik's tiny rock-and-wood home, a stone's throw from the sawmill that gave the village its reason to exist, Nysska tried to keep her heart from breaking as she watched Morrin draw into herself on the cold ground. Most humans inspired only her contempt. Contempt for Staige's drunkenness, for Brux's crude, aimless brutality. But for Morrin, Nysska felt...what? Empathy? Pity? Oceans of frustration, that much was sure.

Brux threw his head back and screamed at the night sky. Greta started at the sudden noise, and ran to Nysska, huddling against her legs. The dog threw fearful glances at Brux as Nysska knelt and stroked her head. "There there," she murmured into Greta's ear. "I won't let him hurt you."

Rounding on Morrin yet again, Brux bellowed, "Well if the fucking dog's as fucked up as your ugly face, how are we supposed to close this out? Huh? If you and that stupid mutt can't find the suspect, then we're all just *fucked*, huh? Aren't we? *Aren't we, Morrin?*"

Morrin curled into a ball and wept.

Staige shifted against the tree trunk and snored louder.

Nysska let a long, rasping sigh escape her lips. As Brux stomped and flailed his arms and screamed, working himself up into a literal lather as bubbles of spit appeared at the corners of his mouth, Nysska took Greta and went back to Henrik's house.

The door already stood open, so Nysska didn't bother knocking. She ducked her head again and stepped carefully inside. Henrik's wife and daughter stood in the same far corner where she'd last seen them, and at the sight of her, the mother pulled her daughter close to her, wrapping her arms around the girl.

Nysska took in the house's interior, paying more attention to it now that she didn't have to concentrate on subduing a suspect. She would have called it "depressing" at its best. The bare dirt floor, the lopsided table with three three-legged stools around it, the butter churn in another corner. The bed—no more than a few blankets laid across a rope net stretched in a wooden frame—and the pallet where the girl no doubt slept. A rough wooden chest underneath one of the windows probably held what few valuables the family owned, along with their clothing.

Nysska moved around the bed and sat down on its edge. She spoke to the mother over the girl's head. "I take it you know why we've come."

The mother's tone didn't quite contain a hiss. "I know you're a demon. You and your kind climbed up out of the metal caves. You're from the under-hell, and you're full of hate, and you want us all to die. You'll sacrifice the men and the women to your vile, vicious god, and you'll feast on the children. No trickery will deceive us. We know your nature."

Nysska sighed. "Experience has taught me how pointless it would be to argue with you." She tapped the white gemstone on the hilt of her longsword. "But you do recognize what this is? What it means?"

The woman's focus had been flickering back and forth between Nysska's eyes and her horns. Now they darted down to the gemstone and back up. She said nothing.

Nysska went on. "Your husband is a suspect in the murder of a young woman who worked in the tavern in Coalbranch. You're familiar with Coalbranch? Village about three kliks west of here? The young woman's name was Layne. Someone raped her and beat her severely and strangled her until she died. That took place six days ago. Our Crucible has been sent to find the person who did that to her and bring that person to justice. Do you know anything about the crime?"

The woman's face wrinkled into a mask of hatred and contempt. "You likely killed that woman yourself. Fiend of the pit. Foul defiler.

Go back to the hell you came from." She made a horrible noise in her sinuses and spat a gray-green glob into the dirt at Nysska's feet.

The action of doing so caused something at the woman's neck, just below the hem of her nightgown, to shift a tiny bit.

Nysska's eyes narrowed to burning slits.

Two minutes later, Nysska and Greta emerged from the house, followed by the sounds of the woman's tears. Nysska realized she'd never gotten the names of either the woman or her daughter, and briefly considered going back in for them, but abandoned that thought when she realized how little she cared. The day's case report was Brux's responsibility, not hers. Before her, Morrin lay on the ground, clenched into a fetal position on her side, next to the still-unconscious Henrik. Staige lay sprawled senselessly under the tree. Brux stomped back and forth several meters away, cursing under his breath and swiping at his mouth with the back of his hand.

Nysska held up the pendant she'd taken from around the woman's neck. "Brux. Look at this."

Brux stopped, and glared at her, and took a good long moment before he approached. His glare shifted from her to the necklace. "The fuck is that?"

"Do you remember when we questioned Layne Wong's parents? In Coalbranch?"

Brux's chest puffed out. "*I* did the questioning." He pointed at the leather band resting just above his eyebrows. "This means I'm in charge, remember? I ask the questions. You just stand outside."

Nysska's yellow eyes glittered as they rolled in their sockets. "Yes, Brux, you are in charge. You are the Crucible's Commander."

"Fucking right."

"But do you remember Layne's mother commenting on the pendant that her daughter wore? The hand-crafted one, given to her as a birthday present?"

Brux's heavy brows drew together. Nysska watched as the glacially slow gears in his mind turned. She imagined she could hear them: *click...click...click...* One painful gear tooth at a time. "The fuck're you talking about? Pendant? So fuckin' what?"

"Brux. This is that pendant." She held it up in front of him. "The one that belonged to Layne Wong. I just took it from Henrik's wife."

Brux snorted. "So?"

Nysska let her eyes close for a moment. Tried to regulate her breathing. "So how did it get around Henrik's wife's neck?"

Click...click...click...ping! Brux grabbed the pendant out of Nysska's hand. She let him. "Holy fuck. Holy *fuck!* This means...this means..."

Nysska nodded. "Henrik probably killed Layne, took the pendant, and gave it to his wife. Unless the wife killed the girl herself. We just need to get one of them to confess."

Brux held the pendant aloft in triumph. "This means we don't need the goddamn dog, or Morrin's stupid fucking face!" He brayed laughter. "You hear that, Morrin? You're off the hook for this one!" He waved the pendant at her, regardless of how tightly her eyes were squeezed shut. "Look what I found! I cracked the whole fucking case!"

Nysska felt Greta nosing at her calves. She bent down and scratched the dog's ears. "Yes, Greta, look at what the big human found. All by himself. Because of his good human brains."

The dog *whuffed* and licked Nysska's hand.

Half an hour later—following multiple vigorous slaps to the face and finally having a bucket of water dumped onto him—Henrik knelt on the grass, awake and sober and penitent, his hands bound behind his back with Imperial bronze shackles. All it had taken to get his mumbled confession was a look at the pendant. Nysska wondered whether, if Henrik had been smarter, or more alert, or both, he might have tried to blame the murder on his wife to save his own skin.

Not that it mattered at this point.

Morrin stood beside a now-awake Staige, Greta sitting alertly between them, several meters away from Henrik. Nysska leaned against the side of the house. She had already told the woman and her daughter what was going to happen and suggested as firmly and tactfully as she could that they be somewhere else when it did. They might have left quietly without her noticing, or they might still be inside, cowering in the corner. Nysska wasn't sure.

Brux had struck a wide-legged stance beside Henrik. This was his element—the closest he would ever come, in Nysska's estimation, to true power. A sword, the pommel of which bore a large white jewel identical to Nysska's, hung at his side, and he drew it with unmistakable relish.

"Henrik Gazer of Nodwin's Mill," Brux called out in his best theatrical voice, which still sounded more like that of an arrogant thug than a figure of authority. "Are you ready to be judged?"

Any fight Henrik might have possessed had left him. Thin tears tracked their way down his dirty face. He nodded silently.

Brux drew the white-jeweled sword and drove it into the ground. He wore a ring on his right hand—a commander's ring—that bore a gem the same white as the one on the sword's pommel, and he tapped the ring stone to the pommel stone three times. "I hereby summon the Council of Arbiters."

Nysska was still a little impressed with what happened next, despite having seen it dozens of times before. After a few seconds' pause, seven ghostly, silver-shimmering figures appeared in a ring around the sword, anonymous in long robes and voluminous hoods that hid their faces. A voice echoed out from the spectral circle, eerie, a single tone made up of seven people speaking in perfect unison. The Voice of the Council. "Who presents the charges?"

"I, Brux Haller, Commander of the Forty-Seventh Crucible."

The Voice of the Council spoke again. "Present your case, Commander Haller."

Brux cleared his throat. "This man—Henrik Gazer of Nodwin's Mill—stands accused of the rape and murder of Layne Wong of Coalbranch."

The Council's combined words echoed again. Rote. Bored. "And has your Crucible's Sensor determined sufficient evidence of the merits of this accusation?"

"No, Lords of the Council. Her participation was unnecessary. I, Commander Brux Haller, found a pendant that belonged to the victim in the possession of Henrik Gazer's wife. When confronted with this evidence, Gazer freely admitted what he had done."

The Council's words came again. "Is this true, Henrik Gazer of Nodwin's Mill? Do you admit the commission of rape and murder?"

Brux poked Henrik with the toe of his boot. Henrik quietly said, "Yeah."

The Voice of the Council rose in volume. "Then, by Imperial Decree, and the auspices of Emperor Valco the Twelfth, we declare the life of Henrik Gazer of Nodwin's Mill forfeit. His execution is to be carried out at once by your Crucible's Enforcer. Is said Enforcer present?"

Nysska pushed off the wall and approached the spectral figures. None of them had moved, or even twitched, and she couldn't tell whether any of them were actually looking at her from underneath their hoods. "I am," she said, and hefted the massive bronze axe she'd unbuckled from her horse's saddle.

"Let the sentence be carried out."

Henrik had stayed slumped, his head tilted forward, his chin resting on his chest. That made it easier.

Nysska brought the axe around and down and took his head off with a single blow.

The screams from inside the house answered the question of where the woman and her daughter had ended up. They were shrill, and hurt Nysska's ears, and made her want to use the axe on them as well, but instead she took two steps back and stayed in place. The way she was supposed to.

"Bronze is law," the Council intoned. "Bronze is peace."

Brux saluted them. "Bronze is law. Bronze is peace."

The seven spectral figures faded away. Just as Brux slid his sword back into its scabbard, Nysska heard the sound of approaching hoofbeats, and turned to see a rider barreling through the center of the tiny village. The treble moonlight glinted off the bronze of his armor.

"Who the fuck are you supposed to be?" Brux called out, still full of bravado from his performance.

The rider—a young man in his mid-twenties, Nysska thought, though she wasn't the best at judging humans' ages—slowed his horse and stopped beside Brux. "Are you the Forty-Seventh Crucible?"

"We are," Brux said, his chest puffing. "What's this about?"

"Word from the Governor," the rider said, handing over a message tube. "You've been summoned to Tember."

3

Morrin stared out the window of her second-floor room with Greta at her feet, wrapped in one of the room's two blankets. The dog always stayed with Morrin when Staige was too drunk to do anything but fall face-first into bed, and after his epic binge in the tavern next door, where Greta would sleep was a foregone conclusion.

There was no fireplace, and the temperature had dropped abruptly with the sunset. Morrin didn't want Greta to catch a cold. Not only because she loved the dog and wanted to make sure she was safe and looked after, but also because Morrin knew that, if not for the insanely expensive argonium runes implanted alongside her nose, the Cathedral-trained dog's life would be worth more than hers.

She hadn't caught the name of the village where they'd stopped. She knew it had to be roughly midway between Nodwin's Mill and Tember, but there were a lot of tiny villages along the Yorke Road. Maybe Thrushing? She thought she might have seen a sign. One village had come to look much like another since she'd been accepted into the Thaumetallicon and given her runes at the Imperial College in Volga. Torches lit the street outside just well enough to see the mud that would swallow a foot ankle-deep if trod upon without care.

Shouts and laughter and the occasional scream floated up and out from the tavern across the street, wedged between what looked like a butcher shop and...probably a brothel. There might have been a narrow wooden bridge connecting the top floor of the tavern to the top floor of the brothel, if that's what it was, or—Morrin squinted—maybe that was just shadows. Her eyesight had never been strong.

Her sense of smell, on the other hand, had always been exceptional, even before the argonium enhancements. She kept the window shut as tightly as the out-of-square frame would allow, but the village's scents threatened to overwhelm her. Mud and sweat and ale and sex and shit, both animal and human. Morrin preferred the wilder places. Places where there weren't so many humans stinking it up.

She knelt and bunched the blanket around Greta. The dog whined softly and covered her face with kisses. Morrin knew the place where Brux had punched her was getting better, because Greta's kisses no longer hurt. "Too bad you can't help me search the room," she murmured, scratching behind Greta's ears. "I know that isn't what they trained you to do." Morrin stood and slowly, carefully made her way around the chamber, simultaneously checking for night-biters and peepholes. She knew no one considered her desirable to look upon. She also knew that desire often had little to do with it.

Especially not when Brux dipped deep into the ale, often trying to match Staige drink for drink. When Brux's steps grew unsteady and his speech began to slur, that was when his cock grew hardest, and sought out whichever of Morrin's holes it fancied. Brux always beat her first. He called it "tenderizing his meat." Usually it was his fists, and usually where no one could see, but sometimes his attention strayed. Sometimes he used his knees and feet and stomped until she was sure bones had broken. Not this last time. Last time he'd hammered his knuckles into her face carelessly, giving her a black-purple-green beauty mark for all the world to see.

According to the Cathedral's rules, what Brux did to her most nights was not allowed. She could report him. She knew she *should* report him. Nysska had encouraged her to often enough.

She also knew how likely it was that such charges would be

ignored. And if Brux found out she had been the one to accuse him... well...then he'd be *truly* angry.

Morrin shuddered as she inspected the bedclothes on the flimsy, creaking wooden frame. From out on the street came the sound of a door slamming open, and the half-shouted words in a familiar voice made her body clenched tight as she stole back to the window. There was Brux, a sloshing flagon in one hand, wavering feet guiding him back to the inn.

Tears started in Morrin's eyes. She hurried to finish her sweep of the room. She knew Brux would throw Greta out into the hallway before he had at her—where the dog would wait, patient, until he'd finished and left—but if Morrin could spot any peepholes and plug them, maybe at least she could keep from sharing her pain and humiliation.

She found one in the floor, next to the room's south wall. Differences in the film of grime told her that, until recently, a piece of furniture had sat there—perhaps placed by a new owner, unknowingly covering up a previous owner's handiwork. Perhaps this had once been the innkeeper's room? But whatever sort of table or chest or what-have-you that had recently stood there had been moved, and Morrin stretched out on the floor and put her eye to the small, dark opening.

She hoped her gasp wasn't loud enough to be heard. This was not a peephole designed to peer *into* her chamber. It was one designed to spy on the chamber below, and had been fitted with a mechanism not unlike that of a telescope, allowing her a broad, wide-angle view...

Of Nysska's room.

Morrin rolled onto her back, her eyes unfocused. The messenger had given them orders to report to Tember, and Crucibles rarely got summoned to a territorial capital without a personnel shake-up. The thought of escaping the Forty-Seventh Crucible—escaping Brux's fists and feet and ghastly breath and giant, surging cock—filled her stomach with flutters of excitement. But if she got caught spying on Nysska? She couldn't even begin to imagine the punishment that would bring. If not from the Cathedral, then from the demon herself.

Demons crept into people's bedrooms and *ate their souls*. She knew they did. Her mother had told her so, and her mother had never been wrong about *anything*. Half the Green Needles Territory spoke of how the demon must have bewitched Governor Anwar and eaten his soul right out of his chest. Morrin's hands covered her heart. When a demon ate your soul, you were just *gone*. Her mother had told her that, too. No ascension to the Dragonlands. No nothing. You just...ceased to be. Morrin could think of nothing more horrible.

And yet...

Her heart chattering against her ribs, she rolled back over onto her stomach and pressed her eye to the lens.

How often had Nysska spoken to her softly? Told her how much she needed to stand up to Brux?

It made no sense, though. Had to be some kind of malicious trick. How could a demon care about a human?

And Morrin didn't dare ignore her mother's wisdom.

Seen through the spyglass peephole, Nysska lay on her bed, directly in the center of Morrin's field of vision, and—Morrin stopped breathing.

She was *nude*.

Morrin hadn't realized it at her first glimpse because the demon's deep-violet skin didn't really connect with Morrin's mind *as* skin. But there she lay, stretched long on the bed as if she were a normal human woman, not a stitch of clothing covering her shame, and...as Morrin watched, lungs barely filled with shallow breath...Nysska reached one unholy hand down, along her abdomen, down between her legs, and began *touching herself*.

If Morrin hadn't been stretched full-length on the floor, she would've clapped a hand over her mouth. Or maybe over her eyes.

Nysska slowly rolled over onto her stomach, her round, taut backside on display to Morrin's spying eye, her hips bucked slightly upward. With a renewed sense of horror and shame and—she could no longer deny it—*fascination*, Morrin realized that whatever sin-filled pervert had installed the peephole had also provided for *sound*. Nysska let out a low, soft moan, her body trembling, and Morrin heard it, heard it piped through some unseen duct, emanating from a crack between two wall boards next to her head.

I can't keep watching this, Morrin told herself, *I can't I can't I shouldn't I mustn't.*

The door to Nysska's room crashed open.

Transfixed, Morrin stared as Brux half-stomped, half-staggered through the doorway and slammed it shut behind him. She expected Nysska to abandon her wicked self-abuse and grab up a bedsheet to cover herself, and she did spring from the bed. But she made no move at all to cover herself, and simply stood, a tower of midnight-violet skin stretched over long, lean, wiry muscles, her horns held as high and proud as a crown.

"Get out," Nysska barked, but at that Brux only laughed.

"Well, now, ain't this an eyeful," he said, leering. "And look at that—got your cooch all nice and wet for me. Knew I was coming, did you?"

Nysska took one step toward him. Morrin watched the muscles bunch and dance across her back and shoulders, where long, black-and-cobalt hair didn't cover them. "I said get out."

Brux shook his head. "Nah, nah, nah, you don't understand. This's our last night together. I heard from a buddy—you're about to get shifted someplace else. And I been eyeballing that tight little ass of yours from day one. Miss my last chance? Pass up fucking a real, live *demon*? Ain't think so. Get you on your knees—use those horns like handles!"

From her angle, Morrin couldn't see Nysska's face, but she watched as the horned head tilted to one side, that long, lustrous hair shimmering as it slid across her back.

"All right," the demon said. Something had shifted in her voice. It emerged from her now like a living thing, cool and tightly coiled and filled with hidden venom. "Take it out, then."

Brux blinked at her. "What?"

"Your cock. Show it to me."

The yellowed grin split Brux's face. "Fucking right," he said, and pushed his trousers down, letting the log-like member that Morrin knew too well flop between his thighs. She watched as Brux glanced down at his cock, and back up to the demon's face—and he must have seen something there that pushed through his ale-soaked haze, because a frown skittered across his features. "Uh…"

The demon crossed the floor to him. She stood half a head taller than he did, and Morrin had known very few men taller than Brux. The demon took his cock in one hand and used it to pull him close, so that their faces almost touched. "Are you certain you want this, *Commander?* It won't happen the way you think it will. I am not like your human cows."

Brux licked his lips, grabbed one of the demon's small, round breasts with one hand, and shoved the other between her legs. He started to say something, something that began with, "Fucking better bel—" but the demon knocked away the hand groping at her crotch, spun him around by the shoulders, and shoved him.

Brux yelped as he all but flew across the room. He landed on the bed and twisted over onto his back, and instantly the demon was on him. She mounted him, and clutched his wrists, one in each hand, and Brux struggled—

Morrin had once seen a horse struck by an arrow, so that it panicked and rose up onto its hind hooves and fell on the madly flailing rider. The rider had struggled, screaming, his leg crushed under the horse's weight, but no amount of his strength had budged the horse's massive weight. He might as well have been struggling to move a giant boulder, or an entire hillside.

That was the way Brux struggled now. Morrin saw his enormous limbs swell and strain, saw his teeth clench and his face turn a horrid purple-red, but Nysska simply...didn't react. For all her body moved, Brux may as well have been lying motionless beneath her. She brought his wrists together, pinned them above his head, and *held them in place with one hand.* With the other, she reached down and quickly, methodically tore his clothes off of him.

Once his shirt was gone, exposing his black-furred chest, the demon said, "Hold still." She released his wrists and slid down and began ripping his trousers off, and Brux surged up from the bed with one enormous fist drawn back, and the demon slapped him on the side of his head so hard it sounded like rock shattering. Brux fell back to the bed, his eyes wild, a great hand-shaped welt rising on his face. Nysska said, "I told you not to move."

When the scraps of his trousers hit the floor, Nysska slid back up his body and took his hard cock in her hand again. "Good. You're persistent." Brux's eyes had not yet re-focused when she positioned herself over him and slid his entire length up inside herself with one motion.

As the demon's hips writhed and rose and fell atop him—Morrin gasped softly, squinting—Brux began to cry. "Stop," he said, and Nysska clamped one hand over his mouth.

"Be silent. This was your decision."

Nysska's hips rose and fell, rose and fell, grinding down on each stroke, grinding Brux into the bed. Listening to the rhythmic, primal grunts that escaped the demon's lips, Morrin didn't think she was watching a man and a woman have sex. She wasn't even watching an act of sexual violence.

This was more like a man being mauled by a bear.

Brux whimpered, and the demon's hips slowed for a moment. "No, no," she said. "You don't get to retreat. Your cock belongs to *me* now." Her chiseled abdominal muscles flexed, and her hips quaked and ground against Brux's flesh. "*There.* Good and hard again. Don't worry, I won't need you for much longer."

She had taken her hand away from his mouth, and Brux whimpered, "*Please,*" but if Nysska heard him, she didn't care. She pumped him, pumped him, harder and harder, and arched her back, yellow eyes fixed on the ceiling as her hips ground and thrust, and Brux covered his face with his hands, but it didn't hide his tears. Again, he said, "Please," and "Don't—don't..." and then a tremor shot through him just as Nysska let out a low, guttural moan.

"*Yes.*" The word escaped her lips in a hoarse whisper. "*Yes!*"

Her body stilled.

Brux's hands fell to the bed, limp. He had his eyes shut and kept them that way as she slid off of him, revealing welts and bruises all around his groin.

Nysska stood up on the bed, astride Brux's flaccid body, towering over him, and took a step so that her crotch was directly over his face. Steadying herself with one hand on the headboard, she crouched and said, "Here, you can have this back," and Morrin stopped breathing altogether as Brux's milky seed emptied out of her, all over his mouth and nose and eyes.

Morrin rolled away from the peephole. Her insides felt…as if they'd been caught in a landslide, tumbling and crashing down a mountain cliff. Part of her wanted to laugh, perhaps hysterically, and she considered letting herself, except she was afraid that might make her vomit. Faintly, from the floor below her, she heard a door slam, and a few seconds later another one somewhere else slammed as well. Morrin sat on the floor, hugging her knees to her chest, long enough for Greta to leave her blanket and come over and whine and nuzzle her hand. She petted the dog absently. Finally, Morrin took one last look through the peephole.

Nysska had left her room. There was no sign of Brux, either.

It took Morrin some number of agonizing minutes to decide what to do, and almost as long to work up the nerve to do it. Finally, she told Greta to stay put, and crept down the short hallway to the stairs that led to the ground floor.

There was still no sign of Brux anywhere. The door to Nysska's bedroom stood ajar, but the room was empty, and Morrin eventually found Nysska in the inn's kitchen, eating a plate of thinly-sliced ham at a small table in a corner. An adolescent boy, whom Morrin recognized as one of the innkeeper's children, stood in the opposite corner, staring at Nysska as if she were an entire pack of wolves.

Nysska was dressed in the simple shirt and trousers issued to Crucible personnel, worn under the much more widely recognizable bronze-inlaid leather armor. She had done her black-and-cobalt hair into a hasty braid that lay draped over one shoulder. Morrin edged into the kitchen and, when Nysska's brilliant yellow eyes flicked up and took her in, she said, "M-m-may I join you?"

Nysska nodded and gestured with her chin toward the empty stool on the other side of the table. Morrin thought that might have been the only response she'd get, but those brilliant eyes shifted to the innkeeper's boy, and Nysska said, "Get this one whatever she wants, too."

The boy jumped and fell all over himself to ask what Morrin's pleasure was, and Morrin indulged herself with a flagon of ale. She knew better than to have more than one, as her tolerance was pitiful, but she thought perhaps a bit of liquid courage would calm her nerves. The boy came back with a large ceramic mug of room-temperature ale. He then scampered back to his corner, and Morrin realized he wasn't like her in that he didn't feel the pressing combination of fascination, fear, and awe that she held for Nysska now. He harbored fear, and nothing else.

"I, uh..." Morrin started, and had to clear her throat and try again when Nysska's eyes fixed on hers. "I saw Brux. Coming, uh, coming out of your room."

Nysska paused in her chewing. She chewed slowly. She always did, Morrin had noticed that before. Nysska ate more slowly than anyone else in the Crucible, and seemed to eat less than anyone else, as well. "Did you, now."

Morrin had done the mental calculus on her way downstairs. *If I tell her I was spying on her in her private room, she's liable to take my head off.* She had decided on some judicious editing of events, rather than complete truthfulness, and hoped Nysska wouldn't be able to tell she was lying.

"I heard. What went on. And I saw him. He...doesn't...usually look like that. When he's finished."

Nysska's eyes narrowed, just a hair. "You mean asshole-naked?"

Morrin almost giggled. She clamped down on it, in part because she was afraid she might not stop if she got started. Seeing what Nysska had done to Brux had set Morrin's entire world into a spin, and it showed no signs of slowing down. "I guess I'm just... well... surprised. That you'd do that. With him."

Nysska shrugged again. A tiny, unconcerned twitch of the shoulders. "Your human pestilences do not touch my kind."

Morrin's jaw fell open. "None? ...At *all?*"

A minuscule shake of the head. Nysska's black-onyx horns glinted in the kitchen's lantern light.

Morrin said, "All right, but...but...what if—" She paused, marveling at the sheer weirdness of the conversation. "What if you got pregnant?"

Nysska set down the piece of ham she'd been about to bite. She straightened her back, her brow furrowing between her horns, and drilled Morrin with a look. "Why in Atiina's name would I do *that?*"

Morrin struggled. "Oh. Oh. I, uh...so, he didn't..." She leaned across the table and pitched her voice low, hoping the boy in the corner wouldn't be able to hear. "Didn't he spurt? In, inside you, I mean? He always does. With me. I've, um...I've already had two miscarriages."

Nysska leaned forward as well, propping her elbows on either side of the ham plate, and her expression softened. "Morrin, I kept my womb closed."

Morrin sat back.

Her tongue felt heavy in her head.

"You can *do* that?"

"Sethyd women *choose* when to accept seed. Just as sethyd men choose when to release it."

Morrin felt her blood roaring in her ears. "So you...can...lie with a man...and *know* you won't wind up with child?"

Nysska took a moment before answering. "It is difficult for a sethyd to imagine *not* controlling exactly when and with whom we bear children."

"Any man. Any time. It doesn't matter if he spurts in you or not, you can just *decide...?*"

Morrin turned the thought around in her mind, over and over and over again. She felt detached from herself. From the world. Finally, after a couple of false starts, she said, "Could you teach me how to...to do that...?"

The horns glinted again as Nysska shook her head. "The human body lacks the proper..." She appeared to grasp for a word. "*Strukturoj.* You do not have the capability."

"But the—wait, what was the name you used? For people like—for your people?"

Nysska's eyes glittered in the lantern light. Morrin couldn't read the thoughts and feelings behind that flame-like gaze. "Sethyd. That is who we are. Not 'demons'." Nysska nudged her plate aside. "This is the first time you have cared to learn our proper name."

Morrin took a long drink of ale. "I just—what happened with

Brux. What you—what you *did* to him. That a woman, *any* woman, could make him feel…it's…" She shook her head as thoughts and words knotted and tangled.

Nysska looked over at the innkeeper's child. "Could you give us some privacy?" The boy yelped and scrambled out of the kitchen. Once he had gone, Nysska reached across the table and took Morrin's hands in hers. Morrin almost screamed, almost jerked away from the touch, but Nysska's fingers held her with a vast gentleness.

"Is there nothing I can do to persuade you to report him?" Nysska asked.

Tears welled in Morrin's eyes. "You know how that would go. My word against his. The claim gets dismissed, and things get even worse."

Nysska squeezed. Not hard. Not painfully. Just for emphasis. "Morrin. Look me in the eyes." It took a few seconds for Morrin to do it, but she lifted her head and stared into those beautiful, terrifying pools of topaz. "I will kill him *for* you," Nysska breathed. "All you have to do is ask me."

The flow of Morrin's tears grew heavier. "No! No, Nysska, if you get caught, they'll *execute* you!"

Nysska shook her head. "I won't get caught. I could dispose of that walking sack of pus in such a way that his corpse was never found." She exhaled. "But I won't do it unless you ask me to. It needs to be *your* decision."

Morrin pulled her hands out of Nysska's, her shoulders quaking. "I can't. I can't ask you to do that. I can't, I *won't*."

Nysska sat back in her chair. She rubbed her face with both hands, stood, and pushed the plate with the remaining ham slices across the table. "Here. Have these. My appetite has abandoned me." She slid her chair under the table and left.

Nysska walked out of the kitchen and turned right, which put her in a short hallway, at the end of which lay the inn's greeting room and the staircase leading up to the second floor. She needed to pass by the stairs, cross the greeting room, and head down another hallway to her own room, but stopped when she saw the innkeeper's boy sitting on the second-to-bottom step. The boy sprang to his feet when he saw her, a collection of wide eyes and fidgeting hands and freckles.

Nysska slowed her stride. The boy had clearly been waiting for her. Now that she paid more attention, she put his age somewhere around twelve. A small twelve, she thought. The kind of size that resulted from too many days and nights without enough to eat. In the back of her mind, she wondered how much sense that made, since the Green Needles Territory was not one of the Empire's poorer ones. The winters here were harsh, yes, but the ground seemed fertile enough the rest of the year, and bronze-clad soldiers made sure the trade lines stayed open. It made her want to find the innkeeper and beat him until he fed his son a decent meal.

Nysska stopped two meters in front of the boy. He barely came up to her breastbone. With shaking hands, he shoved a lock of unkempt, curly hair out of his face and kept staring at her. Nysska slid her watersight lids across her eyes, since she'd been told that the normal sethyd yellow caused great upset among more squeamish humans, and let the blue of the tissue turn her irises a soft, gentle green. *Show them they have nothing to fear.* That was what her mother had said, wasn't it? *Show them that we are all the same.*

Nysska knelt, putting her head slightly below the boy's. "We haven't had a proper introduction, I don't think. My name is Nysska. What's yours?"

The boy turned a shade lighter as blood drained from his face. He opened his mouth to speak, but it didn't work, and his eyes locked on Nysska's horns.

"It's all right," Nysska said, her voice gentler now. She had begun to feel bad for the tongue-tied little man. Especially if he'd been sent to her with some kind of message. She had observed humans using children as couriers for trivial matters before.

"I..."

"Yes?"

The boy swallowed hard and dug his fingers into the material of his shirt over his belly button. "I rebuke you!"

Nysska's eyes snapped back to hard, bright yellow, and the boy backpedaled and almost tripped.

"What did you say?"

Now some blood crept back into his face. The hurdle of getting the first words out seemed to embolden him. "I rebuke you in the name of the Great Silver Dragon!"

Nysska stood, looming over him once again, but now the boy was fearless. He even took a step toward her that might have been meant as threatening. "The majesty of the Silver Dragon compels you! Return to the metal caves you crawled out of! Unholy creature! Vuh-vile beast! Th-the Silver Dragon compels you!"

Nysska watched him shrewdly, realizing with each word that he was reciting something he'd memorized. She wondered if one of his parents, or some other simple, backward human had dispatched him to deliver this stream of bigoted nonsense, or if he'd just picked up the words and phrases from listening to adults. When he paused to breathe, his hands shaking harder now even though he'd bound them up in his shirt, she said, "Have you delivered your whole message? Or is there more?"

She didn't know which had run out first—the words he'd memorized, or the courage he'd mustered—but the boy shook his head, started hyperventilating, and bolted through the greeting room, out the door and into the street.

Silent, Nysska returned to her room, where she pushed a heavy piece of furniture in front of her lock-free door.

Two minutes later, she un-blocked the door, threw her now-soiled bedsheets out into the hallway, and blocked the door again.

Humans.

She hawked up a glob of phlegm that perfectly summarized her feelings on the Empire and its subjects and spat it across the room into the fireplace.

4

Camble Delakroy knew she'd never sneak up on anyone. Unless they were deaf, maybe. She stepped out of the inn's front door onto the street, lifted her left hand, and brought together the rings she wore on her thumb and middle finger. The two tiny metal domes set into the bands collided with a short, sharp click and painted a picture for her.

She knew the streets of Kayjer. She'd never lived there, but had visited regularly, coming into town with her parents to sell their crops. She remembered the deep, filthy scent of the often-muddy streets, the stomps and whinnies of the horses, the whorled texture of the wooden storefronts in the spring. And as always, her grandfather painted pictures for her with words. He described for her the rough clothing of the other farmers. The bronze of the soldiers who kept the peace and collected the Empire's share of the profits.

Cam had listened to her grandfather talk about the days before the Empire arrived. There were soldiers then, too, but they took the Governor's share from the people and then their own on top of that. Now, wherever the bronze of the soldiers' uniforms flashed in the sunlight, her grandfather had said, the people knew they'd give up exactly what they owed, and no more.

Bronze is law. Bronze is peace.

Imperial rule is a good thing, he said. They should be grateful to be Imperial citizens.

Cam heard footsteps approaching and clicked her rings again. Two women—she heard their voices in quiet conversation. Thin, probably very pretty. As they drew closer, Cam got a whiff of their perfume and decided they were headed toward the large building at the end of the street. The building she knew was painted red.

The place she'd been meant to go.

The thought triggered the faintest sensation of a tug in her abdomen. She trailed fingertips across it, over her own Imperial armor. Memories of the frenzied hoofbeats, the rampaging bull bearing down on her, the split-second knowledge that it was coming too fast for her to get out of its way, the jumbled sensations of horns and hooves and blood and broken bones. The pain.

That was the day her path in the world had changed forever. The day her fate had narrowed to the red-painted building with the pretty women and the perfume.

Familiar footsteps approached on the wooden porch behind her, a second before the voice of her commander spoke softly, just over her shoulder. "We should get to the scene. Are you ready?"

Raoul Cullen's was one of the first faces she saw, after her induction into the Thaumetallicon, after the Cathedral's runemasters had bestowed their gift upon her eyes. Even now, with her eyes shut tight, she knew his voice, his deep brown skin, the shape of his tall, rangy body, and the scent of his cropped-off hair. The simmering energy radiating from the luminous white stones on the pommel of his sword and the heavy ring on his right hand. She could have kept her eyes closed and still sculpted him perfectly from clay.

Cam had never touched him. Never touched nor tasted.

She could hear the want in his words all the time now. He thought he kept it hidden, and he'd sooner die than tell her how he really felt about her. She heard it, nonetheless.

Heavier footsteps followed Raoul out of the inn—Theobold Brint, buckling his armor in place as he walked. Cam often thought of Theobold as a broadsword with arms and legs. On the infrequent occasions that Theobold waxed loquacious, he told stories the same way Cam's grandfather had, spinning far-fetched yarns around puffs of smoke from his pipe. He smoked the same kind of tobacco that her grandfather had, as well, and though she'd never admit it, the scent made her want to curl up on the floor at Theobold's feet and listen to his voice until she fell asleep.

Those story-times were few and far between, though. Normally Theobold let his sword do his talking for him. Cam hadn't seen his face in years—the same choice that kept Raoul and Percy and everyone else from her sight—but she remembered his immense shoulders and the shock of white hair jammed under his Imperial helmet.

A steady series of ring-clicks showed Cam the least muddy path along the side of Kayjer's main street. The three of them made their way to the edge of town, where Percy waited with Jax and Flax. If Theobold Brint was a living, breathing broadsword, Percy Bitters was more like...she hadn't ever been able to decide. A living, breathing marionette? A gremlin of some sort, who'd fast-talked his way into the Cathedral's service? Percy only came up to Cam's collarbones, but the assemblage of milk-pale skin and wiry muscle and absolutely no fat that made up his body gave him a speed and strength more like that of a wild animal than a man. Percy's thick, straight hair was every bit as white as Theobold's, Cam remembered, and spilled out from under his helmet, down his back, across his narrow shoulders, matched in flamboyance by the two-pronged white beard that hung down onto his chest.

Cam knelt when they reached Percy and held her hands out to Jax and Flax. "Good morning, kittens. Anyone want some pets? Any chins or ears need scratching?"

She could imagine the two blood lynxes staring at her with their normal air of disdainful apathy. Every now and then they took her up on her offer, but not today. Cam shrugged and stood. Raoul said, "Have any trouble?"

She could hear the grin in Percy's voice. It was his default position. Percy Bitters seemed to find reason to grin no matter what the circumstance or situation. "Barn had lots of hay. That and the kitties kept me warm." Cam heard him scratching something—the back of his neck, she thought. "Don't believe I got any fleas out of the deal. No more than usual, anyway."

Raoul nodded as he spoke. "Good. Ready to get to it?"

Cam could tell Percy had turned, and imagined him holding out an expansive arm. "Perfect morning for a walk, boss."

The four members of the Ninth Crucible—six, if one counted Jax and Flax—made their way out of Kayjer proper and walked half a klik down a farm road. They took a left onto an even narrower lane through a dense stand of trees that opened up onto fields too broad for Cam to judge their breadth. She clicked her rings every ten paces or so, thereby avoiding the ruts and holes in the rough, muddy earth. Soon, another couple of clicks showed her a small structure, and a larger one beyond it. She'd been to enough farms to recognize the farmhouse and the barn.

One of the blood lynxes—she thought it was Flax, but couldn't be sure—growled, soft and low.

A woman came out to greet them. Not as tall as the women in town, and much more sturdily built. More like Cam's mother. She had a harsh scent, like lye soap. The woman gasped, most likely at the sight of Jax and Flax, but cut that breath short and skirted around them to speak to Raoul. "You're the—the investigators?"

Raoul said, "You are Rinda Miller, yes? Wife of Lemuel Miller? I'm Commander Raoul Cullen. This is my Crucible. We're going to find out who killed your husband, ma'am."

Cam didn't need to use her rings to know the woman had been crying. It came through in every word, especially now that she stood closer. "Thank you. Thank you so much."

"If you could show us where you found him?"

"Yes, yes of course, it was—this way—he was in the barn."

Cam clicked her rings much more frequently as they made their way past the farmhouse and approached the larger building. Because of that, she pinpointed a girl—no. A young woman. The same height as her mother, but slender, standing mutely in the doorway of the farmhouse. Cam's sense of smell was, of course, nothing compared with that of the two blood lynxes, but she had learned to trust it, and the scent she caught from the young woman tickled something at the base of her brain. Down where the intuition lived, below organized thoughts or words. Cam began to put together what had happened here before they even reached the scene of the crime.

The woman, Rinda, slid aside the huge door to the barn, and Cam stepped inside, her rings sounding out a staccato beat amid the aromas of hay and animals and manure. She felt Jax and Flax come up beside her, flanking her, and she reached down and stroked the cats' tawny heads, happy that they let her.

From behind her, fear in her words, Rinda said, "Those cats—they're—their eyes are silver..." The words trailed off.

Cam heard Raoul turn to the woman, breaking out the speech he almost always had to give. "Yes, ma'am, they're seraphic animals. And yes, there is a decree banning them from Imperial lands. But as you can see..." She imagined Raoul gesturing toward the bronze-inlaid harnesses both blood lynxes wore. "An exception has been made, and they are in the employ of the Thaumetallicon. Quite legal."

Next came Rinda's voice in what she must have thought a whisper. "And...is she..." Cam picked up on the infinitesimal waver in the word that accompanied a gesture. "Is she *blind?*"

Raoul didn't whisper at all. "Hardly." Then, to Cam, "Ready when you are."

"Everybody behind me?"

"Of course."

Cam took a deep breath through her nose, let it out slowly through her mouth, and opened her eyes, the argonium implants tingling as she brought them up to full strength. She heard Rinda gasp as icy silver flames danced and flared around the runes.

Most of what Cam saw was beyond mundane, rendered to her mind in tones of blue and black and gold and gray as the runes accomplished what her corneas never could.

Hay bales filled most of one half of the large building.

A few stalls stood empty, their walls missing planks and stained with cow shit.

One corner had been converted to a large bin, two-thirds full of potatoes—many having begun to rot, judging by the smell.

Cam concentrated just a hair harder, her eyelids narrowing over the shimmering argonium runes, and—

There.

As she watched, never blinking, a scene played out—a drama with an audience of one.

From a side door in front of the hay bales entered a sight that it had taken Cam some time to accept when she'd first received her runes. It was a thing in the shape of a man...but *only his blood.* The argonium runes did not show her the clothes, or the hair, or the skin or flesh or bones of a murderer. She saw, awash in faint spectral light, a man's veins and arteries moving exactly as they had when they rode around in the rest of his body. Re-enacting the movements that their owner had taken...she squinted...two days ago? Three at most. The pulsing heart, the heaving lungs, the broad red stalks in the trunks and upper arms and thighs, all the way out to the faintest pink filigree at the tips of the fingers. The perpetrator's blood vessels, visible only to her, replayed the fateful actions that had brought the Ninth Crucible to this site.

The living, moving circulatory system walked backward, hunched over, dragging something into the barn—another man. This one's blood had stopped. Already cooling.

The words of her chief instructor at the Imperial College always came back to her when she channeled the runes' power this way. *"Anyone can open their eyes and see the world, Miss Delakroy. You must use yours to drill through it. Peer behind it, underneath it. Learn its secrets."*

Cam watched, corneal runes ablaze, as the perpetrator dragged the victim into the middle of the barn floor, looked around as if to spot any observers, and dashed back out the way he'd come. She let out a long, deep breath and closed her eyes again, the icy fire dissipating in an instant, the brilliant silver of the argonium fading behind her eyelids. She turned to Raoul. "I've got him." Percy and the blood lynxes had fallen back to the big door, next to Theobold, and she beckoned to the cats. "Ready."

Percy leaned down and spoke a quiet word to the felines. They stood and ambled over to her, Flax pausing midway to stretch, and she crouched down to put her face on a level with theirs. "Here it comes, kittens," she said. "Time to earn your keep."

Cam shed tears of blood.

Not hers. Instead, drops of blood from the murderer welled from her tear ducts and ran down her face, almost hot enough to burn, the copper smell sharp in her nostrils. The lynxes came forward one at a time, Jax sniffing and then licking the shining red tear from her left cheek, Flax from her right. Puffs of cat breath in her face let her know that both of the lynxes' mouths had dropped open as they took in the scent and taste and essence of the man who had committed murder.

She heard them spin around and dash back to Percy, and Percy's footfalls as he chased after them. "Come on, Theobold!" the Keeper called. "We got us a hot trail!"

Cam went back to Raoul and Rinda. Rinda said, "I don't understand. Can you explain it to me?"

Raoul said, "Explain what, ma'am?"

"Why anyone would do this! Why anyone would kill Lemuel! They *know* they'll be caught! *Everyone* gets caught!"

Cam heard the tiny sound as Raoul put his hand on Rinda's shoulder. "We can't know the why of it, ma'am. Seems to be something built into human nature, far as I've seen. But we do know we'll bring the killer to justice. Now, the Sensor and I are going to follow the Keeper and the Enforcer while the lynxes do their job. I'd like you to stay here, and we'll come back and update you as events unfold. Can you do that?"

"Y-yes," Rinda said.

Cam heard soft footsteps in the doorway of the barn. She didn't have to use her rings to know that the young woman from the farmhouse had come out to join her mother. Raoul said, "Come on, it's this way," and Cam followed him past the mother and daughter, out of the barn. They had barely walked ten meters before the sound of desperate, wailing tears reached them. They sounded too young to be Rinda's.

"Did you see the girl?" Cam asked quietly.

"I did." He paused. "You've already worked out what happened, haven't you?"

"I could be wrong. But the perpetrator was a young, strong man. Just the right age to be interested in a girl like that. Father objects, tempers flare, young love will not be denied. The suitor splits the father's head open with an axe and dumps him in the barn." They had been climbing a gentle rise, and Cam felt the ground level off beneath their feet. "What do you see before us?"

Raoul sighed. "Another farm. Might as well be the twin of the one we just left behind. Looks as though Percy and Theobold are bracing someone outside the farmhouse. Probably your star-crossed lover boy."

"Star-crossed imbecile. That woman was right. They *are* always caught."

"And yet we still have jobs. As clear as Imperial law is, we'll always have people too stupid, or too drunk, or too lovesick to—"

Raoul cut his own sentence short, and Cam felt something in the air change. Raoul sucked in a sharp, hissing breath, and from somewhere ahead of them, too far for her to get any kind of sense of what was happening, she heard shouting voices and the clang of metal on metal.

"Oh, shit. The imbecile's resisting." Raoul broke into a sprint.

By the time Cam reached the rest of her Crucible, she didn't need to use her rings at all to take in the scene. Theobold and a young, lean man with broad shoulders were locked in combat, Theobold wielding his broadsword, the young man with a machete in his hands. The sounds of the fight bounced off the farmhouse as well as the two combatants. Cam got flickers of their bodies in violent motion with every clang of metal and every harsh breath—

That stopped her. It was Theobold's lungs working so hard. She'd never heard him pant that badly before.

With a mighty grunt of effort, Theobold brought his heavy sword down, and instead of another metallic clang, she heard the unmistakable dense, meaty chop that meant blade had found bone. The young man screamed, staggering, and slammed against the side of the farmhouse. She heard feet moving across muddy earth and knew Raoul had rushed to him, offering aid. He never wanted any of the perpetrators they caught to die before judgement could be passed, and he especially never wanted any of them to suffer.

Cam followed Theobold's panting, which hadn't gotten any better, and arrived at his side where he stood next to Percy. A click of her rings showed her Jax and Flax sitting nearby. Flax was grooming, she thought, as she presented a smaller, denser echo than Jax. Cam went to put a hand on Theobold's shoulder, and realized he was bent over, his hands on his knees.

"Theo, are you hurt?"

"No, lass."

His voice didn't sound good. "Do you need to sit down? Rest a bit?"

The tall, thick-limbed old man heaved himself upright, and gently took her hand off of him. "I'm fine, girl. Just not quite as young as I once was." She heard him direct his voice to Raoul. "We'd best cauterize that."

Cam's eyebrows shot up, and Percy volunteered the information: "Theo took the boy's right arm off, just above the elbow. It's bleeding pretty good."

Cam called out, "Commander? Do you need any assistance?"

A few clicks of her rings showed her a series of images: Raoul kneeling next to the young man, who had slumped to the ground. Raoul standing. Raoul coming back to the team, his head bowed. "Dragon's fire, Theo, did you have to maim the boy?"

Theobold's voice cooled. "Is he dead?"

Bitterness came through in Raoul's words. "The shock took him before he could bleed out. He would have bled out, though, no matter what I did. What any of us could have done. The vessel's thick as a tree branch that high up the arm."

The coolness faded into regret as Theobold spoke. "I had no choice. He had that machete in his hand before I even knew he was going for it. Had it propped just inside the door."

"That may be, but a machete in the hands of a farmer isn't exactly an overwhelming force against a fully-armored Crucible Enforcer with an Imperial broadsword. I'm afraid there'll have to be a report."

Raoul paused before he continued. "Did he confess? When you first got here?"

Percy said, "He might as fucking well have. The kitties went straight to him, and when Theo mentioned the name Lemuel, we could both see it in his eyes. He was screwed, and he panicked, and now he's fucking dead." He sniffed. "Only difference now is how the paperwork gets filled out. It's still one murdering fucker put down, no matter which way you look at it, and I say Theo did what he fucking well had to."

Raoul grunted. "Well...for now...we'd best go back and tell Rinda Miller what's happened."

Cam thought Rinda might be satisfied with the day's conclusion, and that her nubile young daughter would most certainly not be. She opened her mouth and took a breath to say so, and heard Theobold make a strange, whistling groan, followed by a horrible impact as the old man's tall, strong body toppled over into the grass and mud.

"Theo? Theo!" Raoul and Percy were at his side in an instant, frantic to turn him over and try to wake him up.

The shock had made Cam open her eyes.

They flared silver, and showed her the still, lifeless blood in Theobold's great heart.

5

Nysska's stomach clenched tighter and tighter the closer they got to Tember.

She recalled a bit of wisdom she'd heard from her grandmother as a child. Her *avinjo* had said it more than once, usually before a test in school. Nysska had never liked tests. *"Your greatest fears are things that have already happened to you."* The aged woman had gone on to tell Nysska that she'd taken plenty of tests herself, had passed some, had failed others, and not once had a test ever killed her. Therefore, she had no reason to fear them.

Nysska had only ever been to Tember once before. She remained unconvinced that the city wouldn't at least *try* to kill her.

The horses dutifully carried them up to and through the mountain pass to the city's west, and when they exited the canyon and approached the first of the cliffs, Nysska looked far, far down onto a city awash in the crimson of a setting sun. The evening radiance turned the heavy clouds of smoke above Tember a dull brick-red, and the narrow, swift-moving river that cleft the city in two appeared more blood than water.

They would have to make camp again before they passed through one of the territorial capital's heavily fortified gates.

The Ironwood City, humans called it. Square klik upon square klik of wooden buildings, all sizes and shapes, slathered in paint of every color visible to the human eye. Nysska knew the paint had fire-retardant properties—perhaps the only reason the city hadn't burned to the ground yet, considering the attacks from the south its people had fended off over the last several decades—but its utility didn't stop Nysska from finding it extraordinarily tacky. Tember, as a whole, stood in stark contrast to the stately, black and gray block structures of Fajrasxtono. Neither she nor anyone she'd ever known back home had feared for even a moment that one of their homes or businesses might catch fire. The notion struck her as ridiculous. An entire city of wood seemed to her much the same as if it had been built of spider's web.

They had descended the mountain halfway when Staige, not yet completely drunk, pointed to a wide, level spot beside the trail. "Reckon that'll do for a campsite?"

Nysska guided her horse closer and saw the black-smudged earth left behind by previous fires. "Fine," she said, and dismounted.

Staige and Morrin turned to look at Brux, their eyes tight. Nysska watched their faces. She found human emotions pitifully easy to read. Morrin, with her knowledge of what had taken place the night before, gazed at their Crucible's Commander with questions unspoken, along the lines of, *Can you still function?* and *Are you going to fall off your horse?*

Staige didn't have the first clue about Brux's misadventure in Nysska's room. When no one else spoke, including Brux, who simply sat on his horse and stared dead ahead with vacant, hollow eyes, Staige called out to him. "Brux? Do we stop here?"

The question took a good few seconds to make it through Brux's skull, but eventually he did jerk his head up, eyes narrowing at the faded, ash-smeared dirt. "Uh. Yeah. Here's good." He cut his eyes toward Nysska. Just for a heartbeat. Not even that long. Brux hadn't spoken more than a handful of words since they'd set out from Nodwin's Mill, and none of them to her.

Nysska wondered if she'd broken him permanently. Not that it really mattered. Especially not if her teammates' predictions came true, and she got reassigned to a different Crucible. Only slightly less idly, she wondered what other remote, Exemplar-forsaken corner of the territory she'd be sent to now.

No one spoke as they made camp. Even Greta, who normally bounded from person to person and offered her assistance in the form of panting and slobber, simply lay down on a tree stump and stayed there.

Later, once the sun had set, after they'd gotten the fire going and eaten the last of the provisions from their packs, Nysska sat on a rock at the campsite's edge, her back to the fire. Staige had succeeded in getting drunk by then, with Greta curled up beside him. Brux had moved woodenly from the fire to his bedroll and lay on it, silent.

Morrin came and sat down on a smaller rock, facing Nysska. Flames danced in the girl's eyes as she stared at the campfire. Pitching her voice low, Morrin said, "Where could I go if I left the Crucible?"

Nysska pursed her lips. "I would guess…anywhere?"

Morrin shook her head. She ran a finger alongside her nose. "Not with these. I belong to the Empire."

"It's a straightforward thing. If you want to get away from Brux, request reassignment."

Morrin blinked a couple of times and leaned closer. "I'd need a witness. Staige is happy where he is, he'd never do anything to rock the boat. And…I don't know if…"

"You don't know if the word of the first ever sethyd among the Cathedral's ranks would have the effect you want."

Morrin shrugged, a powerless gesture rather than a noncommittal one. She looked smaller than usual.

Nysska slid off the rock and went to one knee beside the girl, her lips at Morrin's ear. "I meant what I said to you at the inn. You have but to give me the word."

Morrin rested her head on Nysska's shoulder, and Nysska realized the girl had been holding back tears. Now the tears fell onto Nysska's armored jacket. "I'm sorry," Morrin whispered. "I can't."

Nysska patted her twice on the back and stood. "Then I will see you in the morning." She left Morrin where she was and spread out her own bedroll on the other side of the fire.

A few minutes after she stretched out and covered herself as much as she could with the inadequate Cathedral-issue blanket, Greta came over to her and, with a soft whine, lay down against her chest and belly.

Nysska draped an arm over the dog and went to sleep, willing herself to ignore the soft sounds of Morrin's tears. It didn't work very well.

The next morning, Nysska woke to the smell of coffee and saw Brux sitting on the same rock where she'd sat the night before. Greta had left her at some point during the night and now slept curled up next to Staige's head. Morrin knelt by the fire. She poured hot black liquid into a metal cup and brought it to Nysska.

Nysska stared Morrin in the eye, shot a look at Brux, and accepted the coffee. Neither of them spoke. Morrin seemed even more miserable than usual in the light shining down over the mountaintops behind them.

Wordless, they rode into Tember under the noon sun. Past the outlying farms, through the ever-more-congested homes and shops that lay outside the city walls, and then finally through one of the massive wooden gates manned by dozens of soldiers in Imperial bronze.

Nysska almost gagged at the city's assault on her nostrils but fought her gorge down.

The smell of the territorial capital battered her with a vile mélange of animal dung, human urine and feces, crudely cooked food, and wood smoke. So much wood smoke. It had amazed her on her first trip here that, in a city known for its measures to prevent fires, so many open flames could be found. Torches in wall sconces, torches in human hands, crudely laid fires in alleyways. Brick chimneys.

Bright morning sun gleamed off the polished, dragon-shaped kites that flew above the various churches of the Great Silver Dragon. She counted eleven of them. Eleven churches around the city, regularly packed with humans who prayed to a giant mythical beast that never existed and could never exist. She hated the kites. She hated the ubiquitous wood smoke.

Just as much, she hated the *noise.*

Her people, by their own admission and with more than a little pride, valued silence and solitude and personal reflection. Not until venturing out into the human world had she even been aware of the concept of "small talk." Humans, lacking anything better to do, would sit around working their mouths for *hours,* and for no other purpose than the "pleasure of conversation." It made her shudder.

Also, when humans grouped together, they invariably grew louder and louder—and if the crowd consisted solely of men, more and more idiotic. So many voices would strive to fill the air with pointless blather, which caused them to increase their volume, talking louder because others were talking louder.

Here in Tember, that seemed to lead to a near-constant *bellowing.* Every human they passed, if they made noise at all—and they *all* made noise—seemed to shout at the very tops of their lungs, whether to signal danger or greet a friend or ask a vendor for a slab of half-burnt meat stuffed in a bun. She wanted to clamp her hands over her ears but didn't want to risk giving herself away if she could help it.

The Crucible had decided, shortly after the Imperial messenger had left and before Nysska had broken Brux in her room, that she should hide her nature upon entering the city. Her bronze-laced gloves did the trick for her hands, but for her face, she pulled a scarf up to the bridge of her nose, raised her leather hood, and lowered her head as far as she could and still see to ride. It wasn't perfect. Her horns left a couple of upward-poking indentations in the leather. But with the sun directly overhead, the hood created a deep enough pocket of shadow that her eyes and forehead could slip through. As an added touch, she slid closed her watersight lids, again masking brilliant yellow eyes as soft green.

"It shouldn't matter if the people of Tember know what I am or not," she'd wanted to say. *"This is why Governor Anwar gave me this post. To walk among you. Show everyone my people are not what you have been told we are. He issued a Territorial Decree in support of this, remember?"* But the words died before she'd even taken a breath to speak them. No matter

how much good will she might eventually engender in the people, it would stand her no stead at all if a mob tore her limb from limb the first moment they saw her.

As they moved deeper into the throngs of humans, Nysska began to wonder why she'd bothered. The Imperial citizens in the outlying territories had shown great respect for the bronze, with a few exceptions here and there, but the people of Tember seemed *allergic* to it. Time after time she watched as a man, a woman, or a child looked up, took in the armor and the bronze-laced tackle on their horses, and either developed a sudden interest in something else nearby or outright walked away. Some even ran. She didn't remember this level of antipathy toward Imperial forces the last time she'd come here, and wondered if she simply hadn't been looking for it then.

They hadn't eaten breakfast, and Nysska's stomach rumbled rudely as they passed a stall selling haunches of some kind of white meat.

"I've never been to the Governor's Mansion before," Morrin said from beside her, giving Nysska the tiniest of starts. She hadn't realized the girl had ridden up. "Dragon's blood...it's *huge.*"

Nysska raised her eyes and took in the home and office of Governor Anwar. She wouldn't have called it huge, exactly. Atiina's Sanctuary back in Fajrasxtono dwarfed it. Well...it had, before getting reduced to a pile of smoking, glowing rubble. Still, Anwar occupied a handsome house, built at the top of a rise in the city's center, three stories of heavy wooden planks painted bronze.

Bronze is law. Bronze is peace.

The words echoed in Nysska's mind involuntarily. How many times had she heard them since accepting Anwar's offer? She couldn't begin to count.

Nysska glanced behind her, confirming that Brux and Staige were still with them, Greta trotting along beside Staige's horse. Staige had already broken out a flask, appointment with the Governor be damned. Brux sat his horse as if someone had taken a life-size wooden replica of the Commander and shoved it into the saddle in his place. For a moment, Nysska thought he was staring at her, until she realized he was staring *through* her instead.

A thought flitted across her mind—*I hope whatever damage I did was permanent*—but fled, chased away, when they passed a boarding house and entered a broad square. A new stench struck Nysska like a rock to the face, and she had to blink suddenly watering eyes before she could focus on the sight that greeted them.

She and Wendell Anwar had entered the city through a different gate when she'd traveled here with him the last time, and had not come this way. She would have remembered. Where she might have expected a market, or rows of food vendors, or perhaps even a circus of some kind, there was no one. Well—no one living.

In the center of the square stood a dozen large, rough wooden frames, little more than limb-stripped tree trunks, so crude that most of them still had bark. Each one forked into a Y-shape at the top, with a smaller log driven in like a peg parallel to the ground a meter below where the fork split.

Each frame held a headless body.

The cadavers' arms draped back over the Y-split, their crotches resting on the pegs. Dangling from the blunt ends of the pegs were placards. Nysska's eyes were not as sharp as usual, since her water-sight lids covered them, but she could still see clearly enough to read each placard. There was "THIEF." Beyond that, "ADULTERER," then "MURDERER," "FRAUD," and another "THIEF."

She passed one with a placard that labeled its corpse, "LIAR."

No wonder the residents of Tember gave the Crucible a wide berth.

At the square's far end—above a broad, ten-meter-high retaining wall, and towering behind another wall beyond that—the Governor's Mansion loomed. Nysska realized it was the rear of the Mansion she was seeing, as if Anwar and the Empire as a whole had turned their backs on Tember and her people. Windows like misplaced, soulless eyes stared down at the corpse forest, at the carnage wrought in the Empire's name.

Nysska held her breath until they'd passed through the square and left it a couple of streets behind, but when she did breathe again, the nauseating smell lingered in her nostrils.

She entertained dark thoughts about humans as the street began an incline and a long, gradual curve that mounted the hill leading up to the front of Anwar's home.

Halfway up the hill, a smaller version of the city's wall blocked their progress. As they dismounted, a handful of adolescent boys in bronze-colored shirts and brown trousers met them and took their horses to some stables off to their left, while a couple of guards in actual armor opened a person-sized door in the wall and ushered them through.

The slopes of the hill leading up to the Governor's Mansion, where not interrupted by gravel paths and wooden stairs, were covered in lush green grass and beautiful, carefully tended flower gardens. The inner wall provided a baffle for the sounds of the city as well. *Allowing those within to pretend the horrors of the square below didn't exist.* The abrupt tranquility did nothing to help her mood, since the quiet and the aroma of the flowers couldn't scrub the stench of rotting flesh out of her nose.

The four of them climbed the hill, while Greta barked happily and sped across the grass and rolled on her back. She returned, obedient, when Staige whistled for her, a few long strands of grass and a single leaf tangled in her fur.

Nysska knew she'd miss the dog.

Two more soldiers opened the Mansion's doors, and Nysska's eyebrows raised when she saw Governor Wendell Anwar himself standing just inside. A vision of the typical upper crust in soft leather boots, crisp gray trousers, a shirt white enough never to have spent any time around a campfire, and a long, dark brown jacket. He'd let his curly black hair grow longer since Nysska had last seen him. His face hadn't changed much, maybe a new line or two here and there. He still looked too young to hold the position he'd been given. Anwar stepped aside and beckoned them in, then gestured for the guards to close the doors behind them.

A steward approached—a man in his fifties wearing brown and bronze livery, with a straight back and ash-gray hair—and as Nysska lowered her hood and pulled her scarf down, Anwar spoke to the rest of her Crucible. "Thank you all for coming at such short notice. Everyone but Enforcer Stonegate, if you'll please follow Dixen here, he'll take you to your quarters. The City Commander is preparing your new orders as we speak, so we won't keep you long."

"As you wish, Governor," Brux said, his words sounding as if they'd originated far back in an empty cavern. Nysska watched him and Morrin and Staige follow Dixen as he led them away. Greta paused near Nysska's feet, and she reached down to scratch the dog one last time behind the ears.

"Go with your Keeper, now," Nysska murmured to her. "That's a good girl."

Greta trotted after Staige. Nysska saw Morrin throw one brief, typically miserable glance over her shoulder before the steward led them through a door and out of sight.

Nysska took a moment to glance around.

Anwar had added a few ornamental touches here and there, but the Governor's Mansion still resembled a massive, overly ornate hunting lodge more than anything else. The interior had been just as unrelentingly built of wood as the exterior—as anything else in the city, really—and everything within her line of sight had been waxed and polished until she could almost see herself in the wall boards and exposed ceiling beams. Rather than a foyer, they stood in a wide hallway that ran the length of the building, with one broad staircase nearby to their left, another one visible on the right at the far end, and doors leading off the hall every few meters. Beautiful, intricately woven rugs covered most of the dark wood floor, and equally beautiful tapestries served triple-duty as decorations, insulation against the Territory's brutal winters, and sound dampeners. She appreciated the lack of noise.

"You look good," Anwar said. He made a show of trying to see over her shoulder. "No axe?"

Nysska regarded him evenly. He wore the same expression as ever—the mix of awed fascination and fear that had sat on his features since the night she'd saved his life on the Tember Road. "The axe is good for taking off heads, and not much else. I don't carry it as a personal weapon. What do you want?"

Anwar grinned and laughed. He almost kept from sounding

nervous. "Are you hungry? Let's go to my study. I can have food sent from the kitchen."

Nysska shrugged, and Anwar laughed nervously again, and then she found herself following him up the closest set of stairs. They passed through a gleaming, dark wood door into a lavishly decorated parlor with multiple animal-skin rugs on the floor, a handful of overstuffed chairs and couches, and a fireplace in the center of the room constructed so that one could see all the way through it. From there, through a door in the parlor's far corner, they entered a smaller room with a large, ornate wooden desk and three walls covered by bookshelves. Another steward, this one a matronly woman, poked her head in from the parlor, and after Anwar spoke a few words to her, she scurried out. The Governor gestured to one of the chairs. "Please, make yourself comfortable."

Nysska prodded the chair with her fingers before settling into it. She had to admit, the humans could build some *really* comfortable furniture. Her people had always favored function over form, and the wooden-and-stone chairs common in a sethyd home bore that out.

Anwar settled into the chair behind the desk. "So. How are you? How have you enjoyed your time in the Forty-Seventh Crucible?"

Nysska narrowed her eyes at him. She knew this would sharpen and harden them into brilliant flame-colored pinpoints. It gave her a tiny bit of perverse satisfaction when Anwar flinched. Before she could answer, the female steward came back in with a polished wooden tray heaped with slices of meat—Nysska smelled both ham and bison—as well as small loaves of crusty brown bread and a couple of ceramic pots filled with strawberry jam. Anwar got up and pulled a small table out of a corner, positioning it between the chairs in front of his desk, and sat down in the other chair. He arranged the tray fussily once the steward had left. "There you go. I can vouch for the bison, and the jam was a gift from my mother, back in Caulspring."

Nysska's stomach growled audibly. She leaned forward and took the thinnest slice of ham from the tray.

"I, uh—I regret not checking up on you more frequently. I was assured the Forty-Seventh was a quality team, though."

Nysska chewed a bite and swallowed. "Assured by whom?"

He had picked up a loaf of bread and torn a small chunk off of it, and was reaching for a knife next to the jam pots, but paused with his hand in mid-air. "Um...by the former City Commander...?"

Nysska ate the rest of the slice of ham, drumming the fingers of her other hand on the armrest. *Remember why you're here,* she told herself. *Remember what your options were.* After a long moment, she said, "I would like to say this without negating your generosity."

Anwar had set down the chunk of bread and abandoned the knife entirely. He held up both hands, showing her his palms. "Please, do speak freely! I value your opinion."

Nysska almost snorted. She wanted to say, *Enough to saddle me with that miserable excuse for a team?* The more she thought about it, the angrier she got. Angry enough to surprise herself. She stood and walked to one of the windows, which looked out onto the sculpted grounds surrounding the mansion. Absently, she tapped on the only-slightly-wavy glass with one black fingernail. "My presence in the Cathedral's Thaumetallicon was an experiment, yes?"

Anwar twisted around in his chair. "Well...in a manner of speaking, yes, I suppose it was. I wanted you to be an ambassador for your people. For the sethyds. As I said the night we first met. I tried to facilitate that with the Territorial Decree announcing that you had joined the Forty-Seventh."

"Yes...the single decree to which citizens in the outer reaches reacted with skepticism at best. Every time I showed up, Governor, it was as if their worst nightmares had been brought to life." Nysska turned and folded her arms across her chest and half-leaned, half-sat on the windowsill. "Your experiment was not supported, nor monitored in any meaningful way. Such that for seven months I had no choice but to work alongside a man who was more pig than human, another man who seemed determined to drink himself to death, and a girl with all the self-respect of a garden slug, Atiina bless her. I had no choice but to endure the stares, and the curses, and the unabashed hatred. And for what? For the knowledge that the only thing the citizens of the Empire fear more than Imperial law is me?"

Anwar came up out of the chair. "Nysska, please—I'm sorry about your Crucible, I didn't realize it was that bad. But I'm trying to make it up to you now."

"By doing what?"

"By reassigning you. To the best Crucible the Thaumetallicon has. Their Enforcer recently passed away, and I believe you'll be the perfect replacement for him."

Nysska said nothing and let silence stretch out between them. "I survived for years by myself in the wilderness. I can just as easily do so again. I do not need any of this."

"Are you—you're not quitting—tell me you're not quitting!"

More silence.

Anwar said, "Just—please. Please, I want to introduce you to some people. They're here, now, literally just downstairs. Come with me. I beg of you."

Nysska sighed, long and slow. "If I do…I have a condition."

Anwar blinked. "Uh…all right? What condition?"

"The Sensor in the Forty-Seventh. Put her in a different Crucible. Somewhere far away from Brux Haller—one where the Commander is a woman. And…send the dog with her."

Anwar cocked his head. "I suppose I can do that. Do you want to tell me why?"

"No. I no longer want to think of any member of the Forty-Seventh if I can help it. Except perhaps the dog. The dog was acceptable."

"Consider it done."

Anwar led her out of the study, through the parlor and down the stairs, apologizing often enough for her to want to tell him to shut up. Once they had reached the ground floor, he stopped outside a set of double doors that, judging by their height, most likely led into some kind of ballroom. "All right. These are the current members of the Ninth Crucible." He opened the doors and threw them wide.

It was, in fact, a ballroom. Or a meeting room—someplace for Anwar to address a small crowd of people. Tables and chairs were stacked against the far wall, except for three chairs set in a half-circle in the middle of the floor, which she figured had contained the asses of the Ninth Crucible until only a moment ago. Now two men and a woman stood in front of the chairs, staring at her, and halfway between the chairs and the right-hand wall...

Lay the two most beautiful animals Nysska had ever seen.

She ignored the humans and focused on the cats.

Each one about two-thirds the size of Greta, the muscular felines were covered with tawny fur, decorated with darker brown spots that ran along their backs. They had tall, pointed, gorgeous ears that swept up to impressive spikes of fur, and *enormous* paws. One of them lay on its side, appearing to nap, while the other casually licked one oversized paw and washed its face. Nysska took a step into the room, and both cats lifted their heads to peer at her—

With *silver eyes.*

They were blood lynxes. *Seraphic* blood lynxes.

Seraphic animals occupied a shifting and volatile place within the Empire, Nysska knew. Some people argued that they were as intelligent as humans and should be treated as such. Others, usually in the more remote regions, maintained that seraphic creatures had been cursed and should all be destroyed. Imperial citizens regarded them with fear, and Nysska had heard of bounties being put on their heads—that the bravest or most foolhardy poachers would capture them, kill them, and strain the argonium out of their blood.

Yet these two wore leather harnesses inlaid with Imperial bronze. Two beasts of the wild, under the Empire's aegis.

Just like me.

Beside her, Anwar cleared his throat. "Enforcer Nysska Stonegate, meet the Ninth Crucible. Commander Raoul Cullen, Sensor Camble Delakroy, and Keeper Percy Bitters. The, ah, the animals—Percy's blood lynxes—answer to Jax and Flax."

Finally, Nysska shifted her attention to the humans. Raoul Cullen immediately struck her as the kind of man whose natural stance was at attention—someone who had been drilled in military procedure and compliance his entire life. He looked young, no more than thirty, more likely twenty-five, with garden-variety brown skin and short hair that was just beginning to curl. About Brux's height, so a handful of centims shorter than her own one hundred ninety-three. He wore the same kind of commander's band around his head that Brux had, of course, and as she watched, he reached up and adjusted it. The motion struck her as a nervous tic. She wondered if he realized he was doing it.

Percy Bitters appeared to be much older, definitely north of fifty, with out-of-regulation-length hair that had once been blond and was now cloud-white, and skin that, if it hadn't been so unusually pale, would have looked like beef jerky. He wore snug black leather gloves instead of Imperial leather-and-bronze. She couldn't tell how tall he was, as he seemed to maintain a permanent slouch, but even if he'd stood up straight, she didn't think he'd make it to her collarbone. His face had split into a wide, toothy grin at the sight of her, pale blue eyes twinkling.

Camble Delakroy...deserved more attention than the other two. Height somewhere between Raoul Cullen and Percy Bitters, athletic build, black hair cropped closely enough that it left only a shadow on her scalp, and skin so dark brown and lustrous that it made Nysska think of the finest cherry wood. Delakroy wore the Imperial bronze, just like Raoul and Percy, but also sported two heavy rings on the middle finger and thumb of her left hand.

She kept her eyes closed.

A Sight Sensor, then, Nysska decided. She wondered if Camble Delakroy had been born blind, lost her vision to disease or an accident, or if—Nysska could scarcely imagine it—she might have voluntarily given up her natural sight for the runemasters' gift. Nysska had heard of such things in her time with the Forty-Seventh.

"Members of the Ninth Crucible," Anwar said, "this is Nysska Stonegate. I mean to appoint her as your new Enforcer."

No one said anything.

Languidly, one of the blood lynxes rose to its massive paws and padded across the floor, followed shortly by the other one. They came and sat down in front of Nysska, gazing up at her with the biggest, clearest eyes she had ever seen. They would have been gorgeous even without the subtle energy put forth by the argonium in their veins. Nysska peered down at them, switching from one cat's gaze to the other's and resisting the urge to try to pet them, until one of them sneezed. The cats glanced at each other, back up at Nysska, and then just as languidly ambled back across to the spot of floor they'd gotten warm already.

"Whoooo, would you look at that!" Percy Bitters exclaimed. "That means you're in the fucking club, that does! Never thought I'd see the day!" He nudged Raoul Cullen, his grin still in place and appearing genuine. "Who knew blood lynxes'd take to consorting with fiends from the pits of Hell, huh? Though, come to think of it, I shouldn't be that surprised."

Raoul took a step toward Anwar, eyeing Nysska. "Governor, would it be possible for us to speak in private on this matter?"

Nysska slowly raised an eyebrow at him.

Before Anwar could respond, Camble Delakroy said, "Depths of Hell? What?" She raised her hand and struck the two heavy rings together. They made a sharp metallic *click*, and her brow furrowed. As brazen and self-assured as if she'd been approaching a simple street vendor, Delakroy walked right up to Nysska and said, "I'm going to touch your face now."

On any other day, Nysska would have slapped away a human hand reaching for her so boldly. But something about the blind woman's demeanor, her confidence, and the sheer *grace* with which she moved, caused Nysska to stand statue-still.

Delakroy started at Nysska's chin, traced the curves of her lips quickly and neatly, ran a fingertip along her nose, and touched her eyes as lightly as a moth's wings. She got to Nysska's horns—paused for less than a heartbeat—and mapped out their shapes, the ridges, the twist from straight forward to straight up, and the needle-sharp tips.

"I'll be damned," Camble Delakroy breathed, and stepped back, but did not open her argonium-amplified eyes. Nysska tried to read her thoughts from the expression on her face but couldn't. She could only identify what was *not* there.

Fear.

Delakroy wasn't afraid of her in the slightest.

"And the Governor said your name was Nysska?"

Trying to decide whether or not it should bother her that this human woman seemed to consider her as threatening as the average puppy, Nysska said, "That's right."

"You can call me Cam," she said, and held out a hand. After a moment's hesitation, Nysska shook it.

"Sir," Raoul Cullen said. "Sir, I don't remember anything about—about this kind of—of development. In the regulations. I need to review the manual—"

Percy, still grinning, piped up with, "Is it true, though? *Are* you a fiend from the depths of Hell? Did you come climbing up out of the metal caves, like they say? You make a habit of killing folks and eating their souls? *Oooh*—do you have a *tail*?"

Anwar covered his face with one hand.

Slowly, deliberately, Nysska pulled off her left gauntlet, drew the slim dagger from the sheath strapped to her right thigh, and cut a shallow line along the back of her arm, down and around the meaty part at the base of her thumb, and ended in the center of her palm. She held the arm up and out to her side, so that everyone there—except Cam—could see the ruby-red blood dripping and splattering on the floor beside her. "Here. Take a good look. I bleed the same red as you do. I live and die, just as you do. No, I do not have a tail. Feel free to draw your own conclusions about whether or not I eat souls."

Percy gave a whooping, delighted laugh. Cam's nose twitched and wrinkled. Raoul Cullen simply stood there, staring at her, until Anwar spoke.

"Commander Cullen, tomorrow morning I will be issuing a Territorial Proclamation. Everyone in Green Needles will be made aware of Nysska's presence as Enforcer of the Ninth Crucible, with full authorization—and protection—of the Cathedral." With a glance at Nysska, he added, "I will issue such a proclamation once a week for a month, in hopes that it reaches everyone."

Raoul couldn't seem to decide whether or not he should be standing at attention. Nysska saw his arm twitch and wondered if he meant to salute—but finally he simply nodded his head once. "Yes, sir."

Anwar beckoned to Nysska. "Enforcer Stonegate, if I may speak to you in private?" He led her out of the ballroom and a short way down the hall, out of earshot of the rest of the Ninth. "Well? Do you find this agreeable?"

Nysska sighed, keeping one eye on the long, shallow laceration she'd given herself. It was already starting to scab over. "I may end up pinching that Keeper's head off, but..." She thought of the two blood lynxes. "I suppose I can give this a try."

"Good. Good. Brilliant! Because there's already a case that needs your attention, that I'll brief you all on first thing in the morning. Now, would you like me to show you to your room? Or would you like to get to know your new teammates first?"

"Right now I could use a hot meal and a bed somewhere quiet."

"That's also available. Here, come with me."

The room Anwar supplied her might have looked plain and utilitarian to someone else, but after the months she had spent in the company of Brux Haller and the rest of the profoundly defective Forty-Seventh Crucible, to Nysska it seemed a small, private, *quiet* paradise.

There was nothing more than a bed, a wardrobe in one corner, a stand with a wash basin in another corner, and a window looking out onto the city—but after the requested hot meal, followed by a hot bath, Nysska sank into the bed, closed her eyes, and debated whether she ever wanted to move again. She fell asleep within seconds...

Her eyes sprang open when a big, stone-like hand clamped down over her mouth.

She couldn't tell how much time had passed. Just that the sun had set. Nysska would have come surging up out of the bed, fists flying and teeth bared, but she saw the pair of gleaming yellow eyes above her and relaxed, scowling.

Gerrit took his hand away. In the room's darkness, aside from his eyes, all she could see of him was his horned silhouette, and that only just barely. Gerrit had undergone training of a very different sort from that which had taken up most of Nysska's life. She knew that if he wanted to enter a place without being seen or heard, he absolutely would not be seen or heard.

Gerrit took a step back as Nysska sat up, and pitched his voice low. "Talk to me."

"Is this how it's going to be from now on? You appear like a ghost whenever you choose?"

"Yes. Talk to me."

Nysska rubbed her eyes and glanced out the window. The level and quality of the moonlight put the hour somewhere past midnight. "Governor Anwar wants to reassign me to a different Crucible."

"Which one?"

"The Ninth."

Nysska saw the briefest flash of teeth in the darkness. "Ah. Very good. *Very* good."

"Why? What do you know about it?"

"I know the case to which the Ninth Crucible has just been assigned. It holds interest for us." Gerrit paused. She saw the tilt of his horns as he gazed up at the ceiling, and knew he was thinking. "You will accept this new role, and you will solve the case assigned to you. Do you understand, Nysska? *You will solve the case.* I want to know the outcome. And I do not want anyone but you and your new team working on it. The information must come to us straightaway."

Nysska let out a raspy sigh. "I'm an Enforcer. I'm not someone who makes decisions. What if something goes wrong with the case? Something beyond my control?"

"Then you will *exert* control." He leaned closer, teeth flashing. "Say it. Say you understand."

"I understand."

"Good. You will see me again."

Nysska sat on the bed, motionless, as Gerrit vanished back into the night.

6

Governor Anwar gave them fresh horses for the short journey from Tember to the Imperial College at Taurus Hill. The Cathedral tended to think of horses purely as a transportation commodity, rather than anything to which a soldier might become personally attached. Nysska admired the thoroughness and efficiency with which the Cathedral trained its horses, though, as she had yet to encounter one that failed to obey the same commands, in exactly the same way, as the one before it. At the same time, it made her sad. She knew horses had personalities just as distinctive as those of cats or dogs or other animals. The Cathedral drilled anything like individual traits right out of them, and now Nysska referred to whatever horse she was given as "Horse," rather than any more imaginative name.

This particular Horse was a mare of an unremarkable brown, but she moved freely and easily and responded to the commands Nysska issued, perhaps just a hair faster than her last Horse had. More important than that, this Horse nimbly avoided the stray rocks and frequent deep ruts in the road on the way to Taurus Hill, for which Nysska was grateful.

She found it easier to think about her mount's disposition than to acknowledge the furtive glances her new teammates kept throwing her way. They'd been on the road for an hour—setting out just after dawn, so that the air still held the prior evening's bite, and their breath plumed out behind them—and she knew she'd have to say something eventually. Nysska felt the Commander's and the Keeper's eyes on her incessantly.

The blind Sensor wasn't a problem, at least. Idly, Nysska wondered if the clop-clop of the horses' hooves gave her a detailed portrait of the landscape around her, or if input from multiple sources only confused her.

The road to Taurus Hill looked much like other roads through the Territory. Badly maintained, slicing through dense forest, and too narrow for more than a couple of riders to move abreast. The woods on either side of them lived up to the name of the region. Countless pine trees, each covered with countless needles, all coated in frigid dew and glistening in the early morning sunlight like emerald sculptures. Nysska drew in a slow, deep breath, tasting the scent of the forest. Wood smoke came to her, so faint she almost missed it, and she spied a thin plume of smoke far off to their right. A hunter's cabin? A logging camp? She had seen how Imperial cities and towns crept out relentlessly from the site of their founding, greedy, hungry, crawling like a dense fungus. How long before the mighty woods of the Green Needles Territory fell to axes and saws?

The Keeper, Percy Bitters, tapped his heels to his mount's flanks just hard enough to make it pick up the pace, and fell in line beside Horse. Nysska glanced around, realizing that she hadn't seen either of the blood lynxes in some time, and caught sight of one of them moving parallel to the road, gliding through the undergrowth just inside the tree line.

The Keeper said, "Perfect opportunity for us all to get to know each other, yeah?"

Nysska shrugged.

Percy went on as if she'd responded politely. "Was kind of hoping we could find out where you come from, what you're like—what you love and don't love, you know? If we're going to depend on you for muscle, and you're going to depend on us to find the filth and refuse, we ought to know what tickles your fancy and what don't, yeah?"

Nysska turned her head and raked her gaze from his toes to the crown of his head. He recoiled a little at that, but only just a very little, and immediately his grin grew wider. "God*damn.* Those things looked amazing last night, but when the morning sun lights them up? No fucking wonder people think you lot aren't human!" He paused, his brow creasing, and a breeze picked up the long twin forks of his beard and flapped them around his face. "I mean to say, of course you're not *human,* but it's no wonder people think you're, that is, not entirely of this world, y'know?"

From ahead of them, the blind Sensor—Cam, she'd said to call her—spoke over her shoulder. "Percy, would you leave the woman alone? She'll open up when she feels like it."

Behind Nysska and to her right, Raoul Cullen spoke up. "Percy's not wrong, though. This isn't Cathedral protocol. Place a new Enforcer in a Crucible and send them on a case this soon? We should've trained together first."

"Exactly!" Percy said, making a dramatic gesture with both hands. "That's all I was trying to say!"

Nysska turned her eyes toward Raoul Cullen, saw him looking back at her with a polite but clear sense of expectation, and sighed. "What do you want to know?" She didn't direct the question to anyone in particular. Just let it hang in the brittle morning air. In her peripheral vision, she saw Percy open his mouth to speak but close it again. After several long moments, Cam cleared her throat and angled an ear back toward the rest of her teammates. The elegant curve of the Sensor's neck struck Nysska—did she look familiar? How was that possible?

"First of all," Cam said, "how did you come to be a part of the Cathedral? I thought all of your people had settled up in the Crags."

Nysska considered her answer for several long moments. "I met Governor Anwar on the Tember Road. He offered me a position. For the last seven months, I have been the Enforcer for the Forty-Seventh Crucible. I was just as surprised as all of you to be assigned to this one."

"I remember when the Decree came out," Percy said. "That we'd have a...uh—you'll pardon me, I haven't heard anybody say the name out loud before. That we'd have a *sethyd* joining our ranks. Nobody knew what to make of it. Reckon most people still don't."

Nysska shrugged again.

Raoul drew closer. "You *met* him. The Governor. And he offered you a position."

"As I said."

"Just like that. He assigned you to a Crucible. No training. No time in the Imperial army."

Keeping her voice flat, Nysska said, "If you question his decisions, I would suggest taking your concerns up with him directly. I'm a Cathedral soldier now, just as you are, and follow orders just as you do."

Another silence fell, and a dense cloud of tension along with it. She had heard that some humans, some of the ones amplified by argonium runes, could hear others' thoughts as clearly as if someone were speaking to them. Nysska boasted no such ability, nor did any other sethyd she'd ever heard of, yet at that moment she felt as if all three members of her team were communicating with crystal clarity. *How is such a thing possible,* she understood them to say, and *What exactly happened on the highway with the Governor,* and loudest of all, *What aren't you telling us?*

No one said anything or tried to stop her as she dropped back and took up the rear, close enough to spring into action should trouble arise, but far enough away to be out of earshot.

After another half hour of uninhabited roadway, Nysska spotted a sign coming up on the right. It was badly painted, decorating a few rough boards crudely tacked together, but legible enough: ROBIN VALLEY.

Aiming her voice generally in Raoul Cullen's direction, Nysska said, "Is Robin Valley the only town between Tember and Taurus Hill?"

Percy snorted. "Don't know that I'd call it a town, exactly. The Empire built a bridge across a gully when the road was going in, and when nobody was looking, some people decided to pitch tents down along the gully's sides. Don't worry, we'll be past it in a flash."

Sure enough, only minutes later the arching frame of a suspension bridge came into view when they rounded a corner and, for the first time since leaving Tember, Nysska saw more humans. Somewhere between a dozen and twenty of them had set up hideous little stalls on either side of the bridge, hawking misshapen fruits and vegetables, trinkets, and in one case, small baskets of dried meat. The humans manning these stalls were every bit as shabby as the goods they sold—dirty, missing teeth, dressed in little better than rags.

As the horses stepped out onto the bridge itself, Nysska glanced over the side, and saw exactly what Percy had described: a shanty town clinging precariously to the sloped sides of a gully, at the bottom of which ran a narrow, swift-moving stream. She couldn't help but agree. Robin Valley wasn't much of a town.

They had almost reached the far side of the bridge when a faint sound reached them. *Drumming.* Distant, but growing closer. The rest of the Crucible stopped, and Nysska wheeled her horse around, trying to pinpoint where the drumming originated. Cam beat her to it, pointing into the gully, downstream from the shanty town. "There."

Percy looked unconvinced. "No way under Dragon's sky they'd be all the way out here."

Frowning, Nysska said, "Who? What does the drumming mean?"

"The Argonium Infantry," Raoul snapped, staring downstream. "And the only reason I can think of for them to be in a place like this—"

An anguished, wailing scream cut him short, echoing up from the gully floor as a woman burst out of a flimsy house and screamed, *"TAAAARN!"*

The house out of which the woman had scrambled *exploded*.

Standing there amid the rubble was something Nysska had never seen before. She had heard stories from her teammates in the Forty-Seventh, but usually when they were drunk, and so she'd never given the details much credit. But as she stared, even from as far away as they were, she felt a tiny thrill of fear.

Under normal circumstances the man would have been unremarkable. Average height for a human, average build, skin and hair both a dull brown. But now the man's muscles flexed with eldritch power, arcs and streams of onyx energy swirling around his arms and legs and chest as the jet-black runes beneath his skin hummed and pulsed. His eyes had vanished, falling away into a lightless void, and his mouth stretched horribly wide, teeth lengthened into knife-sharp jagged shards.

"Is it?" Cam asked, a note of panic in her voice. *"Is it?"*

"Yes." Raoul wasn't panicked, not yet, but he sounded grim. "It's a Tarnished One."

Moving like some kind of animal, a ferocious predator with fear of neither man nor beast, the tarn bellowed and dashed to the next house. He dug his hands into the walls and shredded the structure, and the humans inside shrieked and fled like cockroaches, but one of them was too slow—a white-haired man—and the tarn grabbed him by the throat and one arm and *tore him in half*.

The drums grew louder. The tarn seemed not to care, and ripped through Robin Valley like a tornado, destroying homes, dealing savage, bloody death to any of the villagers he could get his hands on.

"What do we do?" Nysska asked Raoul. "What is expected of us?"

"Nothing," Raoul shot back, and pointed. "Especially not when they're here."

From around a bend at the bottom of the shanty town, a dozen soldiers burst into view. At first glance, they looked like any others in the vast military body known as the Cathedral—except that, instead of bronze, their armor had been inlaid with strips of highly polished tin.

One of them launched himself at the tarn. His feet left a crater in the ground behind him, and he sailed fully ten meters through the air, a heavy bronze sword raised to strike.

The tarn whipped his head around in time to see the infantryman coming. He twisted aside, caught the infantryman's sword arm, braced a foot against the soldier's ribs, and tore the arm off. The infantryman fell, screaming. Three more soldiers reached the tarn, swarming him, but the tarn had taken the bronze sword out of the detached arm's nerveless hand, and he drove it through one soldier's heart, ripped it free, and hacked the head away from another's body in the time it would have taken a normal human to blink. The third soldier tackled him, tried to hold him down, but the tarn seemed aware of the other eight infantrymen bearing down on him. He kicked the soldier away, sprinted upstream, and leapt.

Nysska watched as the tarn rose, rose, higher and higher, until he landed on the bridge not seven meters from where the Ninth Crucible sat astride their horses, staring in horror.

The tarn grinned at Nysska—but whipped around, his hand moving faster than her eyes could track, and *caught* an arrow as thick as a child's wrist right before the barbed, dagger-tipped point would have punched through his head.

Nysska cast a wild look down into the gully and saw five of the eight remaining infantrymen with bows in their hands—bows bigger and heavier than she had ever seen wielded by one archer. Bows that would have looked more at home on some kind of siege engine. At that moment, the sound of the first bowstring reached her ears, a deep thrumming that she felt in her breastbone, and she pivoted back in time to see four additional monstrous arrows rip into the tarn's body, spinning him like a leaf in a windstorm, spraying his blood across half the bridge. A chorus of bone-shaking twangs reached Nysska, reverberating down into her stomach—the lethally final statement of the infantrymen's bowstrings.

The tarn staggered, wheezing, great gory holes in his body, his lower jaw torn completely away—and stayed on his feet.

What was left of his face wrinkled in mad delight, and he lifted the bronze sword high, just as three of the Argonium Infantrymen landed on the bridge, having leapt up just as the tarn had. Two of them had arrows nocked. They drew and fired, faster than Nysska's eyes could follow, and pinned the tarn to the side of the bridge.

The third infantryman approached the tarn, whose arms and legs still twitched like those of a dying insect on a specimen board, drew his longsword, and with no words or ceremony took the tarn's head off.

Breathing hard, the soldier with the sword turned and saluted Raoul.

Returning the salute, Raoul said, "Solid work, Captain."

The captain shook his head. "You can't never tell where they're showing up anymore." With a polite nod to the rest of the Crucible, he returned to his men.

"Come on," Raoul said. "They've got procedures for this. We'd only be in their way."

They left Robin Valley and its carnage behind them, each alone in their thoughts.

Nysska had never been to Taurus Hill, had never had any reason to go there, but she had assumed it was a town like any other in Green Needles, like any other anywhere in the Empire, for that matter. A hub, essentially, filled with markets and taverns and brothels, surrounded by farms or logging operations or mines or whatever took the wealth from the laborers and put in the government's purses. As such, any road leading into a town of any size would be frequented by farmers or loggers or miners or what have you, carrying their goods in to sell, returning home with a bit of copper in their pockets.

The rest of the road to Taurus Hill lay bare and empty.

That emptiness set off question after question in Nysska's head, but no one else on the team seemed anxious to talk to her any further, so she kept her mouth shut.

Eventually the forest peeled away on either side of them, and she did start seeing farmland. But Taurus Hill was home to the territory's Imperial College. How could there be so little traffic between it and Tember?

Why would no one from the capital want to go there?

The questions continued as she got a good look at the town, which did not appear to have anything to do with bulls and wasn't even really on a hill. The entire place seemed to have been built onto and into the slope of a mountainside, in concentric half-circles of homes and businesses that drew the eye up to a massive stone structure against a nearly sheer cliff face. *No shortage of stone here,* she thought, as she took in the contrast of Taurus Hill to the Ironwood City.

Starting with the town's defensive wall, which had been built from huge square slabs of rock, the rest of Taurus Hill followed suit, creating a sort of *de facto* semicircular stone labyrinth. She imagined that anyone who lived there could navigate from one side of the town to the other with ease, but gazing at it from afar made Nysska shudder with a tremor of claustrophobia. They were still too far away to see people, but she imagined them moving like ants, striving to find their way through a maze so as not to be squashed under some gigantic child's sadistic thumb.

Soon they entered the city, and rather than the abject fear that Tember's citizenry projected at the sight of the Imperial bronze, the guards and citizens of Taurus Hill gave them little to no reaction as they rode through the gate. A tall, lean man with captain's insignia on his shoulders stood a few dozen meters inside the gate and held a hand up as they approached.

Nysska had already assumed her "disguise," with her hood up and her scarf around her face, but the captain made a sort of pulling-down gesture at his own chin as he walked up to her. "Enforcer Nysska Stonegate? Am I correct?"

Nysska glanced around at her team, lingering on Raoul to see his reaction. Ordinarily, any kind of liaison or emissary spoke to a Crucible's commander before any of the rest of the team. Raoul looked as if he wanted to say something, but since the guard captain had addressed Nysska, Raoul shrugged and made a subtle gesture with his chin: *Go on.*

"You are," Nysska said to the captain.

"I've been instructed to tell you, ma'am, that Governor Anwar sent a rider last night with a Territorial Decree. You've no need to keep yourself covered up. We know you're a—"

Nysska could hear the word as plainly as if he'd said it. *Demon.* But he backed himself up and started over.

"We know you're a *sethyd.*" Nysska thought the word must have tasted strange in the captain's mouth from the way his lips quirked. "There is no need to cover your face."

Nysska scanned her surroundings. Percy and Raoul both watched her, clearly waiting for her reaction. Cam had the posture of someone listening carefully, like a diner quietly eavesdropping on a conversation one table over.

There were as many soldiers as citizens, this close to the wall. Not one of them looked at her or even glanced in her direction. Her eyes narrowed—there. One man stood in the doorway of what appeared to be an apothecary shop, and he stared straight at her, his gaze level and unafraid. She concentrated, taking in as many details as she could, since he stood at a distance of twenty or thirty meters. Average height for a human, typical curly brown hair, ordinary brown skin. She thought his eyes were brown as well. But she'd never seen anyone dressed the way he was—in boots and trousers and shirt of solid black, within a black coat that fell to his knees. Embroidered into the coat were broad stripes of pure gold, each roughly a hand's width apart, running in a sharp diagonal from collar to hem and down both sleeves. As she watched, the man turned and disappeared inside the shop.

Silently, Nysska pulled her scarf down so that it hung loose around her neck and hooked her thumbs into the hood's hem to push it back. A gentle breeze felt good across her cheeks and forehead, and stirred the jet-black and cobalt-blue of her hair.

The captain's face betrayed no emotion as he gazed up at her. "I am grateful for the Governor's graciousness," she said, because she couldn't think of anything else to say, and because the captain seemed to be waiting for a response.

The captain nodded, once, and pointed. "Take this central street, and at each fork, choose the one that takes you uphill. You'll arrive at the college's doors in no time." A group of young soldiers approached, and the captain made a broad gesture toward them. "These lads will take your mounts to the stables."

"Thank you, Captain," Raoul said, just a bit too loudly. He dismounted and shouldered his pack. Cam and Percy followed suit, and Nysska patted Horse's neck as she put feet to ground once again. Horse turned her head and made a soft *whuffling* sound, and Nysska lightly kissed her soft nose and stroked her ear.

"Eat well, girl, and get some rest," she whispered. "Perhaps we'll see each other again."

Horse *whuffled* again and followed obediently as one of the young soldiers took her reins and led her off along the wall to the left. Percy pulled a couple of leads from his pack and clipped them to Flax and Jax's bronze-inlaid halters, at which both of the blood lynxes hissed and growled. Percy knelt, facing them. "Now, you both know this is for your own good. We've got no choice but to tread among the masses, and I can't have you running off and getting killed. Or eating babies."

One of the cats—Nysska thought it was Jax—made a sound so close to a snort of derision that she could interpret it no other way, but both animals followed after Percy. Maybe not as cooperatively as Horse had gone with the soldier, but follow him they did. Raoul set a brisk pace, and the Ninth Crucible made their way through the streets of Taurus Hill.

Nysska drew in a long, slow breath through her nose once they were away from the gates. The town smelled sharply different from Tember, and it took her a few moments to realize the biggest change was the amount of smoke. That puzzled her, since this place was most of a day's ride north of the capital, and no doubt experienced every bit as much cold weather if not more. She wondered if the thick stone walls she saw on nearly every structure simply insulated the inhabitants better, so that they didn't have to burn as much wood to stay warm. The stone itself had a smell, she realized. Something subtle and clean. Something like the honest scent of a brook in the wilderness, where thousands of years had worn smooth the once-jagged rocks in its bed.

Nysska preferred thinking about that to analyzing the townsfolk's deliberately absent gazes. Averted eyes. Turned backs.

No, the people of Taurus Hill did not seem inclined to gather in angry mobs and tear her apart, but the farther into the town they moved, the more tension she felt. What must that have been like—the rider arriving the night before, telling them that not only was a demon coming, but that it fell under Cathedral protection? That it had the Cathedral's *authority*? Were the humans in cities and towns any more receptive to her existence than the provincial morons she'd policed alongside Morrin and Staige and Brux had been?

Not likely, she thought. *Decree or no decree, nine out of ten of them would rather I burst into flames and die.*

Nysska had heard talk in dozens of taverns over the last seven months. The humans of the Empire *knew* her homeland had erupted in a civilization-ending catastrophe. They *knew* that the survivors had no choice but to flee, as the entire sethyd island-nation had been rendered uninhabitable. They *knew* that the Emperor had granted the sethyds asylum and given them a wide parcel of mountainous land for which humans had no use. But when an actual, living "demon" walked through the door, it triggered something, deep within the human heart. A lock of some kind, impenetrable, unbreakable, a bronze-hard fist holding fast to the idea that the world was made for humans and humans alone, and anything that walked like a person and talked like a person but *was not human* could not be allowed to live.

Along the way, twice, Nysska caught sight of more people in the long, black-with-gold-embroidery coats. One was like the first sighting, a man dressed in black from head to foot, his coat striped, though the stripes were noticeably narrower. The second caught her eye more firmly: a woman this time, same boots and trousers and shirt as the men, but instead of simple stripes, her coat sported a flowing, curving golden pattern. Nysska wondered if the extent of the coat's decoration indicated some kind of rank.

"There it is," Percy said. "And not a fucking minute too soon, you ask me. I've had to take a colossal dump since we rode through the gates."

"Thanks for that commentary," Cam said, her tone both dry and resigned. "I wouldn't turn down a bit of rest, myself, though. What's the place look like?"

For the first time—though not the last, she suspected—Nysska had forgotten that Cam was blind. Raoul jumped in to answer her.

"Bigger than Governor Anwar's mansion. Another stone wall around it, and I'd say at least four levels aboveground. Maybe five, it's hard to judge since the wall's in the way. Looks as if it might go back into the mountainside itself. Architecturally utilitarian. This town does love its square stone buildings."

That seemed to satisfy Cam. No one else spoke until they reached the gate, where two more bronze-clad soldiers waited for them, spears in their hands. Nysska noticed a black insignia on their helmets decorated with gold thread.

One of the guards inclined his head toward Raoul. His eyes flickered over to Nysska but snuck away just as quickly. The other guard had been openly watching her as the Ninth Crucible walked up the broad stone street, but now he lowered his eyes. "Welcome to the Imperial College of the Green Needles Territory," the first guard said, and pushed the gate wide. "You are all welcome here. Professor Greig is waiting for you in the entry hall."

Thirty meters inside the gate, the Imperial College sprang up out of the ground unceremoniously, like a single enormous rock heaved from the earth by some massive seismic event. Nysska craned her head to look all the way up. There were *six* levels, not four or five, dwarfing Anwar's home. The College's face had been constructed so rigidly, so symmetrically, and so *unimaginatively,* that it struck her more like a giant vertical game board than an actual building. A massive wooden door with bronze hinges, set dead center before them, swung open, and a woman in a gold-embroidered black coat strode out to greet them.

Nysska thought that if the sun hit her coat at the right angle, it might blind all of them. It seemed more gold than black, a collar-to-hem frenzy of mad swirls, curves, loops, and arrows. Nysska decided the amount of gold *had* to indicate rank.

The woman herself looked to be in her mid-forties, with short, straight, light gray hair and a broad face marked with a lifetime's worth of lines and creases—more like someone who'd spent decades working on a farm than a sequestered academic. "I am Professor Greig," she said, her words sharp and clipped. "You are here to tell me who killed my runemaster, yes?"

"We have been sent by the Governor, ma'am," Raoul said.

"Professor." Even sharper. "Not 'ma'am.'" Greig's back was spear-shaft straight, and rather than the usual dark brown or black eyes, hers were an unforgiving icy gray, almost white.

Raoul bowed his head. "Your pardon, Professor. Yes, our Crucible has been dispatched to apprehend the perpetrator."

Greig nodded once. "Follow me, then."

The professor led them into a corridor every bit as utilitarian as the college's exterior. Everything here seemed to be constructed of chiseled gray stone—walls, floor, ceiling—and Nysska surprised herself by voicing a thought before she'd even considered it. "This place used to be a mine."

Greig raised an eyebrow at her. "Are the sethyds a mining people, then? I must confess my knowledge of your culture is sorely lacking."

"We've sunk a few shafts," Nysska said, and thought Greig might have a follow-up question, but the professor simply turned and walked away, beckoning them to follow. Nysska got the impression that Greig was the sort of person who, as a rule, distributed knowledge rather than received it.

As they walked, Professor Greig noisily cleared her throat, and spoke as if she were lecturing students. "The Imperial College is divided into three wings: residential, research, and implementation." Several doors down the corridor, which led directly into the heart of the mountain and was now lit by torches placed in regular wall sconces, a group of young men and women in long black coats with gold stripes exited a room and walked at measured paces past the Crucible. Most of them stared at Nysska with open curiosity. Only a few turned their faces away or lowered their eyes. Greig went on. "Some of the runemasters who live here are in training. The rest serve the Empire, using the skills and techniques we teach them."

Greig took them up a broad stone staircase to the level above, where multiple hallways led away from the stairs at odd angles. Nysska realized it would be no challenge at all to get lost here.

Greig made another lofty-sounding statement, but Nysska missed whatever it was, thanks to something brushing past her ankle. She looked down to see one of the blood lynxes keeping step with her and managed not to cry out when the second cat leapt up onto her back. The lynx steadied itself with its claws in her armor and proceeded to drape itself around her shoulders, a deep, rumbling purr filling her left ear and vibrating in her skull.

Nysska glanced over at Percy, to find him gazing at her and her feline passenger with a mixture of amusement and theatrically righteous indignation. "Fucking traitor," he said quietly, and grinned.

"Which one is this?" Nysska asked, scratching her passenger under the chin. "I can't tell them apart."

"That's Flax. This is her brother, Jax. Littermates, I'm almost certain."

Nysska returned her attention to Professor Greig, and found the woman staring at her. Raoul was staring at her, too, openly annoyed. The professor said, "As I was saying, it *is* my understanding that the sethyds do not possess thaumaturgy. Am I correct in that?"

Nysska fought to keep the hostility out of her voice. Greig might have a legitimate grievance, if Nysska had inadvertently ignored her, but Raoul could take that expression off his face and shove it up his ass. "We know of it—we call it *magio*." She was going to say more, but Professor Greig forged ahead.

"Allow me to explain, then. We use argonium runes to amplify the human body's natural abilities. Each rune is crafted by a rune-master specifically for one recipient, such as your Sensor here." Greig allowed no time for a response from Cam. "Thaumaturgical runes correspond to one of the five senses, though the exact effect varies from recipient to recipient. Those with visual implants can see things other people cannot see, just as those with audial or olfactory implants can hear or smell things denied to the general populace. We shy away from taste-related runes, as that tends to complicate eating. A Sensor cannot do their job if they're starved to death, can they?"

Nysska spotted one corner of Greig's mouth twitching upward and wondered if the woman thought she'd said something funny.

"The runes focusing on the sense of touch are the only ones we've managed to imbue with more than one purpose. I'm sure you've seen some of them in use, have you not, since you've been in the Cathedral's employ for...how long?"

"Seven months," Nysska said, vividly recalling the Argonium Infantrymen from the bridge. She opened her mouth to comment on that encounter, but Greig started talking again.

"The effectiveness of troops implanted with what we've come to call *runes of strength* is what has allowed the Empire's glorious reign to extend this far." Greig turned a cold smile on Raoul. "Bronze is law."

Raoul dipped his head, answering as he was obliged to. "Bronze is peace."

They had made several sharp turns as Greig spoke, the doors on either side of them growing farther and farther apart, and finally Greig stopped before one of them. "We are now in the research wing," she said. "This is Professor Olkoff's laboratory."

Raoul moved to stand beside Greig. "This is where he was killed?"

"It is. Do you require privacy to perform your investigation, or may I observe?"

Raoul frowned, and shrugged. "With respect, Professor, it would be best if you were to stay out of the scene. But please don't go far. In this place—" he gestured expansively around them, "—we may need your assistance once the pursuit of the guilty party gets under way."

Greig nodded, and produced a large, ornate key. "Of course. I shall remain in the hallway."

She unlocked the door, pushed it open, and stepped aside. Raoul walked through first, followed by Cam and Percy. Nysska hesitated, and when Greig looked up at her with those icy almost-white eyes, she couldn't help herself. "You select people each year to receive the argonium runes. And yet even my people know the metal is toxic. What do you offer the citizenry? To get them to agree not to live past —what is the upper limit? Forty years?"

Greig's eyes narrowed a millim or two. "We do not *select* the recipients, Enforcer. They come to us each spring and each autumn. Lined up for kliks. Eager to accept the metal."

Nysska didn't think the woman was lying. With Flax purring in her ear still, Nysska ducked her head and walked into Olkoff's laboratory. She heard the door latch as the frenzy of sights within the cavernous room threatened to overwhelm her.

Gone was the College's utilitarian aesthetic. The walls and floor and ceiling were still chiseled gray stone, yes, but thick furs and woven rugs covered the floor, and she couldn't see even a square centim of wall space for the shelving that covered it from floor to ceiling. Half of those shelves contained books and scrolls, while the other half held—she tried to make sense of everything she could see from there, just inside the door—stacks of argonium, beaten into paper-thin sheets; metalworking tools, the variety and complexity of which rivaled anything she had seen back in Fajrasxtono; and, past the tools, row after row of what appeared to be delicate, even spindly machines festooned with gears and lenses and small, numbered handles.

At the far end of the lab, a fireplace massive enough for Cam and Percy to have stood inside it sat cold, stained by smoke, only a few charred lumps of what had once been wood remaining. Near the hearth a couple of fur-covered couches provided ideal locations to stretch out and let the fire warm a body.

The stone-and-metal table dominated the lab, though. A monument to the Empire's power, right in the center of the floor, surrounded by a U-shaped work bench on which rested a half dozen metalworking tools and one of the strange, spindly machines. Flax jumped down off Nysska's shoulders and joined her brother. Nysska watched as the blood lynxes padded about, sniffing, exploring. Now that Flax had taken her near-thunderous purrs with her, Nysska realized someone in the room was breathing hard and fast.

Cam.

The Sensor clicked her rings together—and seemed to grow unsteady on her feet.

Raoul Cullen all but leapt to Cam's side. Nysska saw his steadying hand on Cam's upper arm, saw the way he looked down at her as he spoke soft words of reassurance, and understood in that moment how desperately in love with her he was.

"You all right there, girl?" Percy asked in his normal brassy voice, moving to Cam's other side. "Quite the trip down memory fucking lane for you, coming here, eh?"

Cam removed Raoul's hand from her arm, but not before giving it a quick squeeze. "Thank you," she said to no one specific. "And yes, it's —I can feel the, uh…the argonium." She tapped the base of her skull. "Here. Like a hive of bees." She lifted a hand and pointed at the table. "There *are* restraints, yes? Channels for the blood? A drain in the floor?"

Nysska frowned. She hadn't noticed at first, but now that she looked more closely, yes, there were thick leather straps hanging down off the sides of the stone table, and yes, it had channels chiseled into its surface. She hadn't given much thought to how painful or messy the rune implantation process must be. Little wonder that the College's "volunteers," as Professor Greig had called them, would have to be held down by force.

"That's accurate," Raoul said. He hadn't moved away from her. "The one in Caulspring was similar, I take it?"

"The College there is not as…claustrophobic…" Cam said. "But I'll never forget the scent of the rune lab. The feel of it. None of us will, I expect. Although…there's something different here—something…new…"

"New like what?" Raoul asked.

Cam frowned. "I'm not sure. It's faint—probably nothing." She squared her shoulders and tugged the hem of her tunic. "All right. If you'll give me some room, I'll get to work."

"Everyone stand back." Raoul said *everyone,* but he clearly meant Nysska, as Percy and the blood lynxes were already moving back toward the door. "Out of her line of sight."

Nysska wanted to say, *I've been a part of a Crucible for better than half a year, I know how this works,* but instead silently moved to stand against the wall, next to Percy.

Cam moved out a couple of meters, her back to them. Nysska caught Percy glancing up at her, and when he saw that he'd been caught, just above a whisper he said, "Cam doesn't like to look at living folks when she's using her runes like this."

Nysska's elevated eyebrows asked the question: *Why?* But Percy only shook his head.

The air in the laboratory changed, and Nysska knew Cam had opened her eyes and activated her runes. She couldn't see Cam's face, but something like a white-blue flame glowed and flickered from the Sensor's eyes, and Nysska found herself holding her breath. She wanted to ask how long this process usually took, since her only frame of reference was Morrin and her rune-enhanced sense of smell, but before she could even open her mouth, Cam faltered.

Her back arched, her shoulders and arms spasming, and Raoul

dashed forward again, but Cam must have heard his footsteps because she threw a hand up in his path. "Stay back! *Stay back!*"

Clenching his fists, Raoul said, "What's wrong? Are you hurt?"

"Stay where you are!" Cam shouted. "All of you! Don't get near me!" Her knees trembled and buckled, and she crumpled to a kneeling posture.

Nysska snapped at Percy, "Tell me what is happening!"

"I don't know!" Both blood lynxes growled and hissed at his feet. "I've never seen her do this before!"

Nysska still couldn't see Cam's face, but the silver radiance had grown brighter, and beneath the sleeves of her armor Nysska felt the fine hairs on the backs of her arms stand up away from her skin.

Items on the shelves around the laboratory's perimeter began to shake. Cam's arms moved spastically, reaching out before her, moving so hard and fast they seemed to pull her shoulders with them against her will. She wailed, "There's nothing! There's *nothing there*!"

Flax and Jax backed up tight against the wall. Their ears flattened against their skulls, and in unison they bared their brutal, ripping fangs and screamed.

One of the sheets of argonium rattled against the wooden shelf on which it rested, rose a centim in the air, and shot toward Cam's head, a broad, dull blade aimed square at her eyes.

Nysska felt the fire in her veins come to life.

In less than a second, less than a heartbeat, less than a thought, she braced a foot against the stone wall behind her and launched herself across the floor. Cam had begun screaming, but the din that reached Nysska's ears sounded distorted, attenuated, more like the low, creaking strain of timbers in Fajrasxtono's windmills. She reached Cam before the flashing sheet of silver metal did, got a grip on it with both hands, twisted her body and took the brunt of the impact on her armored chestplate.

Nysska slid to a stop stretched prone on one of the fur rugs, and when she sat up, she found herself staring Camble Delakroy dead in the face, her runes at their full power.

Time had slowed for her in the past.

Now it came to a halt.

Cam's body stopped shivering and quaking as she stared at Nysska with wide silver eyes. In the barely two days Nysska had known her—had known the rest of the Ninth Crucible—she had never seen Cam except with her eyes shut. Now…now that Cam gazed at her, eyes ablaze with silver flame that shimmered and gleamed like moonlight on the sea, Camble Delakroy became something more.

Vastly more.

Nysska felt her lips part, her jaw go slack, as the sights and sounds and scents of the temple in the center of Fajrasxtono slammed into her, filled her up with her mother's perfume and the gentle waves in the air above the candles and the subtle, reassuring rhythm of the drums beneath the floor.

Nysska's gut tightened. Fluttered. Her throat went dry.

Beautiful…

A low, aching groan escaped Nysska's throat, and tears started in her eyes, and she wanted to abandon the rest of the world and spend days, years, decades doing nothing but drinking in the sight because nothing else could be that perfect. Nothing else, no other living being could come close, and Nysska wanted to take Cam's hand and put it over her own heart so that Cam could feel how fast it pumped, how hot, how it made her muscles tremble, made her body tingle from her feet to the tips of her horns.

Nysska set the sheet of argonium aside and rose to her knees, no more than a meter away from Cam. She wanted to say something, to say *anything*, to commune with this impossible, staggering creature—

With a whimper, Cam shut her eyes and buried her face in her hands.

Half the strength in Nysska's thrumming body vanished. She slumped back to the floor, blood rushing in her ears.

Cam snatched her hands away from her face, but kept her eyes tight shut. "Great Dragon! What—" Her chin trembled, and Nysska recognized the signs of panic setting in. "What is this? *What is this?"* Cam's voice rose to a shriek. She waved her hands in front of her, and a whiff of something unholy reached Nysska's nose. "Get it off of me!" Cam screamed. *"Get it off me get it off me!"*

Now Raoul was at her side with Percy right behind him—Nysska wondered how long she'd been locked there, frozen in the force of Cam's silver gaze—and Raoul whipped a handkerchief out of a pocket and wiped at Cam's hands. Immediately Nysska saw something black, there on the white cloth, something like... oil? Raoul paused long enough to give the substance a quick sniff, and his body hitched as he gagged.

Kneeling on Cam's other side, Percy had produced his own handkerchief, and he dabbed at Cam's face—

Where the same black sludge came away from her eyes.

"Great Dragon," Cam said, barely loud enough to hear. "Great Silver Dragon help me, it's my *tears!* What is it, what *is* it, get it off me!" She grabbed Percy's handkerchief and scrubbed at her eyes. "Make it stop! *Make it stop!"*

Flax had crept forward, her ears still flattened against her skull, her mouth hanging open in the way cats have when they smell something pungent. The blood lynx pushed her way between Raoul and Percy, reared up and put her feet on Cam's shoulders, and just as Cam said, "No, sweetie, no, don't—" Flax let fly with a full-throated scream and bolted away. Nysska watched as the big cat fled across the lab and hid in the lowest shelf of one of the bookcases. Jax followed after her, looking between Cam and his sister, growling at no one and everyone.

"There," Raoul said, after working on Cam's hands and face for a few more moments. "I think we got it all. I think it's gone."

Cam fell against him and sobbed. Clear, salty, normal tears welled from her eyes and poured down her cheeks.

Percy sat down hard on the floor and gazed across at Nysska. "What the fuck just happened?" he asked, and since Nysska could tell he wasn't expecting an answer, she didn't bother trying to give him one.

Half an hour later, after Raoul had curtly dismissed Professor Greig's questions and shut the laboratory door in her face, the members of the Ninth Crucible sat on the two couches near the fireplace—Cam and Raoul on one, Percy and Nysska on the other. None of them spoke. None of them looked at each other.

Jax had curled up on the cushion beside Percy and gone to sleep. Flax, after circling her several times and purring loudly, had climbed into Nysska's lap. She remained there, her furry, fifteen-kilgram weight heating Nysska's thighs almost to the point of discomfort. Nysska stroked the big cat's side and scratched her belly, which caused the purring to grow louder.

Finally, Nysska couldn't stand the silence, which surprised her, since in general hearing a human saying anything at all got on her nerves. "What does this mean? Are Cam's—" Nysska broke off when Cam turned her head to hear better. "What's wrong with your runes? Why did that happen?"

Cam trembled for a second, but hugged herself and set her jaw and made the trembling stop. "I don't know. It's never happened before. I don't—I've never heard of it happening at *all*. To anyone. Ever. The runes *work*. They work until they kill you."

Nysska leaned forward. Flax stretched in her lap and pushed one foot up into Nysska's chest. "I've read about Sensors who use their runes all the time. Especially the ones who would be blind otherwise. Why do you activate yours so sparingly? Do you hope to extend your life?"

Raoul shot Nysska a hostile look, but Nysska chose to ignore it.

Cam didn't seem any more bothered than she already was. "As I'm sure you've observed, I can navigate without the runes just fine. And yes, I intend to live as long as possible. What kind of question is that?"

Nysska nodded, but when she realized even Cam's finely tuned sensitivity to sound wouldn't pick up on that, she said, "Understood. Then my question becomes, do you not use them *enough?* Could *not* activating them cause them to...atrophy?"

Cam's shoulders rose and fell. "I have no answers."

"Then...perhaps you can tell us what you *did* see? As opposed to what you expected to?"

"Why don't you leave her alone?" Raoul said, his voice cold. "Why are you even talking? Your position in this Crucible is Enforcer, or have you forgotten that? You do what I tell you, when I tell you. I make the decisions. I interpret the cases for the Council. You are merely a pair of hands and an axe."

Percy said, "Dragon's breath, Raoul, what the fuck?"

Raoul speared Percy with a steely glare, and seemed about to say something else, but instead stood up from the couch and began pacing in front of the fireplace. Percy bowed his head and stared at the floor.

"Normally..." Cam began, and then stopped to clear her throat. "Normally I can see the blood of both the victim and the perpetrator. That's why I refer to my gift as 'Ruby Tears.' Other Sensors have their own names for what they do."

Nysska had never heard Morrin refer to her scent ability with any special name. Of course, Morrin had never seemed to have much in the way of imagination, either.

Jax yawned and stretched and stepped down onto the floor. He gazed around at the three of them still seated on the couches, picked Cam, and hopped up next to her.

Nysska said, "What do you mean, you can see their blood?"

Cam traced the vague outline of a body with one hand. "I mean I can see their blood, the way it was when it pumped through their bodies. Or lay in their veins and cooled, in the cases of the deceased. No skin, no flesh, no bones, but I see the blood vessels as they move. Then the victim's blood..." She touched her face lightly. "Emerges as tears. That's what the blood lynxes key into. My talent, and their enhanced understanding of our mission, is the reason the Ninth holds the record as the fastest, most efficient Crucible in the territory. Maybe in the Empire." She inclined her head toward Jax, who'd been sitting beside her, washing his face. "Isn't that right, partner? Don't you and your sister make this team what it is?"

Jax stopped grooming, looked up at Cam, and held out one paw. Cam clicked her rings once, and bumped Jax's paw gently with her fist. The blood lynx went back to his face-washing. Flax paid no attention whatsoever to that exchange.

Cam said, "But today...here...there was only a, a, a *void*. An abyss—and it sucked out my strength, made me ill—until you..." Her head tilted toward Nysska. "Until you, ah, intervened."

Percy pitched his voice low. "Maybe that Greig woman has her head up her twat? Maybe this ain't the scene of the crime at all, and she set some sort of fucking trap?"

Cam shook her head. "No. No, there's *something* here. Something *happened.* And I believe Greig when she says this Olkoff person was killed in this room. But instead of seeing the blood the way I always have before, it was…" She hesitated. Seemed to be searching for the right words. "Imagine the most frigid winter night—and a pit made of ice, and you're tumbling toward it, and…" She threw her hands up. "It makes no sense. This doesn't happen. Ever. It just doesn't."

Still pacing, Raoul seemed to aim his words at the cold gray stone of the floor. "That is not entirely true."

Every head turned toward him. Percy said, "What'd you say, boss?"

Raoul scowled. "I've heard reports—my father told me. He was in a position to see them when most of the Cathedral wasn't."

Nysska touched Percy on the shoulder and murmured, "Who is his father?"

Percy made a small, negative motion with the fingers of one hand. *Tell you later.*

Raoul stopped pacing and faced them, his arms folded across his chest. "Not like this, mind you. He never mentioned a full failure. Just irregularities. Every so often a Sensor's runes had a—call it a fluctuation. A bit of unreliability."

Cam sat very still. "And what was done about that?"

"Father said, in every case, the Sensor was taken away. Taken to one of the Imperial Colleges, for the runemasters to investigate and research. None of them ever came back."

Percy rubbed the bridge of his nose. "And those were just pissy little twitches, you're saying? Not full-blown fuck-ups. No offense, Cam, I know this isn't your fault."

Cam shook her head. "How? *I* don't know that."

Raoul's shoulders slumped a few millims. "A natural death like Theobold, the Cathedral knows that happens, they make allowances. They send us—" He made an unsuccessful attempt at not wrinkling his nose as he looked at Nysska. "*Replacements*. But for something like this…"

Cam whispered, "Debriefing."

Nysska looked from Raoul to Percy and back. "What? What does that mean? What's involved in a 'debriefing'?"

Raoul's eyes had unfocused. "If a Crucible is judged defective? They'll disband the unit. Isolate each of us. Interrogate us until they understand what went wrong and why, and then they'll reassign everyone."

Nysska didn't move, but her guts clenched and grew icy. "But what about the—the case? Olkoff's murder?"

Raoul made a gesture with one hand, to mimic something flying away. "They'll give it to another Crucible."

Nysska's insides finished freezing over. Flax picked up on her tension, twisted and got her feet under her, and shot off Nysska's lap and across the lab.

Give it to another Crucible.

Nysska could see little in that moment but a pair of flame-yellow eyes boring into her from the shadows. Gerrit's words skittered across her mind like the tiny claws of a spider.

Nysska felt as if her body belonged to someone else as she got to her feet and held out beseeching hands. As if she were watching someone who looked uncannily like her and was using her voice to speak. "Wait. Wait. I'm sure we can figure out what caused this."

A fierce line appeared between Raoul's eyebrows. "What are you babbling about, demon?"

She decided to let that pass. "None of you want the Ninth Crucible to disband. Correct?"

If Cam's eyes had been open, Nysska felt sure she would have seen them rolling. "No, it's fine," Cam said. "Let's let some black-and-gold College freak strap me to a table and write down how loud I scream while they pry out my eyeballs."

Nysska hadn't heard that level of sarcasm from Cam before, and it brought a tiny, surprising, involuntary smile to her lips, which she quickly vanquished before either of the men noticed.

Percy had picked Jax up, holding the cat to his chest not unlike the way a father might hold a baby. "Figure out what caused this *how*?"

Nysska ran her hands through her hair, freeing a couple of strands from one of her horns, and said, "First and foremost, we need to find the killer before the governor comes looking for a status report. Correct?"

Nysska thought Raoul wanted to stamp his foot in frustration. "You're not telling us *how*! The wagon's gone off the road here! How are we supposed to figure out who killed Olkoff if our Sensor can't see what happened, and our tracking animals have no blood to track?"

She cocked her head to one side, just a few degrees. "Can we not try to...investigate the murder...without using the runes or the lynxes?"

Raoul scowled, a black expression that encompassed anger, pity, and outrage all at once. "*That's not how we solve crimes!* What is *wrong* with you? Someone commits a crime, the Thaumetallicon sends a Crucible, the Crucible solves it, and the perpetrator is punished! That's how it works! That's how it's *always* worked! That's why the Empire is so successful—because of the rule of law! There are rules in place. We need to send a report. We need to let Governor Anwar know what's happened and let him decide how to handle it."

Nysska's eyes traveled from face to face as Raoul breathed heavily. She said, "We did not have your thaumaturgy in my homeland. When a crime took place in Fortikajxo, we had to deal with it in other ways."

Raoul barked, "Well good for you!" He started pacing again, but Percy reached out and touched Nysska's wrist.

"How'd you do it?"

Cam had turned toward her as well. "Were you an investigator? In your homeland? Is that why Anwar put you in a Crucible here?"

"I...was not a part of law enforcement, no..."

Raoul snorted.

"But I believe I understand it well enough that we could *try*."

Raoul punched the mantel above the fireplace. "Ridiculous. Ridiculous! You might as well ask a fishwife to write a diplomatic address. Or a lumberjack to perform surgery."

Cam stood. Raoul's labored breathing still sounded out, so she didn't need to click her rings together. She simply went to him, one hand reaching out until her fingertips found his chestplate. "Raoul." Cam let her voice drop, so that Nysska had to work to hear her next words. "Do you want word to reach your father of a Crucible under your command being disbanded?"

Raoul groaned. He roughly adjusted the commander's band on his head and gazed down at her. "That's not—I don't care about—" He faltered and tried again. "It doesn't matter what my father thinks." As clearly as if he had spoken, his expression said, *It only matters what happens to you.* Raoul turned toward Nysska. He seemed to have to work at unclenching his jaw before he spoke. "These *investigators* in your *homeland,*" he bit out. "A situation like this... Fuck. *Fuck.* How would they have gotten started?"

II

THE SLEUTH

7

Professor Greig looked skeptical. Nysska watched from a few paces away as Raoul told the professor what they intended to do and why. She thought he could have sounded more convincing.

"So this is an...examination of Olkoff's life? To what end? And have you or have you not determined who killed him?"

Raoul took a measured breath and squared his shoulders. "Professor, am I correct when I say that you are aware of the Cathedral's influence?"

Greig recoiled. Not a grand, shocked gesture, but enough to dispel any doubts as to her knowledge of the Cathedral's reach and power. "Of course, Commander."

Raoul nodded once. "Then you are also aware of the *latitude* afforded to Crucibles when investigating a crime?"

"W-well, yes, naturally, but is it not of the utmost importance to find Olkoff's killer? If one runemaster died under these circumstances, might not *more* die?"

Raoul made a show of looking both ways, up and down the long, stone corridor, as if to make sure none of the rest of the College's students or instructors were within earshot. "Professor, it has come to our attention that Dr. Olkoff's murder has certain...connections. Certain features and ramifications, that we feel we must look into in order to prosecute it fully. Now, do we have your cooperation in this, and by extension the College's at large? Or do I have to inform Governor Anwar that you have decided to impede our investigation?"

Greig's weathered face got just a touch paler. Nysska saw one of her hands tremble. "We are at your disposal, Commander Cullen. The College wants nothing more than to aid the Cathedral in its pursuits."

"And on behalf of the Cathedral, my team and I express our appreciation. Now. Please allow entry to Olkoff's laboratory to no one but my team and me. We shall also need full and exclusive access to his living quarters, and of course we'll need to examine his corpse."

Panic danced around the edges of Greig's eyes. "His—his corpse? Buh-but, but we cremated it, of course. That was standard. Standard procedure, Commander, we did exactly what we were supposed to do!"

Raoul let that stand for a few long moments, eyeballing the professor. Finally, he said, "All right. Fine. We will let you know if there's anything else. You'll be able to find us either in Olkoff's lab or his quarters." Raoul extended his hand, and Greig shook it—more out of muscle memory than etiquette, Nysska thought. With her hand in his grip, Raoul leaned forward slightly, his teeth reflecting torchlight. "Bronze is law."

"Bronze is peace," Greig said, and hurried away.

Raoul came back and joined Nysska, Cam, and Percy. He glared up at Nysska. "Much as I enjoy terrifying civilians for no good reason, what we're looking at here is a golden opportunity to fall on our faces. Combing through the man's personal effects? Examining every aspect of his life? Do you know how long this could *take*? It could be hours. Days, even!"

Nysska kept her face still. "I suppose that depends upon how thorough we are, and what we find." She glanced down at Flax and Jax, who were wrestling quietly near Percy's feet. "And on how well our four-legged teammates can pick out incongruous scents."

"Yes," Cam said. "Let's hang the fate of the unit on how willing a couple of cats are to help us."

Nysska had no doubt that the blood lynxes heard Cam say that, but neither of them reacted in the slightest.

The conversation broke off when a pale, slight young man in an unstriped coat, gray instead of black, approached them. Or at least *tried* to approach them. His eyes flicked constantly between Nysska's eyes and horns, and he couldn't seem to make his feet carry him any closer than three or four meters.

"Quit gawking, you tit," Percy said to the lad, though without much malice. "What the fuck do you want?"

The young man's voice broke when he finally tried to speak. "Professor Greig, begging your pardons, all of you, I'm very sorry, Professor, uh, Professor Greig sent me to take you to Dr. Olkoff's quarters."

Finding herself possessed of a sudden perverse urge, Nysska locked eyes with the lad and slowly ran her tongue across her upper lip. His face turned a brilliant red, and he abruptly found the floor *fascinating*. "If, uh, if you'll, uh, if you'll all follow me, please?" His cheeks still glowing, he started off in the opposite direction Greig had taken, and the group trailed after him.

Sidling close, Percy said, "I saw that."

Nysska glanced down at him. "Saw what?"

His blue eyes twinkled up at her. "That young man didn't know whether to piss his pants or come in them."

"I'm sure I have no idea what you're talking about."

Percy chuckled—and for the first time, Nysska felt as if one of her teammates was laughing *with* her, rather than at or about her. Considering it as they walked, she thought it might have been the first time she'd felt that way with *any* human.

Nysska never caught the young, gray-coated man's name. He took them up another staircase, down a corridor longer than any they'd seen up to that point, and simply pointed at a tall, wooden door before all but sprinting away.

It was a long enough walk for Nysska's thoughts to travel back to what she'd seen in Olkoff's laboratory. To Cam's eyes. To Cam herself. To the avalanche of emotions and sense memories that had come crashing through her mind and buried her in her childhood and adolescence. She hadn't spoken to Cam since leaving the lab, and neither had Cam attempted to talk to her.

Of course it wasn't what it had looked like. What it had *felt* like.

And yet the image came back to her, vivid, urgent, every time she thought about it. Right there before her, staring at her with luminous silver eyes ringed in icy flame.

Nysska wondered what Cam had seen, staring back at her.

Raoul opened the door to Olkoff's quarters, and the team entered. Nysska paused just inside the door, as she had in the laboratory, and took the place in.

The disconnect between the near-featureless hallways and the opulence on display here was even more striking than when they'd entered the laboratory. The finest bearskin rugs covered the floor from wall to wall, there in the sitting room and on through the short hallway that led to the bed chamber, which maintained privacy via double pocket doors of finely polished hardwood. Likewise, decorative tapestries hung in front of heavy quilts all along the walls, providing some measure of both insulation and sound-dampening, killing off any echo that might have tried to bounce around the chamber's corners. Olkoff's rooms weren't as large as the lab, but Nysska could have easily fit two, maybe even three, of the shack where she had lived with Simana into each of them.

A couch that matched the ones in the lab sat directly in front of the cold, dry fireplace. Across the room stood a huge, masterfully crafted writing desk with a frame of what looked like mahogany and a writing surface of white marble. Stacks of papers, books, scrolls, and opened letters covered every square centim, and more letters bristled from a series of cubbies over the desktop. A quartet of oil lamps sat on a half-circle-shaped shelf just above eye level. Nysska tried to imagine Olkoff sitting there, scribbling away, but realized she had no idea what the man looked like, or even how old he'd been.

Cam, her rings clicking, made her way across the room to the doorway that opened onto to the pitch-dark, windowless bed chamber. Dry as dust, she said, "Give me a room with a view, I always say."

Nysska almost laughed at that.

Raoul clapped Percy on the shoulder. "Get Flax and Jax to sniff around in here. We're looking for anything that doesn't belong."

Percy frowned. "Now, begging your pardon, Commander, but how are they supposed to know what doesn't belong, in the living quarters of some dead fucker they've never laid eyes or noses on?"

Raoul spared a half-lidded glance at Nysska. "According to our investigative expert, they'll know it when they come across it. And no complaining—while the rest of you are busy actually doing something, I'm going to dig through this desk."

Grumbling, Percy knelt down and faced the blood lynxes. Flax seemed to be paying him at least a little bit of attention, whereas Jax had folded himself in half and was vigorously licking his anus. "All right, you two. I know this isn't what we trained you for, but here we are. One man lived in these rooms. I want you to see if you can find anything in here that doesn't belong to him. Understand?"

Jax unfolded himself and sat up straight. He and Flax gave each other a long, slow look, met Percy's eyes again, and walked away from him, each heading to a different corner.

Percy stood up. Over his shoulder from where he'd taken a seat at the desk, Raoul said, "Did that work? Do they get it?"

Percy spread his hands and grinned. "I guess we'll find out."

Nysska took an oil lamp from a wall-mounted shelf near the door, lit it, and moved to follow Cam into Olkoff's bed chamber.

The bed dominated the room. It looked like something imported from Caulspring, an enormous four-poster covered with intricate carvings depicting buxom maidens frolicking through wooded areas. A single nightstand sat beside it—clearly Olkoff had favored one side of the bed—and a huge wardrobe dominated one side of the room, stretching from floor to ceiling. The bearskin rugs on the floor had all been dyed a shade of royal purple that Nysska found repellent. The wall-hangings were a bit more reserved, continuing the forest-frolicking motif from the bed frame, and came off as merely tacky rather than nauseating.

Cam had not waited for Nysska to arrive with the oil lamp before she started searching the room. *Of course she hadn't.* Nysska chastised herself for even having the thought. Cam had been checking under the bed but stood now and opened the massive wardrobe. Nysska watched as she made her way through the garments hanging from a rod, fingertips gliding along each piece of fabric. "How many robes does one person need?" Cam asked, as if talking to herself.

Nysska decided to look through the nightstand. "Right behind you," she said as she slid past Cam.

"I know," Cam answered without turning her head.

Had Nysska imagined it? Had the fascination she'd seen on Cam's face as they'd stared at each other in the lab simply been her *own* fascination reflected back at her? Cam kept her back turned and didn't say anything else, so likewise Nysska kept silent.

Olkoff's nightstand had a drawer set above a small cabinet, both of them closed. The drawer slid open easily, and proved to contain an array of bottles, which Nysska quickly determined to be roughly half colognes and half scented sex oils. She didn't quite drop the bottle she'd picked up, but did replace it quickly, and wiped her hand on one of the quilts covering the bed.

"What's all that in there?" Percy asked from over her shoulder, in a tone filled with the kind of glee that let her know he'd been watching her the whole time.

"Personal items," Nysska said, carefully keeping any trace of embarrassment out of her voice. It would not do, she didn't believe, to let any of these humans know she could even *be* embarrassed like this.

"Hey, I got a question for you," Percy said, sitting on the edge of the bed. "How early do those horns come in? I mean, I don't figure you got them at birth, else it'd make things awfully uncomfortable for your mama, right?"

Nysska realized, to her dismay, that Percy was the kind of person who grew less and less polite the more he got to know someone. She began to regret the sense of mild camaraderie she'd shared with him in the corridor.

"And do they just keep growing? Or do they stop, like when a lad reaches his full height, and you know he ain't ever getting any taller? Ooh, and do you have to trim them, like cutting hair? Are they sharp? What do they feel like? You ever let anybody touch one?"

Nysska took a cue from Cam by not turning to face him. "No."

Still grinning, Percy kept on. "No? No to what? I asked a bunch of questions, there."

Cam did turn this time. "Great Dragon's flaming cock, Percy, don't you have something you could be doing?"

Out of the corner of her eye, Nysska saw Percy draw his legs up under him on the bed. "Place is only so big. You two have the searching well in hand, I'd say, and I wouldn't want to get in the way of the kitties doing their job, would I?"

Choosing to say nothing else in hopes that the wiry little man might lose interest, Nysska opened the nightstand's cabinet—and Flax knocked her hand out of the way with the top of her skull, thrusting her head and shoulders inside. Percy lost his grin. "What's that, girl? You find something? That's a good kitty!"

Flax started growling. Not loud, just with enough volume to be heard. She backed out of the cabinet with something in her mouth that glinted in the light from the oil lamp. Nysska frowned. "What is that? A coin?"

Flax dashed away, out to the center of the first room, and Jax sped out from under the bed to join her. Flax dropped the metal object onto one of the bear rugs, jumped on it, and swatted it into the air with one paw. Jax launched into the air and tried to grab it, and then managed to knock it into one of the wall hangings, where it thumped back to the floor. Flax landed on it again and grabbed it up in her jaws, then spun to stare with huge silver eyes at Percy, who had approached her and hunkered down, hands out. "Come on, girl. You did good, real good, finding something in all this shit. Let me have it, girl. Come on." Flax kept up the growling, her ears flattening, but she let Percy take the thing out of her mouth. Jax immediately barreled into her, and they rolled back into the bedroom together, a writhing, kicking mass of fur.

Nysska followed Cam out of the bedroom, and the two of them, along with Raoul, converged to see what it was the cat had found. Percy held the thing up in the light of the closest oil lamp. "I'd say what we have here is a key."

Cam held a hand out. "Let me touch it." Percy gave it to her, and she frowned. "Is it supposed to look like a copper? It feels like a copper."

The head of the thing had indeed been made to look like a one-copper coin, but with what appeared to be a room number stamped on it instead of the denomination.

Percy said, "So it's a key. A key to what?"

Raoul held up a small, folded piece of paper, from which drifted the scent of a heavy-handed perfume. "If it's a room key, it might belong to the young woman who wrote this letter to Dr. Olkoff. Found it in the desk. It's from one Irene Jasinsky, and she and Olkoff appear to have been…involved." Raoul glanced up at Nysska, and his brow furrowed, though he kept his voice calm. "I don't mind telling you, this is the least efficient, slowest, most bear-shit process I have ever been involved in. We're just guessing. It's…" Disgust filled his words. "It's *speculation*."

Nysska stood there, watching him, and remained silent.

Cam took that opportunity to say, "And yet, if we find out that Irene Jasinsky knows who killed Dr. Olkoff, then we're done and headed back to Tember. Correct?"

Raoul grumbled as he turned and left Olkoff's quarters. Percy gestured to the blood lynxes. "Come on, you two. We're leaving." The big cats stopped wrestling and trotted after him as he followed Raoul.

Nysska didn't touch Cam, but she got close enough to murmur, "I appreciate the support."

Cam turned to face her. Her eyes stayed closed, but Nysska couldn't help recalling the radiant silver she'd experienced earlier, and felt the fluttering tightness in her belly again. "You're an odd one, Nysska Stonegate. By rights, you shouldn't give two slimy eel shits what happens to me, or to this unit. But…the last thing I want is to get sealed away in some Cathedral cell while men in black-and-gold coats pick me apart. And I didn't hear either of these two swinging cocks offer up a single helpful suggestion. So I would say our appreciation is mutual."

Not for the last time, she suspected, Nysska felt relieved that Cam couldn't see the expression on her face. She said, "We had better catch up, don't you think?" Cam nodded, and they left Olkoff's rooms together.

8

Professor Greig frowned. It turned the ever-present lines in her face into valleys. "But *why*?"

Raoul had declared that he'd be the one to do the talking, and Nysska saw no reason to argue with him. He *should* be the one doing the talking. That was part of a Crucible Commander's job. Still, Raoul shot a look around at everyone's faces—even Nysska's—before he settled into the reasoning they had discussed on their way to find the professor.

"It is not always enough to know who committed a crime," he said, in what Nysska felt pretty sure was his best, most authoritative tone. "Catching one murderer or thief is fine, but if we do not understand the reasoning behind the crime, and do not work to remove the underlying cause, then another such crime may be committed subsequently. As I believe you yourself alluded to in our last conversation."

Greig's frown grew even deeper. "Yes, but who would *dare*? Criminals are caught. Why would someone seek to put themselves through the same swift brutality as another criminal? Another *unsuccessful* criminal?"

Raoul hesitated.

Nysska held her breath. It had been her suggestion to supply Greig with that answer, based on a half-remembered conversation she'd overheard when much younger. No more than twelve, creeping to hide beneath the study window, listening to her uncle talk with a visiting friend. That friend had been an investigator, and Nysska had found him endlessly fascinating, but only with the fascination of a child. The draw toward the new, the different. She'd only wanted to hear the unfamiliar man's voice and smell the pipe tobacco wafting out through the open window, and had spent no effort on understanding the conversation's substance. Now she wondered if she had missed something critical in the logic.

Raoul said, "Well…I can't…"

Greig's eyes widened. She leaned closer, her voice suddenly husky with conspiracy. "It's not a tarn, is it?" She looked up and down the corridor where they stood outside her office. "Doing the killing, I mean. I heard the Argonium Infantry put one down, just south of here. Is it a tarn?"

Raoul stood in profile to Nysska, and she watched as his tongue darted out and moistened his lips. "I fear that information is restricted to Cathedral personnel," he said, and Greig's face displayed alternating disappointment and excitement.

"Should I warn the faculty? Should we lock down the students? *Should we evacuate?*"

Raoul put a hand on her shoulder, which Nysska did not think the woman found comforting. "No. If there is imminent danger, you'll be the first one we tell. Until further notice, please carry on with college business as usual." He leaned just a hair closer. "But mention this to no one else. You know only because you have need of it. This information goes no further." Gesturing to the rest of the team, he said, "Ninth Crucible. With me," and marched off down the hallway.

As they followed him, Nysska heard Greig say, "But…you haven't *given* me any information…"

It took a few minutes to make their way back out to the College's main entrance, and Nysska used the time to consider the possible source of Greig's anxiety. *Tarn.* She had only heard the word a few times before and had never seen one until the altercation at the bridge. After several long moments, to no one specific, she said, "What is the origin of the word 'tarn'?"

Percy gave her a sharp, troubled look, but said nothing, instead becoming suddenly very interested in Jax and Flax, who walked on either side of him. Raoul pretended not to have heard her. Finally, Cam said, "It comes from 'tarnished.' A *Tarnished One* is someone who uses deadmetal."

"Oh." She realized she'd heard Raoul use that term on the bridge, *Tarnished One,* when her attention had been focused elsewhere. Nysska blinked several times as they walked out the main entrance into the daylight, her pupils contracting. "And deadmetal is…what?"

Raoul didn't turn his head. "How long were you Enforcer for the Forty-Seventh? Did you receive no training at all? Did you absorb no information?"

"I was Enforcer for the Forty-Seventh for seven months, Commander, as I have mentioned several times. But the members of that Crucible were not as loquacious as you lot."

Flax jumped up into Percy's arms. He stroked her head and scratched along her ears, and the action seemed to give him comfort enough to speak up. "The Thaumetallicon decides who gets the argonium runes. Each rune or set of runes gets customized to the individual. You know that much, right? Like Cam's eyes."

Cam didn't react. Nysska said, "Yes."

Percy kept stroking the blood lynx, who began to purr. "It's supposed to be a big fucking honor to be chosen. The Sensors are… well…the Cathedral's elite. So, if somebody *kills* a Sensor, and takes their runes—it's—they aren't just sentenced to die. It's death by fucking torture. The longest anybody lasted was a *year*."

Nysska's eyes crinkled at the corners, and her upper lip curled, but she kept her tone even. "Understood. And yet there are those who make the attempt, nonetheless?"

Cam picked up the thread. "It's rare—thank the Dragon, it's rare—but every so often…you see…if you take someone else's runes, and implant them in *yourself*…"

"They go haywire," Raoul said, his words even more clipped than usual. "The argonium turns black, and the thaumaturgy isn't channeled properly, and it bursts out. Violently. Like a storm through the skin. You saw it. And the effects go...wider. All the senses get amplified, not just one. All at the same time."

They had drawn close to the wall gate that opened onto Taurus Hill proper. Nysska ignored the guards who gawked at her, even as they hauled the gate open. "All right, the runes go black. Hence 'tarnished.' But is not argonium, by its very nature, toxic? Why would anyone hunt another human down and tear metal out of their body only to poison themselves?"

Cam clicked her rings a few times as they passed through the gate. "Doing that—stealing runes—it increases the metal's poison dramatically. Sensors can make it to age forty, if they're lucky and careful. A tarn has maybe a year before the tainted argonium kills them."

They approached the town's first intersection, drawing near the regular citizenry, and a hush fell over the townsfolk. Nysska felt dozens of eyes on her, maybe hundreds, peering out from windows and alleys and cracked doors. People parted before them, and she wondered whether advertising her presence in the town was wise, or even worth it. The hood and the face scarf were often hot and uncomfortable but might have been preferable to this.

"Again, I ask why?" Nysska pitched her voice low, so that only her teammates could hear her. "Death by torture if one is caught, and no more than a year to live if one isn't? Why would anyone do this?"

"Way I hear it," Percy said, also softly, "it's the highest fucking high you can get. Second the metal slides in, you're in this haze, this euphoria, and once that starts, you don't give two greasy fucks what the consequences are."

Cam said, "Yeah, there's that, on top of the body-wide amplification that Raoul mentioned. But just...*try* to imagine how desperate someone would have to be to go to those lengths. Imagine having that little to lose—and then picture gaining that much power, right when it makes you too brain-addled to feel anything but pleasure."

Nysska did her best to ignore her peripheral vision as the street took them past more and more of the citizenry. "It would seem to me that such a person—a 'tarnished one'—would be...non-viable. Once a tarnished one takes the stolen runes, how would they hide? How would they exist at all among other humans?" She tried to picture it. No one she had spoken to back home had ever heard of such a thing, or if any of them had, they had failed to mention it to her. "Such a person would be akin to a rabid dog, would they not?"

Raoul turned to look at her for the first time since they'd left the College. "An apt comparison. And now you understand what makes them so dangerous." He pointed to an upcoming street that branched off to the left. "Greig said this is the one we take."

The main streets of Taurus Hill were paved with light gray stone bricks, but not all the side streets had received that treatment. The one Raoul led them up consisted of sections of cobblestone and larger sections of bare dirt, and Nysska pondered how filthy the townsfolk must get when it rained. The buildings lining this particular street were every bit as squared-off and utilitarian as the ones she'd seen everywhere else, but now she began to notice that the building materials themselves weren't so uniform. Some of the businesses and row houses used the same huge stone blocks as the more prominent structures, but many more had incorporated rough boulders, wooden frames, and generous amounts of mortar.

They stopped in front of a three-story cube that used so many different kinds of materials that it looked like a patchwork quilt. There was no name visible, no signage of any kind, but in one corner of the front door someone had painted a pair of full, red lips.

Raoul held up the coin key. "According to Greig, this is the only place in Taurus Hill that uses these. If we don't find anything here, it might mean that the key belongs to some other brothel in another town."

Percy said, "It'd also mean we were well and truly fucked, wouldn't it?"

Cam clicked her rings slowly, her head turning as she listened to the building's contours. "It would definitely mean *I* am. Let's hope 'Dearest Naveed' likes his whores local."

Raoul pounded on the door with a fist. A minute later, all four of them, along with the blood lynxes, stood in a small, dingy room that the brothel's proprietor referred to as his office. Nysska thought it looked more like a shabby storage closet. The proprietor, a tall, pale, rangy man who asked them all to call him Rathan, had gotten even paler at the sight of the Imperial bronze, and turned an unpleasant shade of green when he saw Nysska over Raoul's shoulder.

"I-I-I think that's the key to Irene's room," Rathan said, words tripping over each other. He had gone to a shallow box mounted on one wall and pulled a cover off of it, revealing rows of wooden pegs, most adorned with a similar coin key. Rathan rattled through the rows of keys, breathing quickly. "Yuh-yuh-yes! Yes, that's to Irene's room. You want me to show you? I can show you. I'll take you up there myself. I can do that right now if you want."

Nysska walked up right behind Rathan, so that when he turned, he found himself staring at the hollow where her collarbones met, and he yelped and jumped and might have pissed himself a little. Peering at the rows of keys instead of looking at him, Nysska said, "The peg you indicated. The one that belongs to Irene's room. Why is it bare?"

Rathan whipped his head back and forth between Nysska and the key box. "Whuh-what?"

Nysska hadn't moved, effectively trapping Rathan between her and the wall. She lifted a hand and dragged a finger along one of the rows, so that the keys tinkled like wind chimes. "All the other pegs. They have at least one key. And yet the one to Irene's room has none. Why is that?"

Lifting his hands in a gesture as if to ward her off in the most respectful fashion possible, Rathan sidled along the wall away from her. "I don't know, I don't know, that usually means, I mean to say, I let the girls give one key to their best customer, but the other one's for me to hand out."

Nysska looked to Raoul and found him eyeballing her. She backed off of Rathan with a tiny inclination of her head.

Raoul turned his baleful glare on the whoremaster. "And did you?"

Rathan had retreated to a chair but didn't sit. His calves bumped into it, and he almost lost his balance. "Did I what?"

Raoul pointed at the empty peg. "Did you give that key out to a customer? By which I mean, is there a customer in Irene's room with her right now?"

Rathan paused, still breathing fast. "Well...no...I don't think so. I haven't seen her since last night. Sometimes the customers bring their own liquor, and the girls need to sleep one off." Indignation raised his voice. "What? That's so hard to believe? I run a legitimate business here! If one of my girls needs time to recuperate, I give it to her!"

Raoul crossed the office, grabbed a handful of Rathan's shirt, and shoved him toward the door. "Take us there. Now."

Irene's room was on the third floor. Rathan led them up a wooden staircase that creaked alarmingly under Nysska's weight, and a short distance down a hallway to a wooden door painted canary yellow.

"Open it," Raoul said, and handed Rathan the coin key. Rathan didn't speak at all, just slotted the key into the lock, twisted it, and shoved the door wide.

The stench of blood smacked Nysska in the face. She took a fast step back to steady herself and, as Rathan wailed and screamed protests, took in the sight of what had once been a young woman with long, dyed-gold hair.

"Irene..." Rathan cried again. "No, Irene!"

The body lay across the bed, nude, its throat cut so deeply that the head dangled down away from it over the side, the blood-streaked golden locks pooled on the floor below.

The captain of the town guard was a brick-shaped man with a brick-shaped head, on whom the guard uniform—with black and gold braids woven into the deep brown leather at his shoulders—hung awkwardly, like a tarp thrown over a wagon in haste. He said, "But why are you already here?"

It was the third time he'd asked the question.

Raoul said, "And your name was what?"

"Morter."

"Captain Morter, this is Thaumetallicon business. You have been notified. Now let us work, if you will."

Morter blinked. His line of sight twitched back and forth from Raoul to the corpse to Nysska. She imagined she could see a lever in his brain, yawing between terrified and confused. "But we didn't know about it. Her. The, the whore." He pointed at Irene's corpse. "*We* call *you*. That's how it works. We send a message, and then you come. Only you're already here."

Raoul took a slow, deep breath. "Captain, we are in the middle of an investigation. And the last time I checked, the Thaumetallicon's authority exceeds that of a town guardsman. Does it not?"

Morter sounded as if he would've liked to start crying. "The Thaumetallicon's part of the Cathedral, yeah, but—but this isn't how it *works*."

Raoul took Morter by the shoulder, guided him forcefully out the door, and shut it behind him. "We will let you know when your men can come and take the body," he said, just before the door latched. Once it became clear that Morter wasn't going to bang on the door or try to talk through it, Raoul turned and pressed his back to it and rubbed his temples.

"Funny," Percy said, looking up from an open drawer in a shabby dresser next to the bed. "He sounded a little like you."

Raoul stared at him from under his eyebrows. "What?"

Percy grinned. *"That's not how it works! That's not how we do things! Fuck!"*

Raoul thumped the back of his head slowly against the door. "Has anyone found anything?"

Cam, in mid-reach as she felt around under the bed's mattress, shook her head. "Nothing here you wouldn't expect to find in a whore's room."

Nysska couldn't disagree with that. Only a ratty blanket on the floor protected bare feet from bare wood—a far cry from the opulence of Naveed Olkoff's chambers—and aside from the bed and the dresser, on which sat a basin and a dirty towel, the only other thing in the place was an empty metal shit bucket under the single window.

Raoul took the two steps from the door to the foot of the bed. Nysska noticed his eyes carefully avoided the bloodied corpse. "All right. We've got the death of a runemaster that we can't solve by normal means." He gestured with one hand, as if reading items off an invisible chalkboard. "The only things of interest we found there were a key and a letter indicating a relationship with a whore named Irene. And now Irene is dead. Am I missing anything?"

No one spoke.

"Tember will be expecting a report tomorrow." Raoul glanced toward the window, through which deepening late-afternoon sunlight streamed. "If we don't have something to tell them..." He shot a split-second look at Cam, so fast and fleeting that Nysska thought it might have been involuntary. "I don't foresee the Thaumetallicon dragging their feet." His attention turned to Cam fully now, in his official capacity. "Are you willing to try to Sense what happened here?"

Cam had stood, abandoning her search under the mattress as soon as Raoul had started speaking. She shuddered once but kept her chin high. "No, I want to lollygag about and waste enough time that I end up in a dungeon in Caulspring."

Ignoring the sarcasm entirely, Raoul nodded. "Then we'll let you do your job. Percy, gather the cats. We'll wait in the hall." He opened the door. "Enforcer Stonegate."

Nysska walked out of the room, followed by Raoul, and a few seconds later by Percy, who held Jax in his arms while Flax rode on his shoulders. Turning to face the men, she said, "You can call me Nysska."

Percy grinned and winked at her, but Raoul's brow beetled. "Excuse me?"

"Everyone else is on a first-name basis. I am a member of this Crucible, am I not? So you may as well refer to me by my given name."

Raoul squared off with her. His hands curled into fists and came to rest on his hips. "Oh, so we're all familiar now? We don't know a damn thing about you, but you think we should all be best friends?"

Nysska blinked slowly. "Fair enough. What do you want to know?"

Raoul's attitude remained fixed. "Why should we think you'd give us any straight answers? Percy hasn't stopped asking you questions since we met you, and you haven't told him a single goddamn thing."

Scratching Flax's chin, Percy said, "To be fair, I *was* being a gaping asshole about it."

The door to Irene's room swung open. Cam stood in the doorway, her head bowed, her eyes open but staring at the floor. The mesmerizing silver fire from the runes had died down to a soft glow, shimmering around her face like a cloud of tiny fireflies.

Nysska's pulse sped up.

Raoul was at Cam's side instantly. "Are you all right? Did it work? Are you all right?"

Cam's eyes slid shut as she knelt, pushing Raoul gently away. "Bring the cats."

Both blood lynxes had jumped down off of Percy as soon as Cam appeared. He didn't say anything or make any kind of move to signal them. They simply walked up to Cam and sat in front of her as she raised her head.

Drops of brilliant red liquid slid out of the corners of her eyes and ran down her cheeks. The blood lynxes flicked out their rough pink tongues and lapped up the ruby tears, and the silver in their own eyes flashed and glimmered as Cam's dimmed.

"Get ready." Raoul had a hand on the hilt of his sword, staring hard at the cats.

Nysska's heartbeat accelerated further as the cats' eyes grew brighter and brighter, their mouths hanging open, processing what they'd just tasted. They turned to Percy. He nodded and said, "Get to it."

From a full halt, the blood lynxes bolted into a frenzied sprint to the stairs and down, out of sight.

Percy shouted, "Nysska!" but she didn't wait, couldn't wait, and the stairs boomed and creaked under her boots as she tore after the cats. She didn't move quite as fast as she had when the argonium sheet had flown across the laboratory at Cam, but she knew she was speeding after the tracking animals faster than any human could have. Some distant part of her mind admonished her for putting her native-born speed on display in front of so many humans. Flax and Jax were Percy's cats, weren't they? They'd been working with him for years. Surely he was more than able to keep up with them.

But Percy Bitters was not as young a man as once he'd been. She reached the brothel's ground floor just in time to see the blood lynxes disappear through the front door and whip left into the street. Nysska crashed out onto the cobblestones and almost knocked Captain

Morter out of his boots. He yelped and tried to say something, but she had no time to listen.

The cats led Nysska from one cobblestone street to the next, flinging themselves around corners, forcing Nysska to dodge screaming, shouting, cursing pedestrians. She could hear the terror in those screams and picked up a few words in passing. Fragments, such as *demon* and *don't let it* and *kill us all!*

As the cats ran and ran, the sun dipped below the city's walls, and if Nysska's eyesight in the dark hadn't been what it was, she was sure she would have lost sight of them completely. The longer they ran—and how long had it been? No more than a few minutes—the worse the town around her looked. The cobblestones ran out completely, leaving her pelting along a rough dirt road, and the structures on either side of her devolved from businesses and homes to hovels and shacks. Around another corner, a city gate she hadn't seen before—much smaller than the one they'd come through earlier that day—loomed ahead of them. Bronze-clad soldiers were about to close it, but she saw them recoil as Flax and Jax screamed past them, and bellowed, "Hold the gate! *Hold the gate!*"

One of the soldiers cried out and half-drew his sword as Nysska sprinted past. The other one backpedaled away from her so quickly he lost his footing, but she didn't have time to watch him fall.

Nysska bolted out of the city—and came to a skidding halt.

The stark difference between Taurus Hill proper and the area beyond the gate stunned her. By comparison, the hovels of Robin Valley looked palatial. From a distance, when they had arrived on the road from Tember earlier that day, this place had appeared to be some sort of landfill, a dingy mass of refuse thrown carelessly over the wall. Up close, she thought that description still held.

There were no streets. Just jumbled, poorly constructed shacks and lean-tos, scattered about in crushing, abject, chaotic poverty. People huddled near fires, some cooking small, unidentifiable chunks of meat, while others skittered from shelter to shelter, shadow to shadow, like rats or cockroaches. Everyone within sight of Nysska paused, stared hard at her, and scurried away as she stood and raked her eyes across the impoverished masses.

Flax and Jax had disappeared.

Percy, Raoul, and Cam caught up with her moments later. Raoul and Cam seemed fine, but Percy panted ferociously as he said, "Dragon's...boiling guts, Nysska! There was...no need...to fly off the handle like that!"

"I kept up with them as far as the gates." She tried not to let the bitterness overwhelm her. "But now...I don't know where they've gone."

Percy grabbed her arm—more to steady himself than anything else—and panted until he got his breath back. "You think I can keep up with those two little fuckers on foot myself? Maybe if it's a straight path across fucking farmland. No. See, they track the criminal. And I've gotten awfully good at tracking *them*." He let go of her and knelt. "They know how fast they are. So every little bit, one of 'em leaves a squirt of piss for me." Percy sniffed—turned his head, sniffed again—and stood back up. "Come on."

With the shadow of the mountain looming to their left, a massive black void in the dim gray glow left over from sunset, Percy led them into the shantytown. Much the same way the citizens of Taurus Hill proper had parted before them, the rag-clad inhabitants here scurried away as they approached, leaving behind a wake of grunts and curses. Periodically, Percy sniffed again, sometimes kneeling to do so, never wavering from the trail the blood lynxes had left. Nysska kept scanning their surroundings. Her gaze pierced the surrounding shadows, and she turned and checked behind them every few seconds, noting each pair of human eyes peering through the flickering light of makeshift fires.

Cam walked beside her, rings clicking. Nysska said, "What is this place called? Does it have a name?"

"I don't know if there's an official one. I've only ever heard it called 'the Burr.'"

"Why?"

Another click. "It's the part of a piece of metalwork that gets filed off. A burr, I mean. Unwanted. Trash."

"Is there a place like this outside of Tember?"

A faint, joyless smile curled Cam's lips. "You've only ever

approached from the south or west, haven't you? If you'd come in from the east you'd know the answer to that."

"But why? Tember and Taurus Hill both—all of the Empire's towns, from what I've heard—they have plenty of wealth. Why let their citizens live in…in squalor like this?"

Now Cam frowned. "Take a closer look at the people. Try to guess their ages."

Nysska picked someone out. A woman who, rather than flee into the shadows, simply averted her eyes as they drew nearer. White hair. Wrinkled skin. Stooped back. "Are they all…old?"

Raoul surprised her by speaking up. "Too old to work." He wasn't frowning. His tone was that of someone explaining to a child why water rolled downhill. "The citizens of the Empire work. That's how they earn their place."

An image of her own mother appeared in Nysska's mind with such force and clarity that she struggled to keep from wincing. "Don't they have children, though? Someone to take care of them?"

Cam said, "Most of these people? No."

Raoul spared Nysska another of his contemptuous glances. "If you can't contribute to society, and you have no one to pick up your slack, the honorable thing to do is kill yourself."

Nysska understood in that moment that Raoul's contempt wasn't aimed at her. Not entirely, anyway, not right at that moment. "You…*loathe* these people." When he didn't respond, she said, "You hold them responsible for being too old to work, and for not having children willing to care for them." He remained silent. After a moment, Nysska said, "This is the heart of the Empire, isn't it? You work, or you're worthless. You work, or you die. Condemned to the scrap heap."

Noncommittally, Cam said, "In a nutshell, yes."

Nysska blew out a long breath. "That's fucking horrible."

Raoul scoffed. "If I get too frail to swing a sword, and have no one to feed me and keep a roof over my head? I'll gladly put a blade through my own heart." He paused. "Theobold did it the right way."

Nysska heard Cam suck in a sharp breath at that, but before

anyone else could say anything, Percy hissed, "Up ahead. They went through there."

The winding path through the Burr had led them closer and closer to the foot of the mountain, and now they faced a large tent raggedly stitched together from a dozen different hides and fabrics. There seemed to be some kind of commotion inside the tent, and this close, Nysska picked up the odor of cat piss as well. Percy unceremoniously grabbed a tent flap and yanked it open.

Two men whirled to face them. Both stood beside a large flap at the back of the tent. There was nothing else inside the tent besides the two men, a lantern, and a couple of three-legged wooden stools.

Percy said, "Well. You two look guilty as fuck."

Both men were dressed in a higher class of rags than anyone else Nysska had seen in the Burr, but more telling than that were their ages. Neither of them could have been older than thirty, and they appeared to be in perfect health. One had a handful of the edge of the flap, but he dropped it, and without a word both drew long knives from their belts.

Raoul stepped in front of Percy. "That's the dumbest thing you could possibly do. You realize that, yes? Do you both want to get hung on forks? In the name of the Thaumetallicon, lay down your weapons."

Both of them lunged at Raoul. For half a second he just stood there, stunned, and one of the men planted his knife in the upper left section of Raoul's breastplate.

Nysska couldn't tell how far the knife sank in, and she didn't get a chance to find out, because Raoul shoved the man backward and, in a single motion, whipped his sword from its scabbard and brought it around in a perfect flat arc. He might have been aiming for the neck, but the tip of his sword instead raked through the attacker's eyes, both blinding him and shattering the bridge of his nose.

Screams filled the tent, and Nysska saw Percy drop to one side and thrust out a leg. The sweep caught the other man's ankle and took his balance. The man fell, rolled, and came back up to his feet as Raoul staggered backward, only now paying attention to the knife sticking out of his chest. Nysska stepped past him and swung her sword in a brutal vertical arc that sliced through the tent's ceiling. The blade struck the cross-guard of the unwounded attacker's knife and knocked it out of his grip. She sheathed her sword, grabbed the man's throat, and delivered two punches to his face—one to the hinge of his jaw and another straight into his nose. He sagged in her grasp.

Cam said, "The first one—he's—"

Nysska looked over to see the man Raoul had blinded. From somewhere on his person he had produced a short, hook-bladed knife and, before anyone could stop him, he finished the job Raoul had started, slicing open his own throat from ear to ear.

In the abrupt lull that followed, Raoul plucked the knife from his chest. The Imperial armor had done its job, for the most part, as only half a centim at the knife's tip showed bloody. Cam went to him. "Are you all right?"

Raoul moved his arm experimentally and reached up under his armor and shirt. "Yeah. Just a little jab. It's not even bleeding that much." He sniffed the knife. "Don't think it's poisoned, either."

Percy had gone to the flap at the back of the tent. He took great handfuls in both fists and yanked it down, revealing a wall of rock with a roughly circular opening bored into it. Cam's rings clicked. "Is that another mine shaft?"

"Don't know," Percy said, "but my kitties're down there. And I'm betting there'll be more of these fuckers." He glanced at Nysska, who was still holding the second man up with one hand, and his eyes widened. "Shit-fire, woman. I already knew you were fast as fuck, now you've got to be *strong*, too?"

Nysska turned to Raoul and spoke with courtesy that came out only a bit forced. "Commander? Do you want me to wake this one up? Interrogate him?"

"No. Hog-tie him. We need to follow the animals. You do know how to hog-tie a human? You have the restraints?"

Nysska let the dazed man drop to the floor of the tent and, by way of answer, took a length of rope from a pouch at her hip.

Forty-five seconds later, Percy again led the way as the members of the Ninth Crucible crept down the tunnel. Nysska couldn't tell whether it had been dug as part of the mining operation the College had taken over, or as a different mine entirely, or simply by someone with mining experience. The farther they went, deeper into the mountain and down, the more respect she had for the effort such a tunnel had taken. If it were an independent venture—a lair burrowed out by criminals—she thought they'd missed their calling.

Nysska squinted. "There's a light up ahead."

Raoul said, "There is?" She could all but feel him staring into the darkness.

Percy sniffed. "More scent markers, too. Our killer's down here."

Cam's rings clicked together every few seconds, the impact softer than Nysska had heard before. She considered suggesting that she and Cam move ahead of the others and reconnoiter whatever lay ahead of them, but as they drew nearer, the light grew brighter. The flickering of torches. She heard men's voices at the same moment that Cam whispered, "There are people up ahead. I hear them talking."

"Move silently, then," Raoul whispered back. "Strap down any gear you've got that's likely to make a noise. Cam—that means no ring-clicks."

Nysska saw her nod. "I'll use my eyes if I have to."

Half a minute later they reached the end of the tunnel, which opened out into what appeared to be a natural cavern, something like fifteen meters across and half that high. The band of assassins or thieves or whoever dwelled there had brought a few odds and ends of furniture in. Nysska picked out a couple of rectangular tables, more three-legged stools, and bed rolls laid out along one side. She thought the furniture looked like the kind of selection that might have been stolen from a pub.

Against the far wall, someone had taken the initiative to build a rough wooden bar, taking the uneven contours of the floor into account. One man stood behind it. Two more sat on tall stools in front, drinking from oversized, chipped ceramic mugs. All three were dressed in the same kind of not-quite-as-wretched style as the two in the tent had worn, all three aged between twenty and forty. All three armed.

Raoul put his lips right next to Percy's ear, but Nysska could hear him just fine. "Where are the lynxes? Are they here?"

Percy shook his head and pointed. A few paces to the left of the bar, another dark opening punched through a wall, leading Nysska to wonder just how deep into the bedrock this system of rooms and tunnels ran.

A distant voice shouted. For a second Nysska thought it had come from behind them, but then a fourth man ran out from the tunnel next to the bar, said something to the men that she couldn't quite make out, and dashed back through the opening. The bartender and the drinkers abandoned what they'd been doing and ran after him.

Percy sprang out into the room, but Raoul was right behind him and caught his arm.

"My kitties! I can't let them get fucking cornered in here!"

"And we're not going to. But we can't just rush in, either. Come on. Quick but quiet."

Cam allowed herself two clicks as they crossed the cavern. Nysska wished at least one member of the Crucible were carrying some kind of ranged weapon. Crossbow. Long bow. Some throwing knives, at least. But it wasn't the Thaumetallicon's job to engage in actual combat. That's what the Cathedral's regular army was for, or the Argonium Infantry. Nysska promised herself to get her hands on something that could hit a target from across a room.

The second tunnel was much shorter than the first, and a torch halfway along its length meant no one had to guess where to put their feet. It led to another cavern room, this one a bit larger than the first. It seemed to be a storeroom, with shelves around the walls holding crates and chests and barrels and large, lumpy burlap sacks. Torches somewhere to the left spread light across the rocky floor, and unseen people passing in front of them cast long shadows. Tense voices echoed, rising in pitch and urgency—

Somewhere in the room, a cat screamed.

Percy bellowed, "No!" and dashed forward, screaming, *"You get your hands off my cat!"*

Raoul said, "Shit," and pelted after him.

Cam snapped, "Go, I'm right behind you," but Nysska was already hot on Raoul's heels. She burst out into the room, taking in the scene as fast as she could.

The man from behind the bar was holding one of the blood lynxes up, both of his hands gripping the big cat's scruff. Nysska thought it was Jax. Jax screamed again, spitting furious, his whole body twisting and writhing as he sought to sink as many claws as possible into the man's arm. Flax crouched two meters away, ears flat against her skull and fangs bared, making ready to pounce straight over her brother and into the man's face.

Five other men stood around the bartender and Jax. One of them —the oldest and most distinctive, since instead of rags he wore what looked like Imperial surplus leather armor with all the bronze stripped out—had already turned to face the tunnel. Percy stalked across the floor toward the men, his sword still sheathed but a slim dagger in his right hand.

Nysska's eyes ticked over the small crowd, assigning them names. She'd found it useful in keeping track of hostile targets. *Barkeep* held Jax. The four other rag-wearers she dubbed *Snowtop, Braid, One-Tooth,* and *Curly*. The man in the armor looked like a *Hector* to her, so Hector she named him.

Hector grinned at Nysska and her teammates. "I *thought* these might have been Crucible tracking animals. Never seen Seraphic beasts used like this. It's a good idea." His eyes settled on Nysska. "Great Dragon's cock, the rumors are true! The Cathedral really has their own pet demon now?"

"Set the fucking cat down, motherfucker," Percy said in a razor-sharp voice.

Hector shot back, "And if he doesn't?"

If Nysska hadn't been looking directly at Percy's hand, she would've missed it. He flipped the dagger around to catch it by the tip of its blade and threw it underhanded. The dagger sparkled in the torchlight on its short flight to Barkeep's head, punched through his temple, and buried itself up to the hilt in his brain. Barkeep's fingers spasmed open, Jax hit the ground running, and he and Flax disappeared into the shelves. The smug smile on Hector's face vanished. "Kill them!" Hector screamed. "Kill them all!"

Braid came straight at Percy. The bandit had grabbed up an arm-length battle hammer and swung it as if Percy were a giant nail that needed driving into the floor. Percy dodged out of the way as the bronze hammer rang against the stone floor, his own sword in his hand now, and moved in with a series of quick thrusts.

Snowtop and One-Tooth ran past Braid, moving to flank the other three Crucible members, while Curly dashed forward, a long knife in each hand. Nysska's longsword whipped out of its scabbard. She meant to use its greater reach to lop off either Curly's head or one of his arms—

Except Raoul stepped directly in front of her. She took a breath to say *Get the fuck out of the way*, but saw Snowtop coming in from her right, a longsword identical to hers gripped in both hands. Nysska pivoted to meet him.

Bronze clashed against bronze behind her.

Cam?

Snowtop brought his sword down in a diagonal slash. Nysska slipped past it, shoved him off-balance with the flat of her palm against his shoulder, and slid the point of her sword in through his armpit. Snowtop struck the stone floor with a sickening *splat* as Nysska whirled toward Cam.

Percy and Braid staggered past, between Nysska and Raoul—Braid had lost the battle hammer and Percy had lost his sword, but somewhere in the last few chaotic seconds Percy had reclaimed his dagger from Barkeep's temple. He kept stabbing it into Braid's chest as they grappled, the spray of blood turning Percy's forked beard red.

Beyond them, Cam had drawn her Imperial saber, and to Nysska's simultaneous horror and surprise was using it to keep One-Tooth's long knife away from her. One-Tooth kept moving in, feinting, thrusting. Every time he got close Cam knocked the knife away with the saber—but she was solely defending herself, not attacking, and One-Tooth was steadily driving her back toward a corner.

With a scream of effort, Raoul kicked Curly square in the chest with one bronze-heavy boot and followed the blow with a downward sword swing that split Curly's skull open. Curly collapsed backward into one of the shelves, which rocked its contents—

Nysska couldn't move quickly enough to keep the barrel of flour from toppling off the highest shelf. It exploded against the floor, sending white billows everywhere. She heard One-Tooth say, "I can't see! I can't fucking see!" and spotted Cam's saber as it flashed, and One-Tooth's cry turned into a gurgle.

Flour clouds filled the chamber, blocking and distorting the lantern light.

Raoul appeared out of nowhere, not a meter in front of her, wild-eyed and shaking, and dashed toward the tunnel. Nysska lost him behind a flour drift, but heard a startled cry from Cam, followed by the wet, rich, unmistakable sound of a blade tearing through flesh.

Nysska's stomach dropped. She shouted, "Cam!" and made her way through the white, one hand thrust out ahead of her. "Cam, what did you do?" The clouds of flour thinned closer to the tunnel entrance, and Nysska found Cam standing still, panting, her sword on the ground at her feet and one hand clamped over a bleeding wound on the back of her wrist.

A meter away, Raoul lay stretched out on the floor, gasping, his throat laid open. He stared up at Nysska, eyes bulging, the pool of blood around him spreading fast.

"Is he dead?" Cam asked. She was out of breath, but sounded calm, relieved, even, as she answered her own question. "No, not yet, I can still hear him breathing. Fuck, I should've opened my eyes for this shit."

Behind her, Nysska heard Percy coughing. She knelt beside Raoul, but a closer look at the wound in his neck told her there was nothing she could do. Cam's saber had opened a major artery as well as his windpipe. Nysska said, "Cam, I—this is—I don't know how to tell you this—"

Raoul shuddered. His breathing stopped…and his *face changed.*

Raoul's brown skin, his square jaw and broad nose and ink-black eyes all rippled and *shifted,* colors changing and flowing, like...Nysska recoiled in revulsion as she realized where she'd seen this before.

The man's skin changed like that of a *cuttlefish.*

She choked back a cry of revulsion as the colors and lines and contours settled, and the fresh corpse on the floor became the man she had dubbed Hector.

Cam knelt beside her. "Are you all right, Nysska? What're you trying to say?"

She heard footsteps behind her and twisted around to see Percy and Raoul shuffling out of the room with the shelves, emerging from the now-settling clouds of flour like ghosts from a battlefield. Flax and Jax came after them, silver eyes shining out of newly-white fur. Jax seemed none the worse for wear for having been scruffed.

Abruptly light-headed, Nysska put one hand on the floor to steady herself. Forced her eyes to focus. Now that she had the chance to look, she saw that what she had taken for Raoul's Imperial armor was the same tunic, gloves, and trousers that Hector had worn, all the bronze removed from the leather. His boots weren't Imperial issue at all, but badly scuffed and black.

Nysska stood up and turned to face her teammates. "Cam—how did you know that wasn't Raoul?"

Cam frowned. "What?"

Nysska shook her head. "The man whose throat you cut. How did you know it wasn't Raoul?"

"I don't understand. Why would I have thought it was Raoul?"

Nysska closed her eyes. "Please. Humor me. Answer my question."

Cam spread her hands. "I know all your footsteps, for one thing, and for another, this asshole smelled like a wet goat. Why are you asking me this?"

Percy peered up at Nysska, one hand pressed against the side of his face where a blade had cut him. "You look like you've seen a fucking ghost, woman. What happened? Get your bell rung?"

Raoul went to Cam. He was limping, but not too badly, and asked her, "Are you hurt?"

Cam shook her head. "I think I've come out of this better than any of you. Nysska, you want to tell us what the fuck is going on?"

Nysska looked back at Hector's corpse. His face was quite placid now. Just the pale dead flesh of a pale dead man. Flax walked up and rubbed against her ankle, causing small poofs of flour to spring away from her fur. Nysska said, "I...don't know if I can explain what I just saw...but I'm sure as fuck going to try."

9

Emerging from the tunnel into the tent, where the man Nysska had hog-tied still lay on the floor, Raoul said, "All right, let's drag him outside."

Nysska stepped in front of the hog-tied man and faced Raoul. "Drag him outside for what?"

Raoul narrowed his eyes at her. "There's not enough room in here for me to summon the Council."

"Commander, we can't do that yet."

Raoul's already narrowed eyes turned to angry slits. "As I recall, *Enforcer*, I'm the one charged with making that decision."

Nysska pointed at the hog-tied man, who lay on his side, and had either passed out or was pretending to be unconscious. "I'm not disputing that, sir, but this is not the man who killed Irene Jasinsky. Flax and Jax shot right past him. For another—were none of you fucking *listening* when I told you about the man's *face changing?*"

"Yes," Raoul said, anger visibly building. "We were listening. But Irene Jasinsky's killer, whichever one of them it was, is dead now. And this piece of shit on the ground here was part of their crew. Which, under Cathedral law, makes him every bit as guilty as the killer. So we're going to drag him out of this tent, I'm going to summon the

Council and read the charges, and you're going to take his head off. I know you don't have your axe, but I'm sure you can make do with your sword. Now pick him up."

Nysska sighed as her eyes slid closed. "No."

Percy groaned, and Cam said, "Nysska!"

Nysska opened her eyes to find Raoul glaring pure hatred at her, a vein in his temple throbbing. She said, "Commander. I am not trying to defy you. Yes, this man is guilty. Yes, the Council is going to order me to behead him. All I'm suggesting is that we delay summoning the Council until we find out what he knows."

Raoul still scowled at her, but his head tilted to one side. In a manner that made her think he meant to give her enough rope to hang herself, he said, "Elaborate on that."

"We still don't know who killed Naveed Olkoff. We were trying to find that out when we discovered Irene had been murdered. Yes? This piece of shit on the ground, as you called him, might know something about it. Why did his crew want her dead? Was it for the same reason that Olkoff was killed? Why don't we see what he knows, before his head leaves his shoulders?"

Raoul said nothing. He stared at her for so long that Nysska began to wonder if he'd even been listening at all.

Nysska said, "Not to mention we might ask him what he knows about Hector. And what I saw."

Raoul's lip curled in a sneer. "What you saw was a hallucination, Enforcer. Clearly you took a blow to the head, or maybe inhaling too much flour fucks up sethyd eyesight, I don't know, but what I *do* know is that what you claim to have seen happen back there is *not fucking possible.*"

Nysska folded her arms across her chest. "Just like the total failure of argonium runes isn't possible?"

Raoul's jaw clenched hard and tight.

Into that silence, Cam said, "She's right, Raoul. She's definitely right about Olkoff. We weren't assigned to solve the murder of a prostitute, and if we execute this man, we'll be no closer to finding Olkoff's killer than we were before. As to the other thing…what would it hurt to see what we can find out about it?"

Raoul turned to Percy, who had knelt and scooped up Flax in his arms. "That's two against me. Am I looking at a third, Bitters?"

Scratching Flax's chin, Percy said, "Truth be told, boss, I don't see what harm it could do. Maybe that hog-tied motherfucker knows something. Maybe he doesn't. If all it takes is making him chatter, I say we give it a go."

Raoul groaned, a guttural sound that took on gravel and volume until he finally shouted and spat at his feet. "It's against procedure! Do none of you realize that? Crucible procedure dictates that we go to a crime scene, find out who committed the crime, track that person down, and *fucking* execute them! That *works*. That's *always* worked! It's why you can leave a bag of copper sitting in the middle of the street, and it's still fucking *there* the next morning!" He glared at each of them. "We don't *ask questions*! We don't *interrogate* people! We don't *have* to! The citizens of the Empire know better than to... to...misbehave!"

Cam said, "These citizens didn't."

Percy nodded. "I've never seen this kind of—I don't know what you'd call this place. Den of thieves?"

Cam said, "More like den of assassins."

Percy nodded again, more enthusiastically, though his expression remained bleak. "Right. Right. People right outside a town like fucking Taurus Hill, thumbing their noses at the Cathedral. At the whole goddamn Empire. We need to know more."

Raoul rounded on Nysska. He looked as if someone had just ripped a hideous fart in his face. "Fine. Ask him your questions, then."

"I'd rather not engage in an interrogation here, sir. Anyone could approach the tent stealthily and hear every word we say. Someone might have heard too much already."

Raoul's eyebrows shot up. "We're picky now, are we? Where, then?"

Professor Greig's face had drawn up so tightly that it threatened to become a single giant wrinkle. She stood outside Olkoff's living quarters, hands on her hips and every bit of her attention on Raoul. Nysska stood behind Cam and Percy with the formerly hog-tied man thrown over her shoulder. His hands and feet remained bound, and his gag stayed in place, despite his near-constant efforts to talk since they'd taken him out of the tent, hauled him back through the Burr, and carried him into the College.

"Are you sure this is procedure?" Greig asked, sounding quite confident that it was indeed not procedure.

Nysska couldn't see Raoul's face from this angle, but his body language made her think he was about to snap like an over-tightened guitar string. "Our actions remain classified, Professor Greig. I'm sure you understand."

She shifted her weight from one foot to the other. "But it's the middle of the night! Can't this inquiry or whatever you called it wait until the morning?"

Raoul's shoulders quivered. "May I remind you, Professor, that your presence here is not required? Olkoff's lab and quarters constitute an active Thaumetallicon site. We have jurisdiction here. I decided to notify you out of courtesy, not to ask for your permission."

Greig's jaw clenched. Unclenched. Clenched again. She said, "Well. I suppose I shall remove myself from your *jurisdiction*. Commander." With that, she marched away, her footsteps echoing in the empty stone corridor. Nysska imagined the woman hunkering down at a desk to write a sternly worded letter to someone in Caulspring.

His own jaw clenching, Raoul beckoned to the rest of the team. "Get him inside."

Several minutes later, with the door to Naveed Olkoff's living quarters locked, Raoul pulled the gag out of the prisoner's mouth. With Percy's help, Raoul had tied the man to Olkoff's desk chair, but not before carrying the chair into the bedroom. Nysska didn't ask why, but she approved of the choice, since that would put anything the man had to say as far away from the door and any eavesdroppers as possible.

Raoul turned away from the prisoner, who sat still and glared at them all sullenly, and gestured for everyone else to move back into the first room. Percy opened his mouth, presumably to ask why, but the look he got from Raoul was pointed enough that he shut it again. Staying in the bedroom with the prisoner, Raoul slid the pocket doors closed in their faces. Nysska wondered if that was to give the questioning a sense of privacy, or because Raoul didn't know what he was doing and didn't want anyone else to see that.

Her rings clicking, Cam moved over to one of the couches and sat down. Nysska hesitated. If she sat on the opposite couch, speaking to Cam loudly enough to carry on a normal conversation might interfere with the questioning in the bedroom—but she didn't know how comfortable Cam would be if Nysska took a spot beside her. Percy gave no help in the matter, as he appeared to have noticed something on Jax's jaw and was currently seated on the floor in a corner with the blood lynx squirming in his lap.

"What is that?" Percy murmured to the big cat. "Some kind of cyst? Or just food stuck in your fur? Quit fucking wiggling, would you? This would go a lot faster if you'd just be *still*."

Jax continued wiggling. Nysska sat down on the same couch as Cam, at the far end. Cam gave no indication that she was aware of Nysska's presence. After a few long moments, against the backdrop of Raoul's door-muffled voice emanating from the bedroom, Nysska quietly said, "You haven't been talking much."

Cam raised her head. "I suppose I haven't had much to say."

Nysska snuck a glance at Percy. He had produced a fine metal comb from somewhere, and was industriously running it through Jax's fur, while Flax sat nearby and watched. Nysska took a deep breath. "Has that lack been because of me?"

Cam settled into the corner of the couch. It didn't seem like a retreat. Just an effort to get more comfortable. "Oh, yes, the presence of a big bad demon has sent me spiraling into gloom. The very thought makes my delicate constitution shiver. Never mind that I just killed a man."

"Oh—fuck. Cam. I'm sorry. Was that the first time you've killed someone?"

Cam's face softened a tiny bit. She sighed. "No. It's the first time in my role as Sensor, but...no."

Having trouble believing the words were actually coming out of her own mouth, Nysska said, "Whatever's bothering you...would you like to...do you want to talk about it?"

Whatever softness had touched Cam's features evaporated in a heartbeat. "Oh, so you can *comfort* me? Am I tiny pitiful thing, the poor blind girl, so pathetic and weak?"

"What—*no*, I didn't mean anything like th—"

Surprising Nysska so profoundly that she froze into total non-reaction, Cam leaned over, put a hand on Nysska's leg just above the knee, and dug her fingertips between the strips of inlaid bronze, deep into the thigh muscle. The strength of her grip made Nysska gasp. "My grandfather used to do this to me." She turned Nysska's leg loose and settled back into her corner of the couch. "To all the grandchildren—he'd grab our legs like that, and squeeze so hard I swear he touched bone, and he'd say, 'You know what this is? It's a mule eating corn!'"

Nysska felt as if Cam had led her, without warning, into uncharted, dangerous waters. "And...what was the purpose of that?"

Cam scowled. "We were farmers. Dirt-poor farmers—which is to say, farmers at all. We didn't have much in the way of entertainment, nor much time to appreciate it if we stumbled across some. Any little distraction, any silly game, we welcomed. My grandfather had the strongest hands. Like blunt bronze claws, like parts of a machine. As if the Great Silver Dragon had taken the pieces of a sawmill and rearranged them into a man." The scowl faded. "He loved us. He loved all of us. But we had to work. That's the Empire's way, isn't it? Work is life. If you don't work, well, then, what good are you? How do you contribute to society?" Cam cleared her throat. "You may have horns, but your leg doesn't feel any different to me than anybody else's would. And as far as being scared of you, believe me, I've encountered worse."

Carefully, Nysska said, "Everyone works. I understand that philosophy." She paused. "When did you lose your sight?"

"Oh, that's not the right question to ask, Nysska Stonegate. Mighty demon Enforcer. No no no. You should ask when I *gained* my sight. Wondering if I decided to apply to the Thaumetallicon when I went blind, right? Because how's a little blind girl going to do her part? My mother and father had the same question. I was blind when I slid out of the womb. My brothers used to tell me Ma and Pa fought about it—fought about whether or not to drown me. Because they had the same question you do. It made me so mad, Rall and Tomys telling me that. Telling me my parents knew I was useless, and why should they keep me when I couldn't live up to the Empire's standards? Well, they *did* keep me. And I worked. I worked, by the Dragon's scaly cock, I worked till I bled, and it didn't matter if I could see or not."

Nysska wanted to stop her. Wanted to tell her that this was more than she'd meant to ask for, more than she felt at all comfortable hearing, but it was as if a dam had broken, and all of Cam's words flooded into the room and smashed through anything they touched.

"I could've stayed on the farm. Eyes or not, I was better than Rall or Tomys either one when it came to shucking corn, and I'd learned to cook and mend clothes and anything else Ma or Pa wanted me to do. But the Cathedral sent out a message. They said the Empire needed 'solace girls.' Do you know what that term means?"

Nysska swallowed. "I am sure I can guess."

"Demons're smart, huh? Any girls with disabilities that prevented them from being productive members of society were liable to get grabbed up and sent to a solace house. Now, when I was growing up, it didn't matter, because I worked on that farm till my fingers were raw, and my parents always pled my case and kept me. But then the last governor changed the laws for the territory. He said girls like me could stay where they were, *as long as they could have children*. That the Empire needed more upstanding citizens, and if a girl was missing a leg or an arm or, say, a pair of eyes, that was all right, because she could still bear the Imperial fruit, and would be expected to do so. Which is when everything went to shit."

"You're barren? Was that—was it caused by the same thing that took your sight?"

"Fuck no. It was caused by me not being fast enough to get away from an irritable bull." Cam pulled up her jacket and the shirt beneath it and showed Nysska the scar tissue across her abdomen. "The bull gored me when I was thirteen. I was a year shy of twenty when the new law went into effect, and I packed a bag and put on my rings and ran away from the farm and Ma and Pa and Rall and Tomys. And my grandfather. Nobody thought I could, but I got myself to a College, and I applied right there, and you know what? They accepted me." She smoothed down her shirt hem and lowered the jacket.

"You asked me once why I didn't use them all the time. My runes. And I'll tell you." She pointed at her eyes. "Keeping these closed is more natural to me than what I see when I open them. Not to mention that the Thaumetallicon treats me with respect. So what if I only make it to forty? I'm going to live the *fuck* out of the fifteen years I've got left. There. Does that answer all your questions?"

Nysska sat and thought, searching for some kind of response fit for the outpouring with which Cam had just blasted her. Finally she said, "Excuse me," and stood and wandered over to the pocket doors.

The prisoner's voice reached her clearly, this close to the bedroom. It said, "Fuck off, bronze man."

A sharp, meaty impact followed that, and the pocket doors flew open, so that Nysska found herself almost nose to nose with a scowling Raoul, the vein in his forehead pulsing. Over his shoulder, Nysska got a glimpse of the prisoner, face bloody but a smug grin riding on top of it. Raoul shut the doors and stomped past Nysska into the front room, where Percy and Cam both stood and came to him. Nysska drifted off to one side.

Percy said, "Well? Does the fucker know anything?" When Raoul only stood and fumed, Percy offered, "I'm guessing not?"

Raoul rubbed his temples with both hands. "Whoever he works for—whatever crew he was a part of—he's either one loyal little toad, or he's a lot more frightened of them than he is of me. I told him if he doesn't give us what we need, he'll hang on a fork, but he just said he was going to hang on a fork no matter what, so why should he say a word? Then I tried telling him that if what he told us was valuable enough, I could help him *avoid* the fork. He laughed at me. Laughed in my face." Raoul stared up at the ceiling. "And what could I say to that? How am I supposed to convince him of...of anything?" Raoul threw both arms out wide. "This is not what we *do*. It is not what we were trained to do, and with good reason. People who commit crimes in the Empire are drunks, or out of their minds on smoke, or in the heat of passion. But those men in the, the, the lair we found? What *are* they? Who in their right minds would conspire to commit crimes, when they know the punishment is death when they're caught?"

Nysska said, "*If* they're caught."

Raoul whipped his head around to fix her with his usual glare, but it was Cam who spoke. "What was that?"

Nysska took a step toward the group. "You said 'when they're caught.' But unless they are all—*were* all—insane, they were operating under the assumption that it would not be 'when,' but 'if.' They believed they could commit a crime, a murder, and live to tell about it."

Percy nodded. "Yeah. It's like you just said, boss. That fucker in there is more scared of somebody else than he is of the goddamn Empire."

Cam absently clicked her rings together. "So what do we do about that?"

Nysska got even closer to Raoul, and inclined her head toward the bedroom. "Commander. If I may?"

One of Raoul's eyebrows slid up his forehead. "If you may *what,* Enforcer?"

"I would like to try to get through to the prisoner."

Raoul squared off against her. "And how do you propose to do that?"

"I may be able to persuade him to open up to us. Maybe...maybe even see what he knows about the man whose face changed."

Raoul opened his mouth and raised a pointer finger simultaneously, but before he could speak, Cam reached out and put a hand on his elbow. "Raoul. What's the harm? Let her try."

Raoul shut his mouth, dropped his hand, and shrugged theatrically. "Do what you want. It'll be sunup soon. I'm going to have to report to Tember before the day's over, no matter what happens."

Nysska took a couple of long, deep breaths, went to the pocket doors and slid them open.

The prisoner flinched at the sight of her, but only for a second. She noticed his eyes lingering on the details of her armor. "Empire's got themselves a pet demon now. Bronze is law!" His voice rose, mocking. "Bronze is *peace*!"

Nysska slid the doors closed and walked around the man slowly. His ankles were bound together and tied to one of the chair's legs, forcing him into an awkward, angled posture, his wrists lashed to the armrests. The cloth that had been used as a gag now rested loose around his neck. Nysska put his age around twenty-five. Maybe thirty. His sand-brown skin had been somewhat darkened by the dirt ground into it, his hair showed no signs of having been washed in Atiina-only-knew how long, and his fingernails were caked with black filth. She hadn't seen him smile, but she was prepared for what few teeth he had to be morbidly unhealthy. He stared up at her with ink-black eyes as she came into his field of vision again.

"What is your name?" she asked. "Or, better yet, what do your friends call you?"

The prisoner sneered. "I get called 'wife-fucker' a good bit."

Nysska circled him again. Still slowly. "All right, Mr. Wife. Do you believe in the Great Silver Dragon?"

"Hey. I'm not 'Mr. Wife.'"

"Fine. I'll call you Vomit, because that's what you both look and smell like. Do you believe in the Great Silver Dragon, Vomit? The Klik-Long Beast? The Sky Savior? Those are all names for it, correct?"

The man said nothing. Just glared at her.

She went on. "I am told the Great Silver Dragon is what all you Imperial humans worship, with your grand temples and your sacred shiny kites."

"Fuck you."

"And what is your belief about how humans came to be? Something like...the Great Silver Dragon flew across the sky, and breathed fire, and droplets of fire fell to the ground, and grew and became the first humans. Yes? You carry those droplets of fire inside you. Your soul, burning and powerful, ready to serve the Dragon. That is what you repeat to yourselves and to each other when you go to your temples and beg the Great Silver Dragon for His favor."

"Fuck you."

Nysska stopped circling, stood directly in front of him, and bent forward at the waist, so that they could look each other in the eye. She saw the reflection of her own candle-flame irises in his black ones—and this close, he suddenly seemed a bit less sure of himself. Nysska said, "What if I told you all that was a lie?"

This time it wasn't just a rote rebuke. This time he meant it. "*Fuck. You.*"

"A believer, then." She moved around behind him and put her hands on his shoulders. Leaned down to place her lips right next to his ear. "I know the truth, you see."

The prisoner struggled against his ropes.

Nysska whispered, "My people know that the Great Silver Dragon is a fiction. A lie you all tell yourselves so that you can pretend you are worth more than bear shit."

"Fuck you, demon!"

"You did not come from the sky. You are not the progeny of some great, majestic beast. *We are.*"

The prisoner fought so hard he began to bleed from the wrists.

"*We* are the children of majesty, of ferocity, of vast, noble hunger. *We* are the ones destined to rule this world, with pathetic humans like you—the ones we allow to live—bowing and scraping at our every whim." She loaded her words with contempt. "Born of *fire*. Pitiful. While your ancestors oozed up out of the ground, wretched little creatures, scrabbling and squelching through the mud, unaware of how fucking *little* you mean…my people waited. Waited and watched. Waited and grew strong…so *very* strong." Nysska applied pressure to the man's collarbone. It didn't take much to make him squeal in desperate pain. She took her hands away and circled him again, slowly, while he panted and silently wept.

Nysska had picked up the small, sharp, hook-bladed knife the other man in the tent had used to cut his own throat. She brought it out now, knelt, and sliced through the ropes holding the man's ankles. Two more quick cuts and the ropes binding his wrists fell away. The prisoner immediately tried to stand, but Nysska put a hand on one shoulder—the one she'd squeezed—and forced him back into the chair.

"Humans are right about one thing. You do have a soul." She

wrapped a hand around his throat, in much the same way she had back in the tent, and lifted him out of the chair with one arm. He grabbed her wrist and writhed and struggled, but she didn't tighten her grip enough to cut off his air or his blood. She simply pivoted and pinned the man to the wall, his feet dangling off the ground, heels kicking backward into one of Olkoff's tapestries. "We can see it inside you. *I* can see it. Do you know how?"

The man stopped kicking, putting all his strength into his hands as he clung to her wrist, his eyes bulging.

"I'll show you." Nysska let him drop, slowly, until his feet touched the floor again, but didn't loosen her grip on his throat. She let her eyelids slide shut and, while her eyes were hidden, brought her water-sight lids across them, so that when she opened the outer lids again, the prisoner was looking into eyes of green instead of yellow.

He yelped.

"Yes," she breathed, letting the word drag out. "Yes, I see it. Deep down in there. That tiny, sad little spark. If I wanted to, I could reach in there and *snuff it out*. That is the gift of my people. We can kill a human's soul...or we can *feast* on it." Her eyes snapped back to yellow, and as she snarled in the prisoner's face, he lost control of his bladder. "You may not be concerned with what we do to your body. But either tell us what we want to know, or I will *eat your soul*."

Twenty minutes later, having bound the prisoner to the chair once more, Nysska came back out into the front room and closed the doors behind her. Raoul, Cam, and Percy sprang to their feet, and Raoul marched right up to her. "Well?"

Nysska sighed. "He's cooperating, so I'll let him tell you the details himself. But the gist is this—yes, Olkoff and Irene were fucking. That much was not in question. Irene, however, was convinced that Olkoff was about to come into a treasure of some kind, and that he was going to take her out of the brothel. The two of them were planning on leaving together and starting a new life in some remote location. Rathan, the brothel owner, reports to the same people as the chair-bound fellow in there and all his cohorts. Whoever is in charge apparently took a dim view of one of their girls deciding to simply vanish, and they killed her for it."

Quietly, Cam said, "Did you ask him about Hector? About what you saw?"

Nysska's face clouded. "I did, yes. And I believe him when he says he doesn't know what I'm talking about. Whoever Hector was, whatever I saw, he kept our guest in the dark about it."

The thought hammered at her. *Is Raoul right about that part? Was I hallucinating?* Nysska hated the idea that she couldn't trust her own eyes.

Raoul gave out an impatient grunt. "But what about Olkoff? Does the prisoner know who killed him?"

"Maybe. Or who might have ordered it done. Olkoff had some kind of deal with a wealthy patron—a man who made use of Irene and several other girls of Rathan's whenever he came to Taurus Hill."

Cam said, "Grand. Who's this wealthy patron, then?"

"Sergei Benitoff."

Cam gasped.

Raoul said, "Oh...fuck me up the nose."

Percy burst into laughter.

As Raoul, Percy, and Cam fell to discussing what it meant that Olkoff's mysterious partner was a member of Caulspring's Royal Family and a darling of the Empire, Nysska moved silently to the locked front door, opened it, and slipped out of the room.

10

Nysska walked through the gate at the edge of the College's grounds with her hood up, her face scarf in place, and her "soulsight" eyes giving the gate guards a flash of green instead of glimmering yellow. She could tell both of them knew exactly who she was, but neither of them said anything or stared. They just mutely let her pass.

Tears gathered at the corners of her eyes.

For as long as Nysska could remember, if she got angry enough, the tears started flowing—and once they began, they were a goddamn nightmare to stop. Each tear represented something she couldn't control, which made her angrier, which made even more tears flow.

As she moved down into the town below the college, Nysska was *furious*. She swiped the tears away with the back of her gloved hand.

The sun had dropped below the horizon, and torches flickered to life along the streets of Taurus Hill as the temperature plummeted. Nysska had grabbed a long cloak from her pack on her way out of the College, and she swept it about her shoulders, pulling it closed in front. She didn't really feel the cold all that much, but was glad for the air's chill, as it rendered the cloak plausible. This way, unless someone got a careful, up-close look at her boots, nothing about her screamed "Cathedral." At the moment, she craved anonymity.

Nysska let her shoulders slump, let her spine curve in a slouch, taking centims off her height and adding years to her body language. At best, she might be mistaken for a tall, stooped, aged human male. She wondered how wise that was, what with the crushing lack of value the Empire assigned to those whose bones had grown too brittle and creaky to shovel food into the vast Imperial mouth. Maybe if she minded her business, those around her would mind theirs as well.

The hard-working citizenry of Taurus Hill had mostly vanished with the sun, replaced on the streets now by perfumed women with ruby-red lips, and slender boys with heavy eye makeup, and the hungry, wolf-like men who watched them. Here, a working man approached a woman, disappearing with her into an alleyway. There, an old man offered payment to a boy, who then explained what he would and would not do for it. Nysska passed a tavern, where raucous laughter and shrill, excited screams flowed out into the street like breaking waves with a liquor-scented undertow.

A man on a corner bought a small, discreet package from a skinny girl of twelve years.

Figures huddling in another alley whooped as dice bounced and rolled on the cobblestones.

The Empire survives because of the rule of law. That was what she'd been taught. And yes, it had proved true...*for the crimes the Empire cared about.* Murder made the list. Theft did, too, if what had been stolen was deemed valuable by the right people. She remembered the headless corpse labeled "LIAR." Would anyone hang on a fork in the city center for lying to Irene Jasinsky? Would a Crucible be dispatched if someone stole from the pretty, too-thin boy idling on the street corner ahead of her? She knew the answer.

Hypocrisy. All of it.

Nysska's feet navigated the cobblestones without any conscious input from her brain, lost in her own thoughts. One of her instructors had told her that every society embodied contradictions, and she knew the sethyds were no exception, but until she and the rest of her people had been welcomed onto Imperial land, she'd never seen the concept presented so starkly.

Nysska watched it all, saw and remembered it all, her mind churning. Her teammates, her Crucible, got called in when a life was taken or a body maimed too badly to function anymore—but were ignored in the course of the nightly dealings of vice and self-victimization. Clearly the Empire's formula worked, as their bronze-fisted rule controlled every square klik of land from one coast to the other, from the soulless, frozen expanse of the north to the boiling, venomous jungles far to the south. Who was she to argue with their choice of cruelty? Who was she to object when ordered to separate a head from its shoulders?

That was the question, wasn't it?

Who was she?

The taste of the words she had said to the prisoner in Olkoff's bedroom hung on her tongue like poison, like the pain of a blistering burn. *That* was the source of the tears in her eyes. Not the Empire's arbitrary morality, but her own—twisting the words of her people, twisting Atiina's teachings, committing *sacrilege*, and for what? To make one worthless human tell the truth? Everything she had said to him—all the lies—every word she had used to chisel under his skin and lodge in his bones made her want to find a corner and curl up and sob until she fell asleep.

Show them they're wrong about us, Simana had said.

Be an ambassador for your people, Anwar had said.

Well, she had certainly accomplished that. In just a few minutes' time, she had convinced a human that every single terrible, evil, false thing he'd ever heard about sethyds was incontestably true.

And yet...

Her words had held kernels of reality, hadn't they?

How does it feel, to tell a human some of the truth? a voice in her head wanted to know. *How does it feel to walk among them, a monster, a monument to bloodthirst?*

Nysska sniffled and batted away more tears.

A group of young men piled out of a tavern half a block ahead of her. Laughing. Drunk. Half a dozen of them, arms over shoulders as they tried to keep their feet, lurching in a tightly woven brotherhood. Nysska wondered if they all worked together, or had grown up together, or were perhaps part of the same family. She watched them, envy lapping at her heart like a tiny tongue of flame as they drew closer. Had she and her brother ever laughed as freely as these humans? Nysska shook her head at the fanciful notion. Her people's lives had far too much discipline, too much *purpose,* to engage in this kind of juvenile, frivolous display. That was what she had always been taught. She'd even believed it for a while.

The group of young men drew abreast of her.

She wasn't sure whether the nature of their laughter became just a tiny bit forced...or whether one of them looked up at her with a hair too much lucidity...but just as they came within arm's reach of her, Nysska realized she had made a terrible error in judgement, and the six men charged against her as one and shoved her through a narrow opening between two buildings—

And out into empty air.

No—it only felt empty for the half a heartbeat before the back of Nysska's head cracked into stone, forcing her chin down to her chest, and in the second half of that heartbeat she landed on her back with an impact that drove the air from her lungs. The sound of metal slamming onto stone rang out from above as a hatch closed off the shaft down which she had just plummeted.

Gasping, chest heaving, Nysska rolled and got up to her hands and knees. She clawed the face scarf and the hood away with one hand and reached for her sword with the other—and grasped nothing. One of the men who'd ambushed her had dragged her sword from its scabbard in the confusion.

Nysska's teeth ground. *Stupid, stupid, stupid!* More tears started, burning hotter now that her watersight lids had retracted. How could she have had her head that far up her own ass? Sucking air into her lungs, she got to her feet and turned in a circle, staring hard at everything around her.

She'd landed in some sort of subterranean storage area. From the scuff marks and bolt holes on the stone floor, she guessed it had once housed huge barrels of beer or wine. Now it was simply a large room broken up by stacked-stone support columns every five meters or so. The thin light from a few sconce-mounted torches didn't reach far enough to show her any of the walls.

"This is what you might call a two-birds-one-stone situation," a deep voice said from somewhere off to her right. Nysska turned to face it, and a tall, thickly muscled man with black skin and black eyes stepped out from behind a column. He wore the same kind of Imperial-surplus leather armor that Hector had in the mine lair. "Decree or not, I'm sure you can guess how the good people of Taurus Hill feel about being asked to tolerate a demon in their presence."

"I don't think I'm in the presence of the *good people* of Taurus Hill," Nysska said. "Who are you? What do you want?"

The tall man made a gesture with one hand, and four more men emerged from the shadows, two to Nysska's left and right, one in front of her, one behind. All of them carried either swords or daggers.

"We want to be left in peace," the tall man said with a smile full of brilliant white teeth. "And we won't be, as long as you're still breathing, isn't that right?"

The man behind Nysska rushed her, coming in with a dagger strike aimed at her kidney, and Nysska pivoted and struck him on the back of the knife hand so that the blade thrust harmlessly past her ribs. The hook-bladed knife had found its way into her hand again, and she dragged it through the skin and tendons and blood vessels of the man's throat and took his dagger away as he collapsed in a gurgling heap.

All three of the remaining men lunged for her at once. No time to assign nicknames—the flood of fire in her veins made Nysska see them not as individual humans, but as an incoming barrage of weapons and targets, of dangers and opportunities. She had trained for this, just as every sethyd had. But training for situations like these could only take one so far, and though she twisted out of the way of another dagger and ducked under the arc of a sword, the tip of a third blade punched through the bronze-inlaid armor over her thigh and dug into the muscle. Nysska pivoted again, the motion pulling the knife in her thigh out of its wielder's grip, and in a series of fluid movements she buried the dagger she'd taken in the back of one man's neck, hooked the curved blade of her knife into another's guts and sliced up until the blade met his breastbone, and grabbed a sword out of suddenly nerveless fingers. She heard motion, leather on stone, from over her shoulder, and she slipped to the right as another dagger flashed past her ear.

Nysska brought the sword around with both hands. The blade severed the remaining man's forearm and sank into his neck just under his jawbone. She held onto the sword as the man's body dropped to its knees, put a foot on the chest, and pulled the blade free.

The tall man in the leather armor hadn't moved. His grin had grown wider, and to Nysska's pained annoyance, he *applauded*. "That was...that was something else," he said. "Impressive. Truly. Aren't you going to pull that blade out of your leg?"

"No," Nysska said, and started toward him. She liked the weight of the sword she'd taken. She wanted to see how sturdy Imperial armor was without the inlaid bronze strips and thought the sword would make an excellent tool for finding out.

"Ah-ah," the tall man said. "Boys, if you will?"

Shadows writhed around the edges of the room as they disgorged more blade-wielding men. Like the first four she'd killed, they wore simple laborer's clothes typical for Taurus Hill townsfolk. Everywhere she looked, another lackey of the tall man stepped out from behind a column or emerged from some dark corner. They advanced on her from all sides. She counted fifteen, not including their leader.

Nysska let a growl start, down deep inside her. Let it build as it worked its way up from her diaphragm, build as it occupied all the air in her lungs, build as it came up into her windpipe like lava spewing from a volcano. Nysska bared her teeth and let the whites show all the way around the flaring yellow of her irises, and when the breath in her body had reached a crescendo, she *roared*.

The sound exploded through the air like a cataclysmic earthquake, and the men closest to her flinched and staggered back, hands flying to suddenly bleeding ears.

Nysska charged.

She knew the most vulnerable points of the human body. Every sethyd knew, thanks to the same instructors who'd taught them reading and mathematics.

Nysska abandoned any pretense of defending herself, any scant thought of blocking or parrying the blade strikes that came her way. This was about attack. Pure, swift, uncompromising. The sound of her thunderous, crashing footsteps on the basement's stone floor mixed with the dying echoes of her battle cry as her sword found its way to human throats. Stabbed through human eyes. Sought out and opened human arteries in upper arms and upper thighs. She tore a circle through the men, lavishing her attentions on those closest to her first—the ones most dazed by the roar—and along that path of screams and spattering blood, daggers and swords reached out and found her as well.

She lost count of the wounds after the first few seconds. Five? Eight? A dozen? The armor helped, but it couldn't stop an assault from so many, and Nysska felt the lines of agony as they traced across the skin and into the flesh of her calves and shoulders, her back and her abdomen, but she knew the only way out was through. She knew she had to kill them all as fast as she could if she ever wanted to see the light of day again.

If she ever wanted to see…

A dim, primitive part of Nysska's brain slapped the image front and center. Survive…for what?

For Cam.

Nysska roared again.

It didn't have as great an effect this time, as only the two men closest to her winced and jerked back, but she used those two to carve a hole through the line of bronze blades, getting her feet on dry stone and off the blood-slick killing floor. She had no idea how many men she had gutted, or how many were left, but the fiery agony in her arms and legs and chest and belly poured together and coalesced into a fueling anger. Three men in front of her. A sword thrust—too slow—Nysska's blade whipped down and severed the man's arm at the wrist. Slip to the left, so that the thrust meant to spear her skull only sliced through the skin of her cheek, bring the pommel up into the man's jaw and hear the crunching fracture—drop beneath the stroke of a longsword, roll inside its range, drive the point of her blade up into a groin.

A blow that felt as if it came from the hoof of a bull caught Nysska between the shoulder blades and drove her face-first into the floor.

She rolled, blinking blood out of her eyes, and the massive head of the bronze war hammer that had struck her clanged against the stones. Nysska looked up into the raging black eyes of the tall man, the leader of this band of assassins or thieves or whatever they were, and she thrust out a booted foot and turned his ankle sideways.

He screamed, still upright somehow, and Nysska surged up and took the hammer away from him, but the tall man grabbed a sword from the twitching hand of one of his men. He swung it up and over his head and down, straight at Nysska's skull—

The impact as the blade came to a punishing halt jarred the tall man's hand so badly that he almost let go of the hilt. He staggered, barely stayed upright, and she saw his eyes go wide as he stared at what should have been a head split in half.

The sword had come to rest in the crook of Nysska's left horn.

With a toss of her head, she took the sword out of his grip and sent it clattering into the shadows. Nysska choked up on the war hammer's shaft and brought the heavy bronze head straight up into the tall man's chin. He fell in a heap, silent and motionless.

Nysska tottered, trembling, and when she saw that there were no men left, she slid down to the floor, her back against one of the rough stone columns.

Sometime later—seconds, minutes, there was no way to tell—she heard a metallic bang and the creak of rusty hinges, followed by the patter of quick, light footsteps. "Nysska! Nysska, how badly are you hurt? How can I help?"

She dragged her eyelids open. Cam knelt beside her, her eyes shining silver, and Nysska's heart tripped and stumbled. After a couple of hard swallows, she said, "I don't think they hit...anything important. It's just flesh wounds...a *lot* of flesh wounds..."

Cam scampered over to where Nysska had dropped her cloak and came back, ripping strips off of it. "Let me get your armor off." Working together, with Nysska moving very slowly, they unbuckled and peeled off the blood-soaked Imperial armor. Cam slid the cut-to-ribbons shirt and camisole off Nysska's torso and wrapped makeshift bandages around as many lacerations as she could. When she finished, she said, "Come on, we need to get you back to the College."

Nysska put a hand on her arm. "Just…give me a moment…please."

"We don't have any time to waste! I don't know how many more of them there might be!"

"And I'm not…arguing that. Just let me…catch my breath." She peered up at Cam's worried face. "Why are you…using your runes?"

Cam frowned. The silver radiance wasn't as overwhelming now as when she had used them in Olkoff's laboratory. "I followed you. Heard you get ambushed, and—heard that—that *sound* you made. I tried to reach you, but when I got to the door it was jammed shut, and the only way I could know what was happening was to *look*…"

Nysska blinked. "You saw me fight."

The tall man, still laid out nearby, groaned and moved one arm.

Nysska and Cam both looked over at him.

Silent, Cam stood. She picked a blade off the ground, walked over to the tall man, knelt beside him, and cut his throat.

Nysska's eyes almost left their sockets. "Cam—what—why? Why did you do that?" When Cam didn't answer, just wiped the knife on the tall man's armor and dropped it, Nysska said, "We could've questioned him!"

Cam came back and crouched down and looked into Nysska's yellow eyes with her silver ones, and Nysska had to work to keep breathing.

"Yes. He would have known things. He would have talked about those things. That's why he had to die." Nysska shook her head, no words coming to her, so Cam went on. "Nysska, I *did* see you fight. I saw you kill nineteen men. *By yourself.* I didn't know you could do that. I didn't know anyone anywhere could do that. But now I do know, and so did he." When Nysska still didn't speak, Cam went on. "Can all sethyds fight like that? No no, don't try to tell me, because it doesn't matter. The *second* word of what you did here got out to the public, my people would rise up and *kill you*. You can take out nineteen men, yes, but can you beat a hundred? A thousand? Because that's what they'd send. However many it took. And once you're dead, they'll bring together an army of soldiers with argonium runes in their muscles, and they'll go to the Crags, and it'll be genocide." She paused. "The way you fought, Nysska…the way you moved…you killed all these men, and it's left you with nothing more than a bunch of bad scratches. I've never seen anything like it. *No one else can know.* Do you understand? Say it."

Nysska's head had tilted back until it rested against the column. With her eyes closed, she said, "I understand."

"Good. Now. Can you walk?"

Slowly, painfully, Nysska got to her feet. With her ruined armor tucked under one arm and the remains of the cloak wrapped around her, the two of them left the basement and the throng of dead men behind them.

11

Are you sure you're all right to walk?"

Cam had been trying to support Nysska as they climbed up a set of stone stairs from the killing ground below, but as soon as they emerged into a small courtyard, the difference in their heights made that impractical enough that they gave up on it.

Nysska paused and gingerly moved each arm, tested each leg, and bent slowly at the waist in all four directions. "I believe so. As I said down in…that place, I don't think they punctured or severed anything vital. And my people heal fairly quickly." At Cam's raised eyebrows, Nysska added, "It's not a thaumaturgical thing. I'll be a mass of scabs by morning, and I'll feel every one of these wounds for the next two weeks. But yes, I can walk."

They left the courtyard by passing through an ornately carved wooden gate and stepped out onto the cobblestones of one of Taurus Hill's main streets. Nysska watched as the citizenry melted away from them. Heads studiously turning, bodies sinking back into shadows, doors closing and latching.

"Do you think they all know what happened?" she said softly.

Cam's rings clicked a couple of times. She had shut her eyes again as soon as they had left the storage-basement-turned-bloodbath.

"They might know you were set to be ambushed. And since you're alive and in one piece, they can draw their own conclusions. But none of them *saw* you fight. None of them can go running to tell that tale. That's the important bit." After a few seconds, she asked, "Why did you leave, anyway? Where were you going?"

A river of thoughts and feelings and, here and there, actual words washed across Nysska's mind. It was too much. "I…did not enjoy interrogating the prisoner. I wanted some air." They turned a corner, headed for the College. "Why did you follow me?"

Cam said nothing. Only clicked her rings every few steps. Finally, she murmured, "I wanted to apologize."

Nysska felt her heartbeat speed up. She hoped it wouldn't make her voice shake. "For what?"

Another long pause. "For taking your head off the way I did back in Olkoff's rooms. I hadn't said more than two sentences to you since we met, and the first time you ask me an honest question, I rake you over the coals. It was uncalled-for. It's not how teammates are supposed to relate to each other."

They turned right, onto the street that led up to the College's gate. Nysska was about to ask a question concerning how teammates *were* supposed to relate to each other when she spotted a pair of town guards ahead of them. "Up there. Pair of Captain Morter's men."

Cam's rings clicked. "I suppose we need to tell them…hmm. Some version of what just happened."

Nysska's hand settled on Cam's shoulder. "Not a word."

As they passed, the men in Taurus Hill armor averted their eyes from Nysska just as the regular townsfolk had, and Nysska's lips tightened into a thin, flat line. Cam said nothing until they were out of earshot. "Why?"

Nysska turned her head enough to spot the men from the corner of her eye. Both of them had stopped and were staring after her and Cam. "We're dealing with something the Cathedral isn't prepared to handle. Something living right under the guards' noses. And what's the best way to get away with something?"

Cam made a sound of disgust in her throat. "Bribes."

"We have no way to know how many of Captain Morter's men are involved in this thing."

Cam raised her hand to the gate guards at the College's perimeter. Through the gate and halfway to the College's main entrance, she said, "You do know who Sergei Benitoff is, yes?"

Nysska had been preoccupied with a pain in her right ankle that flared with every step, and it took her a moment. "I know he's a nobleman. I know nothing of him personally."

Cam stopped outside the College's front door, pitching her voice low enough so that only Nysska could hear. "'Nobleman' doesn't even come close. He's a royal. A genuine High Family royal from Caulspring."

"You're saying he's the kind of person we won't be allowed to touch."

Cam sucked her teeth for a second. "We'll see." She pulled the heavy door open.

Raoul appeared to have been pacing back and forth across Olkoff's outer room long enough to work himself into a lather. As soon as the door opened he rushed to Cam, and Nysska thought it must have taken every ounce of willpower he had not to sweep her up in his arms. Instead, he put his hands on her shoulders. "Where did you go?" He lifted his eyes to Nysska, and they widened as he took in her bloodied, battered state. "What the fuck happened?"

Nysska let her perforated, blood-soaked armor hit the floor with a sodden thud and slumped onto one of the couches. She had shrugged back into the remnants of her Imperial-issue shirt so as not to be arrested for public nudity, but she didn't think the ripped and bloodied garment covered much more than Cam's makeshift bandages did. Flax immediately jumped into her lap, gave her face a rough, thorough licking, and settled down against her in a huge, loudly purring pile. Nysska stroked the lynx while she related to Raoul and Percy where she'd been and what had taken place.

Percy peered closely enough at her to make her uncomfortable. "It's hard to see wounds on your skin, huh?"

Nysska made a small, dismissive gesture with one hand. "I'm fine. Everything's scabbing over. It all itches more than hurts now."

"Wait," Raoul said, brow furrowing. "How many men were a part of this ambush?"

Cam had her eyes closed, but Nysska felt as if the Sensor was giving her a pointed look nonetheless. Nysska said, "I don't know. It was dark. But the men who ambushed me were part of the same group as the ones we found in the mine lair. Commander, we have stumbled upon something..."

As Nysska groped for the right word, Percy said, "Something fucking immense."

Raoul groaned. He rubbed his hands over his scalp and adjusted his commander's band. "I wasn't trained for this. *No one* is trained for this. Some kind of, of, of what? Cabal? How could any group of criminals be this *bold*?"

Cam had taken a seat on the couch opposite Nysska. She drummed her fingers on the armrest. "The prisoner told us how. Benitoff. Someone in a position of power and wealth, who's given them the freedom to do...whatever it is they're doing. However they're doing it."

Raoul sat down beside Cam but didn't touch or look at her. He slumped forward, staring at the rug-covered floor. "We have to report this. All of it. It's too big. We don't have the authority to handle it on our own."

Percy hooked a thumb at the closed doors to the bedroom. "So what do we do with Happy Fuck-Knuckle in there? Turn him over to the Taurus Hill guards?"

Raoul looked up. Nysska could tell from his expression that he'd come to the same conclusion she had. "No. The guards might be involved. We need to bring him with us...and hope Imperial bronze is still enough to let us get out of Taurus Hill alive."

Percy frowned at Raoul. "Bring him with us? Where are we going?"

Nysska said, "Tember. There's only one person we can talk to about this."

Cam nodded. "Governor Anwar."

Jax had climbed up into Percy's arms, and Percy held the big cat up and looked into his eyes. "All right. What the fuck do we do if Anwar's a part of this, too, then?"

No one said anything. Nysska knew the answer, though.

If Anwar was involved, they were most likely all going to die.

Nysska smelled the familiar wood smoke of Tember long before they could see the city.

The Ninth Crucible had ridden out of Taurus Hill without incident, unless one counted the even more determined than usual fashion in which the townsfolk refused to look at Nysska. To her delight, she had been reunited with the last mount she had named "Horse," and had spent several minutes petting her and scratching her neck and enjoying the softness of her nose. That made up for the binding, uncomfortable fit of the new armor she wore, courtesy of the Taurus Hill town guard. She had been assured, not convincingly, that the leather would stretch out once she'd worn it a while.

Now, as the sun was sliding just past its zenith, the bronze-clad soldiers attending Tember's northern gate snapped to attention at their approach and opened the way for them without a word. Nysska saw the soldiers eyeballing the bound, gagged, beaten-bloody prisoner in their midst, and wondered what kind of rumors his presence might spread.

Nysska said goodbye to Horse as a boy led the animal off to the stables. She wondered what it would take to get the mare assigned to her permanently.

With Raoul in the lead, as usual, the team made their way to the Governor's Mansion, the prisoner stumbling along between Percy and Nysska. She could muster no sympathy for the man. Especially since they had been polite enough to give him water and food and allow for bodily functions along the way. Take off the shackles and the gag, and his journey would have been no different from theirs.

Governor Anwar did not come to meet them this time. Instead, a slender young man in livery opened the door to the Mansion for them and led them to the parlor with the see-through fireplace. Anwar was there, waiting for them, seated in an overstuffed chair and scowling as he read an official report of some stripe, but as soon as the Ninth Crucible filed in he laid the papers down and stood to greet them.

"Gentlemen. Ladies. Who's that rather worse-for-wear chap you've brought with you?"

Raoul had the prisoner's collar gripped in one fist. "Begging your pardon, Governor, but is there somewhere secure this 'chap' might be held while we speak?"

Anwar gave the group a grin with very little humor in it. "Well, this wouldn't be an Imperial establishment without such a place, would it?" He gestured to the servant, who'd been hovering in the doorway. "Jan. Escort this prisoner downstairs, would you? Make sure he's safe and secure."

Jan inclined his head in assent. Nysska thought about objecting to a house servant handling a potentially dangerous prisoner, until the Jan produced a knife as long as his forearm, slipped up behind the prisoner, and let the tip rest against the man's Adam's apple. "Come along, now," Jan said. "Let's not make a fuss."

The prisoner whimpered—he'd been the very picture of cooperation since the talk he'd had with Nysska—and placidly left the room with Jan.

Anwar gestured at the chairs and couches placed around the parlor. "Please, all of you, have a seat. I've been anxious to hear who might have been so bold as to kill an Imperial College runemaster in his own laboratory."

A near-palpable silence fell across the room. Anwar's eyebrows raised, then raised further when no one spoke.

Raoul cleared his throat. "My apologies, sir, I've been trying to decide on the best way to present this information, and I've come to the sorry conclusion that there is no best way. We still don't know who killed Olkoff."

Anwar's eyebrows hadn't stopped rising, and now threatened to disappear into the mop of black hair on his head. He didn't look angry. More like he was simply trying to process that information.

"I...did not think...forgive me, Commander, but how is that possible? Murderers are caught. Murderers are *always* caught." While Raoul struggled to find a way to explain, Anwar went on. "Even when someone dies of poison, or an assassin's arrow, a Sensor always finds a trace. I've seen it myself. Someone sabotaged my father's saddle, intending him to fall and break his neck, and a visual Sensor—very like you, Cam—*saw* the hands that had done the tampering and pointed the tracking animals straight to the culprit." He leaned forward, earnest eyes fixed on Cam. "Has there been some kind of problem, Miss Delakroy?"

Cam's lower lip trembled. Just once, but Nysska saw it, and so did Anwar.

Nysska said, "We encountered something, Governor—some kind of external factor—that interfered with the Crucible's normal function."

Anwar blinked. "You're going to have to elaborate on that."

Cam cleared her throat. "I couldn't see Olkoff's killer, sir. My runes work just fine—I tracked down another killer shortly after that —but something about Olkoff's death kept me from...from doing my job. Sir."

Anwar sat back in his chair, frowning. "Well. That's disturbing. The law dictates that such an incident be reported to Caulspring." Reading the expressions on everyone's faces, he turned his palms up in a *What can I do?* gesture. "People more important than a territorial pro-tem governor are meant to handle situations like this."

Raoul took a deep breath. "I'm afraid it's more complicated than that, sir."

"Oh?"

Over the next fifteen minutes, Raoul explained everything that had happened. How Cam was unable to see the perpetrator and suffered a reaction as if a trap had been laid for her—but also how she was able to see clearly who had killed the prostitute called Irene. How the team had searched Naveed Olkoff's quarters and found the evidence that had led to Irene in the first place. How pursuing Irene's killer had taken them out of the city and into the Burr and down into the tunnels and chambers beneath the mountain.

Raoul described the men they had encountered there, and—in as detached and neutral a fashion as he could manage—related how Nysska had seen their leader's face transform.

Anwar's entire body seemed to clench at that last part. He made Raoul go back over it several times, and finally turned to Nysska.

"You say he actually changed the shape of his face?"

Nysska kept her voice steady. "No—I'm saying the color of his skin changed. Precisely enough, and convincingly enough, that I mistook him for Raoul."

Anwar shifted in his seat, and then shifted again. "Sorry, that's—I—you realize, the implications of that are *profound*."

A low murmur around the group let him know that they were well aware.

Continuing, Raoul related how they had taken the one surviving member of the cave-dwelling criminals back to the College and questioned him. "Eventually Enforcer Stonegate was able to persuade him to open up. And he gave us a name."

Anwar looked as if he had a thousand more questions, but wrestled them down to one with some effort. "What name was that, then?"

"Before we tell you," Nysska said, prompting a brief but potent glare from Raoul, "you should know what happened subsequent to that interrogation. I felt the need for some fresh air and went for a walk in the city. I believed by wearing a hood, a face scarf, and my cloak that I would be concealed enough. I was badly mistaken, because a number of young men took me off-guard and shoved me down a shaft to a place underground. I there encountered another man in the same kind of armor that we saw on the one whose skin changed. He said that it was a two birds, one stone situation—that preventing me from sticking my nose where it doesn't belong went hand in hand with killing a demon—and he and a group of men set upon me."

Cam spoke up. "Governor, we have never encountered this before. This many people, flouting the law in an Empire town."

Nysska watched as gears turned in Anwar's head. The man might have been young, but he was far from stupid. "Such activity would imply the existence of a patron, or patrons. Correct? I can see by your faces that you've all come to the same conclusion."

Raoul dropped his voice. "The prisoner confirmed it, sir. It's Sergei Benitoff."

Percy said, "The rich cunt's bankrolling the whole thing. Offering these fuckers protection."

Before Anwar could react—beyond a small, sharp gasp—a voice rang out from the other side of the fireplace. Nysska watched Anwar's face fall at the sound of it. "My mother always told me filthy language implies a hampered mind."

Nysska heard the creak of leather as someone stood up from a chair. Around the fireplace walked the single most beautiful human girl Nysska had ever seen. She put the young woman's age somewhere between fourteen and seventeen, and...she seemed to be made of gold. Long, thick, golden hair fell in loose waves past her shoulders. Her golden skin gleamed with the kind of unblemished youthful perfection that denied even the possibility of lines or wrinkles. The only thing about her that wasn't gold was her eyes, her enormous, sapphire eyes, that caught a ray of sunshine from a high window and glittered like bits of priceless jewelry.

The girl wore a simple white frock that might have been shapeless and unappealing on anyone else, but which fit the long, slender, gentle curves of her body flawlessly. No doubt it had been tailored for her. Those enchanting blue eyes swept across the assembled faces and lit upon Nysska. As if no one else were in the room at all, she came straight to the chair where Nysska sat, circled around behind it, and began stroking Nysska's hair as if it were the most natural thing in the world to do.

"Amazing," the girl said, in a voice so clear and pure and simple that Nysska immediately wondered if she had some sort of problem with her mental faculties. "I had heard demon hair was quite something to behold, but this is beyond words! So silky—and the *blue*! I've never seen anything like it! You must tell me, is it natural? Or is this some wondrous kind of dye?"

Nysska looked to Anwar for guidance, but the expression on his face conveyed helplessness and little else. Raoul and Percy both seemed dumbstruck as they stared at the girl. Cam's rings clicked furiously.

Slowly, as if dealing with some kind of forest creature, Nysska stood and turned to face the girl made of gold and sapphires. She towered over her, and yet the girl only gazed up at her, unafraid. Open. Simple. "I am not a demon," Nysska said, in as even a tone as she could manage. "My name is Nysska Stonegate. I am a sethyd. Who might you be?"

The girl's wide eyes clouded, cooling. She wandered away, approaching a small table beneath a window, and picked up a hand mirror. "Let me know when you're done talking," she said, apparently to Anwar. "I find all this *dreadfully* boring." Staring into the mirror, the girl primped and patted her hair, and drifted to the door. "Time for a nap, I think," she said, as if talking to herself, and left the parlor.

The members of the Ninth Crucible turned to Governor Anwar, who stood as soon as the door latched. "That is Galena Vachs. Fresh from Caulspring. You may recall that my position here is Governor *Pro-Tempore*, yes? Well, in three months Galena will turn eighteen. At that point she will take over my position."

Raoul's jaw fell open. Percy snorted, and started laughing. Cam seemed to have withdrawn into herself completely. Nysska said, "So… we'll be taking orders from her?"

Anwar's mouth curled sourly. "Everyone in the Green Needles Territory will."

12

After asking the members of the Ninth Crucible whether they had eaten recently, at which point Percy's stomach growled loudly enough to make Flax jump out of his lap and race across the room, Governor Anwar had some of his household staff bring in one big platter piled with meat and cheese and bread, another covered with carefully sliced carrots and ears of boiled corn, and three pitchers filled with strong, dark beer. He discussed the matter of Sergei Benitoff with them as they ate.

After listening for some time, Nysska said, "Please forgive my ignorance, as we do not have this 'royalty' among my people. Is it against the law to punish someone like Benitoff when they commit a crime?"

Percy talked with his mouth full, but she understood him well enough. "Might as fucking well be."

Anwar swallowed hastily, tried to say something, but had to take a swig of beer to wash the food all the way down. Everyone waited for him. "It's not a matter of written laws protecting people like Benitoff," he finally managed. "It's just that his family is...well...you could say monstrously wealthy. They've been that wealthy for as long as anyone can remember, and they hold sway over decisions made. Not just here in Green Needles. Empire-wide."

Nysska slowly chewed a bite. "Exactly how much sway?"

Cam said, "*All* of it. Their word is essentially law. As Percy so eloquently pointed out."

Percy said, "Fucking straight, I did."

Anwar took another swig and dabbed at the corners of his mouth with a linen napkin. "At the same time, Sergei has been working on a reputation, at least here in Tember, for years now. Gambling. Whoring. Drinks himself into a stupor and beats girls until they can't work anymore. Everyone knows about it. Even he's acknowledged he can let things get out of hand, which is why he pays double or triple every time he sends for a girl."

Raoul spoke while scowling down at the beer glass in his hand. "My father served with Sergei's father. Anatoly Benitoff loves his son more than he loves breathing. There's no way he'll let anything happen to him."

Cam had tilted her head toward Raoul. "Benitoff's father was in the Thaumetallicon?"

Raoul shook his head. "Regular Cathedral army. But he had contacts everywhere. To hear my father say it, Anatoly Benitoff had all the wealth and privilege, yes, but he put in the effort, every day in the service. Rose through the ranks the same way anyone else would have. Good man, smart man, knew what he was doing."

Nysska lowered the piece of ham she'd been about to bite into. "And did his son serve as well?"

"No." Raoul lifted his head and looked her straight in the eye, and for the first time since she'd been introduced to him, she saw no malice or scorn or contempt there. Only worry. "So, in a lot of people's minds, that makes you a better citizen of the Empire than Sergei Benitoff." He pushed a carrot stick around on the edge of his plate with one finger. "And yet we can't let this rest. We've still got to find out who killed Naveed Olkoff. And that leads us straight to Sergei." Raoul shifted his gaze to Anwar.

The governor sighed. "You don't figure out who did the killing, and the Cathedral top dogs in Caulspring hang my ass on a fork. You go after Sergei Benitoff, and…they probably still hang my ass on a fork. Even if you've got him cold, with evidence, zero question about any of it—it still means, at the very least, the end of my political career." He rubbed the bridge of his nose with his eyes closed, and in that moment Nysska imagined she could see Wendell Anwar shrugging off an unseen burden—stepping out from under a constant, oppressive weight. When he opened them again, his clear brown eyes flashed with new determination. "But you know what? Fuck it. Fuck all of it. Fuck whatever prevented a Sensor from seeing who did it, and fuck whoever killed that poor girl in the brothel, and fuck Sergei Benitoff. I'll be out of a job as soon as Galena comes of age anyway. If the last thing I do before my own family exiles me to some scorpion-infested corner of nowhere is bring down a smug asshole like Sergei, then so be it. I'll take full responsibility." He drained the rest of his beer and slammed the glass down on the table. "Go do your jobs."

Percy grinned as widely as his narrow face would allow, and Cam allowed herself a small, discreet smile. Raoul hadn't moved, though, and just stared at his plate of mostly uneaten food. Anwar said, "Commander Cullen? Further thoughts?"

Raoul shrugged. "I'll be hearing from my father about it. One way or another. Probably sooner than later." He slowly stood, pushing his chair back, and lifted his glass. "Here's to career suicide."

No one else raised their glass to that toast. Raoul didn't seem to care. He drained his beer faster than Anwar had.

When Percy, the blood lynxes right on his heels—though moving a bit more sluggishly than usual, as Percy had been feeding them a steady stream of table scraps—opened the door to the hallway, he jumped back and yelped. Galena stood right there in the doorway, one hand raised to knock. Percy got out of the way as she traipsed into the parlor.

"Wendell, I am still *terribly* bored. Are there any respectable dressmakers in this Dragon-forsaken town? Perhaps replenishing my wardrobe will stave off this horrid lull."

The Ninth Crucible filed out of the office, leaving the governor in deep discussion over dress fabrics. Nysska let her eyes linger on the golden young woman. The sheer pressure of the gaze would have been enough for most people to realize they were being watched. Galena Vachs seemed not to notice at all.

The road to Sergei Benitoff's private estate branched off the eastern highway into Tember and wound its way into a canyon. Nysska kept an eye on the rock walls on either side of them as they grew higher and higher, blocking the sun and casting the way into shadow. At one of the canyon's narrower points, a high wall of stone blocks barred their progress, a massive gate of wood and black-painted bronze in its center. Men with crossbows peered down from the wall's battlements.

Raoul raised a hand and brought the team to a halt. "Estate of Sergei Benitoff!" he called out, sounding as though he was putting every bit of authority into his voice he could muster. "I am Commander Raoul Cullen of the Ninth Crucible! We demand an audience with Lord Benitoff!"

"Why don't you turn your ass around and go back where you belong," one of the men on the wall shouted in response. "Lord Benitoff is not receiving visitors."

Nysska had been mistaken—that was simply Raoul getting warmed up. When he spoke again, the volume and authority in his words rang off the canyon walls with the clarity and power of a church bell. "By the power vested in me as an agent of the Valconian Empire, either open that gate and grant us access to the grounds and personnel beyond, or face deployment of the Argonium Infantry!"

She couldn't be sure, but Nysska thought some of the paler faces on top of the wall turned a sudden greenish shade.

The man who had shouted before did it again. "You don't have that kind of authority!"

Raoul kept up the intensity as his voice boomed back. "Governor Wendell Anwar of the Green Needles Territory knows of our mission here today and has already approved deployment in the event that we face the kind of resistance you currently present! Now *open that fucking gate!*"

One by one, the crossbows withdrew, and seconds later the massive gate swung open on shrieking hinges.

The road changed on the other side of the wall, from hard-packed dirt to a broad gravel lane bordered by stone blocks on both sides. The horses' hooves *crunch-crunch*ed as they made their way up to what looked, at first glance, like a smaller version of the Governor's Mansion. Nysska wondered if the same architect had designed them both or if this was some kind of conscious imitation. More men with crossbows watched them from the grounds as they approached. A man with one eye came out to greet them, and offered to take their horses to a stable, but Raoul refused.

"Our horses know when to stay if we tell them to stay," he said as he dismounted. "And they'll stay right here, outside the door, until we're ready to leave."

The one-eyed man grumbled. "Don't expect us to feed 'em or nothing, then."

"Rest assured," Raoul shot back. "We expect nothing from any of you."

A servant opened the grand wooden door, and Raoul led the way inside.

The interior of the place looked nothing like the governor's mansion. Rather than the foyer and hallway leading to various parlors and offices and bedrooms, the ground floor of Sergei Benitoff's house —*if one could call such a place a house,* Nysska thought—was a single massive room dotted with long, low couches and small, squat tables. Rugs and animal hides covered almost everything, save one large, central area of bare stone floor. At the far end of the room, a beautifully ornate bar held countless bottles filled with clear and amber liquids, and next to the bar stood an immense round bed.

Cam's rings had been clicking since the moment they stepped into the place, and she spoke to Nysska, frowning. "Am I getting this right? Is it like…what *is* this place like?"

Nysska glanced at Raoul, who simply stood, staring around him, scowling. To Cam, she said, "It appears to be a place meant for regular festivities."

Percy had been eyeballing the bar, and grinned at Cam and Nysska. "She means it's for drinking and fucking." He cracked his knuckles as Flax and Jax wandered around the room's perimeter, sniffing things furiously. Both cats' jaws hung open. Percy said, "I'd wager the best-looking young lasses from Tember have an open invite to this place."

On the other side of the bar from the giant round bed—to which Nysska decided not to get any closer than she could manage—a pair of wooden double doors swung open, and Sergei Benitoff strode out. Nysska had never seen him before, but she could think of no one else in this place who could have that much swagger while dressed in brilliant scarlet silk pants and an emerald-green dressing gown. Benitoff held a glass in one hand. Three people had come through the double doors with him: two women who fit the "best-looking in Tember" description, and a hulking bear of a man with a bald head and a dense, curly black beard that hung down to his chest.

Benitoff himself, aside from the cocky swagger and the conspicuous wealth, wasn't much to look at, Nysska thought. His brown skin, brown hair, and brown eyes were all the color of mud puddles, and even if he'd grown a beard to rival his associate's, she didn't think it could've hidden his weak chin. He held out the hand clutching the glass, and one of the women rushed to his side with a bottle to fill it.

"Well, would you look at this!" Benitoff said. His voice was high-pitched and scratchy, as if he'd been shouting for a long time and strained his vocal cords. "I don't believe I've ever had the pleasure of entertaining a Dragon's-honest-truth Crucible in my home before. Please, everyone, make yourselves comfortable! Have a seat! What would you like to drink? You name it, I bet I have it." He gestured to the two young women—one with long dark hair, the other with short dark hair. Both of them wore what might have been considered sleeping attire, if one were trying to sleep in a tropical climate. "Shella, Garnet, see to our guests' needs, there's a couple of good girls, yeah?"

The young women approached, but as Raoul waved them away, Nysska shifted her attention to the bearded giant. He stood like a statue, thick arms folded across his chest, muscles unmistakable under the long-sleeved black shirt and gray trousers and boots—and he had somehow changed position from near the door to about two meters behind and to one side of Benitoff without Nysska noticing. That piqued her interest. Rarely had she encountered someone of that size who could move with that kind of grace.

"We're not here to socialize, Lord Benitoff," Raoul said. "We need to talk to you about a Cathedral matter. In private, if you don't mind."

Benitoff sat down on the plush couch nearest the bar. He made a show of taking his time, sipping his drink as his eyes crawled across the members of the Ninth Crucible. Nysska felt them settle on her, but Benitoff's expression never changed. She couldn't decide if he looked more bemused or smug.

"Let's call it semi-private," he finally said. "Girls, you can go wait for me in my bedroom. I won't be long."

Cam's rings clicked. Out of the side her mouth, she murmured, "This isn't his bedroom? That *is* a giant bed over there, isn't it?"

Nysska murmured back, "You can't see me shrugging, but I'm shrugging."

Benitoff beckoned them closer. "Come on, come on, if you're not going to relax, at least don't make me shout."

Nysska brought up the rear as Percy and Cam followed Raoul across the enormous room, until they stood a couple meters in front of Benitoff. The bearded giant still loomed behind him. Nysska put him at a couple of centims taller than she was, which made him one of the biggest humans she'd ever seen. Benitoff had caught sight of Flax and Jax prowling around the room, and his eyes glittered in a way that made Nysska's skin crawl.

"All right. Anything you want to say to me, there's no reason Darlo can't hear it as well."

The giant—presumably that was Darlo—didn't move. Nysska could barely even see him breathe. Raoul said, "Lord Benitoff, you have been named a citizen of interest in a Thaumetallicon investigation. I'm going to need to know where you were on the sixth of this month, as well as two nights ago."

Benitoff smiled and settled back farther into the couch's pillows.

He sipped his drink as he rested one ankle on the opposite knee. "Well, now, this should be the easiest investigation you've ever had to conduct, Commander. I haven't left these premises in the last ten days."

Raoul dipped his head. "All right. Then please explain to us how you know the Imperial College runemaster Naveed Olkoff, as well as the prostitute Irene Jasinsky."

Benitoff's smile slowly faded. It looked as if he were consciously turning it down, degree by degree, and as it left his face, his eyes narrowed. "No, no, no, no, no. This isn't how the Thaumetallicon does its business, Commander Cullen. Maybe you've forgotten? See, it works like this: someone commits a crime—that is, someone commits a crime the Cathedral gives a fuck about—your people go out, find the criminal just *immediately*, chop his or her head off, and everyone's home for dinner. You don't spend your days riding around *talking* to people." He set his drink down on a nearby table. "Would you like to know what I think, Commander?" Benitoff still addressed Raoul, but his attention slid over to Nysska and stayed there. "I think you don't know what you're doing. Come in here, acting all official, got your chest puffed out, when you're making every bit of this up as you go along. That just *fascinates* me. What could have thrown one of the Thaumetallicon's oh-so-high-and-mighty Crucibles off its game so badly?"

Raoul's words came out brittle. "Are you refusing to answer our questions, Lord Benitoff?"

Nysska didn't blink, no matter how long Benitoff stared at her—though, as the seconds dragged past, she began to think she might have underestimated him. Under that debauched façade lurked something more than just the demands of the id.

Benitoff said, "I know your father, Commander Raoul Cullen. Were you aware of that? Many a time I accompanied my own father when he joined yours on hunting expeditions. Good old Boris. You were off being the ambitious son, working hard, rising through the ranks, doing your best to make your father proud. And yet who sat around campfires with him, listening to his stories? Who got to ask him for all kinds of advice? That would be me. Yours Truly. Quite the rapport he and I formed."

Raoul had begun, very slightly, almost beneath notice, to tremble. "Lord Sergei Benitoff, you are to accompany me to the Governor's Mansion forthwith for further questioning."

Benitoff made a tiny motion with his left hand. It might have been nothing—a fidget, a mere tic—and Nysska would have dismissed it as such, had not the dozen men in chain mail, every one of them holding a loaded crossbow, come pouring through the double doors. They fanned out, staying along the far wall, and though they weren't pointing the weapons directly at the team, the threat could not have been clearer.

Percy made a soft kissing sound. Flax and Jax trotted across the floor and sat on either side of him.

Sergei Benitoff leaned forward on the couch, dividing his attention between the blood lynxes and Nysska, but still pitched his words to Raoul. "I must say, Commander, yours is the most interesting Crucible I have ever seen. I know your Sensor has the runes, but seraphic tracking animals? And then a *demon* on top of everything else?" His eyes flicked up to Percy. "You know how much it would be worth to crack those cats' skulls open and dig out the shine? I have friends who'd give you a pretty penny for the privilege."

Jax and Flax both started growling.

Raoul said, "Lord Benitoff, you are interfering with a Cathedral investigation. That in itself is enough to take you in."

"As if you've got any fucking evidence," Benitoff snapped, looking annoyed for the first time. "You say I've got something to do with all this bullshit, you come into my home and harass me with it, I say it's *your* hide that'll get the caning. At least. So get out."

A silence fell across the room. Thick. Oppressive.

Benitoff frowned. "Am I stuttering? Take your asses out the door! Go!"

No one moved.

Raoul took a deep breath...the crossbowmen's grips on their weapons tightened...and Benitoff said, "All right, all right, wait. Wait. You don't want to leave? Then I've got a *splendid* idea. Rather than have my men turn you all into pincushions—what if we place a little wager?"

Raoul glanced over his shoulder at the rest of his team, just for a second. "What are you talking about?"

Benitoff had lost the annoyance, but the glitter in his eyes had returned. He grabbed up his drink, drained it, and threw the glass carelessly over his shoulder. It smashed against the wall behind the bar. "Yes—*yes*—this is brilliant! I've always wanted to see a demon fight!"

Raoul said, "No, no, whatever you're—" but Benitoff talked over him.

"If your Enforcer—she *is* your Enforcer, yes? If your demon back there can take out my bodyguard, one on one, then what the hell, sure, I'll go with you and answer your questions. And if she loses...well, that'll just give me all sorts of valuable information, won't it?"

Raoul was shaking his head and waving both hands, all emphatically in the negative. "Forget it. That's the most ridiculous suggestion I've ever heard. You can't just sit there and dictate what—"

This time Nysska broke in. "I'll do it."

Raoul, Percy, and Cam all rounded on her. Jax stayed where he was, but Flax came and started winding around Nysska's ankles and purring. Raoul spoke through gritted teeth. "No. Absolutely not. Private citizens don't dictate to the Cathedral! *We* are the authority here!"

Speaking just loud enough for the rest of the team to hear him, Percy said, "Isn't that exactly what we said the royals do, though? Dictate shit?"

Cam's rings had been clicking, but she let them fall silent. "I don't like this any more than you do, Raoul, at least on a policy level. But if Nysska fighting one man is going to get this case solved, and she's good with it, I say let's take the quick way out."

Nysska gently bumped Cam's shoulder with her elbow. "You're certainly willing to let me enter the fray, aren't you?"

Cam's mouth crimped. Pertly, she said, "I've seen you fight."

Raoul might have been on the verge of hyperventilating. He said, "I hate this. I *hate* this. The very thought of it makes my stomach cramp."

Percy inclined his head toward the crossbowmen. "Another thing to consider. If this fucking asshole is as connected as we think he is, Nysska could win the fight, and he'd still turn us into pincushions. And it's his fucking word against ours, with him swearing we never even made it here today. Or that we came in and attacked him, and he only gave the order to defend himself."

Nysska raked her eyes up and down Darlo. Skin several shades darker than Benitoff's. Green eyes—unusual, but not unheard-of among humans. "Benitoff's man is big, and he moves well. But Benitoff is a gambler, correct? He won't go back on his word. Not when this many men are around to talk about it." She stepped out of their huddle and spoke to Benitoff directly. "I'll do it on one condition. No matter what happens, the rest of the team leaves unharmed."

Someone had brought Benitoff another drink. He raised it to Nysska in a mocking, one-sided toast. "Here's to favorable odds! Now, your little playmates need to clear out of the way—back against that wall, please. Kitty cats, too." He pointed at the roughly circular, six-meter-wide patch of bare floor in the middle of the room. "You two can mix it up right there."

Slowly, with visible reluctance, Raoul and Percy and the two blood lynxes moved to the far wall. Cam came over and, to Nysska's astonishment, took both of Nysska's hands in hers. "Listen. Maybe you shouldn't do this after all."

Nysska tilted her head down to get it closer to Cam's ear. "You said you'd seen me fight."

"And I have—but you're also still beat to hell. I shouldn't have encouraged this."

Nysska squeezed her hands gently. "As you said. It's one man. The fight's all but over already. Now go—please. I don't want to swing at him and hit you by mistake."

Her face clouded, Cam clicked her rings and made her way over to stand between Raoul and Percy. Nysska turned to Benitoff and saw that Darlo had come to the edge of the patch of bare floor. She said, "Weapons? No weapons?"

Darlo still hadn't spoken and gave no indication that he would.

Benitoff waved a dismissive hand. "Darlo clearly isn't armed, so it would hardly be fair if you were."

Nysska unbuckled her sword belt. "Rules?"

"Hmmm." Benitoff tapped his chin. "How about, the one who can still walk off the dance floor wins?"

"Is there a signal for when to start?"

"Yes," Benitoff said, and Darlo snapped across the floor like a striking viper. Nysska saw the punch coming, *barely*, and moved to avoid it, so that instead of connecting with her chin Darlo's fist clipped her shoulder.

The impact slammed Nysska sideways, knocked her off her feet, and her shoulders and the back of her head crashed into the bare stone. Agony shot through her skull, and she felt half a dozen of the lacerations from the ambush pop back open. Darlo's boot filled her field of vision, and she jerked to one side, rolling out of the way as he brought down a stomp where her face had been. The vibration of the blow rattled her bones.

Nysska rolled over backward and came up to her feet, breathing hard, blinking, and Darlo turned to face her. Not advancing now. Circling. Stalking.

Benitoff laughed with the joy of a child and clapped his hands.

Through the ringing in her ears, Nysska heard Percy say, "What the fuck was that? How'd he hit her that hard?" She didn't have to wait long for an answer. Darlo rolled up one sleeve, then the other, revealing the long, deadly, silver-glimmering runes under the skin of his forearms.

Raoul bulled across the floor, waving his arms at Benitoff. "No! You can't do this! We never agreed to this!"

Benitoff lost the laughter and speared Raoul with a glare. "The agreement was that your demon had to beat my bodyguard. There were no specifics beyond that."

Nysska couldn't pay attention to anything else as Darlo lunged at her again. She slipped to one side, avoided his looping roundhouse punch entirely, but wasn't prepared for him to spin nimbly in place, and though she got her arms up in time to block, the back-fist strike smashed into her and sent her flying. Nysska crashed into a couch, flipped toes-over-temples, and landed on one shoulder and the side of her head. She surged back to her feet, the room spinning around her, but Darlo remained on the dance floor. Waiting.

His face had yet to change expression, but he beckoned to her with one hand.

Nysska took a few seconds to catch her breath and think. She'd seen runes like his before, in exactly one place: the Argonium Infantry. She had never heard of an Infantry soldier serving as anyone's private bodyguard, but even if that were common practice, she couldn't imagine that such a soldier would *ever* use his or her runes out of uniform. And yet Darlo stood before her, dressed like any other civilian, with the strength of a wild horse running through him.

That's what his blows felt like, Nysska decided. Being kicked by a horse. Or getting struck by that damn warhammer from the ambush. She came around the couch but stopped at the edge of the dance floor.

"Now now," Benitoff said, "no delays. Get back to it or consider our deal null and void."

Nysska racked her brain, trying to remember anything and everything she could about the Argonium Infantry. She'd seen them take out the tarn at the bridge...how long ago was that? It felt like a lifetime, but she knew it had only been a couple of days. The Infantry represented the Thaumetallicon's elite fighters, in the same way that Crucibles represented its elite investigators. Imbued with far greater than normal human strength, drilled in the fiercest, most efficient fighting techniques.

Human fighting techniques.

Human.

Nysska stepped onto the dance floor and said, *"Mi pasigis tro multe da tempo for de hejmo."*

Darlo frowned. Benitoff leaned forward and shouted, "The fuck did you just say?"

Nysska closed on Darlo. He came at her with another fist like a sledgehammer, which she slipped, but instead of pushing him away, or getting out of reach, or bringing a knee up into his midsection, or even trying to snap his arm—all of which she could have done—

Nysska grabbed double handfuls of his shirt, lowered her head, and pulled herself straight into him—

So that her right horn drove into the side of his neck.

Someone gasped. Maybe Cam.

Benitoff screamed, and Darlo fought her, slammed his elbow into her, but Nysska held on long enough to twist her head, gouging her horn deeper into the wound before she sprang away from him.

Darlo kept his feet, but his face had gone blank. Great gouts of blood sprayed from the ragged wound in time with his rapid heartbeat, and he sank to his knees. One hand lifted, drifting toward the hole from which his lifeblood pumped, but it had no strength and dropped to his side.

Darlo collapsed onto the stone. Nysska stood, watching, as the rhythmic spray from his mortal wound slowed and stopped. She turned to Sergei Benitoff, and a flick of her head sent drops of Darlo's blood spattering across his face.

Benitoff had lost every bit of cocky swagger. The look he gave her now, Nysska had seen before, in other places. That distillation of fear and horror—as though she were an actual, genuine, mythological demon.

On some humans, that look prompted them to take up arms and light torches and attempt to vanquish what they perceived as an unholy, otherworldly threat. Benitoff was not a human like that. He sat there, his drink forgotten, his jaw slack, and when she spoke to him, she knew he would do exactly as he was told.

"Send your men away."

The lord of the manor needed no further prompting. He twisted in his seat and gestured emphatically at the crossbowmen, who all but stampeded to get back through the double doors. The last one closed and latched the doors behind him.

Percy and Cam were at her side in a heartbeat, Percy congratulating her on being such a fucking beast of a fighter, Cam making sympathetic noises as she tried to mop away the worst of Nysska's blood with what looked like a bar towel.

Nysska paid them very little attention. She was focused on Raoul and Benitoff, as Raoul hauled Benitoff up off the couch by one arm. "Here's to favorable odds," Raoul said. "You're coming with us."

"What was that?" Cam asked, close to Nysska's ear.

Nysska lowered her head. "What was what?"

"You said something. Right before you killed him. What was it?"

Nysska blinked. "Oh—I said, *I have spent too much time away from home.*"

13

Raoul allowed Sergei Benitoff to ride his own horse on the short trip back to Tember, but Imperial shackles bound his hands. Several times during the ride, Benitoff seemed on the verge of speaking, but each time appeared to think better of it. Nysska paid him little attention—she was much more concerned with making sure her bandages stayed as snug as possible. It felt as if every cut she'd sustained in the ambush had split wide open. Plus, her ribs were killing her, and she feared she might have one or two hairline fractures in her forearms.

Nysska rode at the back of the group. She only caught a few glimpses of Raoul's face, and only in profile, so she couldn't really tell what he was thinking. His usual scowl seemed stapled to his face. Percy kept his eye on Flax and Jax, who crept along through the underbrush beside the trail as usual. Cam said nothing. She didn't even click her rings.

Once they reached the city, it became obvious that, somehow, word of Benitoff's arrest had preceded them. Gone was the deference to the bronze, along with the fearful, sidelong glances at the strange demon woman. The citizenry still kept their distance, and got the hell out of the way as they passed through the gate and set hooves on the main road to the Governor's Mansion, but now the people openly stared.

Nysska wondered if they were all thinking, *"Look at those fools who just signed their own death warrants."* She tried to make out the words as a wave of whispers washed over the city, but her ears still rang enough from landing on her head that she couldn't understand any of them.

Raoul waved away the young soldiers who offered to take their horses. He wanted to get their charge in front of Anwar as quickly as possible, so they rode straight to the wall around the Mansion. Raoul made sure Benitoff didn't fall as he dismounted, and simply ordered the gate guards to look after the horses. Neither guard looked happy about it, but neither complained.

The five of them, along with the two blood lynxes, marched straight to the Mansion's front door, the shackled nobleman in the center of the group, and Nysska thought she could see Raoul's lips moving, perhaps rehearsing what he planned to say to the governor. The front door swung open, revealing Wendell Anwar, as they had anticipated—and swung wider still, so that over Anwar's shoulder, everyone could see the tall, gaunt, gray-haired soldier with the deep-set eyes standing halfway down the hall.

Percy murmured, "Oh...Dragon fuck me."

Anwar had the look of a child whose best friend had just gotten caught breaking a rule. Nysska squinted, concentrating on the soldier, and realized he had the bronze bands of a general on the shoulders of his Imperial armor.

"Father," Raoul said, his voice close to breaking.

Cam whispered, *"Oh shit. Oh shit."*

They all watched as General Boris Cullen silently turned and walked away, down the hall and up the grand staircase and out of sight, leaving only Wendell Anwar.

Speaking as if the words were causing him actual physical pain, Anwar said, "Please remove Lord Benitoff's shackles."

Benitoff turned to face Raoul and held his hands up, his face split wide with an obscene grin, every bit of his bravado returned in full force. "What'd I tell you, little man? Your daddy's looking out for me."

Raoul's shoulders trembled, but he kept his words strong and calm. "Governor Anwar, we have taken this man into official custody. He is part of the investigation into the death of runemaster Naveed Olkoff. Removing his shackles would be against Thaumetallicon procedure."

Now a pair of servants appeared beside Anwar. The Governor said, "This decision came straight from Caulspring. Delivered by General Cullen himself. Benitoff is to be released at once."

Nysska watched as Raoul slowly, mechanically pulled the shackles' key from a pouch at his belt and unlocked the restraints. Benitoff's grin stayed in place as he rubbed his wrists. "I'm awfully tired from that ride, Wendell. You got a room where I could relax a bit? Maybe spend some time with a bit of female company?"

Anwar let his eyes close. "I'm sure that can be arranged. Zerri, will you show Lord Benitoff to the eastern suite?"

The servant—a sturdy woman in her late fifties—bowed her head. "Of course, Governor." She led the still-grinning Benitoff away, in the same direction General Cullen had headed.

Anwar spoke to the rest of the group but looked specifically at Nysska. "I'll have someone set the rest of you up with rooms. Nysska, do you require medical attention?"

Cam said, "She needs a fucking tailor to sew her skin back together," but Nysska put a calming hand on Cam's shoulder.

Raoul broke his silence, and now his voice did tremble as he spoke. "Governor, this is unacceptable. This is *criminal*. That man is in our custody! Why would Fath—why would Caulspring do this? Do they even know what's going on?"

Anwar let out a long, uneven exhale. "I am also obliged to ask the four of you to take rooms here."

Percy scoffed. "Why? Are *we* under arrest?"

The Governor shook his head, but to mean *I don't understand* rather than *I'm saying no*. "Until everything is sorted, just—at least let me make you comfortable. Take the rooms. Rest. Nysska, I'll have my physician come and see you. Trevor here will show you the way." The other servant, a gray-haired man with light brown skin, bowed his head to them.

Nysska felt stunned. More so than when she'd fallen down the shaft in the ambush. More so than when Darlo had thrown her onto her head. Every cut on her body burned, and in the face of this...she couldn't put a satisfactory word to it. Farce? Joke? Crime? In the face of this gross miscarriage of justice, she abruptly felt exhausted enough to sleep for days.

As the Ninth Crucible followed the servant Trevor into the Governor's Mansion, Nysska turned her head and, without meaning to, made eye contact with Raoul.

He looked hollow. As if someone had scooped out his soul and thrown it away. For the first time, Nysska thought she understood how he felt.

The shuffle of footsteps outside Nysska's door woke her a few seconds before the tentative knock. She rolled over in her bed—dragging the sheet with her in a few places where blood had seeped through her bandages and stuck to it—and focused on the space beneath the door to the hallway.

Anwar had put the Ninth Crucible in rooms in a wing of the Mansion she hadn't even realized was there. Aside from windows, each one featured an enormous domed skylight—and the one above Nysska's bed let in light from all three moons, filling the room with a cool blue radiance that seemed to creep into every corner.

Only one pair of feet cast shadows under the door. They looked small. Nysska said, "Cam?"

The door cracked open. "May I come in?"

Sitting up, Nysska wriggled and scooted until her back was to the headboard, the blood-stained sheets bunched around her. "Is something wrong?"

Cam slipped in and shut the door. Nysska would have been able to see her clearly in much dimmer illumination, but the treble moonlight surrounded the Sensor in a glow as she stood and clicked her rings, getting a feel for the room. "No. Not with me, I mean. I couldn't sleep, and I wanted to come and see if you were all right."

Nysska let a second or two pass before she said, "Really?"

Cam came to the foot of the bed. "Did the governor's physician treat you well enough?"

Nysska held up one arm. All of the lacerations she'd suffered that had come loose in the fight with Darlo had indeed been neatly stitched back together. "He stared a bit more than I would have preferred, but he had steady hands and was good with knots. I don't know that all of this was necessary. My people scab over quickly, as I've said before."

Cam hesitated. She had left her armor in her room, along with her boots, and now wore the standard Cathedral-issue trousers and the same kind of camisole that Nysska had given up on and thrown away. The moonlight seemed to cling to Cam's closely shorn scalp. It made Nysska think of a crown. Cam said, "May I sit?"

"Please."

As Cam settled onto the end of the bed, she said, "I keep going back to General Cullen, when we first arrived. The way he just stood there, and then walked off. Poor Raoul—if your own father won't even *speak* to you? It made my stomach drop into my toes."

Nysska folded her arms across the tops of her knees and rested her chin on her forearms, careful to avoid any bandages. "He did appear to be taking the situation hard."

"So now I can't help but think this whole case, everything we've tried to do, it's all about to turn to shit. I don't know what that will mean for me." She paused. "And I'm fucking terrified."

Nysska opened her mouth to speak—to give voice to the words that had been slamming around in her skull ever since the fiasco in Olkoff's laboratory. *Say it. Say it! Tell her!* The words were *right there*—but she stopped herself. Instead, she said, "How long has Raoul been in love with you?"

Cam turned her head sharply, her forehead creased. "Wow. Is it that obvious?"

"I've seen how capable you are. You ride better than Percy, and you filled your hands with bronze immediately when we fought those men in the lair. No hesitation. But to ask if it's obvious that Raoul would *die* for you?" She couldn't resist. "You'd have to be blind to miss it."

Cam's eyebrows shot up, and her mouth dropped open in comical outrage. "Oh, so now it's *make fun of the girl with the metal eyeballs,* is it?"

Even more drily, Nysska said, "So few humans appreciate sethyd humor."

Openly smiling now, Cam said, "Well, *you're* just a big, horn-having, smelly..." She trailed off and spread her hands. "I can't think of anything to compare you with." Then, softer: "And you smell pretty good, to be honest."

Realizing Cam couldn't see her smile made it easier to let it happen. Nysska truly could not remember the last time she had smiled unselfconsciously. "Do you feel the same way about him?"

Cam pursed her lips. "I feel...grateful. I'm grateful to him. He got me this position. The Thaumetallicon had already accepted me, but he's the one who got me into the Ninth Crucible. Otherwise, I might have been doing something completely different."

"Not everyone with runes works for the Empire?"

"No, they do, I just mean, maybe not as part of a Crucible. Sensors are really fucking good at locating the best spots to dig wells, for example. Some help build roads...others go into medicine. I'm doing what I wanted to be doing."

"How did you meet?"

"Part of the program. Soldiers training for assignment to the Thaumetallicon get paired up with someone learning to be a Sensor. You can say a lot of things about the Cathedral, but they've more or less mastered the efficiency of it all. Which is part of why Raoul has never said anything to me about how he feels. It's against policy for two members of a Crucible to be together. And, no joking, I think it might kill him to break the rules like that."

"So you've known Raoul for...how long? Years?"

Cam nodded. "Four and...a half. When we met. Then for the last four years it's been him and Percy, and Theo, and me. And the cats." Her face clouded. "Dragon's bones, I miss Theo. He was so kind, and so sweet to me. Made up for having to endure Raoul's more... hmm...*stringent* moments."

"I am sorry for your loss. Theobold sounds like a good man."

She nodded again. "The thing is...my grandmother took a long time to die. Most of a year. She had something wrong with her lungs, and the coughing just got worse and worse. Then she had a stroke, and it got *really* bad. But...all right, I never said this to my family, but her taking that long? It let us all say goodbye. Make our peace with it. She didn't leave a single bit of business unfinished when she finally died in her bed."

Nysska had picked up on the direction Cam was headed. "Theobold didn't go like that."

"Mmnnn...no. No, we were tracking down this idiot farm boy who'd been denied the hand of the girl he wanted to marry, so he'd killed the girl's father. The cats led us right to him, of course, but he put up a fight, and Theo had to take bronze to him." She swallowed hard and took a couple of deep breaths. "It was too much for his heart. He'd gotten too old. He was still strong as any bull you could pick, but...he fell down dead, right there at the scene. Nice and peaceful for him, honestly—one second in a good, straightforward fight, the next second, gone. No muss, no fuss." She lowered her head. "And it's been fucking *hell* on the rest of us. You know how much more I wanted to say to him? How much I wanted him to tell *me*? I loved him to pieces. Then he was just...gone. Lingering or sudden, I...can't decide which one's shittier."

Nysska didn't know what to do. She smoothed out a place beside her, but then took three tries to speak. "Would you—I don't mean to be—I'm not trying to be inappropriate. Would you like to come here? And sit with me? Just be aware, there are a few blood stains..."

Nysska couldn't read all the emotions that flitted across Cam's face. For a moment she thought Cam might jump up and run out of the room. Instead, after hesitating, Cam crawled up to the head of the bed and settled next to her, and Nysska's breath locked in her chest when Cam leaned her head on Nysska's shoulder.

Cam said, "The conversation sort of veered away from Raoul."

"You can talk about anything you'd like."

The words appeared again, right there in Nysska's mouth, right on the tip of her tongue. She bit them back.

"It's not really his fault," Cam said. "Raoul. Being the way he is. His father's one of the most powerful men in the Cathedral, which means he's one of the most powerful men in the Empire."

"The general seemed...unyielding."

Not very delicately, Cam snorted. "That's one way to put it. Another way would be that he's got a massive pole up his backside and held his son to an impossibly high standard ever since Raoul could walk. That's why Raoul is all *rules, orders, procedures* all the time. Twenty-eight years of trying to please a father who can't be pleased."

Nysska tried to think of a good response to that, and while she tried, a silence descended. Outside, a stiff wind blew, and the ceiling creaked and popped, and she almost yelped when Cam's hand touched hers. Nysska didn't resist as Cam lifted her hand, running her fingertips along the lines of the palm and the undersides of the fingers.

"Your hands are big. But not huge. They're smaller than my grandfather's hands." Cam's head still lay against Nysska's shoulder, and she snugged in tighter to Nysska's body. "Yet I've seen their strength. Are all...sethyds? *Seth ids*. Am I saying that correctly?"

"You are."

"Are you all that strong?"

The words came again, and this time Nysska couldn't stop them. Didn't try to stop them. "Cam, listen—if the Crucible is disbanded—if they decide to take you away." She took Cam's hand in both of hers. "I can protect you. I know how to live outside of, of cities, outside of the Empire. If you want, you could come with me, and I'd keep you safe."

As she spoke, Cam's breathing had become harsher. Cam moved away from her, pivoted to face her—but left her hand in Nysska's. "Why?" When Nysska didn't answer, she said it again. "Why? Why would you do that? Why would you *say* that?"

Unexpected, unwelcome tears started in Nysska's eyes. "I... suppose this is...a confession I must make."

Cam didn't seem angry. Or repulsed. Just confused and, with her next words, even urgent. "Go on."

"I...my whole life...I was trained for one thing."

"To be a fighter."

Nysska shook her head, then realized Cam couldn't see that. "No. Well, no more than any other sethyd. No, I was trained to be a—I don't think an exact translation exists in Plainish. The best would be 'priest-singer.'"

Cam's eyebrows climbed up her forehead. "You were a *priest?*"

"A priest-*singer*. Except 'priest' isn't an exact translation, either—I know about your religion. The Faith of the Dragon. The belief that the Great Silver Dragon created humans. A vast, fearsome, yet ultimately merciful god who answers the prayers of those who follow its teachings most closely. Yes?"

"There are others, but yeah, the Dragon Faith is the most common religion in the Empire."

"Well…sethyds do not technically have a religion. There is no supernatural entity we claim to have created us. We do not send thoughts up into the sky and hope a deity hears and answers them."

Cam had not tried to take her hand back. It became important to Nysska to keep hold of it as she tried to explain this. Cam said, "And yet you were something like a priest, you said."

"In our culture, there are what we call…I believe this word does translate properly. 'Exemplars.' Figures who embody the best traits a sethyd could have. Figures we try to emulate. Over the centuries, I suppose some of them have been elevated to what would seem to be god-like status, but they are not gods."

"Ultimate role models, then."

"Exactly."

"What does this have to do with you offering to help me become a fugitive?"

Nysska exhaled, long and slow. "Part of that elevation to god-like status involves a measure of…idealization, you could say. The Exemplars are depicted, in paintings and statues and such, with physical traits not typical of the rest of us."

"All right…?"

"This is difficult for me to say."

Cam brought Nysska's hands up to her lips, and kissed them, and Nysska's breath shuddered and almost stopped. Cam said, "Please go on," and the tears spilled over and coursed down Nysska's cheeks.

"I was brought up as an attendant of the Exemplar of Wisdom. Her name is Atiina. Every nineteen days, those of us who have dedicated ourselves to the ideals that Atiina represents gather, and a scholar of her wisdom talks to us about what it means to follow the examples she set. Part of those gatherings involves singing her best-known proverbs."

Cam whispered, "Priest-singer."

Nysska almost nodded, but instead said, "Yes. From my earliest memories, I was taught the songs, taught the best ways to sing them, the best ways to bring honor to Atiina."

Her voice must have hitched, because Cam's grip on her hands tightened. "Nysska—are you crying?"

"You...you've seen me. You know what I—what sethyds look like. Our skin, it's a deep violet, and in dim light it looks...it looks a lot like *yours*, and..."

Cam must have intuited what was coming. Her breathing sped up.

"...and as part of her commitment to wisdom and peace, Atiina filed her horns down until they were little more than black circles against her skin, and—Cam, please understand—Atiina has *silver eyes*."

Cam pulled her hands from Nysska's. She moved away, but stayed on the bed. Just out of arm's reach. Nysska could only watch, a fist squeezing her heart, as Cam drew her knees up to her chest and wrapped her arms around them. Neither of them said anything for what felt like a long time, and Nysska took the opportunity to wipe her tears with the hem of the blood-stained sheet. The distance Cam had just put between them made that a futile effort.

"You want to save my life because I look like the goddess you grew up worshiping?"

Misery colored Nysska's voice. "Not a goddess."

"But just as good as?"

"It's not just that. It's not just that you looked like Atiina when you were using your runes. It's everything about you. It's how you've not just survived but thrived here. I have seen how the Empire treats women. But you, Cam, your strength, your intelligence, your determination. I..." She let her words trail off.

Cam began to rock back and forth, just a little, just a couple of centims either way. She said, "I saw you."

"...What?"

"In the laboratory. Olkoff's laboratory. When you stopped the sheet of argonium from taking my head off, I—I saw you. I *saw* you."

"I'm sorry, I don't understand what you mean."

Cam uncoiled her body and crawled back across the bed. She didn't bother clicking her rings, just held her hands out until they found Nysska, found her hands again, and held them tight to her chest. Nysska could feel Cam's heart beating quickly, almost whirring.

"You know the talent the runes give me. How I can see…I see the *truth* of what happened in a place. The raw nature of the thing. Nysska, I saw you. I saw the truth of you. And it scared me shitless, that's why I avoided you, why I was so nasty to you for so long, because I couldn't make any sense of it. I was afraid to make sense of it."

Nysska had to force herself to breathe. "What did you see?"

Now tears had found their way to Cam's eyes as well. "People—humans—they call you demons. And I saw the horns, and the yellow eyes, and the violet skin. I know how tall you are, and I've witnessed how strong you are, how fast. But Nysska, I didn't see a demon. I saw *you*. Dragon above, you looked like…I don't know how to describe it. I've thought about it often enough, but I can't—it's just—you looked like an *angel*."

Nysska saw the silver light start behind Cam's eyelids, and a sliver of that aching, perfect radiance as Cam began to open her eyes, and Nysska pressed her palm over them. "No. No! Cam, don't you do it. Don't you do it when you don't have to."

Gently, Cam grasped Nysska's wrist. "I want to see you again. The real you."

"But you can't! Using the runes hastens your *death*." She did her best to stifle a sob. "Don't you cut your life any shorter than you have to. Not for me. Not…not when I want you to live as long as you can. As long as…as long as I can have you."

Cam carefully pulled Nysska's hand away from her eyes. They were closed again, the silver light gone out. Cam skimmed her hand along Nysska's collarbone, glided up her neck, and her fingertips found the line of swelled, scabbed tissue where a blade had sliced into her cheek. Cam hissed. "Your poor face…"

Nysska pushed her cheekbone into Cam's hand. "It's nothing."

"But…you'll be scarred…"

She kissed Cam's palm. "We don't scar."

Cam let out a shuddering breath. She slid her hand farther up, along Nysska's temple, and over to the nearest horn. Nysska softly gasped as Cam's fingers ran over the ridges, pressed the pad of her thumb against the dagger-point tip. "Can you feel this? Are they sensitive?"

"Not the horns themselves. But the pressure…yes. I can feel it."

Cam grasped the horn and used it to tilt Nysska's head back, and her lips and tongue found Nysska's neck, and Nysska pushed the sheet down and away. She wrapped her arms around Cam and pulled her in tight, and the curves of their bodies melded as Cam's lips found hers.

The brightest of the moons had set, plunging Nysska's room into a comforting twilight. She could still see Cam well enough, but didn't need to, didn't even want to. Nysska wanted to feel her. Explore every bit of her with fingertips, with tongue and lips. Cam lay on her side, her lean back and round, muscular ass and long, taut thighs pressed against as much of Nysska's body as she could manage. Nysska trailed one finger along Cam's ribs, slid it lower, drew spirals along her hip.

"You know what made me realize you were nothing like people say?"

Nysska frowned. "People talk about me?"

Cam chuckled. "Not you, specifically. Your people. All that business about being demons. You know what let me know you weren't a demon?"

"My sparkling personality?"

Cam laughed again. "Well, sort of. It was how you were with Percy's cats. You paid attention to them before you even acknowledged the rest of us."

"I've always loved animals. I know they're Percy's cats, but they make me think of my dog. His name would translate to…let me see… Springer, I think."

Delight in her words, Cam said, "You have a dog named Springer?"

"I did. I lost him in the *Krizo*. I miss him. A great deal."

"*That* should be what goes out in the Imperial Decrees about you. 'Welcome our new sethyd neighbors. They love dogs.'"

Nysska kissed Cam's earlobe. "Those who follow the Dragon Faith believe in a life after death, yes?"

"That's an abrupt change of subject. But yes. The Dragonlands."

"Not so abrupt. You see, we don't hold such beliefs. In sethyd culture, the life you have is the life you get, and it's your obligation to make the most of it. But I'll tell you this much…the idea that an afterlife would let me see Springer again?" She closed her eyes and sighed. "That makes me *want* to believe in one."

Cam turned, so that she lay on her back, and Nysska was about to draw gentle spirals around a nipple when Cam said, "Sing something to me."

Nysska's hand paused in mid-reach. She rose up onto her elbow, gazing down at Cam, and let her palm come to rest on Cam's flat belly. "I don't know about that."

Cam reached up, ran her fingers into Nysska's hair, and pulled her face down for a lingering kiss. "Please?"

Nysska chuckled. A smoky sound. "I doubt you'd get very much out of Exemplar hymns."

"You've got to know other songs, though. And you trained for it your whole life, you said. I just—it's another part of you. I want to know *all* of you."

Nysska trailed kisses from Cam's lips down to her shoulder. "All right. Just a little bit. Here's something my mother used to sing to me when I was a girl." She cleared her throat, took a deep breath, and started with the low tone. Kept it rich and smooth—then brought in the middle tone with a flowing vibrato—

Cam sat up abruptly. "What was *that*?"

Nysska allowed herself a languid smile. "Clearly you've never heard sethyd singing before."

"All right, first, when would I have had the chance to? And second, *what was that?*"

"Relax. Please. Lie back down."

"Are you going to answer my question?"

"Yes." She patted the pillow and waited until Cam's head rested on it again. "With a little training...all right, with a lot of training, which I've had, sethyd voice boxes can produce three different...ah, we'll call them 'tones.'"

Cam covered her face with her hands for a moment. "*Three*? And that was what, the first two? Nysska, it sounded like—like a *choir*."

"Do you like choirs?"

"All right, all right, I won't stop you again. Please. Sing me a whole song."

"You won't know the language."

"That's fine! Just—I have to hear this. Please. Go on."

Nysska took another deep breath, letting the air fill her lungs completely, all the way down, and started again. This time, with the low and middle tones complementing each other, she brought in the high tone, or verse, and sang Cam a song about a sethyd woman who lived alone on a cliffside—who watched the sea, every day, waiting for her son to come back. The woman lived to be very old, waiting, always waiting, but her son never returned, because he had ventured out too far and been claimed by Those Who Dwell Beneath the Waves.

She knew Cam didn't understand any of the words, but Nysska had always been good with infusing her songs with emotion, and when she finished, Cam had to turn away and dry her eyes and regain her composure. Finally, she nestled close again, and spoke with her lips near Nysska's heart.

"That was...I...I can't put it into words. Not words that'll do it justice. That was the most beautiful thing I've ever heard."

"It's a sad song."

"It may be, but...Great Dragon above, Nysska. It sounded like thirty people all at once." Nysska felt Cam's forehead wrinkle against her skin. "Is this how you were able to scream the way you did? When you got ambushed?"

Nysska nodded. "I can get really loud when I want to." She ran gentle fingernails along Cam's scalp. "But I was thinking about what you said, when I fought Benitoff's bodyguard. No one else knew I could do that. And since I figured out how to beat him another way, I decided to keep the battle cry secret."

"Battle cry."

"Call it whatever you want to."

Cam snaked an arm around Nysska's waist and pulled her closer. "Sing me something else."

Nysska opened her eyes to the butter-yellow light of the sun making its way through the shutters over the window and in through the skylight. She lay on her right side, curled around Cam, her right arm under Cam's head, her left arm draped across Cam's ribs, and her left hand cupped one of her absolutely *splendid* breasts. Nysska kissed the back of Cam's neck, felt her stir—

From the door, Raoul's voice struck at them, harsh and flat like knuckles on wood. "You're both awake now? Good. The governor wants us."

Cam bolted upright, gathering the sheet around her, and Nysska rose up on one elbow to see Raoul standing there, just inside the doorway, sidelong to them. His head turned away.

Cam said, "How long have you been standing there?"

"About five seconds," he shot back. Nysska's guts clenched at the torture in every syllable. "I did knock. Now hurry up. Anwar wants to talk to us." He risked a glance in their direction, and Nysska felt pummeled when his eyes settled on her. "All of us. I'll wait in the hall." He stepped out of the room and shut the door behind him.

Cam twisted on the bed, her eyes squeezed tight shut, her forehead a mass of worry. "What have we done? This isn't allowed! Members of the same Crucible can't fraternize! And, and Raoul *caught* us, he caught us in *bed*, what have we *done*?"

Nysska sat up beside her and put her hands on Cam's shoulders. "There's nothing we can do about it now. All we can do is get dressed and find out what's going on." She moved her hands up and touched

Cam's face. "But my offer still stands. If they try to take you away... well...first they'll have to go through me. And then we can disappear. Together."

Cam pulled Nysska to her for one brief, fierce hug, and then leapt out of bed to start looking for her clothes.

Eight minutes later—made even more awkward, as Cam had to pass by Raoul in the hallway to get back to her room for her armor—the members of the Ninth Crucible gathered in one of the downstairs parlors. General Cullen was nowhere in sight, but Governor Anwar stood in the middle of the room, waiting for them. The look on his face made Nysska's heart sink.

Anwar said, "Lord Benitoff has returned to his estate."

Percy snorted, but didn't react otherwise. Cam covered her face with her hands. Nysska didn't bother keeping the edge out of her words. "Then his involvement is to be, what, just *ignored*? The prisoner we took implicated him directly. He threatened a Crucible with deadly force!"

Anwar stared at the floor. "It is General Cullen's position that the prisoner was lying, and that, whatever personal shortcomings Lord Benitoff has, he is not involved in any widespread criminal activities."

Raoul appeared to have lost the ability to speak. He simply stood, statue-like, his arms folded across his chest, eyes on the ceiling. Nysska surprised herself by sputtering. "He had a member of the Argonium Infantry acting as his personal bodyguard! How many laws does *that* break?"

"Nysska, I—" Anwar caught himself. "Enforcer Stonegate, General Cullen was dispatched here with the full authority of the Emperor's Council in Caulspring. There is nothing more I can do." He moved closer to them, close enough that he had to crane his neck to look Nysska in the eyes. "For what it's worth, I believe you, and I find it alarming in the extreme that there's something out there that can defeat an Imperial Sensor." Directly to Cam, he said, "I'm truly sorry, Sensor Delakroy."

Nysska stepped between Cam and Anwar, looming over him. "Sorry for what, exactly, Governor?"

Anwar sighed. "Word of the situation has been sent to Caulspring.

They will decide what is to become of the Ninth Crucible collectively, and its members individually. Until then, you are all to continue your confinement here. I will have food brought to you." He reached out, as if to put a placating hand on Nysska's arm but drew it back before he made contact. "I'm sorry. I'm *truly* sorry. My hands are tied."

Cam made no sound. No tears, no whining, no harsh words. But she found Nysska's hand with hers and clung to it with what felt like all her strength.

14

Half an hour later, the members of what would soon no longer be the Ninth Crucible gathered in Raoul's room. The governor's house guard had relieved them of their weapons and armor and confined them to the single hallway, but did allow them to meet and talk. As much as Nysska hated the situation, and as much as she wanted to take it out on Anwar, the rational part of her brain kept telling her it wasn't his fault, which made the rest of her want to throttle the rational part of her brain.

Percy sat on the floor with his back to a wall, absently scratching Jax between the ears. Flax sat in a corner, grooming, but her eyes stayed focused on Nysska—which, after a few minutes, Nysska began to find unnerving.

Cam sat in the room's other chair, slumped forward, her face in her hands. Raoul stood in front of the single window at parade rest. He stared out at the city. Wordless. A living tower of tension.

The silence grew oppressive enough for Nysska to break it. "Are they listening to us?"

Percy turned his head. "Are they what?"

"Rooms like this." Nysska gestured broadly. "Are they fitted out with secret spying lenses? Tubes that let distant ears hear what we say?"

"I already checked," Raoul said. He didn't move as he spoke the crisp words. "The room is free of such blemishes."

Nysska leaned forward and rested her elbows on her knees. "Then let me be the first to say that this is all bear shit. They asked us to find out who killed Naveed Olkoff. We worked our way through it until we got our hands on a human who would know, and now we're being punished for it."

Raoul still didn't move. "No. We are being punished because we broke with procedure. There are rules, regulations for every situation, no matter how rare such a situation might be. When Cam's runes failed, we should have reported that failure to Governor Anwar immediately. And since I am the commander of this Crucible, the blame for all this falls squarely on my shoulders. As it should."

"It wasn't a Dragon-damned failure," Cam snapped. "You saw what I did at the scene of Irene's murder. What I've done in every other case we've ever worked. Something interfered with my eyes. They didn't *fail*. If someone shoots a horse and kills it, you don't say the horse *failed*."

Jax left Percy's side. He padded over to Cam, nuzzled her shin until he got her attention, and when she reached down to pet him, he licked her hand. The ghost of a smile haunted her lips, but only for a heartbeat. "I appreciate the gesture," she murmured to the big cat. "But I'm afraid there's not much you can do to help."

Nysska felt something against her own leg and looked down. Flax had come over to her and stared up at her with those wide silver eyes, and when Nysska sat up straight, the blood lynx jumped into her lap and settled down and started purring. The wide, vertically-pupiled eyes still stayed open, though, fixed on Nysska.

"It might be all right," Percy said. "Like you've been saying, we don't know what the fuck happened with Cam's peepers. Maybe we explain everything, and it turns out this is something they've known about for years. And they'll tell us, 'All right, you got fucked up by whatever-the-fuck-it-was, and this is what you do about it, now get back to work.'"

Cam tilted her head in Percy's direction. "That's uncharacteristically optimistic of you, Mr. Bitters."

Jax had returned to Percy and flopped down on his side. Hollow-eyed, Percy said, "I can't work with anybody else. Put us with some band of skull-damaged mouth-breathers, and Dragon knows it, one of them will try to hurt one of my kitties. I can't let that happen." He thumped his head back against the wall. "I fucking won't."

"There's no point in flagellating ourselves," Raoul said. He still hadn't turned around. "All we can do now is wait. Word will come back from Caulspring soon enough. Until then…try to relax. Get some sleep if possible."

Nysska shifted, and when Flax understood that she meant to get up, the blood lynx hopped down from her lap. Nysska went to Cam's side and touched her lightly on the shoulder. "May I have a word? In private?" Nysska was watching Raoul out of the corner of her eye as she said that, and she had no doubt that he heard her, but he didn't move or otherwise indicate that he had. She wondered if that was why he wouldn't face them. Because he couldn't look at the two of them.

Cam nodded, silent, and rose to follow as Nysska opened the door and stepped out into the hallway. She nodded at the guards stationed at either end—keeping watch over the stairs, and their charges' only exit—and moved down to her own room, Cam right behind her. When they stepped inside, Nysska saw that someone had taken away her blood-stained sheets and replaced them with perfect, snow-white new ones. She found herself irritated that her mind had spent time recording such a mundane detail.

Cam closed the door and leaned against it. Nysska couldn't read the expression on her face, but she sighed with relief when Cam pushed off the door and crossed to her and flung her arms around her. With Cam's breath hot against her chest, Nysska returned the embrace.

"What are we going to do?" It wasn't quite a wail, but it wasn't far off.

"Come on." Nysska guided her over to the bed and sat down on the edge. Cam sat beside her, and clung to her arm, and Nysska felt hot tears on her skin. "Listen. We can go tonight."

"What? …How?"

"Out a window. I can get us to the roof. From there it's just a matter of making our way through the city to the wall unseen."

"Just that easily."

"Hey." She put a finger under Cam's chin, lifted her face up, and planted a kiss on her lips. "I mean it. I can get you out of here. I lived in the wilderness for a year and a half before I stumbled over Governor Anwar. Two able-bodied women? We can make a place of our own. Far away from the Empire."

Cam let go of Nysska's arm. She dabbed at her eyes and turned sideways. "I don't think I can."

Nysska blinked. "What do you mean? I'll help you through any tricky parts."

"Yes, I know—I know, but you're talking about…living, just, in the woods? In some kind of hut or something? Just the two of us, for the rest of our lives. Seeing no one else. Going nowhere else. Nysska, I know you're trying to help me, but what kind of life is that? For either of us?"

Nysska took a moment. Slowly blinked. Every word Cam had just spoken felt like a nail driven into her chest. "It would be a *life*. It wouldn't be what you talked about. Strapped to some table with rune-masters picking you apart."

Cam put a hand on Nysska's chest, over her heart. "But the Empire would never stop looking for us. These runes…the argonium, it's—I'm an *investment*. That was the deal I made, that I'd work for them until my death."

Nysska covered Cam's hand with hers. "Yes, until you die of the poison that metal puts inside you. No one should have to make a deal like that."

"But I *did*. I did make that deal. It's what I agreed to."

Now Nysska pulled Cam's hand away and dropped it back in her lap. She stood, leaving Cam there on the bed, and paced back and forth across the floor. "I don't understand this. I don't understand why you're rejecting an offer to save your freedom. To save your life."

Cam bowed her head. "What kind of a life could we have as outcasts? It wouldn't even matter if the Empire never found us, *someone* would find us. What would they think? Nysska, it would be bad enough to see a human and a—a sethyd living together, but what would they think of two women?"

Nysska stopped and turned to face Cam. "Why would anyone care about that?"

Cam sighed. "Do you not know what people think about women, or men, living as lovers? Is it normal, among—among your kind?"

Nysska's eyes narrowed. She had not missed that stutter in Cam's speech.

"It's still natural for you to call us demons, isn't it?"

Cam stood and came to her. "That is not the point. I'm asking you. Can two sethyd women live together, the way human husbands and wives do? Can two sethyd men?"

"Yes! Look, we don't *have* husbands and wives. When a sethyd woman becomes pregnant, she gives birth to twins. A brother and a sister."

Cam's eyebrows lifted. "Every time?"

"*Always*. That brother and sister have a—a bond. A special bond. And when the sister reaches maturity, if she takes a lover and becomes pregnant herself, she and her brother raise the children." Nysska started pacing again. "We are much alike, brothers and sisters. Men and women. Sethyd men and women, I mean. At maturity, every male and female stand within a centim or two of each other. Our body mass hardly varies. Every sethyd woman is just as strong as any sethyd man."

Cam frowned. "Wait, what're you saying? Cocks and quims, it's all just the same to you?"

Nysska squeezed her eyes shut and sighed. "No—*yes*. In a way. We don't even think of it in those terms, it's—it's about who a person *is*. What's between their legs is *incidental*."

Cam folded her arms under her breasts. "Well. That's very nice. But it's not like that here. Not where the Empire holds sway."

"Are you telling me there are none among you who prefer to bed those like themselves?"

"Of *course* there are. And it's illegal. Punishable by death." She waved an arm toward the far wall. "You've seen what it's like out there. Any crime the Empire decides is worth prosecuting, you lose your head for. Any crime it sees fit to tolerate, on the other hand, does a brisk business. But as long as the Emperor lives—and he seems pretty damn healthy—if you and I were *together,* together the way you want us to be, we risk losing our heads."

Nysska hesitated. "The way *I* want us to be? Is it not the way *you* want us to be as well?"

A fresh tear spilled out from the corner of Cam's eye and tracked down by her nose. "What kind of a relationship *is* this, Nysska? You want to fuck me because I look like the goddess you grew up worshiping?"

"Cam—that's not what—"

"And I want to fuck you because I had some kind of rune-based *vision*? We hardly know each other! I don't know a goddamn *thing* about where you grew up, or what your family's like, or anything! And you want us to say 'fuck the Empire, we're going to go live in the woods for the rest of our lives,' just because we made each other come?"

Nysska stood there, staring, nostrils flared, long enough for Cam to shift her weight from one foot to the other. Then Nysska went to the door and opened it. "I would like to be alone now, thank you."

Cam took a tentative step forward. "Nysska—"

"I would like to be alone so that I can think. Thank you."

Cam's lower lip trembled. But she clicked her rings and walked past Nysska into the hall with her head held high and her shoulders square. Nysska closed and latched the door behind her.

Once the sun had set, Nysska pulled on a dark overshirt she'd found in a drawer, wedged a chair under her room's doorknob, and swung open the window. It had been first painted shut and then nailed shut, but she had pulled one of the nails out and used it to scrape and punch through the paint, then worked the window in its frame enough to loosen the rest of the nails. The window overlooked a stone-paved courtyard a good ten meters below, and nothing but sheer wall above led up to the overhang of thin stone plates that covered the roof. It would take an idiot, she knew, to try to get up to the roof from that window.

After Nysska sprang from the windowsill, gripped the roof's edge, and swung up onto it, she thought, *Only a human idiot, perhaps*. Staying low, she crept up to the crest, which gave her a view of Tember's rooftops stretching out before her.

Nysska squinted. Blinked. Squinted harder—until the low-slung animal she'd spotted moved out of the shadow of a chimney and came padding toward her: Flax the blood lynx, strolling along the roof's crest as if it were the most natural thing in the world to do. The big cat stopped a meter away from Nysska and sat down, staring up at her, silver eyes glinting the light of the first moon.

"What are you doing here?" Nysska hissed. "How did you even get *up* here? Go back to Percy! He's going to be worried sick!"

Flax tilted her head. Still staring. Then, to Nysska's combined surprise and bemusement, the blood lynx gestured with her head in the exact direction Nysska had been planning to go.

Nysska crouched. "I cannot believe I'm having a conversation with a cat." Flax's ears flattened, and she narrowed her eyes. "All right, all right. Yes, I can believe it. I know how smart seraphic animals are. Fine. If you can understand me, wink your left eye."

Flax stretched, yawned hugely, and winked her left eye.

Nysska almost laughed. "Good, then you can understand me when I tell you that you need to go back to Percy. I'm busy." She pointed. "You go that way. I go this other way. Got it?" The cat did nothing but stare. "All right, all right, do what you want. Just—don't follow me. I'm about to do something that will, at best, bring the wrath of the Empire down on my head, and at worst get me killed. Got it? Stay there, go back to Percy, find some rats to eat, whatever. Good? Good night, then."

Nysska crept away along the roof, keeping low so as not to provide anyone with a recognizable silhouette. Neither the second nor third moon was out at that point, but the light from the first was still bright enough to get her caught. She made it to the edge of the Mansion's roof, sprang across a gap to a tree, climbed the tree's trunk a couple of meters, and jumped from there to another rooftop. She rolled as quietly as she could and made it to the other edge of the roof before she checked behind her.

Flax sat there, not two meters away, grooming a paw.

Nysska heaved a sigh and went and knelt in front of the blood lynx. "Look, what I'm doing is important. I'm trying to help us—all of us—but I *really* can't get caught."

The cat stopped grooming, looked up at her, and winked her left eye again.

It hit Nysska. "Wait, are you—do you want to *help*?"

Flax yawned again and padded past her to the edge of the roof. She put her front paws up on the low wall that ran around it, looked back at Nysska, winked her left eye again, and moved her head in a jarringly recognizable gesture: *Come on, let's go.*

Nysska joined Flax, scanning the street below for passersby. When the way had cleared, she said, "You follow me, all right? Match my pace, because once we're outside the city wall, I'm going to move fast, and I don't want to have to worry about you keeping up. And then once we get there, you do what I ask you to do. Got it?"

Flax didn't wink this time, but she did rub her face against Nysska's elbow and lick her hand.

"All right, then. Not how I was planning this evening to go, but let's see what we can accomplish."

They leapt to the next rooftop together.

It had taken the team most of the morning to ride to Sergei Benitoff's estate, but they had followed the roads, and hadn't pushed their horses at all. Now, just as the third moon rose, Nysska and Flax ran full-tilt through the forest, heading straight for their target in as true a line as a crow would have followed. The hazy blue of the moonlight streaking through the trees made Nysska think of the night she'd spent with Cam—which led to a re-living of the fight they'd had. She found herself gritting her teeth hard enough to make her jaw ache.

Halfway to Benitoff, she glanced over and saw that Flax had begun to pant, and without breaking stride she swept the blood lynx up and slung her over one shoulder. Flax struggled, digging her back claws into the fabric of Nysska's shirt, but Nysska stroked her and said, "Grab hold of my hair. Between that and my grip on you, you'll be steady enough." She felt big feline paws on her neck, and the pressure on her scalp let her picture Flax's formidable claws sinking into her thick braid. Flax calmed down, and half an hour later they reached the perimeter of Benitoff's grounds.

Nysska circled around, giving the wall a wide berth, and found a spot near the back of the property where an aged tree hung a massive limb out far enough. She scaled the trunk, crept out onto the branch, and whispered, "Are you all right to drop this far?"

Flax let go of her braid. Nysska set the cat down on the branch, and watched as she immediately leapt to the ground, landing lightly. Nysska scanned the grounds and, when she was sure no one was watching, hung from the branch and dropped beside the blood lynx.

Twenty meters of moss and low-growing ground-cover grew between the wall and Benitoff's house. Nysska had only seen the front of it, and of the inside only that enormous single room where she and Darlo had fought. Looking at the massive house from the rear, she was able to pick out what were almost certainly bedrooms along the second floor, below which she expected to find the kitchen, along with rooms dedicated to whatever else Sergei was interested in. Judging by his choice of companionship, perhaps a dormitory for willing—or well-paid—young women.

Nysska spotted movement near the house. She pulled Flax back with her into the deepest shadow. "Wait," she whispered. "He's got guards patrolling." She remembered the crossbow squad that had come out to watch her fight Darlo. Individually they didn't worry her all that much, but there'd been a lot of them, and tonight especially she wanted to draw no attention whatsoever. Nysska counted the beats of her own heart in between the two-man patrols that circled the house. She studied the lights in the windows.

The third moon rode high now, rendering true shadows scarce, and in its illumination she saw thin tendrils of smoke rising into the night sky. Tracing those back to their source, she spotted small chimneys protruding from the roofline above each of the bedrooms.

Except for the one at the far corner. No smoke from the chimney. No lights from the windows. Nysska crouched with her back to the perimeter wall and pulled Flax up onto her thighs. "All right, smart kitty," she said, as the blood lynx stared up at her. "I need to get inside that house. And I need to do it so quickly, and so quietly, that no one knows I'm there. You see those men, walking around the house?"

Flax looked in the direction Nysska was pointing. She yawned.

"I'm going to consider that a yes. Now, I think I can make it across the grounds here and climb up to one of those windows before the guards see me, but taking the time to get a locked window open would leave me exposed. So. Do you see that last chimney, up there on the roof? The one with no smoke coming out of it?"

Again, Flax followed Nysska's pointing finger. She winked her left eye. Nysska allowed herself a tight smile. "Do you think you can climb up to the roof, shimmy down that chimney, and unhook the latch on the window from the inside?"

Flax's jaw dropped open, and she began the loudest purring Nysska had ever heard. The big cat hopped down from Nysska's thigh, pointed herself toward the house, and her hindquarters wriggled as she got perfectly set. "Wait," Nysska whispered. "I'll tell you when to go. Wait...wait...*now*."

Flax shot across the mossy ground like a furry, silent arrow just as the last pair of patrolling guards rounded the far corner. Nysska lost sight of her as she disappeared into the darkness where the house's foundation met the ground, but seconds later spotted the low-slung feline shape gliding across the edge of the roof. She held her breath as the cat leapt to the top of the chimney, peered down into its depths, and dropped out of sight.

Nysska waited. She could barely breathe, despite her heart beating double-time against her ribs. Nightmares played out in her head. What if someone was there, in the room, and preferred not to have a fire? What if Flax got caught in the chimney and was unable to escape? What if she couldn't figure out how to open the window? Nysska imagined the horror and shattering loss Percy would suffer if one of his cats died—followed, no doubt, by the homicidal rage he'd take out on her for causing that death.

"Come on," Nysska whispered. She'd come to care about the blood lynxes a great deal, Flax especially, and if something did happen to the cat, she'd deserve every bit of Percy's wrath. For a few seconds, each of her breaths hung in front of her face, visible in the chill air. *Surely anyone asleep in a bedroom on a night this cold would have lit a fire.* "Come on, little kitty, smart kitty, you can do it. You can do it."

Three patrols had come and gone when, with a tiny *pop* that she hoped would garner no notice, the window in the lightless, smokeless bedroom swung open. She couldn't tell if it framed a triumphant feline face or not, and she had to wait while another patrol passed below it—*Don't look up don't look up for Atiina's sake don't look up*—before sprinting across the ground almost as fast as Flax had.

The window's ledge was a good four meters off the ground. Nysska bounded up the wall, touching it once with a foot, hooked her fingers around the sill, and hoisted herself inside all in one fluid motion. With a glance back out to make sure the next patrol hadn't made it there yet, she shut the window and locked it.

The latch was a simple hook-and-eye affair. Definitely something a cat as smart as Flax could figure out. It took Nysska's eyes a few seconds to adjust to the darkness, and when they did, she saw Flax sitting on a rug in the middle of the floor, coated from ears to tail with soot. Only her silver eyes gleamed. Nysska took a step toward her, but in another shockingly human gesture, Flax held up one paw: *stop*. The cat stood, stretched, and shook like a dog, dislodging a cloud of soot and largely returning to her natural coloration. Nysska scooped her up, gave her a fast hug, and whispered, "I owe you a steak for this." The cat's purrs returned, and she licked Nysska's chin. "But you stay here now, all right? Stay here, out of sight, and perfectly quiet. Maybe take a nap. I'll be back for you."

Nysska set the cat down and watched as she curled up underneath the bed. At the door, Nysska pressed her ear against the wood and concentrated, listening. She heard nothing at first...then, faintly, very faintly, voices. She couldn't make out any words, but she heard two men talking. Conversational. Nysska opened the door, just a crack, and peered out at an empty hallway. Sticking close to the wall in an effort to avoid loud floor joists, she crept from the empty bedroom and moved closer to the door from which she was pretty sure the voices emanated.

Rarely had she felt more exposed. A staircase yawned at the end of the hall, and anyone climbing it would see her immediately. For that matter, anyone coming out of any of these rooms would see her immediately, too. Nysska paused, right outside the door in question, and listened hard. She feared pressing her ear against it, in case it might rattle in the frame, and part of her mind walked through the comically implausible explanations she might give if confronted. *Oh, don't mind me, I'm just the new maid, yes, demon maids are quite popular in the larger cities, didn't Lord Benitoff tell you?* Or perhaps *The solace house sent me, absolutely, Lord Benitoff has decided to explore non-human options now.* Or even *I'm not really here. You're drunk and this is just a figment of your imagination, run along now.*

One of the voices moved closer to the door. She recognized it as Sergei Benitoff when he cried out, "God damn it, man, the whore had to go!"

Then, from farther into the room, a voice so deep it made her bones hum: "Agreed. She was supposed to go. As in *disappear*."

Nysska sucked in a quick, silent breath as footsteps began to ascend the stairs. Another two seconds, maybe three, and one of Benitoff's people would get an eyeful of out-of-place sethyd, at which point she had no doubt every alarm in the Green Needles Territory would go off. Nysska took a step backward, turned the doorknob of the room next to the one where Benitoff was talking, thanked Atiina that it wasn't locked, and slipped inside. She had barely latched the door, as quietly as she was able, when the footsteps passed by right outside.

Nysska glanced over her shoulder and saw one of the young women she'd first seen Benitoff with—her name was something like Shella—sitting up in a narrow bed, lit by a tiny lantern on a nightstand, staring at Nysska with a jaw slack from shock.

Shella appeared to be the sole occupant of the room, and seemed to have just awakened, as she blinked sleep from her eyes and maybe tried to decide whether or not she was having a blistering nightmare. Nysska didn't give her the chance to find out. She crossed the room in two rapid, silent strides, clamped one hand over Shella's mouth, and pulled her neck into the crook of an elbow, where a few seconds' pressure cut off the blood supply to her brain. The woman went limp in Nysska's arms.

Nysska grabbed up an article of clothing off the floor—something lacy, she didn't have time to figure out what—and stuffed it into Shella's mouth. Over the next thirty seconds, Nysska bound Shella at the wrists, elbows, ankles, and knees with her bedclothes, and used another, larger lacy item to tie the gag in place. By the time she'd finished, the young woman's breathing had returned to normal, and when Shella's eyes opened and filled with tears, Nysska laid a finger over her lips.

Leaning close, Nysska said in the tiniest of whispers, "I'm not going to hurt you. *Unless* you make noise. If you make noise, I'll have to hurt you very, very badly. Do you understand? Nod if you do." Shella nodded. "Good. Now, just lie there and be still, and you'll have no worries."

Shella did as she was told, lying frozen, only her eyes moving as they tracked her captor. Nysska left her on the bed, went to the wall shared with the room next door, and pressed her entire body against it ear-first. After a few seconds' concentration, the voices came to her, faint but coherent.

"I tire of arguing. Your money and influence go only so far."

"Mr. Lockridge, it is *not my fault* that somebody started putting the Olkoff thing together!"

Nysska felt an ice-cold ball form in the pit of her stomach. She listened harder.

"And yet, if not for *my* influence, your headless body would be hanging from a fork. I will say this one more time, since it does not yet seem to have penetrated your skull. I wanted her to *disappear*, Sergei, not be left to bleed out in her room like some gaudy theater prop. This display of ineptitude draws more from your account than you have deposited. Do not harbor the notion that I will forget any of this."

Heavy footsteps crossed the floor.

"Where will you be? If I need to reach you?"

"Send a messenger to Altamar—but *only* if your over-valued life is in jeopardy."

"Look…sir…despite any, ah, misunderstandings, I promise you, I've done my level best to follow your instructions."

"And you will continue to do so. Good evening, Sergei."

Nysska heard the door to Benitoff's room open and close, and then more heavy footsteps heading away toward the stairs. She meant to crack the door open and try to get a peek at this *Mr. Lockridge,* but when she turned away from the wall, Shella leapt off the bed, her bonds in tatters and a knife in her hand. The girl hadn't bothered taking the gag out of her mouth, so intent was she in using that knife on Nysska, but Nysska reached out and caught her in mid-leap. One hand on her wrist, the other on her throat, Nysska squeezed—the knife dropped as wrist bones ground together—

Nysska almost cried out when she felt Shella's windpipe collapse. The young woman's eyes rolled back in her head, her body twitching as her bladder emptied on the floor beneath her, and Nysska came close to dropping the corpse when Benitoff pounded on the wall between them.

"Shella! Get your ass in here, girl!"

Nysska's heartbeat had already accelerated, and now it kicked into a rhythm like the thundering hooves of a stampede. She whispered, *"Shit shit shit god damn it, why couldn't you have stayed down,"* and flung Shella's body back onto the bed. Nysska grabbed up a sheet and slipped out into the hallway. As Benitoff pounded on the wall again, she knotted one corner of the sheet around the doorknob to his room, crossed the hall, tied another corner around another doorknob, and pulled the sheet tight till it was taut as a guitar string. She knew it wouldn't hold Benitoff for long, and anyone outside his room could cut through it in seconds, but he shouldn't be able to open his door. At least not until she'd made her escape. Nysska moved as fast as she could to the room where she'd left Flax while still maintaining at least a nominal amount of stealth.

She had just ducked into the room when, down the hall, Benitoff realized something was wrong. He started bellowing for someone to let him out, and Nysska dropped to the floor next to the bed to find Flax's silver eyes peering out at her. "We're leaving now," she said. "No more sneaking. We need to get across the grounds and over the wall and back to the Mansion as fast as our legs will carry us. You understand?"

Flax surprised her yet again, this time by actually *nodding*.

"Then let's go."

The sounds of running feet came to her from what sounded like every part of the house, converging on Benitoff's room, and Nysska paused in the window just long enough to make sure there were no patrols directly below them. She didn't see anyone at all—presumably since they were all rushing to see what was happening to their employer—and she leapt out the window, landed rolling, sprang to her feet, and sprinted for the wall. Off to her right, Flax streaked past her, and Nysska and the blood lynx both arrived at the top of the wall at roughly the same time.

The trees swallowed them up as they left the Benitoff estate behind.

15

Most of a klik from Benitoff's estate, Nysska slowed to a stop and leaned against the trunk of a tree, panting softly. Flax streaked on ahead of her, but noticed that Nysska was no longer keeping pace, and circled back a few moments later. She twined around Nysska's ankles and meowed softly.

Nysska knelt and stroked Flax's head. "You did really well back there," she said softly. "I don't think I could've asked for a better partner."

Flax looked up at Nysska—and froze, growling, staring past her. Before Nysska could rise and turn, Gerrit's voice made its way to them from the darkness. "I've never seen anyone with a bigger soft spot for animals."

Nysska stood and faced him. He was little more than a lean, horned silhouette among the trees, the yellow of his eyes glinting in a stray beam of moonlight. "What do you want?"

Gerrit drew closer. "The same thing I've wanted from the beginning. Information. What did you learn on that flashy little jaunt?"

Nysska's jaw clenched, along with her fists. The rush of fire in her veins hit her hard enough to make her stomach hurt. "Why should I tell you? What assurances do I have that you've done what you said you would?"

Gerrit chuckled. "You mean *haven't* done what I said I *wouldn't*." He held out a fist, from which dangled something delicate and silvery that reflected the light of the three moons. "You're so predictable. Here."

Carefully, slowly, Nysska reached out. Gerrit let the necklace fall into her palm. "You recognize that, don't you? You should. Atiina knows, she never took it off." He moved a step closer. "Now tell me what you saw and heard in Benitoff's home. Or next time I'll bring you a severed ear."

With Flax clinging to her shoulders and hair, Nysska crept across the rooftop of the Mansion, got a firm and careful grip on the edge, and dropped down until her feet hit the windowsill of her room. She reached up and carefully detached the blood lynx from her shoulder perch, passed her in through the window, and slipped inside herself—

To find Percy and Jax waiting for her. "Nice fucking trick with the chair," Percy said. Nysska couldn't tell exactly what his frame of mind was. "Unless someone slips a poker under the door and jabs the chair legs loose. Which I did."

Flax crossed the floor and nuzzled Jax's face. They licked each other for a few seconds, then Jax jumped on Flax and they started rolling around and wrestling.

Nysska said, "Flax followed me. She wanted to help."

Percy inhaled slowly and exhaled even more slowly. "And did she?"

"Yes. I couldn't have done it without her."

"Whatever the fuck 'it' was."

"Percy—"

He shook his head, closed his eyes, and held up his left hand. Taking hold of the gloved fingers, he pulled the glove off—revealing a hand with an intact pinkie finger, a ring finger that ended just before the tip, and no other digits at all. The rest had been sheared off, along with a third of the palm.

Nysska tried to remember any time when she'd seen Percy do anything with his left hand and came up empty. She settled back against the windowsill. "What happened?"

"I was a miller. Nothing special. Filled enough meal bags to sell—enough to put food on the table. Then we had a hard winter, and our little boy's lungs filled up too fast for him to cough it out, and he died. My wife's love for me died along with him."

Nysska had never heard Percy speak the way he did now. He had always seemed ready to make fun of everything and everyone around him. Eager to, even. Now, standing there in her bedroom, Percy seemed smaller and...dimmer. The lines on his face deeper.

"With my boy gone, and my wife unwilling to look at me anymore, much less touch me...I guess you *could* say it happened because I was distracted. My hand, I mean. The accident. I can't say for sure. Maybe I didn't mean it to happen at all. Maybe I meant to go further and shove my head into the mill instead." He held up his mangled left hand. "Whatever the reason, I couldn't work anymore. Not the way I needed to. Not enough to keep the mill going. I think the wife was relieved, really. Maybe not as much as if I'd died outright, but... anyway, you know how the Empire does things. If you can't work, you don't deserve to live. I might not've been brave enough to kill myself, but I wasn't about to end up in a place like the Burr, either. So, I just—wandered off into the woods. Figured I'd either starve or let a bear take me. Either way, it'd make the decision for me, and Katie could get remarried if she felt like it."

Percy put his back to the wall and slid down to the floor. He made the kissing noise with his lips, and Flax and Jax stopped wrestling and came to him at once. He put Jax in his lap and gathered Flax up in his arms, all fifteen kilgrams of her. Both cats started purring loudly.

"These two found me," Percy said. "I don't know where they came from, or why they decided to care about me. But...well...they saved me. Saved my life. And it wasn't long before a Cathedral patrol ran across us, and word got back to somebody in the Thaumetallicon, and before I knew it, I had a man in bronze telling me how rare it is for one seraphic animal to cooperate with a human, let alone two, and how exceptions could be made for me and the kitties, and would I like a job." Percy set Flax down and slowly pulled his glove back on. "Never thought I'd be doing work for the government. Never in a million years. But my kitties are good at the job, and I'm good at taking care of them." His bright blue eyes locked onto her yellow ones. "Or at least I thought I was."

"Percy, I'm sorry. I didn't set out to put Flax in any danger. She came to me—followed me, wanted to help—"

He held up his right hand, palm out. "I understand that. They both get strong-willed, but Flax is the more pig-headed of the two, and a little smarter, I'd say." Jax, lying on his back in Percy's lap, reached up one paw and swatted Percy on the chin. Percy looked down at him. "Sorry, boy, but we both know it's the truth." He started scratching Jax's belly. "There. Does that make it better?" Jax closed his eyes and purred. "You can have a child that's smart and capable, ready to do things out in the world. Maybe things that need doing. But it's still *your child*. And they're my children now. I'd rather die than let them get hurt. You should've told me."

Nysska could think of nothing worth saying. She nodded.

"And if you ever, *ever* put either of my kitties in danger again without talking it over with me first...then you're going to have a problem with me. A *big fucking problem*. Do you get what I'm saying?"

"I do."

Percy stared at her for a few more seconds, until he seemed satisfied. Then he reached over, rapped on the door with his knuckles, and called out, "All right, I said what I had to say."

The door swung open, and Raoul, Cam, and Governor Wendell Anwar all filed into the room, carrying with them a near-palpable cloud of recrimination.

Nysska said, "Well, shit."

"This is unacceptable," Raoul gritted out. "I let Percy have his say, but now I'll have mine. You violated direct orders from the governor. Such behavior is not tolerated in the Cathedral, not in the Thaumetallicon, and especially not in my Crucible. Enforcer Nysska Stonegate, you are hereby formally—"

"Wait, now, hold on," Anwar broke in. "Before anyone makes a pronouncement they may have cause to regret later. I, for one, am keenly interested to hear exactly where Enforcer Stonegate has been and what she was doing."

Cam crossed the floor to her. She didn't touch Nysska, but got close enough to whisper, "Are you all right?"

"I'm unhurt," Nysska murmured back, her heart thumping harder in her chest. *I hate the way we left things,* she wanted to say. And *I only suggested running away to the wilderness because I want you to be safe,* and *I'll die before I let anyone hurt you.* Nysska watched silently as Cam went back to stand between Percy and Raoul.

Nysska exhaled slowly. "This might take a bit of time."

Anwar sat down in a chair, folded his hands in his lap, and looked at Nysska expectantly. Cam sat down on the edge of the bed, but Raoul remained standing, his arms folded across his chest, a vein popping out on his forehead and the muscles of his jaw rippling. Nysska took a moment to gather her thoughts.

"Benitoff is obviously involved in all of this," she said, "and would have been prosecuted if not for General Cullen's interference."

Anwar said, "For the sake of my nerves, can we call it 'involvement,' rather than 'interference'?"

Nysska frowned. "I don't think so." She shifted against the windowsill. "I went back to Benitoff's estate tonight." Anwar groaned loudly, but she pressed on. "We never had a chance to find out what he knew, and I wanted to take that chance. Flax came along, helped me get inside unseen. Once in there, I heard Benitoff talking to someone I couldn't see—someone he referred to as 'Mr. Lockridge.' This Lockridge is, beyond any doubt, Benitoff's boss. That's one thing. Another thing is that Benitoff is the one who had Irene killed, on Lockridge's orders. They were supposed to abduct her, make her disappear, Lockridge said, so as not to trigger a murder investigation. No dead body, no Crucible assigned to it. Benitoff also confirmed that he and this Lockridge were responsible for Naveed Olkoff's death, though I wasn't able to figure out the how or why of it."

Percy's eyes had gotten huge, and he laughed with only a touch of hysteria in it. "Holy fucking *shit,* Nysska."

Cam was frowning, thinking hard, and Anwar's jaw had dropped open. He closed it, and after a couple of false starts said, "Do you have any proof of any of this?"

On the heels of Anwar's question, Raoul said, "Did you leave any trace of yourself there?"

For the first time, Nysska let the guilt touch her. Her shoulders seemed suddenly much heavier. "I had to subdue one of Benitoff's women. I was going to leave her unharmed, but she attacked me, and...I might have accidentally...crushed her throat."

Raoul rolled his eyes. The vein in his forehead began to throb visibly. "You *killed* someone. You killed a civilian."

"A civilian who tried to stab me in the face, yes." She tapped her foot a few times. "And...I suppose someone might find a cat hair or two..."

Cam buried her face in her hands, and Nysska realized she was losing her audience. "Wait, wait, there's more. You want to know who this Lockridge is, and about this cabal that's infiltrated the Empire, and how they obscured the identity of Olkoff's murderer? Yes? Lockridge told Benitoff that he could reach him at a place called Altamar. We go there, we find Lockridge, and we bring him back so he can answer for all of this."

Cam said, "Where the fuck is 'Altamar'?"

Anwar's frown had deepened. "Never heard of it."

Percy looked up from petting Jax. "So your mystery man is in a mystery place with a mystery location."

With an expression one might have upon biting into an apple and discovering it filled with maggots, Raoul said, "It's an outpost. Up on top of a mountain—" he pointed north, "—around twenty kliks that way. *Barely* an outpost. More like a hunter's camp."

Nysska felt her face harden. Her lips pressed into tight lines, and she could tell from Percy's response when he looked at her that her eyes were flashing. "Then I would say we have a choice to make. We can stay here, under house arrest as ordered, and let the Thaumetallicon do whatever they want with Cam—as she's 'their property'—while the reason for all of this sits up on top of a mountain and continues to kill people and undermine the fabric of the Empire."

Percy picked up where she left off. "Or we can say *fuck it,* hike up that mountain, find this Lockridge fucker and beat his ass till he lays it all out for us."

Raoul threw his hands in the air. "Unbelievable. I let you—*you*—" He jabbed an accusing finger at Nysska. "You're the one who talked us into breaking the rules in the first place. That was bad enough. Now you want us to do it again, but on a scale that…that…it wouldn't just finish our careers, *Nysska*. They'll *execute* us for this. It's gross insubordination, it's flagrant disregard for everything the Cathedral stands for! This is not why we signed up! We agreed, all of us, to serve the Cathedral in general, and the Thaumetallicon specifically, and they gave us the bronze in exchange for our obedience! Does it not—*how* can it not get through that thick, horned head of yours? *This is who we are!* We obey! We swore we'd obey, and we fucking *do it*! How else can we—how else can I—"

To Nysska's astonishment, she saw tears start in Raoul's eyes, and he fell silent. She said, "For Cam."

Cam lifted her head. "What?"

Nysska kept speaking directly to Raoul. "Forget about solving this murder. Forget about preventing some sort of clandestine cabal from enacting a coup. If we stay here and do nothing, you know what will happen to Cam."

Cam stood up from the bed. "Don't make this about me."

Nysska narrowed her eyes at Raoul. "But it *is* about you. It's been about you from the start." She saw the realization in Governor Anwar's expression and body language. "If you obey, Cam spends the rest of her life in a laboratory. If you obey, you'll never see her again. Yes, we can solve a murder. Yes, we can protect the Empire. But in your heart, Cam is the one worth dying for, don't you agree?" Nysska paused. "I know *I* do."

Raoul's lips skinned back from his teeth in a snarl of rage and frustration. He spun on his heel, jerked the door open and stormed through it, slamming it behind him.

The rest of the room's occupants remained there, in silence.

Twenty minutes later, an undeniable fatigue had settled over Nysska, made worse by the wordless, oppressive silence that had filled the room since Raoul had left. Anwar sat in a chair, motionless, staring at the floor—staring *through* the floor—visibly detached from his present surroundings. Percy stayed where he was, next to the door, back to the wall, giving the two blood lynxes all his attention.

Cam sat on the edge of the bed, her shoulders slumped. Every bit as motionless as Anwar.

Nysska went to the other side of the bed and lay down, stretching out, her feet dangling off the end. After a minute or two, she rolled onto her side, facing away from Cam, and bent her knees so that all of her was on the mattress, and thought perhaps she might doze off.

Nysska's eyes sprang open as Cam settled in against her back. Nysska turned her head, Cam's face close to hers, and spoke in the tiniest of whispers. "Cam…there are people in the room…"

In just as soft a voice, Cam said, "I'm not trying to get your trousers off. Just hold me, will you?"

With those words, Cam acknowledged what hadn't been said yet. They weren't a Crucible of the Thaumetallicon any longer. They were simply a group of people, adrift. Lost. Anwar just as much as the rest of them.

Nysska rolled over onto her back, and Cam molded her body to Nysska's, her head on Nysska's chest. Nysska lifted her head and saw that neither Anwar nor Percy were looking at them, or even seemed aware of them.

Cam stayed silent for a bit. Her warmth and the weight of her body began to lull Nysska back toward sleep—but then she said, "Why were you living in the wilderness to begin with?"

When Nysska didn't immediately answer, Cam lifted her head, frowning, and sat up.

Nysska said, "What's wrong?"

"You tell me. As soon as I asked the question, your heartbeat doubled."

Nysska sat up as well, a chasm yawning in front of her, between her and Cam. A chasm she knew was too wide to cross. "Cam…I—"

Governor Anwar said, "Will you two please stop talking? My head's already pounding as it is."

Half relieved at the distraction, half worried that she'd never heard that much stress in Anwar's voice before, Nysska scooted closer to him on the bed. Behind her, Cam gave an irritated sigh, but Nysska said, "Governor, what is it?"

He lifted his head and focused on her. It appeared to take significant effort. "Do you know what will most likely happen to me, if it's discovered that I let some sort of wide-ranging subversive cabal get established in this territory? Worse yet, do you know what will happen if this cabal spreads beyond Green Needles? The more I think about it, the more it...it just doesn't happen! The Valconian Empire has been in power for three hundred years! Enforcement of the Imperial Codes is...it's more than just a system of rules and regulations. It's what we live and *breathe*. It's our culture! Bronze is law. Bronze is peace."

Percy didn't look up from scratching and stroking the cats. "Bronze is fucking oppressive bullshit."

Anwar's head snapped toward him. "I beg your *pardon*, sir?"

Percy still didn't look up, but his words filled the room. "What? I thought we were telling the truth now. Well, except for Nysska, who clearly doesn't want to talk about why she's not hanging her hat with the rest of the tall-dark-and-horned crowd."

"I knew he was listening," Cam muttered.

Percy said, "Sure, Emperor Valco the whatever-number-he-is sits over there in Caulspring and hands out decree after fucking decree, and shit, you'd better not defy him, better not speak up, or next thing you know you're on a fork in the town square with your neck stump hanging out. That's not fucking *order*, Governor, forgive me for being so bold. And I wouldn't be, because I've got a pretty fucking sweet job here, and I don't want to see it go away. But it's about to go away, isn't it? Because this Lockridge motherfucker's pumped up enough sets of balls that people finally stopped caring what Emperor Valco says. And we've been running around the continent, telling people that 'Bronze is law, bronze is peace' and chopping off their heads for so long that we started to believe it ourselves. So now that somebody's about to stand up, not a damn one of us knows what to fucking do about it. Except maybe her." He pointed at Nysska. "And none of us smooth-headed types are about to listen to her, because we're all too fucking scared."

Anwar said, "Then what is it?"

Percy said, "What is what?"

"You said the Empire's laws had not brought about order. Then what? What have they brought about?"

Percy shrugged. "Fear. You want to talk about the Empire's fucking culture? It's a culture of fear." He thumped his chest. "And I'm a fucking hypocrite, because I've been wearing bronze along with the rest of you for years now, but it's the truth. We've got people so fucking cowed—nobody obeys the laws because they love the Empire. They obey the laws because they're fucking *terrified* all the time. It's seeped into everything. Down into the marrow."

He looked Anwar in the eye. "And you know what's going to happen, if Lockridge's big-balls brigade shows up in enough numbers, and tells the people there's a better way? Tells the people, 'Hey, we had *one* member of the fucking Argonium Infantry working for us—what do you want to bet we've got a lot more that nobody knows about? We got the upper hand here. So why don't you take a pitchfork to all those regular soldiers out there and throw in with us, and we'll give you some of that fucking *respect* you've heard rumors about.' You know what's going to happen then?"

Anwar's breathing had grown shallow. "It wouldn't—they, they can't—the Argonium Infantry would be dispatched, and—" He stopped.

Percy gave him a mirthless grin. "See, you couldn't help it. It's ingrained. Any threat, anything real, the Empire's solution is *send in the fucking Argonium Infantry*. But what if they *can't*? What if the Infantry turns out to be taking orders from Lockridge?"

Anwar's forehead had wrinkled into something like an angry prune. "Then why even try to defend the Empire? If you hate it so much?"

Percy continued as if the governor hadn't spoken. "But never mind the Infantry. Nysska took out one of them herself. *Unarmed*. What if

Mr. Big-Balls Lockridge goes up there to the Crags, and tells Nysska's people the same thing? Throw in with me, and you won't have to live on this Dragon-forsaken stretch of rock anymore. I'll give you your own fucking *city*."

Nysska said, "Hey, Percy, why don't we leave my people out of this—"

Anwar sputtered. "But—but the sethyds are full citizens of the Empire! We took them in when they had nowhere else to go! Gave them the same rights as anyone else! They wouldn't commit *treason*!"

Percy didn't quite sneer. "Oh, so that's why they got shuffled off to a big stretch of barren fucking land that nobody else wanted, is it? Because they're so equal? Treated so fairly?"

Anwar faced Nysska, his face seized with sudden, heartbreaking fear and desperation. "Is he right? Do you think your people would—would turn against us? Turn against the Empire?"

The chasm that had been yawning before her swallowed Nysska up. Filled her lungs so that she couldn't speak, filled her eyes so that the room turned dark. She pressed her hands to her face. "Look, Anwar, I—"

The door burst open. Raoul came through, breathing hard. He reached up, pulled the commander's band off his head, and chucked it into the far corner of the room.

"Wait," Cam said, clicking her rings, "I missed something. What just happened? Raoul, what did you do?"

"I came to my senses," he said, his words practically vibrating in the air. "Also I heard most of what you were saying, Percy, and you're right." He turned to Anwar. "I love the Empire, sir. I've given it my whole life. It's not perfect, not by a long shot, and I mean to do everything I can to fix it. But I can't fix it—" He looked around the room. "I can't ask any of you to help me fix it if it's dead. And if we don't get off our asses, right this goddamn second, we might as well put a knife in its heart ourselves. Governor, how long till word gets back from Caulspring about what to do with us?"

Anwar rose to his feet. "Probably another couple of days. Maybe three."

Raoul nodded. "Is there a way for all of us—my team, I mean—can we get out of here without anyone knowing we're gone?"

Anwar tilted his head, his eyes narrowing. "There is, actually. More than one. Imperial architects don't like the thought of their royalty being trapped."

Raoul turned to face Percy, Cam, and Nysska. "Look, I—I know I've been an insufferable ass for...well, I've been this way since before any of you even met me. But if we just sit here—that's just it. We *can't* just sit here. So, who wants to set some rules on fire and climb a mountain with me?"

Cam's hand found Nysska's and squeezed.

Nysska squeezed back.

Before she could speak, Percy stood up with both blood lynxes in his arms, the cats staring at Raoul with wide, round, silver eyes. Percy said, "To answer your earlier question, Governor, yeah, maybe I do hate the Empire. But I know I hate this Lockridge fucker more." He turned to Raoul. "So we wait here for some bear-shit judgement from Caulspring, or we go stick a sword up Lockridge's ass? Shit, boss. Why even ask the question?"

16

Nysska climbed with a measured pace.

She brought up the rear as the Ninth Crucible made its way up the trail that Raoul had described more in terms of hazard to life and limb than of accessibility. "They'll see us coming if we take the mountain road," he'd said. "It's much easier going—broad enough for two carts to pass, carved into the stone in a long series of switchbacks—but it's also highly visible and exposed, and takes at least twice as long. If Lockridge or his people keep even one eye on the road, the element of surprise is lost entirely."

Instead, Raoul had told them, it would be much better to take an old trail that he'd hiked a few times with his father as a boy. Cam had immediately asked why Lockridge wouldn't be watching that trail the same as he would the road.

"Well..." It was the closest Nysska had ever seen Raoul to coming off as sheepish. "There was a landslide a few years ago. Part of the trail sort of isn't there anymore." And, after Percy's profane but legitimate protests, "We can get around it! We'll just need to be careful."

They had left the Governor's Mansion via a hidden tunnel that took them from Anwar's personal chambers to a cleverly concealed door that opened just outside the city walls, far from any of the gates.

Anwar had suggested they squeeze whatever sleep they could out of what remained of the night and depart at daybreak.

It had only taken them half the morning to get to the foot of the trail, thanks to the horses Anwar had arranged for them, but the trail itself was not horse-friendly. They knew they'd have to spend the rest of the day climbing.

Now—wearing baggy, non-descript civilian clothes and hooded cloaks over their armor, thanks to Anwar—the four of them wound their way up what Nysska thought Raoul had been overly generous in calling a "trail." She hadn't seen any part of it for the last hour less steep than thirty degrees, and while rock-and-timber steps had been dug into the mountainside in a few places, and every so often they encountered a knotted rope anchored to a tree, most of the climb so far had involved grabbing saplings and scrambling on all fours. Raoul, at the head of their minuscule column, climbed like a machine. Cam was almost as good at it, rings clicking constantly. Percy panted like a dog on a hot summer's day, but he hadn't slowed them down.

The blood lynxes kept pace with them effortlessly. Watching them climb, Nysska thought the cats might as well have been traversing level ground.

They had agreed not to raise their voices unless absolutely necessary, so Percy spoke just loudly enough for them all to hear him. "Could anyone else use a couple of minutes' rest? I have to piss like a racehorse."

Raoul stopped and turned to face the rest of them. "Five minutes."

Nysska wasn't hungry yet, and didn't have to empty her bladder, so she found a shady spot in the lee of a rock outcropping and sat down to enjoy the view. The road that had brought them here, and that had dead-ended at the mountain's foot, ran parallel to a swift-running river. From her vantage point, Nysska had a breathtaking view of where the river came from: a deep-blue lake, around which a small town had cropped up, and at the far end of that, a mammoth waterfall cascaded down a sheer rock face at least half a klik high. Maybe higher.

Cam sat down next to Nysska. "What do you see?"

Nysska was about to answer, but Raoul had come up behind Cam to lean against the outcropping, and he spoke before she could. "Sawtooth River. That's the one we were following all morning. Comes out of Gar Lake—can you hear the falls from here, Cam?"

Cam frowned, concentrating. She shook her head. "Too far away, I guess."

"The town around the lake is Barleenek, and the falls are called Dragon's Pain. Nysska, you see where it comes out? Way up there?" He pointed at the top of the cliff. "It looks closer from here, but that spot's about six kliks north of us. That's where we're headed."

Nysska squinted. "That's Altamar?"

"Yeah. Or at least that's where it used to be. I haven't heard of anyone going up there in at least ten years. At one time it had good hunting, but too many people found out about it and over-hunted the hell out of it."

Neither Cam nor Nysska responded to that, and a silence bloomed and spread among the three of them, the kind of void made all the more awkward for its sudden appearance. Nysska thought Raoul might have more to say, but he dropped his eyes to stare at the ground and turned to head back toward the trail.

Nysska followed him and stopped him with a soft hand on his shoulder. "Commander, I—"

Raoul shook his head. He didn't look angry, she didn't think, or sad or heartbroken, just...calm.

She tried again. "If you want to talk about—"

Another silent void swallowed whatever the rest of her sentence might have been.

Raoul picked up where her words failed. "It's all right. There's nothing to talk about."

"But..." She faltered again. "Are you certain?"

"The only thing I need to be certain of is what we're doing up here. Maybe we're not on a Thaumetallicon mission. But it's a mission in the Empire's best interests, and I trust you—I trust you both—to carry it out."

Nysska groped for something to say, and yet again came up empty.

Trust.

When had a human ever said they trusted her? *Had* a human ever said that?

How could she stand there and let Raoul trust her? How could she let *anyone* trust her, most of all Cam? Nysska felt as if her internal organs were being stuffed into a massive mortar and ground into paste by an equally huge pestle.

Raoul stepped back onto the trail, where Percy was emerging from behind a tree, buttoning his trousers. "Five minutes is up," he called out. "Let's keep moving."

No one spoke much on the rest of the climb. It left Nysska alone with her thoughts more than she was comfortable with. None of them knew what they were heading into. None of them knew how many enemies they were likely to face, or what the mysterious Mr. Lockridge even looked like. The one thing Nysska expected each of them to dwell on, as they sweated and grunted and hauled their weight higher and higher, was the likelihood that they were all about to die.

They might not have died if they'd stayed in Tember, stayed under house arrest, but that choice would relegate Cam to a fate just as bad as death and possibly worse. She didn't think Raoul ran any risk of being executed, but he'd never see Cam again, and would probably get demoted to the lowest rank the Cathedral offered.

If Percy got separated from Flax and Jax, or assigned to a unit that would put the cats in danger...Nysska wondered what the odd little man would do. Run? Live the kind of life she herself had lived, in the wilderness with Simana—the kind of life Nysska had offered to Cam? Or would he lock himself and the cats in a room somewhere, cursing and spitting at the soldiers who came to drag him out, resisting until one of them buried a knife in his heart and solved all his problems for him?

And what would you do? a small, sinister voice in the back of Nysska's mind asked her. *You know what will happen if you fail to gather the information Gerrit wants. Could you live with the consequences?*

Nysska pushed the thoughts away and, as much as she could, concentrated on climbing.

Just as the sun had begun to dip toward the west, Raoul signaled for the group to halt. Percy and Cam sagged against a couple of trees, breathing hard, but Nysska made her way past them. She was about to ask Raoul why he'd brought a halt to their progress—until she got close enough to see for herself.

"This is where the landslide happened," she said. It wasn't a question.

A couple of meters ahead of them, where the trail should have been, a sheer cliff dropped away. Nysska moved closer to the edge, and Raoul said, "Careful. No reason the ground couldn't give way again." Nysska nodded and stretched out on her belly on the rocky earth so that only her head poked out over the lip of the precipice.

It looked as if some unfathomable giant had taken a colossal spoon and simply scooped away a section of the mountainside, leaving a half-globe-shaped void directly ahead of them. Raoul mimicked her, lying down beside her to take a look. He pointed to their left.

"We can skirt the area. Just have to watch where we put our feet."

Nysska followed the rim of the slide around with her eyes. She thought she might have been able to see where the trail, such as it was, picked up on the other side.

Raoul said, "But not tonight. This trail, if you want to call it that, is dangerous enough in the daylight. Going around the fall, I don't know what we'll run into, but I'd rather do it when we can all see."

Cam's rings clicked from slightly farther down the slope. She said, "You people and your limitations."

A sad smile crept onto Raoul's lips. "There's no good place to pitch tents, but make yourselves as comfortable as you can. We'll start out again at first light."

A rustling from nearby caused Nysska and Raoul both to look to their right, where Flax and Jax hopped out of the underbrush, each with a big, fat, very dead rabbit in their jaws. Raoul's smile grew more genuine. "Are they going to expect to eat those themselves, Percy?"

Nysska rolled over and sat up, her back facing the cliff, and saw Percy's normal wide grin stretch his face. "They already ate, Commander. Those are for us. And I think you've just insulted them by not accepting the food right away."

Raoul scooted down and away from the cliff and put his back to the trunk of a tall pine tree. "No offense intended," he said to the cats. "We appreciate your generosity."

Jax dropped his rabbit at Raoul's feet, but Flax took a couple of moments to stare at the Commander with unreadable eyes. Finally, she made a noise very like "*Hmph*," and flung her rabbit at him.

Percy started a small fire after the sun had set but before more than one moon had risen, when the carefully shielded flames and thin plume of smoke would be least visible. They ate the rabbits, along with some vegetables and crusty bread they'd brought with them, and soon had very little to do except wait for the dawn.

Nysska moved carefully along the edge of the landslide until she found a massive piece of relatively level exposed bedrock. She unrolled her blanket, lay down and stretched out, and stared up at the stars with her fingers laced behind her head.

She heard Cam approaching before she saw her, ring-clicks and footsteps, touched by the pale blue moonlight now that two of the moons were up. It made Nysska think of the night they'd spent in her bed. It seemed like...weeks ago. An entire life ago. Her heart beat faster the closer Cam got.

Once at Nysska's side, Cam said, "Mind if I join you?"

Nysska lifted her head, glancing back at their—well, she couldn't call it a campsite—back toward where she'd seen Raoul and Percy laying out their own bedrolls. Nothing moved back that way, and she'd walked far enough to be out of the men's earshot. Quietly, Nysska said, "I was hoping you would." She slid over to the edge of the blanket, making a space that would barely fit Cam's trim body.

Once Cam had settled in—both of them lying on their backs, shoulders touching—she said, "I wasn't sure if you'd want me to be with you tonight."

Nysska sighed.

Cam turned her head, brow creasing. "What was that sigh for?"

"'Be with me'. That could be taken to mean different things. So much of your language is based on context."

Cam rolled over to face her and propped up on one elbow. "Are you saying the sethyd language is free of ambiguity?"

"I have heard humans say that we call our tongue 'the true language.' As if we think the words we say and write somehow render us superior to you."

"But that's not accurate?"

"No. It's a misnomer. We call our tongue *la lingvo de vero*. The language of truth. Not the true language."

Cam smiled. "Well, your Plainish is excellent. When did you learn it? And how long did it take you?"

Nysska's stomach wound itself into a painfully hard knot. It was the kind of feeling she'd gotten on the few occasions when she'd come close to falling from a great height, only to catch herself at the last second. "I wish you could see the moons."

Cam hesitated, but she lay back down, her shoulder touching Nysska's again. "Oh, I've seen them. When I first got my runes, I spent a couple of weeks doing what most visual Sensors do—looking at things. Looking at everything. And yes. The moons were spectacular. Most of the people, on the other hand, were...less so." A pause. "What's it like? Where you come from? You haven't told me anything about it. I don't even know the sethyd name for your own country. Is Stonegate a common surname there?"

Nysska laughed softly. "My name is not Stonegate. Not my real name, anyway. A lot of us came through a port city called Stonegate when Emperor Valco let us in, and that's what they put on all the paperwork."

"Oh! Shit, now I feel bad, calling you by the wrong name all this time."

"It's fine. I've gotten used to it. We all have, more or less."

"Then what *is* your actual surname?"

"Kaur. Nysska Kaur. Kaur means 'princess.'"

"Dragon's scaly ass—are you *royalty*? Are you Princess Nysska?"

"Hardly. It's just a name."

"Well...all right, then, Princess Nysska Kaur. Tell me about your homeland."

Nysska slowly turned her head toward Cam. The question seemed to be asked sincerely. "It might be easier to approach that subject in another way. What have you *heard* about where we come from?"

"Propaganda, I'm sure, and little else, now that I've gotten to know you."

"Please. Indulge me."

"Hmm." Cam drummed her fingertips on her flat belly. "It's an island. A really big island. According to my grandfather, until something like five hundred years ago, it was just a part of what would become the Empire—then, and these are his words, not mine, the demons showed up out of nowhere and slaughtered everyone and took over and didn't allow any humans to set foot on the shores anymore. Until..."

Nysska closed her eyes. "Until the *Krizo*. You would translate that word as 'Crisis.'"

"Right. Yes. Um...I know this is horrible of me, but I don't know exactly—what I mean is, I don't know *anyone* who really knows what happened. All we heard was that something went really, really wrong, and a lot of your people died, and something made the land uninhabitable. Which is what turned you all into refugees—sent you asking Emperor Valco for help. The best speculation I've heard is that a volcano erupted in the middle of the island and spewed out poison gas everywhere. *Is* that what happened? Was it a volcano?"

Nysska took her time answering. "Of sorts. Yes. We had no choice but to leave. Anyone who tries to go back succumbs to the poison. Quickly."

"How quickly?"

Nysska thought about her mother. The once-powerful body rendered frail. The once-keen eyes robbed of their sight. "Days. Less time if you get closer to the island's center."

"So what do you call it?"

"What do I call what?"

"Your homeland. The, uh, island nation. Home of the sethyds."

Nysska let a tiny chuckle escape her. "We actually named it after the mountain that ended up driving us out. *Patrinamonto*. Mother's Mountain." She fell silent, staring up at the moons as they performed their glacial dance across the sky. The third and brightest one had joined the other two. "I grew up in one of the larger towns. Not as large as the capital—*Fortikajxo*—that translates to 'Fortress.' My town, Fajrasxtono, was about halfway between the mountain and the coast. The name means 'fire stone.' We mined coal there."

"So you lived with your mother and her brother, right? That's what you told me before—the mother and the uncle raise the children?"

"Glad to see you listen to me when I talk."

Cam nudged her playfully with an elbow. "That also means you have a brother. Correct?"

"I did. We grew up together. Went to the temple together, went to school together. We were as close as any sethyd brother and sister."

"Where is he now?"

Glad Cam couldn't see the details of her face, Nysska fought off the grief and rage that had overtaken her for a moment. "I lost him. In the *Krizo*."

"I'm sorry." Cam rolled over again but didn't bother propping herself up this time. Instead, she snuggled against Nysska, resting her head on Nysska's broad shoulder, and slid one arm across Nysska's body in a sideways sort of hug. "You must miss him."

Nysska lowered her face as Cam lifted her own, and their lips met. Pressing harder, Cam's tongue found Nysska's. The kiss didn't go on long enough for Nysska, and her fluttering heartbeat sent her mind spiraling up into the night sky. "I didn't know if we were going to do that again."

Cam slid over on top of her, and they shared another kiss, longer this time, the heat between them building. Nysska sat up, taking Cam with her, and her tongue found a place on Cam's neck that made her gasp.

"Great Silver fucking Dragon," Cam breathed. "You have got *skills*."

"It's nothing," Nysska said, nuzzling her earlobe. "Nerves are easier to find in humans."

Cam stopped moving. Stopped making any sound. If Nysska hadn't been pressing their chests together, she might have thought Cam had stopped breathing as well.

"Cam?"

Cam put her hands on Nysska's shoulders and pushed. Not hard.

Not roughly. But she pushed away, and Nysska let her, and Cam twisted off of her and came to rest seated on one corner of the blanket. Knees pulled up to her chin and arms wrapped around her shins.

"Cam, what's wrong?"

Cam had begun rocking back and forth a tiny bit. When she spoke, her words came out hollow, like an echo far down inside a cave, the ghost of a thought. "How many humans have you been with?"

Nysska blinked. "What? Cam, you're—I—the way I've been with you? No one. No others."

Cam nodded. "I believe you. And that makes it worse, doesn't it?"

Nysska moved closer to her, reached out to take one of her hands, but Cam snapped her own hand away as if she'd touched a glowing coal.

"I don't understand."

"I don't either. But I think I'm about to. The sethyd island. Patrinamonto. Your people never left it, and never allowed any of us to go there. You stayed totally separate. And yet you speak perfect Plainish."

"I—what does that have to do with—"

Cam shook her head, as if to dislodge unpleasant images from her mind. "And then I saw you fighting. You've got the strength and the speed, yes, but I saw where you put your blades. And then tonight... nerves are easier to find in humans, are they?"

Nysska sat back, the weight of the error she had made crushing her lungs. "Cam...I would never hurt you, you *know* that, don't you?"

"The only reason I'm not running away right now is that I know you could catch me."

"Cam, please, I—"

"There's one way that I can think of. One way for you to have learned Plainish well enough to speak it like a native. Plainish and however many other human languages you know. One way for you to pinpoint every single weakness the human body has. One way for you to understand the patterns of our nerves well enough to do what you can do with your tongue...and your fingers." Cam turned her face up toward the sky, and the light of all three moons shined and refracted through the tears on her cheeks. "You've been studying us. Haven't you? All that about no one leaving Patrinamonto, no one from the outside being allowed there. That's all lies, isn't it? You've been—what—abducting us? Testing us? *Dissecting* us? You have, haven't you? Don't lie to me, Nysska."

Nysska's hands trembled in her lap. A cold wind came rushing up from the landslide, caught her braid and whipped it around so that it stung her cheek.

"Yes."

"Great Dragon." Cam lowered her face until her forehead rested on her knees. "Great Dragon save me. Save us all."

Nysska risked moving closer to her. "What do you want me to do? To say?"

Without lifting her head, Cam said, "Well, I don't fucking *know*, do I? Nysska, I saw *you*. The real you, when I looked at you with my runes. And what I saw was *not* someone who'd lie to a person they care about. Except you *have* been lying to me, and your people have been poking and prodding us for…how long, exactly?"

Nysska didn't shy away from the truth. It felt like taking her great bronze axe and chopping off parts of her body with every word, but at the same time she felt *free*. Lighter and lighter with every drop of blood spilled. "I'm not sure exactly. At least a hundred years. But you have to understand, everything changed with the *Krizo*."

"Huh? Changed how?"

"We weren't born to be conquerors. Not all of us. At the beginning, all we wanted to achieve was peace. Harmony. We call it the First Age—that's when we recognized Atiina's wisdom, along with the other Exemplars."

Cam sniffled. "But then?"

"But then…a faction arose. A movement, an order, called the Mountain Bulls. A group of sethyds who made the argument that since we are stronger, faster, more intelligent, in every way better than humans…that we should expand. Leave our tranquil home and venture out into the world. Reshape it in our image. Take what rightfully belongs to us."

"And what rightfully belongs to you…according to the Mountain Bulls…"

"Is everything. Yes." Nysska paused. Cleared her throat. "They were only a few years away from being ready. They had built and trained an army."

"Great Silver Dragon above," Cam said, just above a whisper. "An army of sethyds."

"But then the *Krizo* happened. Nine out of every ten sethyds died a swift, savage death, and the rest of us had no choice but to flee. To appeal to Emperor Valco."

Cam lifted her head. "Fine. All right. Fine. But why are *you* here? If you think we're so inferior, if you think we need to be conquered, why are you wearing the bronze? Why are you spending time with *me*? Am I just an easy fuck? Something to pass the time while you're waiting to slaughter us all?"

"Cam…my mother's name is Simana. I told you not every sethyd agreed with the Mountain Bulls. Some of us were vocal in their opposition. My mother was such a one. She was…injured…very badly. In the *Krizo*. But her attitude, her belief, never changed. And when we arrived here, when the Emperor gave the sethyds the Crags to live in, my mother began beating that same drum again—but found herself in the minority. They banished her. I chose to go with her. Help her. Take care of her."

"Great Dragon save us," Cam murmured. "Most of the sethyds in the Crags are Mountain Bulls?"

"It's…at this point it's philosophical. They're too busy trying to catch and grow enough food to keep from starving to death to put their army back together."

"For now."

"Well…yes. For now."

"So—you agreed with her? Your mother? You were part of this opposition, too?"

"I stayed out of it. I was a priest-singer, remember? We're not supposed to take sides. But I couldn't let my mother crawl off into the wilderness to die. So I went with her. And I was there, in the wilderness with her, when Governor Anwar and I ran across each other. *That* is why I am here now. And…Cam…I'm here with *you* because…"

"Because I look like your goddess. Your *Exemplar*."

"Because I've never met anyone who's taken hold of the world by the balls and *squeezed* as hard as you have. Your mind, your heart. Your sharp tongue, backed up by a sharper wit. Yes, I love the way you taste, and yes, when I see the silver blazing in your eyes it makes me want to fall to my knees and worship you. But I'm here because of you. Because of Camble Delakroy. You've shown me what humans can be. What humans *are*."

"And your mother? Simana? Where is she? Did you just leave her to fend for herself in the wilderness?"

"No." Nysska shivered, even though the chill of the wind didn't touch her. "My mother is dead."

They both fell silent.

When it became clear that neither of them had anything else to say, Cam got up and made her way back to the campfire.

Nysska lay back down on the blanket. Though her eyes were aimed at the stars overhead, the only thing she could see was the lie she had just told, the mass of it, the weight. She wondered how long it would take to squash her flat.

17

It was an hour shy of noon, by Nysska's reckoning, when they walked into what had once been Altamar. They'd sent Flax and Jax to scout ahead, and when both felines had returned and given no indication that they'd seen anyone, Raoul reconnoitered the place himself.

Now, entering the former outpost, Percy let a low whistle slide out between his teeth. "Your father brought you here? Was he angry with you?"

Raoul's face didn't change as he answered. "Most of the time, yes. But when we did come here, there was...a *here* to come to."

Nysska paused by Cam, scanning the scene before them as Cam's rings clicked like mad. Clearly there had once been some kind of settlement, spanning the ten-meter-wide rushing river that sped past them and threw itself over the falls to crash into Gar Lake, far below. Now, there was little more than bare earth. A few scorched wooden stubs protruded from the ground here and there. Nysska spotted several broken foundations. Even the well had been destroyed, leaving nothing more than a hole in the ground ringed by worn stones flush with the surface.

Cam walked over to the well and knelt, rings clicking. "This has been filled with dirt."

Raoul turned in a circle. "There never was much to the place. It wouldn't have taken a lot to raze it. I just wasn't expecting the job to be so thorough."

Nysska concentrated. Listened as hard as she could. "All I hear is the river."

Percy gave her a short, barking laugh. "All *any* of us can hear is the river."

"Not true," Cam said, coming back from the well. "Some of us pay more attention to sound than others. But Nysska's right. I don't hear any birds. Anywhere."

Nysska's right. The words rang in her ears. Nysska had awakened that morning with her guts in knots and spent the rest of the journey to this place waiting for Cam to open up to Raoul and Percy about what Nysska had told her the night before. But she hadn't. Cam had not, in fact, said more than two words to anyone until they arrived in Altamar. Did that mean she accepted what Nysska had told her—that Nysska would never hurt her? Or did it mean that she was simply biding her time, waiting to roll out the truth when it would do the most damage?

Nysska had yet to unclench.

Percy made a broad gesture with both arms. "So what the fuck are we doing? I don't see any kind of criminal mastermind squatting in the fucking woods up here. The place is deserted."

Nysska looked around until she spotted Flax and Jax. She caught Flax's eye and beckoned to her, and after stretching and then grooming for a moment, the blood lynx sauntered over. Nysska knelt. "When we sent you and your brother in the first time, we wanted you to tell us if there were any people here. And you performed the task perfectly. But now we need to know if anyone has been here in the last few days. Can you point us to any recent scents?"

Flax cocked her head. She looked around at Jax, and the two cats locked eyes for several seconds before Flax turned her gaze back to Nysska. The blood lynx gave her a left-eyed wink and scampered with

Jax to the edge of what used to be Altamar. Nysska stood, watching as the lynxes made a great show of sniffing the ground and underbrush.

She hadn't realized Percy had gotten so close until he said, "And just what the painful bleeding fuck was that? Didn't we talk about you and the kitties?"

Nysska regarded him with a mild expression. "Come on, Percy. You know how smart they are. Plus, Flax and I—I suppose you could say we bonded when she helped me get into Benitoff's place."

He pointed a finger at her nose, but she didn't think his heart was in it. "Yeah, well, they're *my* cats. *Mine*. They take requests from *me*."

Nysska considered saying *I think those cats belong to themselves* but thought better of it. "Absolutely. Whatever you say, Mr. Bitters."

"What'd you tell her, anyway?"

"That we wanted to know if anyone had been up here in the last few days."

"Huh. Yeah, good idea." Percy's head turned as he watched the blood lynxes making their way around the area's perimeter, and he couldn't seem to keep a proud smile off his face. "Damn fucking straight, whatever I say," he mumbled and followed after the cats.

While the lynxes searched, Cam drifted over to talk to Raoul, too low and too close to the river for Nysska to make out any words. Nysska's intestines coiled around themselves again. *It doesn't matter now,* she tried to tell herself. *We're too far from the Cathedral for Raoul to do anything about it, and too close to finding Lockridge to care.* But she did care. Nysska made her way to the top of the falls and peered over the edge.

For just a moment, she forgot everything else. The view took her breath from her, held it in icy, clawing hands as the water plunged straight down into the deep blue lake below. The homes and businesses around the lake's edge looked like toys from this height, the marina like a collection of matchsticks. The largest of the boats no more than something a child would play with in the bath.

Off to one side, Nysska got her first unobstructed view of the road Raoul had warned them away from. As he'd described, it made its way up the side of the mountain in a broad, leisurely zig-zag, tilted stone-paved terraces dug into bedrock. She squinted. It was hard to tell from this distance, but parts of it looked eroded—suffering from a lack of upkeep—and one of the hairpin turns had been obliterated by another, much smaller landslide.

"What are you looking at?" Cam said, at Nysska's elbow.

Nysska successfully played off the surprise as if she hadn't almost jumped out of her skin. "The road. The real road. The one we had to avoid."

"See anyone on it?"

"No. I don't even know if horses could get up it at this point. But Raoul was right, if we'd taken it, and anybody up here had been keeping watch, they would've seen us coming as soon as we left..." She had to take a moment to bring up the name. "Barleenek." She turned to face Cam, trying and failing to read her expression. "May I ask what you were talking to Raoul about?"

Cam moved away from the falls, and Nysska followed. Cam said, "I don't see that that's any of your business. Unless, of course, I was telling him about the impending sethyd invasion, and that purple-skinned, yellow-eyed berserkers were going to come and rip us all to pieces."

Nysska exhaled, long and slow. She'd already covered the reasons that wasn't going to happen any time soon. "*Are* you going to tell him? Are you going to tell anyone?"

Cam shook her head slowly. "Nysska, I...I don't know. I don't know what to do with the information you gave me. I don't know anyone who *would* know. Maybe Governor Anwar? Sure as fuck not that empty-headed teenage girl who's taking over for him." She took Nysska's hand, but it felt more like the touch of someone looking to hold on to something solid, rather than any kind of affection.

"Until I met you, I thought I knew my place in the world. I thought, maybe, if I were really lucky, I might meet a man who didn't beat the shit out of me, and maybe I'd get married. Maybe even have a child or two, before I turn forty and they put me in the ground. But now—now I'm standing in an abandoned hunting camp, trying to find someone who may or may not be planning to overthrow the Empire, and the one person I can see spending my life with...*also* may or may not be planning to overthrow the Empire."

"I promise you, I'm not."

"Stop smiling."

"I'm *not* smiling."

"Maybe not, but you *want* to. I can hear the smile in your voice."

"Apologies."

Her grip on Nysska's hand tightened. "So right now, my whole world goes about as far as finding Lockridge. Let's just focus on what we came here to do, all right? And worry about everything else if we survive."

Nysska ran her thumb over the back of Cam's hand. "I accept your proposal."

From the tree line at the far end of the barren space that had once been Altamar, Percy waved his arms and beckoned to them. Nysska said, "Looks like the cats might've come through."

Percy and Raoul stood, conferring quietly, when Nysska and Cam reached them. Flax and Jax, having fulfilled their task, both sat at Percy's feet and groomed themselves. At Nysska's inquiring look, Raoul pushed aside what she had taken for a chest-high shrub—but which was actually a cleverly constructed screen, behind which the ground dropped into a slot canyon less than a meter wide. The cleft in the earth angled steeply downward, though not quite steep enough that it couldn't be navigated, and cut off their line of sight when it crooked to the right after twelve or thirteen meters.

Raoul let the screen drop back into place and beckoned everyone away from it. When they'd gotten far enough to put them out of anyone's earshot who might have been listening from deeper in the slot canyon, he said, "I don't like this. None of it. If Lockridge is the head of some vast conspiracy, then where are his men?" He made an expansive gesture around them. "This is nothing more than a bald spot on top of a mountain."

Percy shrugged. "It's public. Anyone could wander up here. Just like we did. I'm in charge of something secret? I'm going to keep it fucking *secret*." He pointed at the brush screen. "If anybody's here at all, I'm betting we'll find them down at the bottom of wherever that hare-lip in the bedrock takes us."

Raoul ran his hands over his scalp—careful not to dislodge the commander's band, which he'd retrieved from the corner of Nysska's room—and stared at the ground. "Could the cats scout for us again?"

Percy put his hands up. "Whoa, hey, now, they're fucking smart—you know that—but they're not going to be able to spell out *exactly* what they see. Could be two of Lockridge's thugs. Could be a couple of civilians who got really fucking lost. Could be who knows what. Better to send somebody down there who's got thumbs and speaks Plainish."

"I...could..." Cam stopped herself, then started again. "I...could tell...I think I could *look*. You take my meaning?" She tapped the outside corner of her eye with one fingertip. "I've never tried it before, but I might be able to look...*through* some of the stone...see what's around the corners...?"

Raoul's eyebrows had shot up, and Percy's mouth fell open. He said, "Fucking Dragon's *balls*, woman, are you telling us you can see through *rock*? You didn't think this was information we could fucking *use*?"

Cam punched Percy in the shoulder. "Are we a combat unit? Have I ever *needed* to see around corners before?"

Nysska said, "I'll go."

Cam spun to face her. "Why? I just said I can probably see whoever's down there, if I get close enough. Do *you* have eyeball runes?"

Nysska grunted. "All right, first, *anyone* can see something if they get close enough." Cam sputtered in protest, but Nysska kept going. "Second, if you get down there and break out the argonium, *they're* going to see *you*. Hey, what's that silver light shining from around the corner? Oh, I don't know, probably an intruder, let's go stab them repeatedly." She dipped her head closer to Cam. "Also, if you think I'm going to let you shorten your life when there's an alternative, you've lost your mind."

Cam's face wrinkled into a sour mask, and she folded her arms, but didn't say anything further. Nysska looked to Raoul. "Commander? Do you find this plan acceptable?"

Raoul swiveled his head between Nysska and the brush screen a couple of times. "I suppose." After a pause, he said, "But listen. Cam's right. We're not a combat unit. We're an investigative unit. All four of us can fill our hands with bronze, as we've demonstrated, but it would be idiotic of me to pretend you're not the Ninth Crucible's biggest muscle."

Percy said, "What he means is, don't leave us up here with our asses hanging out."

Nysska gave Raoul a tiny, experimental smile. "Don't worry, Commander. I won't abandon you."

Raoul nodded. "Good. Also—Nysska. For fuck's sake. Call me Raoul."

Nysska's smile got marginally wider. "Just sit tight, Raoul. I'll be back soon."

Percy held the screen aside for her. Flax let out a tiny trill and acted as if she were going to follow, but Nysska crouched down and looked the blood lynx in her silver eyes. "No no, kitty cat. You and your brother need to stay here with Percy. All right?"

Flax cocked her head, and gave Nysska a slow blink, and yawned. Nysska scratched her between the ears and, when she was sure neither of the lynxes were following, entered the slot canyon.

She had only made it halfway to the sight-obscuring turn when she noticed how much both light and sound had dampened around her. It was broad daylight up above, but down in this rock crevice the sunshine seemed to die, and moss growing on the walls and underfoot absorbed any noise she might have either made or heard. Nysska paused at the corner and concentrated, listening hard—

And heard nothing.

Taking care that a horn didn't clatter or scrape against stone, she peeked around the corner, and saw the canyon path continue down the same steep grade, just shifted ninety degrees to the right—and going far enough and deep enough into the gloom of the mountain's heart that she couldn't see what lay at the far end. Nysska took a deep breath, kept her hand on the hilt of her sword to make sure nothing rattled, and crept downward.

After at least a hundred meters, maybe more, the slot canyon took another sharp turn to the right. She peered around the corner and had to take a moment to process what she was seeing. The canyon itself ended in a vast rock wall, but the lowermost three or four meters of it remained open, becoming the entrance to what looked like a cave. From somewhere inside, deep within the darkness, firelight flickered.

Nysska paused. The approach to the cave mouth was ten more meters of narrow canyon, with sheer walls on both sides stretching all the way up to the tiny strip of blue at the top, and would give her zero cover. If anyone who might be inside the cave bothered to glance out, they'd see her, with nothing she could do about it.

Nysska weighed her options—go back now, bring everyone down here, and take their chances as they entered the cave...or try to get inside and get the lay of the land first, while risking being discovered and losing any element of surprise.

Nysska already knew the answer to the dilemma. There was no way between earth and sky that she would risk bringing the rest of the team into an unknown situation. She approached the cave entrance silently and stepped inside.

Darkness enveloped her. Immediately after the entrance, the walls on either side opened out sharply, and she hugged the one to the left, taking the few seconds she needed for her eyes to adjust to the diminished light.

One by one, details came to her.

This was no mere cave. It was a *cavern*. Not only the walls, but the ceiling as well, sprang away from the narrow entrance, lit here and there by guttering torches, some in wall sconces, a few in free-standing racks. Far above, fifteen or twenty meters over her head, she could just barely make out the shapes of stalactites. The true width of the place escaped her.

In the center of the cavern, canted at five or ten degrees off level, was a...she groped for words. A *structure*, yes, certainly. But not one she'd ever seen the like of before. It appeared to have three stories, but part of the bottom story had sunk into the cavern's floor. That wasn't the strange bit—the bit that made her stare and stare until she had to blink. The structure was rectangular on its face, at least superficially similar to the Imperial College in Taurus Hill, but...it seemed to be made of *one enormous stone*. She could see no evidence of any seams or joints or lines of mortar anywhere—though the building did seem to be moored to a much larger, perfectly flat, very thin black stone that spread out from it, so that the whole thing looked like a sculpture seated on a table. More torch light glimmered inside the building, but she saw no movement in its windows.

Well. If Lockridge were here, that was where he'd be, no question.

Nysska slipped noiselessly out of the cavern and sprinted back up the length of the canyon.

18

Percy let a long, low whistle escape from between his teeth. "Well hold me down and plant petunias in my asshole."

"*Please* be quiet," Nysska said, keeping her voice low. "We don't know who might be inside that thing, or how many of them."

"But you don't see anyone outside?" Cam asked softly. Her rings clicked, clicked again, and kept on clicking as she turned in a slow circle. "I would very much like to get closer to whatever this thing is."

Nysska glanced over at Raoul and, for the first time, saw that he seemed at a genuine loss for words, rather than simply choosing to sulk. In the dim light of the torches his eyes had taken on a shimmering sort of wonderment. "I'm guessing your father had no idea this place was here," she said.

Raoul spoke as if forming the words took a great deal of effort—effort he'd much rather spend staring at the bizarre gray structure. "He might've known about that slot canyon, but the opening to this place—" Raoul gestured vaguely behind them, "—has been recently excavated. What kind of architecture are we looking at here? What kind of *stone* is that?"

They had made it to the edge of the "table" on which the building perched. The edge itself was rough, irregular, as if broken out of a much larger piece. Percy knelt and ran his fingertips across the broad, flat surface at their feet. "It's like—I don't know, it looks like somebody melted a bunch of rocks into porridge and just fucking *poured* it here. Poured it and let it cool, and it turned into this." He took a tentative step out onto it. "And look at this—someone's painted *stripes* across it."

Nysska stepped up beside Percy. Sure enough, very faint, as if painted eons ago, yellow stripes crisscrossed the surface.

Raoul had let his gaze travel from the building's foundation up to the roof. "See how the whole structure sits at a slant? My mother told me once about an earthquake, in a town down near the southern border. She said, when it was over, some of the homes wound up at a slant. Kind of like this."

Cam said, "That is truly fascinating. Can we please get closer?"

Flax and Jax had left the group and begun sniffing around the outside wall, drifting far enough away that they were almost lost in shadows. Percy snapped his fingers and made his *come here* sound with his lips, and the blood lynxes bounded back over to him.

Raoul faced the rest of them. "We circle the structure once. Make sure there aren't any surprises on the other side." He took a deep breath and let it out slowly. "Then I guess we see what's in there."

Cam grunted. "Fucking finally."

With Nysska in the lead, yellow eyes gleaming in the dim interior, the Ninth Crucible made their way around the perimeter. The odd, cracked, "melted rock" surface gave way to what appeared to be the cavern's natural floor, and soon they found themselves picking through stalagmites. Halfway around, Nysska paused. "I'm not seeing bedrolls or anything out here. No trash, no shit buckets. Any people staying here long-term are going to be inside."

They finished their circle, tightening their path as they came around the building's far side, and arrived at the door. It was nothing more than a tall, wide, empty rectangle built into the bizarre seamless stone, except that halfway through, a vertical, floor-to-ceiling slot had been carved into the wall on both sides of the doorway. Cam examined it, rings clicking, fingertips probing. "It's like a pocket door," she whispered. "At some point, some narrow door slid out of here."

Nysska took a step inside, touched one of the walls, and jerked her hand back.

Cam touched her arm. "What is it? Are you hurt?"

"No. The walls are covered in...I think it's moss?"

Percy had taken a few steps ahead of them and waved his hand to get their attention. "Bet your ass it's moss," he said, gesturing with his chin farther inside. "Anybody ever heard of moss that fucking *glows*, though?"

What the strange building's interior had looked like before the earth shook and left it in its current state, Nysska had no idea. Now moss grew everywhere, and when Percy waved his arm at it, it gave off a faint pale light. Nysska stepped up beside Percy, and the moss around them glowed a tiny bit brighter.

"It looks like fireflies," Raoul said quietly from right behind them. "The glow. It's like a firefly's abdomen."

Nysska waved her hand slowly near the ceiling, and the glow there intensified. Still weak, but ever so slightly brighter. "Seems as if it knows we're here."

The corridor stretched away into darkness. "I brought lanterns," Raoul said. "Should we even bother?"

Nysska addressed the group. "If you'll allow me. I should go first, for all the same reasons that I took point in the canyon."

Raoul shrugged. Flax walked up and nuzzled Nysska's ankles, but Percy said, "Ah-ah, kitten, you're staying here with me."

Cam pressed against Nysska's side and squeezed her arm. "You just make sure you stay in one piece."

Nysska crept down the hallway, just as she had in the slot canyon, but this proved to be a much shorter journey. Not fifteen meters from where the rest of her team stood, she discovered a door—a hastily, sloppily constructed door made of wooden planks lashed together with twine—and when she peered through one of its many cracks, she drew in a sharp breath and walked quickly back.

"Any people?" Raoul asked.

"No live ones. Place is tomb-silent. But you all need to witness this." Nysska led them back down the hallway, took a good look through the door again, and pushed it open. All four of them stared.

Percy said, "Fuck me sideways."

Quietly, staying together, the team entered a broad, low-ceilinged room that had been very clearly set up to mimic the laboratory of Runemaster Naveed Olkoff, brightly lit by at least a dozen lanterns hung from the ceiling on chains. The shelves were arranged in the same way as Olkoff's lab. The same style of work benches were bolted to all four walls. Olkoff's taste in furniture remained consistent, and the same kind of table he had used occupied the center of the space. The only real difference, aside from the location, was the *seven other tables* neatly arranged around the room's perimeter.

Cam's rings hadn't stopped clicking, but she stuck by Nysska's side. "Are—are they…?"

Five of the tables, including the one in the room's center, were occupied. Nysska got closer to the center table. "Dead," she said with a quiet finality. Scanning the other bodies, she saw that they were all in a similar state. "Throats slashed. Doesn't look as if a drop of blood remains in any of them."

Behind her, Raoul made a noise of deep disgust in his throat. Nysska saw him nudging a bucket below a table with his toe. The bucket sloshed, deep red liquid oozing down the side, and the stench of rot and death washed over them.

Cam laced her fingers through Nysska's as Percy and Raoul joined them, the four of them forming a small, tight circle. Flax and Jax stepped into the middle of that circle and sat, looking up with their great silver eyes, paying attention. "What do we do?" Cam asked.

Raoul gestured with one hand. "Well, someone lit all those lanterns. And no one simply walks away and lets a dozen lanterns burn. There's someone here. Somewhere. But until that someone gets back, we…" He trailed off.

Nysska said, "We search the place? See what kind of information we can turn up?"

The oddest smile curled Raoul's lips. Nysska thought it was a perfect dual embodiment of bitterness and good-natured humor. Raoul said, "Just as we've been doing since we were assigned this case, yes, Nysska. I suppose this is as good as time as any to say, 'You were right.'"

Percy chuckled, but Nysska said, "I'd feel better about it under different circumstances."

Raoul actually let his teeth show. "And yet here we are. All right, let's see what we can find. Everyone go to one corner and work to your right. When you're done..." He did a quick count of the shelves. "Pick a row of books and see if anything jumps out at you. Cam—you can stick with Nysska for the book part."

Cam put her hands on her hips in mock indignation. "Are you saying I can't read?"

The words took Nysska off-guard, and she laughed.

She really, truly *laughed*.

It felt as if some kind of obstacle had just broken loose—some blockage in the gears—not between her and her own laughter, but between the four of them. Looking from face to face, she thought the others felt it as well—a kind of release, a warm, comforting flood of familiarity. Of friendship. Of *trust*. For the first time, Nysska knew she could simply stand there with these people, people who accepted her, and *belong*.

She had never felt that way before. Not with humans. Maybe... maybe not with sethyds, either. Not like this.

Nysska held her arm out, bent at the elbow. "Flax? Want to come up here and help me look for things?" The blood lynx's eyes fastened on Nysska's elbow, her hindquarters wiggled, and she leapt up and settled into the crook. "There's a good girl. Let's go find some information, would you like to do that? Would you? Hmm?"

Nysska walked off toward one of the corners, the big cat purring against her chest, and heard Percy say—a grin in his words—"Turns out demons from the pits of Hell are big softies."

Nysska rifled through stacks of papers and carefully-rolled scrolls of parchment on the first worktable. Every square centim was covered in tiny, tightly scrawled handwriting in a language that Nysska had seen before but couldn't read. She thought it might have been Estmani, but thanks to the terrible penmanship it was difficult to tell. Half the sheets and all of the scrolls were thick with numbers, sequences, and equations using symbols and mathematical conventions with which she was unfamiliar.

She set down the last scroll and moved to her right, which put her directly in front of one of the dead bodies on the lab tables. The corpse was male, human, and in life would have looked like a woodsman, perhaps. Tall, thickly muscled, with a dense black beard that hid the upper part of his chest. Aside from the ear-to-ear incision that had opened up all of his major vessels—a cut that Nysska confirmed by lifting up his beard with the blade of her dagger—he also had long, fresh wounds running down his arms and legs. Those had been stitched shut, though Nysska judged that to have been performed post-mortem, since a thick black suture line had been used to close the incisions with all the skill and finesse of a child playing doctor. In fact—she looked more closely—she thought she saw the same kind of knots that had been used to put together the wood-plank-and-twine door to the lab.

Moving past the corpse, she came to another worktable. This one had much less of the strange, tiny kind of notation she saw at the first desk. Instead, its writing surface had been modified with bronze brackets at the edges, and after a few seconds of examination, Nysska realized they were pivot hinges.

Flax seemed to have come to the same realization. She hopped off Nysska's arm onto the desk and pushed at the lower edge of the writing surface—which gave way, revolving—and Nysska pulled Flax back so that it wouldn't hit her on the head as the top edge swung down.

The writing surface came to rest with a click, and Nysska's eyes narrowed.

A single large piece of paper had been affixed to the writing surface's underside, the entirety of which was taken up with a strange pattern of connecting rectangles: one narrow rectangle running horizontally, with smaller boxes attached, above and below it.

Flax had been staring at it. At the same instant that Nysska said, "Oooh, *shit*," Flax hissed. Nysska called out, "I've found something."

The rest of the team crowded around her, Jax on Percy's shoulders. Cam said, "What? What is it?"

Nysska touched the long, central rectangle. "Am I crazy? Or is this a floor plan of the Governor's Mansion in Tember?"

"New toys," said a voice from the laboratory door. Nysska whirled around to see a small, gaunt old man standing there, dressed in a long, gray robe. His pale skin was blemished with broad age spots, and his wispy white hair had almost all fallen out. Yet his pale green eyes gleamed and flashed in the lantern light, and he raised a walking staff—a polished length of pale wood, with a fist-sized dark red stone set at one end—and punched it down into the floor. "How delightful."

Horrible, grinding screams filled the air as the five corpses on the tables woke up.

19

Nysska's world slowed to a crawl.

The corpse directly in her line of sight was tall, lanky, with long arms and legs and a long neck supporting a head with a narrow skull. It sat up, its head swiveling toward her, and something about the way it moved made her think more of a stick insect than a human. It might have been trying to talk, or perhaps scream, but she couldn't tell because what came scraping and grinding out of its throat were like no sounds ever made by humans or sethyds.

Smoke rose from it as the runes buried underneath its skin began to glow.

Nysska knew how closely argonium and thaumaturgy were tied—that the energy of thaumaturgy was the color of argonium, the gleaming silver, the frozen blue-white sparks, the godlike flames that poured from Cam's eyes.

She remembered the corrupted energy of the tarn killed by the Infantry on the bridge, too, the flares of ebon lightning that shot from his skin, the runes shining black like onyx.

The light bursting forth from this corpse's limbs and chest and face glowed *red*.

And it *was* a corpse, there was no doubting that, with its blank milky eyes and its chest that neither rose nor fell, never mind the gaping wound in its throat. And yet the corpse's hands curled around the metal edge of the table on which it sat, and Nysska watched as the runes along its arms glowed brighter, and its fingers dug into the metal, crushed it, crumpled it, as if it were little more than paper.

That same horrible, unholy sound wrenched itself from the throats of the other four corpses in the lab as they all sat up, all of them glowing with the hideous, malevolent blood-red light, all of them twisting and jerking heads on horribly damaged necks as sightless eyes focused on Nysska and her teammates.

At that moment, Nysska realized the corpses weren't the only ones screaming. She tore her gaze away long enough to get a good look at Cam's face, and her heart shattered, became glass-sharp fragments that ground into her soul.

Cam had opened her eyes, the divine silver light gleaming—and thick, oily black liquid ran down her face…the same putrid tears that had come to her in Olkoff's lab.

"There's nothing there," Cam said, the words as brittle and fragile as Nysska's heart. "What I saw—in the lab—this is what I saw!"

The long, lean corpse shoved itself off the table and lunged for Nysska's throat, metal-gouging fingers hooked into claws, and Nysska sidestepped and brought her longsword down on the corpse's outstretched forearm. The red runes under his skin flared, blinding-bright, and Nysska's sword jumped away from the limb as if she had struck a block of solid marble. She barely held on to the weapon, her fingers singing with pain, and another of the corpses flung itself directly onto Raoul.

Nysska pivoted, brought the hilt of her sword around in an arc parallel to the floor, and connected with the back of the thin corpse's head with more than enough force to kill a normal human. The blow rewarded her with the sickening crunch of breaking bone. Oily gray matter sprayed from the huge rent in the corpse's skull, and it whirled, moving with the force of the blow, and punched her in the chest.

Nysska sprawled backward and slammed into the nearest corpse table, gasping for breath, trying to refill her suddenly airless lungs.

Raoul and the second corpse had crashed to the floor, and Raoul tried to shout something, but she heard the twisting snap of a bone giving way, and the commander's screams added to the unholy cacophony from the corpses.

The other three had backed Percy and Cam into a corner, along with Flax and Jax, advancing on them with outstretched arms. Nysska tried to gather air for a battle cry, but it was all she could do to suck in enough to keep from passing out, and she realized that if they tried to fight these creatures here and now, they were going to die, swiftly and horribly.

She vaulted backward over the table, grabbed a lantern off its wall hook, and heaved it at the floor between the advancing corpses and her cornered teammates.

Flames splashed out, roaring and crackling as the lantern shattered, and the corpse on top of Raoul looked up, its grip loosening. Nysska rushed at the one that had struck her, dropped low and swept her leg around in a swift, brutal arc, knocking its legs out from under it. She rushed past its sprawling body and slammed straight into the one mangling Raoul, bashing it away, and as she helped Raoul up, Nysska finally got enough air inside her. She bellowed, "*Ninth Crucible! Fall back! Fall back!*"

She'd lost sight of the old man in the robes but didn't much care about him. Every bit of her attention centered on her teammates, and as Percy scooped up the two blood lynxes, Nysska took Cam's wrist with one hand, steadied Raoul with the other, and the whole team barreled toward the door. Nysska didn't know how far behind them the corpses were but knew they couldn't take the time to find out. She had one of Raoul's arms over her shoulder, mostly carrying him, and as they pelted out into the hallway, Nysska screamed, "Back outside! Back outside!"

The short length of hallway between the lab door and the strange building's exit stretched out in front of them. Alone, Nysska could have covered that distance in three seconds, maybe two, and she was determined not to let Raoul slow her down much more than that—

Halfway between the lab door and the entrance, the wall exploded in a shower of gray bricks, dust, and shredded moss, and one of the corpses stepped through the gap, its body alight with red runes and the hair on its head on fire. Another corpse followed the first one—the big bruiser Nysska had seen first when searching the laboratory—and another after that.

"They've got us blocked off," Percy cried, and Nysska wheeled, Raoul's feet leaving the floor as she spun.

"That way!" she screamed, pointing down the hall on the far side of the lab door. "Go! Go! *Run!*"

"We don't know what's down there," Raoul said, strained with agony, his left arm hanging useless at his side.

All five corpses piled out of the hole in the wall and started after them. "Doesn't matter," Nysska barked. "Just go!"

Moving as fast as they could, the Ninth Crucible scrambled down the corridor, deeper into the unknown structure, as glowing red death came shambling after them.

"Move," Nysska said, as much to herself as to the rest of her team. "Move!"

Raoul cried out but clamped down on it as soon as the sound had escaped his lips. Percy stumbled past, Flax and Jax still clutched to his chest, both cats squirming and growling. Cam kept pace with Nysska and Raoul, her eyes open and silver runes shining, but the black tears kept coming, and from the hollowed-out expression on her face, Nysska feared that every second Cam's sight remained active did more damage to her.

The corridor dipped, a long ramp taking them down to a level below the laboratory. Empty doorways passed by on the right and the left, yawning portals of darkness lit only fleetingly by the luminescent moss. Nysska didn't slow down. She could hear the corpses' footsteps behind them and reckoned it pointless to duck through any of the openings, as it would offer them no way to halt their pursuers and likely as not leave them trapped in a dead end.

"Up ahead," Cam croaked out, and pointed. "Up there."

Nysska squinted but, try as she might, her eyes couldn't penetrate the dark. "What? What do you see?"

"Door." Cam hurried ahead of the group, the glowing moss coming to life around her. "Door! Come on!"

The blood lynxes finally broke free of Percy's grip, hit the ground, and streaked ahead after Cam. Percy stopped for a heartbeat, blinking, as if his entire purpose had been to protect the cats. Nysska barked, "Go after Cam! Make sure she's all right!"

Percy grunted and bolted away down the corridor.

From behind them, a wordless, scraping groan echoed, but with all the moss on the walls Nysska couldn't judge how close the reanimated corpses were. Raoul said, "I can walk. Turn me loose."

Nysska picked up the pace instead. "We don't need to walk. We need to run."

"Either turn me loose or carry me! This isn't getting the job done!"

At that instant, Nysska saw the door Cam had shouted about. The hallway dead-ended at it—a massive thing of metal, standing most of the way closed, only a crevice of darkness between its edge and the doorframe. Cam popped back out from the other side, her silver-gleaming eyes a beacon. "Run! *Run!*"

"Forgive me, Commander," Nysska said, and picked Raoul up entirely, tucking him against her with one arm around his waist. She broke into a sprint and covered the remaining ground in a flash, slipping through the opening to find Percy and Cam on the other side, both of them straining as they pushed to close the massive door.

Footsteps and grinding voices grew louder from the hallway.

Nysska set Raoul down and joined Cam and Percy in pushing. The door moved a scant centim, unseen hinges howling in protest. Raoul pushed as well, setting his good shoulder against the metal. The door moved another two centims and ground to a halt.

"Come on!" Nysska bellowed. The floor under their feet was the same strange, smooth, stone-like material as the rest of the building. She wished it were dirt—something she could dig her feet into. "Push!"

The door moved another fraction. Not nearly fast enough.

The corpses were almost there. The blood-red glow from their runes seeped around the door's edge.

Nysska screamed, *"Come on! Put your tits into it!"* She pushed hard enough that she thought her bones would break—

As one of the corpses reached past the doorframe, the hinges shrieked like a dying animal, and the massive metal door slammed closed. The corpse's reaching hand, severed at its elbow, hit the ground and flopped like a fish on a dock.

A handle shaped like a ring half a meter across was set in the door's center, and when Nysska didn't hear any locks engaging, she grabbed it and spun it clockwise, in hopes that it would work like tightening a screw. To her vast relief, the handle turned without much resistance, and after three revolutions she heard multiple deadbolts sliding home.

Nysska turned and collapsed against the door, sliding down until her ass hit the floor's cool, smooth stone. Raoul didn't bother putting his back to the door. He just sank to his knees. Nysska thought the only thing keeping him from collapsing entirely was the pain that made him wince and hiss when the hand of his broken arm touched the floor.

The walls on either side of the huge metal door supported strips and clumps of the luminescent moss, but it only lit their surroundings well enough to see for a dim two meters.

Cam had collapsed nearby, curled into a fetal position on the floor, her body trembling with sobs. As Nysska scrambled to her, she heard Percy say through panting breaths, "Where the fuck are we?"

20

Nysska gathered Cam up in her arms. Her body still trembled, and Nysska wiped the black sludge away from her cheeks, but the physical contact seemed to give Cam something to hold onto. She planted a hand on the side of Nysska's neck, stared into her eyes, and Nysska watched as the icy fire dimmed, flickered, and went out.

Cam looked up at her with eyes of silver, not too dissimilar from the blood lynxes' eyes. Her ragged breathing slowed and evened out, and her jaw clenched and rippled with concentration. "All right," Cam breathed. "All right. I think...I think I've got this." She slid out of Nysska's arms, propping herself up with one hand and wiping further at her face with the other. "Hell of a way to learn to control something. God*damn* this stuff stinks." She got to her feet, Nysska following her a second later, and they both flinched as a tremendous impact from the other side of the huge metal door rang like the strike of a gigantic bell. The door itself did not move. At all.

Nysska wondered if they were going to be able to get back *out*.

She put a hand on Cam's arm. "*Are* you all right?"

Cam glanced around. Blinked a few times. "I think so. That's why everything went crazy in Olkoff's lab—one of those dead fuckers killed him. That's why I couldn't *see* it. And this is the second time they've caught me off-guard, but…I'll be damned if they do it again." She glanced around. "You know the way I felt, there in the lab? When I said I could sense the argonium, but there was something different about it? That feeling is much, *much* stronger here."

Nysska had a hard time focusing on Cam's words. "You're still using your runes."

Cam gazed up at her. "I've got them toned down. This way they work like regular eyes, more or less. No solving murders or anything. We'll find out what happens if I look at one of those fucking corpses again."

"But using them at *all—karulino,* they're toxic."

When Cam spoke, her words held a flat, hard edge that Nysska hadn't heard her use before. "It's a little late to worry about taking years off my life. Those were dead bodies out there. *Cadavers.* And they got up and attacked us. If a walking corpse is going to rip my throat out in the next ten minutes, I fucking well want to see it coming." She softened her expression, grasped Nysska's arm, and lowered her voice. "I did like the sound of whatever name you just called me, by the way."

Nysska couldn't think of anything to say to that. A ball of dread appeared in her stomach and settled in.

Raoul called out from where he sat with his back against the huge metal door. "Cam—can you see in here? What is this place? More important, are there any other entrances that those glowing dead fuckers can get through?"

Cam turned and stared out into the darkness. Nysska watched, fascinated and terrified, as the radiance of her eyes increased bit by bit, like a silver sunrise. "I do see a door, but it's got a pile of rocks in front of it—looks as though the ceiling collapsed."

"Nothing else?"

"I don't think so, but there are a few spots I can't see from here. Let me check."

Nysska almost stopped her. Instead, trying not to sound as if she were on the edge of hysteria, she said, "Don't go far."

"Don't worry." Cam went up on her toes, gave Nysska a quick kiss on the lips, and disappeared into the impenetrable dark. Nysska strained to hear her footsteps, which scuffed off to the right, then to the left. "I'm pretty sure we're alone in here," Cam called out to them, her voice fainter with distance than Nysska liked. "Hey—got a couple lanterns." The footsteps approached again, and Cam came back into the weak glow of the moss. She held two ordinary Imperial lanterns out to Nysska and Percy. "Either one of you have firesticks?"

"I've got it," Percy said, and took both lanterns. He rummaged in a pouch, knelt to set the lanterns on the floor, and seconds later, both of them lit up bright. Percy sat back, putting away the two metal rods that had provided the necessary sparks.

Raoul said, "Good work."

In response, Percy's face wrinkled up. "Holy fucking shit, boss. You look like hell."

Percy wasn't wrong. Nysska went to one knee beside Raoul, taking in his waxy complexion and the sweat trying to soak all the way through his armor. "Can you tell how bad it is?"

Raoul tried to move and gritted his teeth against the pain. "My shoulder's dislocated. The break is halfway between the wrist and elbow. Pretty sure it's both bones."

Another deafening *clang* sounded out from the other side of the metal door, but the door itself didn't even vibrate.

Cam knelt on Raoul's other side, bathing him in the silver glow of her eyes. "Both bones are broken, yes," she said. "I can see them through the skin and muscle. Clean breaks." She looked up at Nysska. "We're going to have to cut his sleeve off."

Percy grunted. "You were serious, back there in the canyon, huh? You really can see through shit with those?" When Cam didn't answer, he said, "Good thing I've got a giant cock, then! ...Nothing? Really? Fuck. I thought that was funny." He backed up, giving them room to work, but paid close attention to the proceedings. After half a minute, he said, "So you're just going to fucking use those things now? Let your light shine all the time?"

Cam didn't turn her head. "We'll see. I could get used to it. Percy, can you find us something to splint a forearm with?"

Percy scuttled away, taking one of the lanterns, as Nysska tried not to dwell on the new attitude Cam seemed to have adopted. The two blood lynxes came and sat on either side of Raoul, and Jax popped up and put his feet on the side of Raoul's chest and licked him a couple of times on the jaw. Raoul worked up the faintest of smiles. "Is that supposed to help me feel better?" Jax meowed once. Raoul said, "Well, thanks, friend. I appreciate i—"

He would have finished the word "it" if Nysska hadn't chosen that moment to pop his shoulder back into its socket, causing Raoul to erupt into a long, impressive string of curses. Jax bounded away from him, retreating to the edge of the lantern light, where he turned and peered at Raoul and Nysska with huge, reproachful eyes. When Raoul could breathe again, he glared at Nysska and Jax in turn. "Did you two plan that? Distract me so I'd be relaxed when you did it?"

Jax yawned, walked over to his sister, and he and Flax began to wrestle. Nysska hadn't moved, and said, "If we had, would you have approved of the decision?"

Another ear-ringing *clang* sounded out. Both of the cats bolted away into the dark, passing Percy, who came back with a couple of flat strips of green, corroded bronze. "Look what I found," he said, sounding proud of himself, and handed them to Cam. "Bronze is fucking law, huh?"

Cam wasted no time applying the makeshift splint to Raoul's arm. She'd torn off a few centims from the bottom of her shirt, now leaving a span of her midriff bare, and Nysska chastised herself for thinking grossly inappropriate thoughts given their present circumstances. "How does that feel?" Cam asked.

Raoul moved his arm gingerly. "Feels like it's broken," he said, but at the look on Cam's face, he quickly followed that with, "But now I know the bone's not going to come poking through the skin or cutting any major blood vessels, so it's much better, thank you." Using his other hand to brace himself, he got to his feet and looked around the space. "What exactly are we looking at, with all of this?" Another resounding impact struck the door, and Raoul winced. "With any luck, something that will help us get *out* of here?"

Cam beckoned to them, and walked out ahead, talking over her shoulder. "I don't even know how to describe these things." She pointed, and Nysska raised a lantern high. "There's all this...wreckage? I suppose you'd call it? And then the new versions over here."

Now that they were away from the door, and had a couple of decent sources of light, Nysska could make out the rest of the room they were in—though she didn't think the word "room" did it justice. More like "chamber," or "artificial cavern," or maybe even "temple."

The remains of rusted metal lay everywhere around them. Fittings and brackets in the walls all the way up to the ten-meter-high ceiling had no doubt once held bolts and beams. Mostly crumbled piles might have been fallen walkways, as Nysska spotted a halfway-gone set of steps. In the middle of the vast space they saw outlines and rusted metal chunks of rectangular tray-like objects, and beyond them, something huge and round seemed to have crashed to the floor and burst apart.

"How fucking old is all this shit?" Percy said, asking no one in particular.

Nysska peered up, caught sight of a few links of chain dangling from the ceiling, and said, "There was at one point some kind of enormous metal...pot? Or cauldron? Hanging from up there?"

Raoul and Percy had moved past the dilapidated bits and pieces and stood looking at what Cam had referred to as the "new versions."

One corner of the colossal space contained a massive oven, an intact cauldron-like piece hanging from unbroken chains, and a long series of trays, though these were much smaller than the ancient ones elsewhere in the room. Every piece of this newer equipment was made of bronze.

"This is a smelter," Raoul said. "Heat metal up till it's molten, then use this..." He tapped the side of the cauldron. "...to pour it into molds." He turned to face the rest of the group, as Flax and Jax came out of the darkness and sat down at Percy's feet.

Percy had picked up a piece of the rusted metal and begun digging and chipping at it with the tip of one of his daggers. A chunk of rust fell away, and he frowned before he held it up near one of the lanterns for the rest to see. The surface under the rust shone a dull silver in the light. "Feels like I'm losing my Dragon-damned mind in here. The fuck kind of metal is this?"

Nysska's jaw tightened. "Everyone. Listen." At the note of command in her voice, the rest of the team did turn to her—Raoul with his brows raised. Nysska paused. "Commander. My apologies."

Raoul shook his head carefully. "No—no, you go on. I'm doing the best I can right now not to vomit. Say what you have to say."

Nysska ticked off points on the fingers of her right hand. "First, as far as we can tell, there's only one way out of here. Second, that scrawny little man in the robes, if he's still here, is the only one who can confirm what Lockridge is planning, but it seems clear from that layout of the Governor's Mansion that Anwar is in danger. Third, all five of those glowing dead fuckers are between us and saving Anwar's life."

"There's a fourth point," Cam said quietly. "We all know what normal argonium looks like. And we know what it looks like when somebody tears it out and puts it in a tarn. Nobody's ever seen *red runes* before."

Nysska spoke just as quietly. "Which means what?"

Cam gestured around them. "I can see traces of it. Someone has taken argonium and alloyed it with…I don't know what with. Something I've never seen before. Something new. And when it's active, I can't see it at *all*, which is how I wound up with fucking corpse juice running out of my goddamn tear ducts." She pointed at the smelter. "So where *is* all this—I don't know what to call it—this new thaumaturgical alloy?"

Raoul looked even more nauseated. "They took it with them. Lockridge and his people worked up who knows how much of the stuff and took it with them."

"We have to get out of here," Cam said. Not in a panicked, desperate way. Just a statement of fact. "We have to tell people about this…Dragon help me, I'm scared to say it, but…"

Percy finished the sentence for her. "We have to tell people about this new kind of thaumaturgy."

The words hung there between them. Obscene. Terrifying.

Raoul said, "You're right. We have to let the world know. Because the world just fucking *changed*."

Nysska took a deep breath. "Yes. And to make it out...I'm going to need Flax and Jax's help."

Percy's face clouded. "You need what, now?"

"You've said—we have all said—that this is not a combat unit. But those creatures out there are slow, and..." she pointed at the severed arm lying near the door, "...that is clear evidence that they can be hurt."

"My cats can be hurt, too!" Half-hostile, half-pleading, Percy put a hand on Nysska's arm. "They're trackers, not fighters. Please."

"I wouldn't even suggest it if the corpses were any faster, but as it is, the blood lynxes and I are the swiftest members of this team. And we will deal with this threat. If I may?" Percy didn't look convinced, but Nysska knelt and called out. "Flax! Jax! Come here, please. It's important."

The two big cats came slinking out of the shadows and sat in front of Nysska, peering up at her with their great silver eyes like tiny moons. She explained what she needed them to do. "It is crucial that you do exactly what I'm telling you," she said when she'd finished. "Your lives depend on it. All our lives depend on it. Can you do it? Do you understand?"

Jax yawned and stretched, but Flax, staring straight at Nysska, lifted one paw and held it in the air. After a couple of seconds, Nysska reached out her own hand, and Flax put her paw in Nysska's palm—and extended all of her claws. Five hooked razor-sharp daggers on display, as if to say, "*This* is what I can do."

Nysska nodded, and scratched Flax between the ears. "Does your brother understand as well?"

Jax meowed once and winked his left eye at her.

Nysska stood and faced Percy. "Are you satisfied?"

Percy had his arms folded, gazing at the cats. "Those two never cease to amaze me. But with them—and you—fuck, we might get off this goddamn mountain alive."

Nysska pointed at the far side of the chamber, beyond the ancient, collapsed cauldron. "Then the three of you get over there. It's time to open a door."

Nysska felt a deep-seated dread at how smoothly the ring-shaped handle of the lock spun back to the left. She whispered one of Atiina's proverbs—"*Dwell in peace in the home of your own being, and the Messenger of Death will not be able to touch you.*"

She didn't feel at peace.

The lock made a *clunk* sound as it disengaged. Taking long, deep breaths, Nysska drew her sword and retreated into the shadows, just beyond the ring of light thrown by a lantern sitting on the floor.

It only took a few seconds. Something on the other side of the door pushed, and the massive metal slab began to swing inward on its enormous hinges.

At the far side of the ring of light, two pairs of silver eyes glinted back at her.

A crack appeared between the door and the frame, and the malignant red light glowed through, along with the grinding moans of the shuffling corpses. An arm breached the gap. Fingers grasped the edge of the door and pushed, and the twisting, shimmering, ruby malevolence burst into the chamber as the first of the corpses stumbled in.

A feline howl echoed around the walls as a tawny blur flashed behind the corpse, followed by another less than a second later, and the corpse *screamed* and collapsed to the floor. A second animated cadaver stomped in, heels crunching down on the first one, blind eyes seeking, glaring, and the same thing happened—first one flash, then another, and the corpse wobbled, stumbled, fell headlong beside the first one.

"I want you to hit the tendons, right here, right above the heel," Nysska had told the cats, pointing out the spot on her own ankle. "Do not slow down. Do not let them get their hands on you. Slice through this part—" she tapped it again, "—and keep going. Can you do that? Are your claws sharp enough?"

Before the third corpse could make it into the chamber, Nysska darted forward. The first corpse had pushed itself up onto its elbows, and when it saw her coming, it reached out for her with the same metal-crushing hand that had done such damage to Raoul's arm.

Nysska's sword flashed, and the reaching arm flew away from the corpse, separated at the elbow, skidding off into the shadows. She danced back, out of reach of the second hobbled cadaver, out of the blood lynxes' way as the third glowing red horror pushed the huge door wider and came through.

One by one, bit by bit, Nysska and Flax and Jax took the corpses apart. She knew her plan only worked because the corpses were naked—if they had been wearing any kind of armor, even boots, the cats' formidable claws couldn't have found the purchase they needed. But against naked skin and flesh, putting every measure of strength they had into it, they severed the crucial tendons on the ankles of all five corpses, allowing Nysska to come in and dismantle them with sharpened bronze. First the arms. That was a lesson her instructors had given her early on, a lesson taught to every sethyd. *If you take away an opponent's hands, he cannot strike you with them.* The instructors had been talking about breaking bones, not improvising amputations, but given the corpses' unnatural strength, Nysska wanted to take no chances.

First the arms, then the heads.

The entire plan took just shy of four minutes to play out. Once the last of the five corpses fell, Nysska didn't wait for the rest of the team to make their way to the door. She dashed through it, listening, staring hard, and caught both the sound of rapid breath and the flicker of moss-light farther up the corridor. A two-second sprint let her overtake the man in the robes, and when he spun on her, a knife in his hand, she smacked the weapon away so hard that it buried itself point-first in the nearest wall.

Nysska clenched the robes' collar tight around his neck with one fist and lifted him off the floor. She made sure not to slam him into the wall hard enough to knock him unconscious, but his sandaled feet still drummed against it at the pain, and his gnarled hands clawed at hers, weak as a kitten's paws.

"Tell me everything," she said, putting her face close enough to him to see the reflections of her yellow eyes in his black ones.

The old man smiled at her. As the rest of the team caught up to them, he said, "If you haven't figured things out by now, nothing I could tell you would do any good."

Keeping the old man pinned to the wall with one hand, Nysska put her other hand over his mouth as she turned to Raoul, Cam, and Percy. "You want to question him?"

Raoul frowned. "Why're you asking us?"

Nysska could hear the rest of the question in his tone: *Where are you going?* She said, "Do you want him conscious or not?"

Cam peered at the old man, then at Nysska with eyes of pure silver. "Sure, we can see what we can get out of him, but it sounds like you don't plan to be here for that."

Nysska took her hand away from the old man's mouth. "Where is Lockridge? How long ago did he leave?"

The old man had stopped trying to pull her hands away, and simply hung there in her grip, his mouth twisting into an even nastier smile. "If you're asking how long, then you already know his destination."

Nysska snarled, and this time covered his mouth and his nose. He struggled for several seconds before going limp. She let him crumple to the floor. Percy said, "I thought we were supposed to question him? How do we do that if he's fucking dead?"

Nysska nudged him with the toe of her boot. "He's not dead. I only cut off his air a little bit. But listen. That layout of the Governor's Mansion tells us where Lockridge is heading—either himself, or his people. No one was here when we got here but this wrinkly piece of shit, and we didn't see anyone leaving, which means they've got at least a twelve-hour lead on us. And the only way to save Anwar's life is to get there before Lockridge."

Cam said, "That's impossible. You couldn't make up that lead even if you sprinted back down the trail, never mind using that washed-out switchback road."

Nysska's face darkened. "I'm not taking the trail or the road." She toed the old man again. "Question this geezer or don't, but get back to Tember as fast as you can, all right?"

Percy's face had gone from a puzzled frown to the darkest of scowls. He said, "You can't be fucking serious."

The realization hit Raoul and Cam at the same time, and both of them tried to speak, both making noises of protest, but Nysska stepped forward, swept Cam up in her arms, and gave her a kiss that lacked no heat for its swiftness. "I can do this," she said. "Sethyd bones are stronger than a human's. Don't worry."

Nysska set Cam back on her feet and, before she could talk herself out of what she'd decided to do, turned and sprinted up the hallway and out of the strange poured-stone structure, her teammates' cries echoing after her.

Nysska's feet picked up speed as she bolted out of the cave and careened up the slot canyon. *Am I lying?* The question flared in her mind as her legs pumped and her lungs heated up. *Can I really do this?*

If she didn't make it back to the Governor's Mansion before Lockridge and his assassins got there...well...not much else would matter, would it? Nysska Stonegate's place in the Ninth Crucible—in the Thaumetallicon—for that matter, in the Valconian Empire, would blow away like winter fog under a noonday sun.

Nysska exited the slot canyon and barreled across the broad, empty space that had once been Altamar. She picked up even more speed as she dashed along parallel to the river, and in one final, breathless leap, flung herself far out and over the falls.

21

Nysska might have been screaming on the way down.

All she knew for sure was how much everything hurt.

She'd hit the water feet-first, the way her brother had told her to if she ever decided to go cliff-diving, an activity he'd highly recommended. His face swam before her, the brilliant yellow of his eyes, the perfect symmetry of his cheekbones. The horns that swept forward and then up and out and back, curling from his forehead to just above the tips of his ears.

The memory brought her pain, just as everything else had become pain.

Pain and cold.

She couldn't breathe. Why couldn't she breathe?

I am Nysska Kaur, daughter of Simana Kaur, granddaughter of Olympea Kaur. Stonegate is not my name. Stonegate is merely a status.

Neither Nysska Kaur nor Nysska Stonegate could breathe.

Getting darker around her. Darker and colder. None of her limbs obeyed her. Why had her watersight membranes snapped shut over her eyes? She couldn't recall. Nothing made any sense.

Her brother's mouth opened, and a multitude of voices poured out of it, talking over one another, so that she could only comprehend snippets here and there. All the voices, the great mad choir, saying things like:

height of folly to ignore our destiny

and

superior people, superior species, to ignore that would be to ignore the moons rising

and

lived with this ridiculous notion of pacifism for too long

and

no human drawing breath will be able to resist

Drawing breath. Drawing breath…

Her brother's face floated before her, encased by the darkness that surrounded her as well, but as she watched, that darkness resolved into something sharper, something cleaner—something lit by the shine of the three moons, broken by the broad vertical brushstrokes of a forest, defined by the faint firelight struggling to escape the windows of the shelter she shared with her mother.

"You will accept the human's offer," Gerrit said, signaling to the other sethyds who brushed past Nysska and pushed into the shelter. "You will become a part of this Thaumetallicon. You will ingratiate yourself to its leaders. And you will give us information, whenever we require it."

Nysska stood, rigid, straining against the fear that had spread itself across her face. She didn't budge as Gerrit's companions moved inside the shelter, didn't budge though she heard her mother's cries, didn't budge as they brought Simana back out, bound and gagged.

When she finally could speak, she said, "Gerrit...please don't do this. She's your mother, just as much as she is mine."

Gerrit stepped closer, looking her dead in the eyes, yellow to yellow. "We both know that's not the truth, fratino. *Not anymore, not after what she did. What is very much the truth, though, is that if you resist this mission in any way, the life of the traitor known as Simana Kaur will end abruptly."*

Nysska broke the surface of Gar Lake, gasping, coughing, her body a scalp-to-toenail collection of bruises and possible hairline fractures. She floated on her back for a minute, a tranquility broken by frequent coughing spasms. Finally, she retracted her watersight membranes, groaned and flipped over and swam toward the marina with long, powerful strokes.

She wasn't sure how bad she looked when she hauled her water-logged carcass up onto the closest jetty, but a few affluently dressed humans spotted her and screamed as they ran away. Nysska shrugged off the shirt Anwar had given her and let it drop to the weathered wooden planks. Her armor and boots followed, landing in the first boat she came to that she felt confident to pilot by herself.

Nysska cleared the lines of the mooring cleats, pushed away from the jetty, and eyeballed the far end of the lake. There, the water flowed through a gap and became the Sawtooth River, which smashed and crashed its way down, ever down, beds of whitecaps announcing its speed as it rushed toward the city.

Somewhere on the shore, someone—perhaps the owner of the little boat she'd taken—shouted something about personal property.

Nysska paid the voice no mind as she pointed the prow toward Tember.

The swift-flowing river took her back to Tember faster than the fastest horse could gallop. Repeated travel from Gar Lake had led the Empire's citizens to wade in and remove the worst of the rocks and overturned trees most likely to snag a boat's hull, and once she'd cleared the whitewater, she cruised past a few fishing boats in calmer eddies, never losing any speed.

Never moving as fast as she wanted to.

Soon, the outskirts of Tember crept down to the river's banks. She flashed past huts and lean-tos at first, then houses, each growing larger with their proximity to the city walls, and finally the wooden gate that barred watercraft from free entry to the capital hove into view. Bronze-clad soldiers stood guard there—four of them, just enough to roll the gate back along its tracks—and all four stood rooted to the spot, staring as she rode the water closer and closer.

Nysska knew what she must have looked like. No trace of Imperial armor. No hood to hide her skin or her horns. Her hair loose from its braid, her clothes still damp, more like a giant purple waterlogged yellow-eyed rat to their eyes than anything else. She called out to them to open the gate, but still no one moved. And why should they, she asked herself. Without her armor, which still lay in the bottom of the boat, no one knew she belonged to the Thaumetallicon. She was just some strange demon with a bronze longsword strapped across her back, crawled out of a watery grave and demanding entry to their city.

Nysska steered the boat closer to the river's edge, which by now had become walls of stacked stone, grabbed up her armor and boots, and leapt free, grabbing hold of the wall's lip by just the tips of her fingers. It was enough to gain purchase. She clambered up, sprinted past the soldiers onto a cobblestone street, and bulled her way through the crowd as she streaked toward the Governor's Mansion, stopping only long enough to slip her armor and boots back on. She buckled the tunic as she ran.

Screams followed in her wake. Some of anger, some of fear. Men and women cursed at her. Children burst into sobs at the sight of her. Nysska didn't care about any of that—she only cared that no one tried to stop her.

Scant minutes later, she burst out into the city center, where the broad square still played host to the two score headless bodies hung on tall wooden forks. A dim part of her mind registered that they were different headless bodies now—a new wave of the recently executed. The Governor's Mansion loomed to her right, the ten-meter-high retaining wall and then the property wall and the building itself beyond that. It would have taken her an extra twenty minutes to circle all the way around to the approach that led up to the Mansion's gates.

Nysska flung herself halfway up the retaining wall, dug her fingers into crevices between the stones, and climbed. She reached the top in eighteen seconds, scaled the property wall in half that time, dashed across the strip of grass to a small side entrance and, without checking to see whether or not it was locked, kicked the door completely out of its frame. Nysska's feet pounded across it before it had settled fully to the floor. She bolted down a narrow hallway and up a flight of stairs to the Mansion's ground floor.

Bursting out into the central hall, she scared the hot piss out of one of Anwar's servants by bellowing, *"Where is the governor?"*

The young man squeaked out, "In his office!"

The wooden floor beneath her barely made a sound as she all but flew to the stairs. She took them two, sometimes three at a time, reaching the second floor in a tiny handful of heartbeats, bronze-clad soldiers and house staff alike getting out of her way in a chorus of shouts and shrieks. A tall, burly soldier stood outside the door to the parlor with the see-through fireplace, his eyes getting wider and wider as she hurtled toward him, and he tried to say, "You can't go in there, the Governor's—" but she brushed past him and threw the door wide.

Anwar sat at a small table in front of a window, a scroll half-unrolled before him and a pen held gracefully in his right hand, nib in mid-flourish.

Standing at his side, peering down over his shoulder, was a tall, gaunt, dark-skinned man with iron-gray hair and heavily bronze-inlaid armor.

General Boris Cullen.

Both Anwar and Cullen looked up at her as she stood there panting, their expressions placid. Half a dozen soldiers in Imperial bronze came crowding into the office, all of them with weapons drawn and leveled at Nysska, all of them barking orders at her.

"Boys, boys." Anwar set the pen down and raised his hand in a peaceful gesture. "This is Ninth Crucible Enforcer Nysska Stonegate. She's one of our own and has every right to be here." He made a flicking motion. "So out. Out with you, all of you. Go now. Go." The soldiers hesitated, but Anwar was clearly serious, and they filed out one by one. He added, "Close the door behind yourselves, would you?"

Once Nysska was alone in the office with Anwar and Cullen, Anwar stood and came around the desk, beckoning for Cullen to follow him. "What's wrong, Nysska?" Anwar asked. "What's got you so agitated?"

Nysska took a few steps toward them and slouched over, hands on her knees. "I just…need to…catch my breath. General Cullen…isn't it…sir?"

Anwar smiled. Broad, genuine. The smile she'd seen dozens of times before, that made his already boyish face look about twelve years old. "Of course! Nysska, this is General Cullen, Raoul's father. He's been seconded to me here in Tember as—what would you call your position, General?"

Cullen's eyes hadn't left Nysska. "I would say 'Special Advisor,' sir."

"Yes! Perfect. Special Advisor."

Nysska straightened up. Her breath had returned to normal, but her skin crawled. "I see. And on what kinds of special things will you be advising the Governor, General?"

Cullen got closer to her. Close enough for his near-black eyes to glitter as they took her in, scalp to toes. "Well, I dare say I could impart a few bits of wisdom concerning sethyd-kind. Perhaps you could join me in that, Enforcer Stonegate? Diminishing the general public's ignorance of your people?" He glanced over at Anwar. "I have no doubt those documents can wait. Is your study free, Governor? Might we retreat to a venue more hospitable for informative conversation?"

"A splendid idea!" Anwar shot back at once. He tilted his head toward the door to the office in the parlor's back corner. "Come with us, Nysska. You can fill us in on what's brought you here in such a state."

Nysska took another few steps forward. "I believe I might be able to do that right now, sir," she said. "I believe, in fact, that you know full well what brought me here, Governor. And I hope you can appreciate how much sadness my arrival brings me."

Both men frowned. Neither moved, but Anwar said, "Sadness? Why?"

Nysska said, "Because you are left-handed, sir," and in a single motion drew her longsword from its scabbard and swung it in a long, broad arc, so that its tip bit into Anwar's forearm just above the wrist and sliced upward through cloth and skin alike.

A harsh, grating squeal filled the room as sparks struck, the sword's tip having dragged along the length of the deep red, metallic rune implanted under Anwar's skin.

The Governor's face wrinkled into a dead-eyed mask of rage, every hint of his personality dropping away from him like a heavy icicle falling from a branch, and runes lit up along his arms and legs and from beneath his hair like burning coals. The blood-red light—exactly the same as the light from the shambling corpses in Altamar—blazed through his skin and clothing and lit up the stitches along his hairline where his scalp had been peeled back and re-fastened.

The corpse of Wendell Anwar growled, an inhuman, scraping sound that came from deep inside him, and he raised hands with fingers curled into talons and lunged for her.

It took every bit of skill and strength she had, but Nysska timed and aimed the sword stroke exactly right, and when she side-stepped so that the corpse rushed past her, she took Anwar's head off his shoulders.

Without a further word, Cullen turned and fled across the parlor and through the door to Anwar's study. Nysska sped after him while Anwar's head still rolled and bounced on the floor.

Cullen had a dozen steps' lead on her. She came through from the parlor just as a concealed wall panel was swinging shut, and she thrust the blade of her sword through the gap before it could latch. Nysska wrenched the hidden door open to the sound of footsteps retreating down a narrow spiral staircase, and she plunged after them, the heavy falls of her booted feet echoing on stone.

The spiral staircase wound down one level and opened into a long, rectangular room, lit by sunlight streaming in from a series of narrow horizontal windows set just below the ceiling. Lying on her side like a pile of discarded rubbish, hog-tied and gagged, was Galena Vachs. Cullen knelt beside her, a dagger clutched in his fist, arm raised high and poised to drive it down through flesh and bone.

Nysska hurled her sword at him as hard as she could.

Swords are never meant to be thrown, and the Imperial Enforcer's longsword was no exception. The weapon spun end over end, and rather than impaling Cullen or severing a limb as Nysska had hoped, the flat of the blade cracked against the side of his head. It still had enough power to make him falter, and she needed only that half a second to cross the space and slam into him like a boulder crashing down a cliff. Cullen's dagger went flying.

Nysska and Cullen rolled, limbs tangled, fists and elbows and knees trying to find targets. Nysska had one split-second, crazy view of General Cullen's eyes locked on her, and then Cullen's hand reached up and found its way to her throat. Sudden agony made her vision turn red around the edges as his fingers tried to crush her windpipe.

Nysska surged up, Cullen lying beneath her but his gripping, vise-like hands seconds away from grinding her neck to shreds, and she brought both her palms together on the sides of his head with enough force to crack a human's skull. Cullen screamed and let go of her throat, but before she could get a better grip on his head, intent on jamming her thumbs into and through his eyeballs, he bucked her completely off of him with strength like that of a wild horse. Nysska's shoulders and the back of her head slammed into a stone wall, and while she blinked away the red-tinged spots before her eyes, Cullen got to his feet.

His armor began to smolder. He shrugged it off as Nysska regained her equilibrium, eyes seeking her sword, which lay in a corner beyond Cullen. When the Imperial armor hit the floor, revealing Cullen in only a thin shirt, boots, and trousers, Nysska took in the sight of the black metal runes lining his arms and his chest.

"Oh…shit."

"You have no idea," Cullen said, and Nysska watched in horror as his face changed.

Exactly like Hector's had, in the lair under the mountain.

Exactly like a cuttlefish.

Cullen's skin shifted from the same rich, dark brown as Raoul's to the palest pink. The shape of the nose, the contours of the cheeks, the width of the brow. Everything changed, until she found herself looking at a completely different man—a man with low, flat cheek-bones, a narrow nose, and a mouth with thin, cruel lips. He ripped the gray wig off his head, revealing a smooth scalp, and his light blue eyes mirrored the bloodthirsty grin that skinned his lips back from his teeth. "You're quite the thorn in my side when you want to be, aren't you?"

"Lockridge," Nysska whispered.

The man's brow rose. "It was *you*. At Benitoff's estate. You're the one who snuck in and murdered his whore. You'll have to explain that trick with the chimney." Sparks and ribbons of jet-black power flowed and writhed along his limbs, exactly like the tarn she had seen executed at the hands of the Argonium Infantry. "Tell you what. I'm going to present you with a once-in-a-lifetime offer." He tilted his head toward Galena Vachs. "You let me do for her what I did for Governor Anwar, and you and I can put our differences behind us. Truthfully, I would welcome you by my side. And, down the road, let us say, perhaps if *your* people were to come to an understanding with *my* people? Oh, Nysska. What we could *accomplish*." He seemed genuinely pleased with himself. "Ambassador Stonegate...that feels good on the tongue, does it not?"

Nysska got to her feet, her back to the wall and her mind spinning.

On the one hand, the bastard standing there, *right there,* had caused her and her teammates immense trouble, and—she hadn't let it hit her yet, but she knew it would—he had killed and violated the body of Wendell Anwar, her first-ever human friend.

But if she struck a truce with Lockridge...wouldn't that be exactly what Gerrit would want?

Wouldn't that get her mother back, safe and unharmed?

Lockridge's sharklike grin grew even wider. "Oh, you're thinking about it! Look at those wheels turning! Better yet, *look around you*. All these people *hate* you. Join me, Miss Stonegate. Help me bring down this corrupt, loathsome empire. I'll make you a princess. No—better yet. I'll make you a *general*."

Nysska tried to steady her breathing. "And the price is nothing but a little murder. Correct?"

Lockridge's smile faltered. "Forget about *murder*. People die in wars. People die every day. I should think you would understand that better than most. And if it's *Vachs* you're concerned about—be realistic. What's one empty-headed child, versus the chance to re-make an entire society?" He gestured wide, using both arms. "Do you not see what we've already *done?*"

Nysska seized the question. "Explain that. You're a *tarn*. How are you still lucid?"

"Join me, and I'll show you." He took a step toward her. "This power can be yours. Imagine it. The already fearsome strength and speed of the sethyd, amplified a hundred-fold. I can hear the blood in your arteries. I can see the thoughts firing in your brain. *I can let you have this.*"

Nysska lifted one foot. Braced it against the wall behind her. "And the corpses? How did you control those dead bodies in Altamar? How did you control the Governor? What are you doing to the argonium?"

Lockridge slid forward. His fists clenched and unclenched, sending waves of ebon energy dancing and sliding up his arms. "The world is bigger than even the sethyds realize. But...you've decided to remain small, haven't you? Yes, you have. I can see that just from your pretty face. Ah, well. I know where to find more of your kind."

Nysska launched herself off the wall, shooting past him, her body lengthened into a spear, her hands outstretched, ready to grab up her sword. Ready to deal with Lockridge the way she had the corpses in the strange subterranean laboratory, the way she'd been forced to deal with poor Governor Anwar's puppeted body.

She didn't see Lockridge move.

His hands simply appeared, clamped around her upper arm, and the crushing power he'd shown her when he'd gripped her neck was nothing compared with the godlike strength that dug into her skin, through her muscles, ground against her bones—

Nysska abandoned the sword, twisted beneath him, dug one foot into his chest and, with her back against the floor, thrust Lockridge *through the wall.*

Bricks and mortar exploded as he crashed out into the sunlight, sprawling on the strip of green between the Mansion and the property wall above the city center. Nysska shot out after him, teeth gritted hard against the pain in her shoulder, fighting back the thought of what he would have done if she'd given him even a second longer.

He would have torn your arm from your body, her mind insisted. *He would have killed you.*

She didn't know the extent of the damage he *had* done, but her arm still worked, and before Lockridge could rise fully to his feet, Nysska rammed her good shoulder into his gut, sending them smashing through the property wall and out into the open air.

The ten-meter fall seemed to take a very long time as Lockridge struck at her and clawed at her face, but Nysska tucked her head, kept him underneath her, and drove Lockridge's body into the broad flagstones of the square like a slaughterhouse hammer crushing the skull of a cow. The impact cracked the stones beneath them, but as Nysska rolled away, the shadows of the tall wooden forks passing over her, Lockridge howled and slammed his fists into the stone and rose like a specter from a fresh grave.

The citizens of Tember screamed, fleeing, and Nysska heard the first of many cries: "Tarn! *Tarn!* It's a tarn, get away, *run!*"

Lockridge's eyes had become bottomless pits in his face. He came forward in a half-crouch, talon-fingers curled and ready, as the townsfolk streamed out of the square. From the corners of her eyes, Nysska saw them huddling in windows, in doorways, staring in morbid awe as a Tarnished One stalked a demon in their midst.

"Looks as if your secret schemes are no longer secret," Nysska called out, backing away from him.

Lockridge wedged the fingers of one hand into a crack at his feet and pulled up one of the square's great flagstones. Nysska's eyes widened to brilliant yellow circles as jet-black energy crackled around Lockridge's body, and she threw herself as far as she could to her left, but not quite fast enough—the huge, flat stone hurtled past and clipped her right foot while she was in mid-air. It spun her body like a top and sent her crashing into one of the tall wooden forks. A deafening, splintering roar filled the city center as the flagstone mowed down more of the wooden forks, but Nysska's whole world had narrowed to the pain in her foot and the rotting, headless corpse that had come slamming down on top of her, dislodged by the impact of her ribs against the fork's trunk.

She rose to one knee as Lockridge charged her, and flung the corpse into his face, but he batted it away and launched a fist at her jaw that boomed like thunder. Nysska slipped the fist, wrenched her body to one side, got solid grips on his shirt with both hands and lowered her head, her right horn plunging toward Lockridge's neck like the tip of a dagger—

Lockridge's hand snapped up.

Grabbed her horn—

And broke it off.

Nysska screamed and exploded away from him, blinding agony in her head. She ran, stumbled and fell. The pain in her foot forgotten but still slowing her down, she surged back up and ran again.

A horrified glance over her shoulder made her wish she hadn't looked. Lockridge had picked up a fallen corpse fork and swung it like a staff, breaking off more of them left and right as he came after her, headless cadavers raining to the flagstones around him.

Nysska fetched up hard against the side of a building. She was sure he had shattered her skull, that a great gaping hole had opened in her forehead, that her blood and brains were sliding out. Only when her hand touched the jagged stump where her horn had been did she dare believe that Lockridge hadn't killed her outright.

Lockridge appeared before her. Stalking her now. Grinning. Enjoying himself.

From somewhere far away came the sound of drums. It took her a second to place them—*the Argonium Infantry*.

The cry of *Tarn!* had gone out wide, and in minutes they would arrive.

"Don't mind the drums," Lockridge called out, drawing closer and closer, the crackling black death around him like a lightning storm. "They won't get here in time to save you."

She knew he was right. Nysska's shoulder throbbed. It hurt to swallow. Especially without a weapon, the second Lockridge got a grip on her, he'd finish the job he'd started.

A grip.

The idea sparked in her head—took hold—came alive.

Nysska unbuckled her armor jacket and let it fall. Lockridge paused, one eyebrow rising. Watching. She shrugged off the long-sleeved Imperial shirt, as well as the camisole, leaving herself nude from the waist up—then she lowered her head, raised her left arm, and with the tip of her remaining horn, pierced the skin just below her elbow. Yellow eyes boring holes in Lockridge, she dragged her arm down, the tip of the horn slicing through violet skin all the way to her wrist.

Even from their hiding places, she could hear the townsfolk's gasps.

Lockridge stopped dead still. Frowning.

Nysska repeated the same motion with her other arm. The jagged stump of her broken horn pierced her skin easily, opening a rent from elbow to wrist.

Her face dripping red, both arms bleeding freely, Nysska raised her fists above her head and let the blood run down. Slowly, provocatively, she passed her arms across her chest, across her abdomen. Slid them along her neck, until she glistened ruby red.

Lockridge spat a curse word and charged.

Nysska was fast, faster than any human, but Lockridge was a human no longer. She didn't know what to call him, how to think of him, she only saw him as pain and rage and punishment, and she tried to side-step, tried to bring a knee up into his solar plexus, but one of his hands reached out and locked onto her blood-slicked wrist—

She wrenched it free.

Leaving Lockridge, for the tiniest fraction of a second, off-balance.

A dim, flickering part of her wished she could take more time to enjoy the surprise on his face, but she *had* no time to do anything but react, and in the split-second before he could adjust, Nysska drove the point of her elbow straight into the bridge of his nose.

Lockridge screamed and staggered, but came back even faster, a fist like the head of a flail driving at her face—but she turned her head, and though the impact made her see flashing lights, his knuckles slid across her bloody cheek, tearing no skin, breaking no bones.

This time, Nysska's knee found its target, rising fast as a striking cobra straight into the bottom edge of his ribcage, and she heard bones crunch. Lockridge staggered again, and Nysska's leg flashed out, catching him in the side of the knee.

Lockridge screamed and drove his good leg down, launching himself at her face, a flurry of punches landing, a swarm of pain driving into her like the stings of a hornet hive. And yet none of them caught her square. She moved just fast enough, and the blood that coated her proved just slick enough, that he couldn't find the mark that would have sent her into darkness. His strikes grew wilder and wilder, less and less precise—

Until she saw one of them coming, and dipped her head at exactly the right moment, and the tip of her left horn pierced Lockridge's palm and tore through the side of his hand.

He screamed again, and fell to one knee, and she took his back and rode him to the ground. With all her weight on top of him, his chest grinding into the stone, Nysska snaked her arms around his throat and locked him in a choke she had practiced hundreds upon hundreds of times. A few seconds' worth of pressure and Lockridge would black out. Another few minutes of it, and he wouldn't get back up. Nysska tightened her grip.

Lockridge turned his head.

He shouldn't have been able to. *No one* should have been able to. But he turned his head until his closest eye could focus on her, and said, "I'm about to kill you."

Nysska sank the choke in even harder—and yet she could feel the muscles of his throat working, forcing air past, allowing him to speak.

"You can't stop me," he said, and Nysska almost let him go when she felt the snap and sizzle of power flowing along his body, stinging her, ripping at her skin. "All your strength. All your *might*. Humans are as nothing to you...and yet you are as nothing to *us*."

That jet-black, burning, tearing power *grew*. Suddenly Nysska wasn't pinning down a man. It felt as if she'd grabbed hold of a beast, a tiger, impossible to overpower. The rune-strength in Lockridge's body grew with every second, and soon he would throw her off, take her body in his hands, bloody or not, and rip her to pieces.

"Us?" she gasped, her muscles spasming with the energy emanating from him. "There are more of you?"

"Oh, yes," Lockridge whispered. "An entire *world* of us."

His shoulder moved, his body turning in her grip. A few more seconds and he'd break free, and her life would end, and Nysska made the only choice left to her.

She drew an immense breath, put her mouth to Lockridge's ear, and *screamed*.

Nysska's earliest memories were ones of singing. Of learning to harness the breath, to bend it, shape it, make it into the instrument of one's will. She had never considered herself a master singer. Not even the best one in Fajrasxtono. But she had always had *power*. A strength in her lungs that none of the other priest-singers could match. She had used a portion of that power in the ambush beneath Tember's streets, when she'd needed to conserve her breath.

Nysska had no reason to hold back now.

The sound slammed out of her like lava blasting from a volcano. Tiny bits of gravel trembled and danced around her, and townsfolk along the square's perimeter flinched and held their ears and gritted their teeth against the pain. Windows in the nearest buildings cracked and shattered.

Lockridge's eyes bulged from their sockets as Nysska's scream continued. Blood burst from his tear ducts, ran from the corners of his mouth. The black runes implanted below his collarbone vibrated, edges slicing through his skin, and as the scream rose and rose and rose in pitch and power, the top of Lockridge's skull cracked and split, and in a horizontal geyser of blood and skin and gray matter, his brain erupted and spewed across the flagstones.

Her breath gone and her blood spreading fast across the stones, Nysska collapsed beside the body, dropping away into welcoming darkness.

22

When Nysska opened her eyes the first time, she could do little but stare at the ceiling. She felt as if all the meat had been taken off of her bones and replaced with... what? Rendered fat? Grave dirt? Whatever her body had become, it did not possess the strength to move her limbs.

She heard someone say, "She's waking up!" and Cam's face filled her field of vision, her wide, beautiful eyes shining silver.

"You shouldn't be doing that," Nysska whispered. Her throat felt as if someone had carefully scraped all the soft tissue out of it with a garden trowel.

"We can talk about it later," Cam said, and even as weak as Nysska was, some part of her shrank from the finality in Cam's voice. "For now, just get used to the idea that I want to see as much of you as I can." She smiled, and kissed Nysska's lips, and Nysska would have wept if her body had been capable of producing tears.

Beyond Cam, Percy and Raoul crowded close to the bed, and Nysska realized that she was back in her room in the Governor's Mansion, the room out of which she and Flax had sneaked on their secret mission. Something about that thought made her focus on an itching sensation in her knuckles, and when she glanced down, she saw Flax lying there on the bed, curled up asleep on her left hand. *I didn't want to move that hand anyway,* she thought vaguely, and managed to whisper, "I would very much like some water."

Percy disappeared. He came back seconds later with a glass, and Cam carefully lifted Nysska's head and let her drink. "Not too much. There. That's good. You can have more soon."

"Well?" Nysska asked, her voice marginally stronger now. "How do I look?"

"Tough as a *motherfucker,*" Percy said through his usual grin. "Cam wasn't lying about how fast you horn-bearing types scab up. Speaking of horns, is that one going to grow back? Or did you just get a fucking great battle scar?"

"It'll grow back," Nysska said, and took another couple of sips of water. "Might take a while, though."

Raoul moved closer. He had his arm in a sling, but he looked at her with a welcome blend of admiration and simple friendliness. "Impressive work, Enforcer."

Nysska inclined her head a degree or two and let the corners of her mouth twitch upward. "Thank you, Commander."

Jax leapt up onto the bed, sniffed the side of Nysska's face, and began kneading her shoulder with his forepaws.

"All right," Nysska said. "Can I have a couple extra pillows?"

Raoul went to a far corner of the room and came back with the pillows as requested. He and Cam lifted her, gently and together, at which point she saw who was standing in the doorway and almost yelped.

"Governor," Nysska said. "I see you managed to free yourself."

Galena Vachs walked slowly across the room to the foot of the bed, studying Nysska, but...*was* that Galena Vachs? The young woman watching her was the same height, her body shaped the same, but the expression on her face and, more than that, the light in her eyes had changed completely. Governor Vachs said, "Would you all excuse us, please? I'd like a private word with Enforcer Stonegate." As the rest of the team made polite assenting noises, Vachs said, "Take the cats with you, if you would. I know how bad blood lynxes can get when it comes to gossip."

"Wait." Nysska put her hand on Cam's. "Lockridge. He was masquerading as Cullen. *He changed his face.*"

"Oh." Vachs seemed amused. "And now you're afraid someone's done that with me? That I'm some kind of skin-changing spy?"

Percy stepped nearer. "Flax. Jax. Is that really Galena Vachs?"

The two blood lynxes converged at the end of the bed, both of them staring at the young woman, both of them sniffing deeply. Flax turned to her brother, conferring wordlessly with him, and then looked over her shoulder at Nysska and nodded. Vachs reached out and scratched both cats between the ears, stroked their backs, and when Nysska heard them start purring, she finally unclenched.

"We'll see you soon," Cam said, eyes flashing, an easy smile showing off her flawless teeth. The rest of the Ninth Crucible, felines included, left the room.

Alone now, Nysska peered at the Governor, trying to make sense of this abrupt transformation, and Vachs startled her with an unexpectedly deep, throaty laugh.

"The look on your face," Vachs said.

"I...would say that it's...well-founded, Governor."

Galena Vachs came around and sat on the edge of the bed, her chin up, her back effortlessly, perfectly straight. "You're wondering how much of what's gone on here I even understand, correct? That's fine. I rather enjoy letting people underestimate me, you see. Always have. And when Father sent me out here to get some first-hand experience with governing before I took over, I decided the best way to do that was to appear so simple-minded that no one would think to modify their speech or behavior around me. I must say, I learned a great deal in the few short weeks I got."

Nysska realized her jaw had fallen open. She closed it.

Vachs went on. "Regarding exactly what *has* taken place, please allow me to sum it up, and you can correct any errors. Acceptable?" Nysska nodded. "Very good. First, there is a surprisingly large and well-organized criminal element operating in Imperial territory. A cabal whose ultimate goal is very likely the overthrow of the Empire itself. How am I doing so far?"

"I...have yet to hear any inaccuracies, Governor."

"Ugh. *Governor.* I suppose I must use that title, but it's so unwieldy. What do you say, when it's just the two of us, that you call me Galena?"

Cam had left the glass of water on a bedside table, and carefully, very carefully, Nysska reached over and picked it up. It took every bit of her strength and coordination not to drop it. After a long sip, the blessed coolness of which she felt all the way down into her stomach, she said, "Whatever you say, Galena."

"Splendid. Now, to get a bit farther into the weeds. Within this criminal cabal, you have encountered evidence of an entirely new kind of thaumaturgy. Alloyed argonium used in ways that the Imperial College has never even dreamed of. Runes that re-animate the dead and render our Sensors powerless. Yes?"

Nysska's eyes slid shut. She could see the glowing red of the corpses' bodies, reaching, clawing. "Yes. I believe that's what Naveed Olkoff had been working on. Then, when he lost his nerve and tried to take his favorite whore and run, they killed him. And the whore."

"Troubling. Extremely troubling. But not so troubling as the existence of a breed of person able to become other people."

Nysska opened her eyes again. "Not completely. These people are excellent mimics, but I don't think their ability would hold up well enough for, say, a husband to fool his wife." She paused. "They could do my skin and eyes, but they'd have to wear false horns. I'm fairly sure."

Vachs nodded. "Not a hundred percent convincing, but still enough for a Crucible Commander to look down a hallway and believe the man he saw standing there was his father."

"Yes."

"But it's not just that, is it? One of these camouflage people *was also a Tarnished One.*"

Nysska paused before responding. "Yes and no. Yes, he had—I believe the term is 'deadmetal' runes—runes taken from the body of the intended user. But he wasn't out of control the way tarns are, and he activated them at will."

"All right, then, answer me this. Are these new kinds of runes what allowed the people to change their skin?"

"Oh…I don't think so. The first one we encountered—the one Cam killed in the mountain lair—didn't have any runes at all."

Vachs sighed, long and harsh. "So Lockridge came here, killed Anwar, implanted the runes in his corpse, and was going to have him issue a raft of proclamations."

"Before the body started noticeably decaying, yes, that seems to have been the plan."

"And once Anwar was no longer of use, he was going to do the same thing to me."

"I would think so."

Vachs scooted a bit closer on the bed, her posture relaxing slightly. "We have witnesses who said that this Lockridge—before you killed him in a way that's going to be sung about in ballads—"

Nysska groaned.

"—Lockridge confirmed that there are more like him. Do you know what he meant by that? More people who can do what he did with argonium? Or more…skin-shifters?"

"I would have to say both."

Vachs's eyes slid shut. She groaned louder than Nysska had. "There are supposed to be three kinds of intelligent creatures in this world! Humans, sethyds, and seraphic animals. That's it. That's what we're all taught in school. So what does it mean, this—this camouflage talent?" Vachs stood up and began pacing in a horseshoe pattern around the bed. "Do you know what kind of nightmare this is going to cause? A fourth kind of intelligence? Especially a fourth kind of intelligence that can look like us, and seems to want us all dead? Where did they come from? How many of them are there? What do we do about them?" She stopped and faced Nysska. "Which brings me to the question of those Imperial citizens with horns and yellow eyes and violet skin."

"Ah…excuse me?"

Vachs gripped the top of the bed's footboard and leaned on it. "I know Wendell was trying to do a good thing by making you an 'ambassador for your species,' as he put it. But you've demonstrated—publicly, and to fanfare that shows no signs of dying down—that you,

Nysska Stonegate, possess skills and abilities that *we didn't know sethyds had*."

Nysska lifted one arm and draped her bandaged wrist across her eyes.

"And that's fine. Yes? Because we gave the suddenly nationless sethyd people a new home. Gave them full citizenship. They'd have no reason to rise up against us, would they? Except now, people are beginning to talk. People are beginning to say, 'Well, what if they *did* rise up? What could we do about it?' It's a fair question, Nysska. What *could* we do about it?"

Nysska didn't reply.

Vachs went back to pacing. "And that, of course, leaves us with the much more prosaic issue of the Ninth Crucible disobeying direct orders." She waved a dismissive hand. "All of that is rendered null and void, of course, since those orders came from an imposter."

Nysska moved her wrist. "Wait. Where is the real General Cullen?"

Vachs allowed herself the hint of a smile. "On his way here. He had no idea any of this was happening. Was on the other side of the continent, in fact. The imposter was able to do what he did through some strategic interception of Imperial couriers. Once things had been explained, General Cullen seemed impressed with the Ninth Crucible's actions."

"All right. Well. Good, I guess? So…Galena…what happens now?"

Vachs stopped again, and her smile fled as she faced Nysska. "In less than a week, your actions—all of you, collectively—have turned the Empire on its ear."

"I understand that. What I'm asking is what exactly happens to *us* now? As a unit? There was talk of reassigning us. Of…taking Cam and…maybe vivisecting her to find out what went wrong…"

Vachs's face creased in horror. "Great Silver Dragon, no! Of course not! No, no, no. There'll be no reassigning. The Ninth Crucible stays together—and from now on, you'll report directly to me."

Nysska thought back to how Vachs had been in the room when Cam had leaned over and kissed her. "So…you have no problem with Cam and me?"

Vachs laid a hand against her heart. "Personally? Not even a little.

Also, in case you didn't realize it, I was awake, lying hog-tied in that room with you and the imposter. I heard him try to tempt you. And I know I'm alive because of you. As far as I'm concerned, Nysska, you can do no wrong, and I'm *eternally* grateful. But I'm also not the Emperor. I can't issue Imperial Decrees, so you might want to keep what's private private. Maybe no kissing and fondling in public. Can the two of you live with that?"

"I suppose we can."

"Good. Also, as soon as you've recovered?"

Into the pause that followed, Nysska injected a tentative, "Yes?"

"You'll be going to Caulspring. You've got an audience with the Emperor. Asked for the Ninth Crucible specifically. Something about explaining to him in person exactly what Sergei Benitoff had to do with all this." As Nysska tried not to choke, Vachs said, "Tell him hello from me."

Later that night, after her teammates, both human and feline, had spent a great deal of time in her room, and after several bottles of wine had been poured, Nysska and Cam lay in bed. They had not made love. They had barely even kissed, as Nysska was still too weak to move for more than a few moments at a time. But Cam lay snuggled against Nysska's side, one arm thrown over her chest, eyes closed and breath deep and even. Someone had extinguished the lantern, and the dark seemed to cradle them.

Nysska hadn't had much wine, but in her weakened state the little she did have was enough to make her sleepy, and she wasn't sure how long she'd been out when she opened her eyes.

There was someone else in the room with them.

Before Nysska could decide what to do, a column of darkness detached itself from the corner, and Gerrit's towering shape glided to the head of the bed. His eyes—the same candle-flame yellow as her own—gazed down at her.

He didn't speak. Didn't seem to want her to speak.

He was just letting her know that he was still there. Still watching. A beast in the night, waiting to be fed.

As silently as he'd arrived, Gerrit turned and vanished. Nysska never heard her window open. Never heard any footsteps retreating across the roof above.

"You awake?" Cam mumbled. "Something wrong?"

With a yawning pit of guilt and desperation in her gut, Nysska said, "No, no. I'm fine. Go back to sleep."

TO BE CONTINUED

ACKNOWLEDGMENTS

To say that writing a book in a genre I'd never tackled before -- at least, not in prose -- was a daunting task would be a grave understatement. The project would have suffered greatly without the help, input, and encouragement from the following people:

Tracy Jolley, for being the best and most patient sounding board on Earth.

Haris Orkin, Clint McInnes, and Maciek Binkowski, Beta Readers Extraordinaire.

John Hartness, for his brilliant edits (and for saying "yes" to a convention pitch).

Melissa McArthur, for her insightful and valuable perspective.

Tuppence Van de Vaarst and Alisha Grace, for mercilessly hunting down and killing typos and continuity errors.

Suan H. Roddey, for delivering a fantastic cover.

ABOUT THE AUTHOR

Dan Jolley began writing professionally at age 19. Starting out in comic books, Dan has worked for major publishers such as DC (*Firestorm*), Marvel (*Dr. Strange*), Dark Horse (*Aliens*), and Image (*G.I. Joe*). He soon branched out into licensed-property novels (*Star Trek*), film novelizations (*Iron Man*), and original novels, including the science-fiction/superhero *Gray Widow Trilogy*.

Dan began writing for video games in 2007, and has contributed storylines, characters, and dialogue to titles such as *Transformers: War for Cybertron, Prototype 2,* and *Dying Light,* among others.

His latest work includes *The Storm,* a mystery-thriller inspired by actual events in Dan's hometown, and the best-selling Audible Original audiobook *House of Teeth.*

Dan lives with his wife Tracy in northwest Georgia. Readers can learn more about him on his website, www.danjolley.com.

ALSO BY DAN JOLLEY

ADULT FICTION

The Gray Widow Trilogy:

Gray Widow's Walk

Gray Widow's Web

Gray Widow's War

YOUNG ADULT BOOKS

The Alex Unlimited Trilogy:

The Vosarak Code

Split-Second Sight

True Chemistry

MIDDLE-GRADE BOOKS

The Five Elements Trilogy:

The Emerald Tablet

The Shadow City

The Crimson Serpent

House of Teeth (Audible Original audiobook)

FRIENDS OF FALSTAFF

Thank You to All our Falstaff Books Patrons, who get extra digital content each month! To be featured here and see what other great rewards we offer, go to www.patreon.com/falstaffbooks.

PATRONS

Dino Hicks
John Hooks
John Kilgallon
Larissa Lichty
Travis & Casey Schilling
Staci-Leigh Santore
Sheryl R. Hayes
Scott Norris
Samuel Montgomery-Blinn
Junkle

www.ingramcontent.com/pod-product-compliance
Lightning Source LLC
Chambersburg PA
CBHW020258030826
48979CB00026B/1389/J

* 9 7 8 1 6 4 5 5 4 1 2 7 1 *